THE
DISCIPLE

Also by Stephen Coonts

The Assassin
The Traitor
Saucer: The Conquest
Liars & Thieves
Liberty
America
Saucer
Hong Kong
Cuba
Fortunes of War
The Intruders
The Red Horsemen
Under Siege
The Minotaur
Final Flight
Flight of the Intruder

With William H. Keith

Deep Black: Terror at Sea
Deep Black: Arctic Gold

With Jim DeFelice

Deep Black: Conspiracy
Deep Black: Jihad
Deep Black: Payback
Deep Black: Dark Zone
Deep Black: Biowar
Deep Black

Nonfiction

The Cannibal Queen

Anthologies

On Glorious Wings
Victory
Combat
War in the Air

THE
DISCIPLE

STEPHEN COONTS

Quercus

First published in 2009 by St Martin's Press
First published in Great Britain in 2010 by

Quercus
21 Bloomsbury Square
London
WC1A 2NS

A CIP catalogue record for this book is available
from the British Library

ISBN (HB) 978 1 84916 293 7
ISBN (TPB) 978 1 84916 294 4

This book is a work of fiction. Names, characters,
businesses, organizations, places, events and incidents are
either the products of the author's imagination
or are used fictitiously. Any resemblance to

Printed and bound in Great Britain by St Ives Plc

10 9 8 7 6 5 4 3 2 1

To Deborah

God willing, with the force of God behind it, we shall soon experience a world without the United States and Zionism.

—Mahmoud Ahmadinejad

THE
DISCIPLE

CHAPTER **ONE**

MAY: SYRIA

The dark green bombs fell from a milky sky. There were six of them, weighing a ton apiece. They had been dropped from an altitude of about twenty-six thousand feet, so the fall was going to take a while.

On the ground, Mikhail Toporov heard the distant, fading thunder of the three warplanes. Although he didn't know it, they were Israeli F-15s. He scanned the sky. The visibility was excellent in the dry air under a high cirrus layer, which made the sky look a dirty white. Toporov saw nothing. If he had looked harder, he would have seen the aircraft as black dots against the white clouds, but his eyes were not focused for really distant objects. Even as he looked, the falling bombs were accelerating to terminal velocity.

Mikhail Toporov was offended by the airplane noise. There should be no aircraft at all in this prohibited zone.

Toporov flipped away his cigarette and walked quickly back into the air defense command and control bunker. Meanwhile the GPS modules on the tails of the bombs located their satellites and began issuing steering commands to canards that protruded from modules screwed into the noses of the weapons. Each bomb steered toward its designated target.

As the warplanes completed their postrelease turns and steadied out on course for home base, Mikhail Toporov leaned over the shoulder of one of his Russian colleagues seated at a radar console and looked at the display. The radar was sweeping . . . and there were no returns.

"Select the local area display," Toporov said.

"That *is* the local area display."

It didn't compute. Toporov had just heard the planes. "Select fifty kilo-meters," he said.

A flip of a switch, and still the scope was empty.

"Something is wrong," Toporov said, his mind racing.

Now only three miles above him, the bombs plummeted down.

Inside the administration building for the Syrian nuclear reactor, which was just next door, less than fifty yards away, Dr. Raza Qureshi was eating lunch at his desk while he scrutinized the latest draft of the government's Top Secret plan to stockpile enriched uranium for future nuclear warheads. He had written the plan upon direction from Damascus; it was almost ready to be signed and forwarded to the ministry.

Dr. Qureshi gave little thought to the political implications of the plan—he was concerned with the technical aspects. Still, he knew that Syria and her allies in the Middle East had many formidable enemies, with the most formidable, Israel, not very far away. It was his belief that the national leaders were prudent and correct to plan for the future.

He used his fingers to select a piece of cold meat as he scanned the text. He was a compulsive editor, one who was never satisfied, even with his own words, and now he saw a word that perhaps should be changed. He abandoned the food plate in midgrope. He drew a careful line through the offending word and wrote the one he wanted immediately above it.

That done, he laid down the pen and checked his watch. He had another half hour before he needed to go to the control room.

Qureshi reached again for the food plate and resumed reading.

There were seventeen people in the reactor control room. A dozen technicians monitored dials and gauges and made meticulous notes in logbooks. Behind them, four electricians were trying to find the fault in a relay panel, which seemed to have developed a short. They had the front of the panel off and were working with voltage meters.

The technicians were engrossed in their work. The reactor had been down for a month for maintenance, and they were engaged in the prestart checks. They were almost finished. Just now they were pulling the rods from the pile one at a time, then reinserting each one, checking to ensure that they had complete control of every rod. So far, everything was working just as it

THE DISCIPLE — 3

should, praise Allah, but Dr. Qureshi was a demanding taskmaster who insisted on no shortcuts. Intently focused, they continued their work.

A man from the ministry in Damascus was watching and taking notes. He spoke to no one, asked no questions. Even though this was his very first visit to the reactor, he acted as if he knew everything, so there was nothing to ask; most of the people in the room suspected that he asked no questions because he was afraid to reveal the depths of his ignorance. In their experience, political people rarely knew anything about the reactor or how it worked. This one, they had concluded hours earlier, was like all the others.

Seventeen people, all of whom had only seconds more to live as the bombs fell toward the earth, toward the reactor, toward them.

An F-15 and two F-16s banked into a lazy right-hand circle around the reactor, twenty-two thousand feet above the ground, still well under the cirrus layer.

The reactor off their right wings had been constructed under a large pitched roof, which resembled that of a barn, or even an old factory. The roof was there to hide the reactor from satellites and aerial reconnaissance. A half mile to the northeast of the building was the Euphrates River, a broad, brown, placid, meandering highway that stretched to the horizon. The reactor had been under construction for six years, so the disturbed area above the ditches in which the water pipes were buried that carried river water to and from the reactor were no longer discernible from this altitude.

The single-piloted F-16s were merely escorts for the F-15, which had a two-man crew. The man in the rear seat of the F-15 Eagle centered his handheld camera on the roof of the reactor. Fortunately, the visibility was excellent today. The camera was a digital one with a long lens, one designed to take five photos a second automatically if the shutter button was depressed and held down. The pilot in the front seat was counting down the seconds. "Six . . . five . . . four . . ."

At four, the cameraman depressed the shutter button and held it down. He concentrated on holding the camera steady and keeping the reactor centered in the viewfinder.

In the antiaircraft defense control center, Mikhail Toporov was still baffled. Something was wrong—he had heard jet engines, and there should be no aircraft in the prohibited zone, none whatsoever. He reached down beside the man at the scope and pushed the red ALERT button on his console. Instantly a siren sounded in the control room.

A siren also sounded in the reactor administration building. Startled, Dr. Qureshi looked up, just in time to see his secretary walking into his office. That was the last thing he saw as the first bomb penetrated the roof of the building, plunged through all five floors and detonated in the basement of the structure. The floors heaved before they buckled. The desk on which he had been working was flung upward and struck Dr. Qureshi in the head, knocking him unconscious. He was killed when the building collapsed around him.

In the reactor control room, a siren also went off. Shocked, the technicians stared at the gauges in front of them, trying to understand. The reactor was cold, so this couldn't be the nuclear alarm.

Even as they realized it was an air raid alert alarm, the bombs smashed into the roof of the reactor and penetrated deeply, one at a time, two-tenths of a second apart. The bomb fuses were set to explode before the weapons penetrated all the way through the structure into the earth; they actually exploded just above the massive concrete floor that formed the support for the reactor. The trip-hammer explosions—a total of five tons of high explosive—destroyed the pile, destroyed the coolant pipes and pumping systems and rods and rod machinery and the hydraulic systems that controlled them, destroyed the walls and machinery and ceiling, reduced everything to molten rubble. The explosions were so hot that steel and concrete ignited.

In the adjacent control room, everyone died instantly as the control panel, which faced the reactor, was driven into them by the successive shock waves. The control room was completely crushed, which was fortunate, because anyone surviving the initial blast would have been cremated alive by the resulting inferno or quickly poisoned by the radiation released from the nuclear pile.

In the F-15 the photographer was capturing all of it. Later, technicians examining the photos would be able to count each individual explosion. The guidance system in every bomb had worked flawlessly. The Americans made good stuff.

Now, through the viewfinder, the photographer saw smoke pouring out of the reactor and adjacent administration building. Soon the rising smoke obscured the buildings, so he released the shutter button. He waited a moment, watching the smoke column, which he knew was radioactive. It seemed to be drifting off toward the desert to the southeast, just as the weather gurus predicted it would.

"Let's go home," he said to the pilot, who banked the jet smoothly around onto a heading back to Israel.

Mikhail Toporov heard the explosions over the wail of the siren. He ran outside. The antiair defense center was on a low ridge two miles from the reactor. He stood stupefied as black smoke roiled up from the place where the reactor and admin building had stood. Their remains were hidden by the smoke.

That was no meltdown—he knew that. Airplanes. *Bombs!*

The Syrian in charge of the facility joined him. "What happened?" he demanded in Russian, the only language that Toporov spoke, as he jerked at Toporov's sleeve.

"Look for yourself, fool," Toporov roared, gesturing wildly with his free hand. He jerked his other arm free and went back inside, the Syrian trailing closely.

"Why didn't your radars detect the planes?" the Syrian screamed over the high-pitched blast of the siren. He, too, had leaped to the conclusion that the facility was bombed.

"I don't know," Mikhail Toporov replied bitterly. He was very worried. The people in Moscow, he knew, would be apoplectic when they heard the news. First and foremost, he must get possession of the tape that recorded everything the radars saw during the last hour. Only with that tape could he prove that the S-300 air defense system—a combination of radars and computers that controlled batteries of SA-20 antiaircraft missiles—failed to detect the incoming bombers. Only with that tape could he save himself.

When the warplanes landed in Israel, two men in civilian clothes stood outside the operations building watching them. One was about five and a half feet tall, heavyset, with a rounded tummy and a crew cut. He wore khaki trousers and a white short-sleeve shirt with buttons down the front and a pocket protector in the left breast pocket. His name was Dag Mosher, and he was a senior officer in Israeli intelligence, the Mossad.

The man beside Mosher was an American. A half foot taller than Mosher, he was lean, with graying, thinning hair combed straight back. His face was not handsome; he had a square jaw, gray eyes and a nose that was a trifle large. His face and arms were tanned. He was wearing blue jeans and a pullover golf shirt with a logo on the left breast that he had apparently acquired at some summer festival in the States. He was the new CIA head of Middle Eastern Operations, and his name was Jake Grafton.

They watched the planes shut down in revetments. The crews were picked up by a little van, which brought them to this building and let them out in front of it. Still in their flight gear, the pilots and Weapons Systems Operators straggled into the building carrying their helmets and chart bags. Mosher and Grafton followed them.

The civilians sat in the back of the room and listened to uniformed intelligence officers debrief the flight crews. Neither asked a single question. An hour later, as the crews gathered their gear to leave, a technician brought in bomb-damage assessment photos of the target reactor and taped them to the blackboard. Mosher and Grafton strolled to the front of the room and, when the flight crews had had their looks and left, adjusted their reading glasses and studied the photos carefully.

The intelligence debriefers packed up their gear and departed. When only Mosher and Grafton were left in the room, Grafton dropped into a folding chair and asked the Israeli, "Are you guys going to do Iran?"

"You know we can't without aerial tankers. We'd need to borrow some of yours."

"Anything you bomb in Iran will release radioactivity. Lots of it."

"Their problem," Dag Mosher said and dropped into a chair beside Grafton. He sat looking up at the row of photos.

Finally he turned to Grafton. "All the choices are bad—every one has a great many negatives attached. I certainly am not one of the decision-makers, but I can tell you this: If Israel is destroyed, it will only be because we gave every last drop of blood and that wasn't enough. We Jews got in line and shuffled into the gas chambers once—but never again. Never!"

Mosher turned back to the photos and sat staring at them.

"I think the driving force in Iran for the acquisition of nuclear weapons," Grafton said conversationally, "and perhaps the destruction of Israel, is Mahmoud Ahmadinejad. One wonders what might happen in Iran if he died unexpectedly."

Dag Mosher turned slowly to face Grafton. He sat silently, examining his face. Finally he said, "Was that thought hatched in Washington, or did you dream it up?"

"Well, I'm kinda new to the Middle East," Jake Grafton drawled, "and, I confess, I thought that one up all by my own self. There're probably a hundred good reasons not to pop Ahmadinejad. Not cricket, bad form, and all that. You won't hold this against me, will ya?"

A trace of a smile appeared on Mosher's face; then he turned back to the photos.

"Same country, different subject," Jake Grafton continued. "I've sent one of my best men to Iran, and he's going to need all the help he can get. I was wondering, do you folks have a few people there who can discreetly watch his back? I would appreciate a heads-up if he appears to be getting in too deep."

Dag Mosher looked amused. "Tommy Carmellini, perhaps?" he asked casually.

"Why, yes," Grafton said with a smile. "Let's hope the Iranians are not as well informed as the Mossad."

"We can always hope," Mosher admitted.

CHAPTER TWO

The air attack upon and destruction of Syria's nuclear reactor was a media nonevent. Nothing about the attack appeared in either Syrian or Israeli newspapers or broadcasts. The Syrians quickly began cleaning up the reactor site, using the expedient of pushing dirt into the hole with bulldozers, then pouring in concrete. Syria did, however, ask the UN for sanctions against Israel for violating Syrian airspace and attacking a "military storage area." These sanctions failed when Syria refused to allow an inspection of the attack site and, attempting to silence rumors, denied that it even had a nuclear reactor.

Still, whispers swirled through the diplomatic community worldwide. Unable to stonewall any longer, the Syrians decided to change the lie. A week after the event, the Syrian minister of information acknowledged that Syria had had a reactor under construction, a reactor at least seven years from completion, and that was the site bombed by the Israelis.

Still, the Western press generally ignored the story. Without verifiable facts the story had no legs, and, after all, even if there had been a reactor, the Syrians didn't have one now.

The unofficial, nonpublic reaction in various capitals around the world was less tepid.

In Washington the president was briefed on the attack over breakfast by his new national security adviser, Dr. Jurgen Schulz, and the director of the CIA, William S. Wilkins. Rounding out the foursome was presidential aide Sal Molina, who this morning was togged out in a sports coat that didn't go with his trousers. Schulz was dressed as usual in a tailored wool suit and silk tie; he was trim, with a full head of dyed hair, thickened, some suspected, with hair implants. He looked like a natty Harvard professor on government leave, which he was.

Wilkins never made that kind of effort. He was a career intelligence bureaucrat and looked it. He was balding and slightly overweight and wore trifocals, a suit from Sears and a cheap, out-of-date tie.

Since he had just come from his morning workout, the president was wearing sweats.

As breakfast was served by the White House staff—yogurt with fruit, cereal and 2 percent milk—Wilkins asked Schulz, "How come so many of the national security advisers have had German names?"

"It's fashionable," Schulz said with a straight face.

When the staff had retired, leaving the four alone, the president said, "What do you have, Bill?"

Wilkins ran through the facts of the attack and the poststrike assessment.

"So the Israelis are at it again," Schulz remarked. "What are the chances they'll decide to derail Iran's nuclear program?"

"The distances are too great," Wilkins said. "They'll need our help, and it won't be a one-location strike. The Iranians have two reactors, three enrichment facilities—centrifuge, laser and heavy water—and an underground bomb-making plant that is impervious to conventional attack."

"I thought the National Security assessment was that Iran didn't have a weapons program."

"Your predecessor thought so," Wilkins said drily, "and you know how that came about."

Indeed, they all did. After the American intelligence community concluded, based on circumstantial evidence, much of it manufactured by Saddam Hussein in the hopes of deterring Iranian aggression, that Iraq had nuclear weapons, the administration had used the erroneous assessment as justification for invasion. The discovery that Saddam did not possess, nor was he building, nuclear weapons had proven to be a major embarrassment. The intelligence agencies were even more embarrassed, and the discredited professionals had decided to insist on verifiable facts before they would again put their reputations on the political chopping block. The entire basis of a sound foreign policy, good intelligence, had gone off the track. Arguably, the assessments immediately went from too aggressive to too conservative—and one was as bad as the other.

"To the best of our knowledge," Wilkins continued, "the Iranians are enriching uranium. They are not presently manufacturing weapons."

"What will it take to convince you?" Schulz asked.

"An explosion with a mushroom cloud," Sal Molina said heavily. A Hispanic lawyer who had been with the president since he started his political career, Molina didn't have a big title at the White House. In fact, no one seemed to know just what his title was; his refusal to make speeches, attend parties or fund-raisers or talk to the press added to his aura of mystery.

The president broke the silence that followed. "I have read the assessments, read the raw reports the assessments were constructed from, and I've looked at the satellite photos. It is beyond dispute that they are spending billions on enrichment facilities. I am convinced Iran is gearing up to make bombs. There is no other logical explanation."

The president paused to gather his thoughts, then continued. "A nuclear Iran may well prompt other nations in the Mideast to go nuclear. Iran's leaders are unstable men. Ahmadinejad is a megalomaniac, and God whispers to Khamenei. It's within the realm of possibility that they could go on a nuclear jihad to wipe out Israel and conquer the Middle East."

"We can't attack those nuclear sites," Schulz said. "If we do, we are likely to release a cloud of radioactivity that will drift God knows where. The Israelis did it and got away with it, but if we do it, the political fallout in this country will be awe-inspiring. Every tree-hugger, green weenie, peacenik and left-wing radical between Canada and Mexico will go ballistic. The firestorm will be even worse in the Middle East; it'll bring down every pro-Western government, shatter the Middle East like Humpty Dumpty. All the king's horses and all the king's men won't be able to put the Middle East back together, not in our lifetimes."

The president glanced at Schulz, measuring him, perhaps. "No doubt you're right," he said, "but I'm not going to sit on my thumb doing nothing while those religious crackpots nuke Israel. When we know precisely what the threat is and how much time we have, then we can figure out the best way to get this mess unscrewed."

"How much time *do* we have?" Sal Molina asked the CIA director, who was frowning at his cereal, which tasted, Wilkins thought, like ground-up cardboard.

"I don't know," Wilkins said. "Six months, a year, two years . . ." He shrugged. "Getting good intelligence out of Tehran is extremely difficult."

"We need it in spades this time," Jurgen Schulz remarked.

The president put down his spoon and stared at Wilkins. "I know they are gearing up to make bombs. I accept that as proved. I want the CIA to answer two questions: When will the Iranians get operational warheads for their missiles, and, once they have them, what do they intend to do with them?"

Wilkins nodded.

"I don't want reports quoting some unhappy Iranian scientist or guesses from the analysts. I want absolute, incontrovertible proof. In writing, signed by Ahmadinejad, with his and Khamenei's fingerprints all over the paper."

Wilkins looked from face to face, then returned his gaze to the president. "You are asking the impossible."

"Absolute proof," Schulz said.

Wilkins took a deep breath, then let it out slowly. "We'll do our best."

"Keep Sal advised," the president said. "He can brief me and Jurgen."

"Yes, sir."

Wilkins glanced morosely at his cereal, then reached for his coffee cup, which was empty. Sal Molina snagged the insulated decanter and poured him another cup.

Two days after the attack, in downtown Jakarta, Indonesia, a limo with dark windows drifted to a stop by a sidewalk café. A man sitting in one of the chairs near the street rose carefully to his feet and motioned to the waiter. He tossed several bills on the table, then hoisted two attaché cases from the chair beside him as the driver held open the rear passenger door. The man seated himself, the driver closed the door and resumed his seat, and the car pulled away into traffic.

Inside the car the man with the cases sat looking at the backseat passenger, a middle-aged man in an army uniform, one with short sleeves. He had stars on the flaps of the shirt and an impressive array of ribbons on his left breast.

"General Darma. Good to see you again," the man said.

The general nodded. He knew the man as Hyman Fineberg, but knew that was not his real name. He took his time examining Fineberg's face. The left side was heavily scarred and didn't match the right, and his left eye didn't track. It was artificial, of course, inserted into the socket merely to fill it. Fineberg also had an artificial left foot and ankle, but he walked so well that his gait was normal to a casual observer.

Fineberg's left sleeve was longer than usual to hide some of the scars on his left hand. The general, who had never seen a day of combat in his life, wondered—again, for this was the third time he had met Fineberg personally—what the rest of Fineberg's anatomy looked like. He would have been shocked, had he known. Fineberg was the sole survivor when a sabot round destroyed his tank, and there had been days when he wished he had also died. That was years ago, though, when he was young. Now Fineberg lived with his disabilities and tried to ignore them.

The car glided expertly through traffic, even though it was armored and weighed almost four tons. Meanwhile, the general realized his scrutiny of Fineberg was impolite and averted his gaze to the aircraft-aluminum attaché cases.

Fineberg glanced at the back of the driver's head.

"My son," the general said.

Fineberg pulled the closest case onto his lap, used a key to unlock both the locks that held it and moved it over to the general's lap.

The first case was filled with U.S. currency, packs of hundred-dollar bills stuffed tightly inside.

The second case was as full as the first.

"Your down payment," Fineberg said.

The general closed the cases and arranged them in the middle of the seat. Fineberg handed him the two keys.

"So," said the general, "have you decided where it will occur?"

Hyman Fineberg took his time answering. "The lobby of the hotel, I think. He stayed in the presidential suite on his last visit. Your people kept the lobby empty for his arrivals and departures. There will be no witnesses, no cameras, no innocent bystanders."

"He may choose a different hotel."

"He might," Fineberg acknowledged, "but he is a creature of habit. One suspects it will be the same hotel, the same suite."

"He had four bodyguards," the general mused, "and they were armed. We allowed them their weapons as a courtesy."

"Of course."

"How many of you will there be?"

"Four," said Hyman Fineberg. "We have the money to purchase only one chance, so we must prepare for it wisely and use it well."

The general smiled and ran his left hand over the top of the attaché cases. "You may not wear uniforms. Civilian clothes only."

"Of course."

"No one else must be harmed."

"I understand," said Hyman Fineberg. He pushed the button on his left armrest to lower his window an inch, then removed a pack of cigarettes from a pocket. He offered one to the general, who refused, then lit one for himself.

They discussed the murder as if it were a magazine photo op and agreed that whenever another visit was announced, Fineberg would again make contact.

General Syafi'i Darma was philosophical. "No one lives forever," he muttered. "Life must go on."

Dag Mosher's office in downtown Tel Aviv was in a drab, nondescript building a few blocks from the sun-washed Mediterranean. His guest today, Jake Grafton, got the only padded chair in front of his desk. The two technicians who joined Mosher and Grafton sat in metal folding chairs and held their graphs and reports on their knees. They talked for ten minutes. Summing up, the senior tech, a woman in a print dress with iron gray hair that she pulled back in a bun, held a graph where Grafton and Mosher could see it and said, "There was no increase in Syrian electronic activity immediately before or during the attack. This graph shows activity in ten major wavelengths, and as you can see, the lines are essentially flat."

Mosher nodded.

The junior tech, a man wearing eyeglasses so thick they distorted other people's view of his eyes, said, "The ECM tapes from the planes show nothing but routine search radar scans were detected. The pilots reported no antiair activity. No interceptors were scrambled by the Syrians. The conclusion is inescapable; the Syrians never detected our planes."

Mosher nodded and glanced at Grafton to see if he had any questions. He didn't. Mosher thanked the techs, and they gathered their stuff in their arms and left, closing the door behind them.

"That ALQ-199 is quite a gadget," Mosher said.

"It is until someone steals the software and sells or gives it to the Russians," Grafton remarked. "After your attack on Syria, I have a sneaking suspicion that acquiring an operable ALQ-199 or the software that drives it became the number one priority of the Russians."

"And the Iranians . . ." Dag Mosher mused.

"And the North Koreans and Chinese. We could make a list."

"So how are we going to get them one?"

A smile flitted across Jake Grafton's face. "I am sure you and I can think of something," he murmured.

A week after the destruction of the Syrian reactor, a tall, lean man in an expensive suit stepped out of a hotel in Tehran and, despite the severe air pollution, lit a cigarette. He had only had a few puffs, however, when a black limousine pulled up in front of the hotel. A man got out of the right front seat and held open the rear passenger door. The tall man flipped his cigarette onto the sidewalk and climbed in.

The tall man was Janos Ilin, and he was a very senior officer in the Russian Foreign Intelligence Service, the SVR *(Sluzhba Vneshnei Razvedki)*, the bureaucratic successor to the First Chief Directorate of the Soviet-era KGB.

After an hour's creep through horrendous traffic, the limo eased to a stop in front of the headquarters of the Ministry of Defense. The man on the curb who opened the door was in his late twenties and clean-shaven and wore a suit without a tie. Ilin noticed a bulge under his left armpit.

"This way, please," the man muttered and gestured toward the door. Then he led the way.

Inside the foyer stood two desks, one on either side of the room. At each desk sat two armed soldiers in uniform. Their AK-47s lay on the desk in front of them, and they wore sidearms in belt holsters. A wire mesh ran from floor to ceiling in front of the desks so that visitors couldn't grab at the weapons. Today there were three people in front of one desk and one in front of another, all in earnest discussion with the uniformed officers.

Trying to talk their way in, Ilin thought.

His escort didn't bother with the guards but walked straight to the door at the rear of the room. It opened as he approached, and he led Ilin through. There was no visible magnetometer or X-ray machine.

Five minutes and four flights of stairs later, Ilin was ushered into the office of the minister of defense, who was there waiting. His name was Habib Sultani. He was of medium height and wore the fashionable short beard and, although he was a major general in the Islamic Revolutionary Guard Corps—the IRGC—a cheap, rumpled dark suit that looked as if it came off the rack of a Moscow department store. The escort stood in the back of the room with his arms folded across his chest.

Ilin nodded at Sultani and paused to survey the room, which was large. On one wall was a banner that proclaimed in English, in letters a foot high, DEATH TO AMERICA. On another wall was a large portrait of Ayatollah Ali Khamenei, Iran's Supreme Leader.

Ilin glanced back at the escort. This must be the minister's nephew Ghasem.

General Sultani shook hands perfunctorily, motioned toward a chair and pushed an ashtray across his desk. "You may smoke, if you wish," he said, then seated himself behind his desk.

Ilin settled into the indicated chair, crossed his legs and took out his silver cigarette case from an inside coat pocket. He selected a cancer stick and snapped the case shut. "Being a good Muslim, of course you don't smoke," he said as he stored the case back in his pocket.

"No," Sultani muttered.

"Too bad," said Ilin, then lit his weed. When it was giving off smoke, he added, "Every man should have at least one antisocial habit."

"This attack on the Syrian reactor . . . The Syrians tell us that the S-300 antiaircraft defense system did not function. Not a missile was launched at the attacking planes; not a single shot was fired."

Ilin nodded his head once, a silent yes.

"You sold us the same systems."

Ilin's nod was barely discernible. He puffed at his cigarette.

"General Ilin . . . May I call you that?" Habib Sultani paused, then rolled on. "General Ilin, we have the great misfortune, like the Syrians, of dealing with you incompetent, perfidious Russians. The Americans are on three sides of Iran—in Afghanistan, Iraq and the Persian Gulf. Even as we speak warplanes may be on their way to attack us."

Ilin examined the glowing tip of his cigarette. "You people are producing highly enriched uranium, and you promised you wouldn't."

"Iran must have a stable, modern source of electrical power."

"Don't give me that! We both know the mullahs want nuclear weapons and they've squandered billions on the facilities to make them."

Sultani's voice rose to a roar, and he came out of his chair. "Lies, all lies! You justify an attack on the nation of God with lies! We will not listen. Russia took our money, made promises, and we are left with useless hardware, defenseless against powerful enemies. You tell your Premier Putin that he cannot play us for fools. If he wants cooperation and respect, he will have to earn it. So far he has earned nothing but contempt. Tell him that."

Sultani sat and mopped his face with one hand.

In the smoky silence that followed, Ilin said, "Obviously, the Israelis were using secret American electronic countermeasures technology to shield their planes from detection."

"Americans invent, innovate, research . . . and Russians lie, cheat and steal. Your ambassador assured us that the S-300 system could detect and defeat the latest frontline American and Israeli fighters. We wouldn't have bought it without that promise, and you and the ambassador and Vladimir Putin know it." His voice began to rise. "We do not need any more long-winded technical explanations of how clever the Americans are or how they outwitted

you Russian geniuses. Nor do we need any more worthless, obsolete equipment that doesn't work—we already have hundreds of millions of dollars'
worth of *that*." Sultani opened the top button of his shirt.

"General Sultani, if your reactors are used for peaceful power generation
and you don't enrich the spent fuel for fissile material," Ilin said coolly, "as
you promised us and the international community, you probably have nothing to worry about from the Americans and Israelis."

"Don't lecture me or try to dictate foreign policy to the Iranian government," Sultani snarled. "We are surrounded on three sides by enemies of
God. Keep your promises. Give us an antiaircraft defense system that works
as you said it would."

Janos Ilin was still as cool as he was when he walked into Sultani's office.
"The latest American CIA assessment, which they made public, said Iran
does not have a nuclear weapons program. Is that true or false?"

Sultani's eyes narrowed to slits.

Ilin stubbed out his cigarette in the ashtray and rose to go.

Habib Sultani stared at Ilin's back as he walked out, followed by the escort, Ghasem.

CHAPTER THREE

There were two of them standing on the sidewalk ahead, two young men, watching me as I approached. We were in a working-class neighborhood—read slum—in Tehran, Iran. They stood there watching me, then glanced at each other.

I was out for my morning run, wearing shorts and a sweatshirt, and I stuck out like a sore thumb—clean-shaven, barbered, fair skin. Obviously I was a foreigner, European or American, and consequently rich. No doubt they thought I had something worth stealing. I did—my wallet, diplomatic passport, and cell phone.

I kept my eyes on them as I trotted toward them. I sized them up as working-class guys, rough clothes, unshaven, who thought they were tough. Well, all three of us would soon find out.

I glanced over my shoulder to see who was watching or following, just in case this might be a setup. No cars following, none parked nearby, no cops, three or four men in sight, all busy doing something else.

The distance closed rapidly; then I was there and they came at me, one from each side. I veered toward the one on the left, set my feet just so and kicked him in the crotch. Caught him solidly. He hadn't expected that move and doubled over.

I spun around and went at the other one, who had started to come at me. Only then did I see the little knife he had in his right hand. My charge was unexpected. I grabbed his right wrist with both hands, half turned and threw a hip into him. Using his momentum, I pulled him into me and threw him, still holding on to that right wrist with both hands. The bones in his arm snapped with an audible crack. As he hit the sidewalk and the knife skittered away, I released his wrist. His lower arm was twisted and turned about sixty degrees from its proper angle.

I was tempted to tell him, "Bad break," but stifled myself.

It was all over in less than eight seconds and I was trotting on. I glanced back. Both of them were writhing on the sidewalk, with a couple of bystanders staring at me.

Running in the megalopolis of Tehran was an adventure. Not so much the running, but crossing the streets.

Like most cities in the third world, Tehran had grown exponentially as the population exploded in the aftermath of World War II. The dearth of contraceptives meant large families, the medicine men used just enough modern medicine to keep more of the kids alive, and rural peasants moved to town looking for a job. Today Tehran and its sprawling suburbs contained somewhere between fifteen and twenty million people, about one-fifth of the Iranian population. The population explosion meant the Iranian economy needed to create eight hundred thousand new jobs a year, and that wasn't happening.

The streets, avenues and boulevards, all built for one-fifth the amount of traffic they were carrying, were clogged. Gridlock was the proper description of morning and evening rush hour. Road rage was endemic. Many of the drivers and motorcyclists regarded a pedestrian, especially one moving quickly, as a sporting challenge. Crossing the street became an exercise in terror.

There was heavy air pollution, too, so bad it made Los Angeles' smog seem like an unattainable dream. It seared the lungs, burned the eyes and limited visibility on windless days to no more than two miles.

Today, as usual, I managed to get back to the hotel in one piece, with more close calls in my logbook.

After a shower, I dressed and walked the three blocks to the Swiss embassy annex, a small building just down the street from the real Swiss embassy. Although America and Iran had not resumed diplomatic relations since the takeover of the American embassy in 1979, the United States had recently opened an American Interests Section in the Swiss embassy annex. Of course, my little corner was in the basement.

The room was small and divided by a waist-high temporary wall, the bottom of which was plywood nailed to two-by-fours and the top of which was latticework. The whole thing was painted a hideous brown. In the wall were two windows, one for me and one for my colleague, Frank Caldwell.

Here Frank and I took applications from Iranians asking for visas to visit America. We also were supposed to interview folks who wanted to permanently immigrate to the good ol' U.S. of A., but since our government was worried that jihadists might slip through, they had declared a moratorium on immigration requests. Consequently we took only tourist visa applications, none of which the State Department would approve unless we were absolutely sure the tourist would indeed come flying home to this mud-hut Islamic paradise when his vacation was over.

I probably should pause to introduce myself. My name is Tommy Carmellini, and although I was stuck here in this basement four hours a day interviewing Iranians who desperately needed a vacation in the heart of the infidel empire, the United States, I didn't work for the Department of State. Nope. I was a CIA operative. I was pretending to be a State visa guy while I tried to steal the deepest secrets of the mullahs. So far I hadn't found any secrets to steal, deep or shallow. I had, however, met a lot of Iranians with fathers, brothers, cousins, uncles, nephews and children safely lodged in America whom they wanted to visit; see before they died, either the host or the visitor, and renew those precious family ties; then, you betcha, come on home.

"Hello," I said in English to the one-legged man who seated himself before me. He had been waiting upstairs since the annex opened. He had a crutch, no artificial leg. He was maybe forty-five, with a big mustache and grizzled jowls.

"Hello," he said back, also in English, and passed me his form.

I looked at it. His name was Abdullaziz Nasr Qomi. I didn't recognize the name of his village, so I asked him about it in Farsi, or Persian. I attended a crash course to learn the language before I came over here—but more on that later.

His face brightened a little as he told me about his village, a little place near Takab, which I knew was west of Tehran and up toward the big lake, Urmia.

I listened to him talk, getting most of it despite his regional accent. I glanced at his hands and saw they were heavily callused. This guy wasn't a bureaucrat or apparatchik.

He worked in construction, Qomi said, was a day laborer. He paused and then said heavily, "I want to go to America." Since we were praying over a tourist visa application, he added, "For a visit."

"How'd you lose your leg?"

"The war with Iraq. I was in the Martyrs Brigade. I stepped on a mine. I was ready to die, ready to go straight to Paradise, but I didn't. I am still here, with only one leg."

"Must be difficult for a one-legged man to make a living in Iran."

He didn't reply to that, merely lowered his head.

I confess, I liked the guy. Qomi was tough, and he'd obviously been through the mill and survived. I have little sympathy for victims, but I really like survivors. My ambition is to be one myself.

"You married?" I asked, then glanced at the form. He had marked NO.

He still had his head down.

"Whom do you know in America?" I asked, not waiting for an answer. "Who are you going to visit?"

He started telling me about his cousin who finished concrete in Queens. As he talked I sat back and glanced around, at Frank Caldwell, who was interviewing a weeping woman in a chador, and at this dingy, damp little room.

I recalled the day that Jake Grafton called me in, told me he wanted me to do an intensive course in the Persian language, then go to Iran. Three months later, I got the language completion certificate, written in English and Farsi; I was ready to trade insults with Cyrus the Great. I reported back to Grafton at the Company headquarters in Langley.

Jake Grafton was a retired naval officer, an attack pilot, retired as a two-star, and for years he had been the go-to guy when . . . shall we say, "situations" developed and the politicians or Pentagon brass needed some serious help with their hot chestnuts. Finally they gave him a job in the Company. He was smart and tough as shoe leather, and if he was ever afraid, it never showed. In addition, he was a genuine nice guy, but I don't think he wanted anyone in the agency to know that. Believe me, this outfit operated on the theory that nice guys finish last. In the spy game, they often did, so maybe Grafton was the exception that proved the rule.

Me? Of course I'm a nice guy—my mother would sign an affidavit to that effect. However, there is a lot she doesn't know. In fact, she is in the dark about 99.9 percent of the stuff I do. She knows that I live in suburban Maryland; she sends me birthday and Christmas cards. I think she knows that I work for the agency, but maybe not. I might have lied about that. She didn't mention it during my last visit, so I didn't either.

The sad fact is I tell a lot of lies. Most of them are professional, in the line of duty, so to speak, but every now and then a personal lie slips out. Maybe it's habit; the darn things pop out before I can stop them, more smirches on my character. Perhaps it's just my criminal mind. Whatever, I'm still a nice guy, and you can take that to the bank.

One April Tuesday a few days after I finished the language course, we were settled in Grafton's office talking about the state of the planet and the people on it, just covering the ground, so to speak, when he said, "I want you to go to Iran next week. You'll be attached to the American Interests Section as a visa officer."

I nodded. I'm not the swiftest guy you ever met, but after doing the language course, I had an inkling this was coming. I had hoped it would come later, much later, but my luck doesn't run that way. Persia, which is presently the Islamic Republic of Iran, complete with mullahs, religious facists, holy warriors and throat-slitters, plus tens of millions of folks just trying to pay their bills and stay alive. Am I lucky or what?

Grafton's desk phone buzzed and he got it. "Yes."

He listened a moment, then hung up. "I have to go to a meeting," he said as he unlocked his safe, which was beside his desk. He pulled the safe door open and handed me a sheet of paper from the gloomy interior.

"Here's the access codes to the file I want you to read. Look it over, then come back to see me."

I went to the converted broom closet the Company so blithely labels my office and shoved aside the mountain of read-and-initial crap that had accumulated on my desk during my absence and I hadn't had time yet to go through. I fired up my desk computer.

The Company is trying to go digital, but very carefully. The last thing on earth anyone in the building wants is a hacker getting into our files. Or worse, a foreign intelligence service. Still, the advantages of going digital are so attractive that we are trying.

Three or four screens into the file, my hands started to sweat. Then my forehead. I had to take off my sports coat and hang it over the back of my chair.

Mahmoud Ahmadinejad, the current president of Iran, was a real piece of work. Born in the provinces, his devout father changed the family name to Ahmadinejad, "virtuous race" or "Muhammad's race," when he moved to Tehran in search of a better life. Young Mahmoud studied mathematics at a private school, then went off to the university in 1975. By all accounts he was very devout. In any event, he fell in with the religious political movement, which was moving toward revolution against the shah. The head revolutionary was Ruhollah Khomeini, who preached a vision of a society led by zealous, uniquely qualified Islamic leaders who would control the "simple-hearted" lower classes. This Islamic Bolshevik went further: He believed that anyone who rejected his ideas, which one critic, Alireza Jafarzadeh, said were "dogmatic, rigid, feudalistic, medieval ideas contrary to the true teachings of

Islam," was not a Muslim. Like Vladimir Ilyich Lenin and the legion of tyrants who had slashed their way through history before him, Khomeini was an all-or-nothing guy. Ahmadinejad signed on early; he was one of the first to join the Islamic Revolutionary Guards Corps while at the University of Science and Technology.

After the shah was routed in 1979, Ahmadinejad joined the Intelligence Unit of the IRGC, which Khomeini put together to defeat his political enemies following the collapse of the shah's secret police service, the SAVAK. This Iranian version of Hitler's Brownshirts operated with no constraints on their methods. Ahmadinejad was right in the middle of it. He was in Khomeini's inner circle in those days and probably helped plan the takeover of the American embassy in November of 1979. There was some debate about whether he was in the first wave that scaled the walls, but he was definitely there shortly thereafter, in charge of the guards and watching the interrogation of American prisoners. He might even have been in charge of interrogations.

There were a couple of photos in the file of Iranians mobbing the U.S. embassy. A figure in each had been circled and labeled as "possible." I whipped out the magnifying glass that all good agency employees keep in their desk and studied the faces within the circles.

Even after I had enlarged the circles as much as possible before they dissolved into individual pixels, I decided that I would have to take the experts' word for it.

I put the glass back in my desk and continued reading.

In the years following the revolution, during Khomeini's consolidation of power, Ahmadinejad was involved in the interrogation, torture and execution of enemies of the regime at the Evin prison, where he was known by the pseudonym of "Golpa," among others. The interrogators tried to stay masked and change their *noms de guerre* regularly so that their victims wouldn't know what they had told to whom. The prodemocracy political movement Mujahedin-e Khalq, or MEK, supplied many of the victims.

For his loyalty and ruthlessness, Mahmoud Ahmadinejad became a senior commander in the Qods (Jerusalem) Force of the IRGC. The report I was reading said he had been a key figure in the formation of the Qods, a terrorist special forces unit that had been linked to assassinations in the Middle East and Europe. Ahmadinejad personally carried weapons across international borders to assassinate political foes, among them the Kurdish leader Abdul Rahman Ghassemlou, leader of the Kurdish Democratic Party in Iran. On occasion this young Iranian Stalin reported directly to and got his orders from the Ayatollah Khomeini, who had sole and complete control of the Qods.

I didn't read the whole file. I scanned enough to realize that Ahmadinejad was involved in every aspect of the fundamentalist Islamic takeover of Iran. According to Jafarzadeh, he interrogated U.S. hostages, led the closure of universities, questioned and tortured political prisoners, engaged in battles on Iran's western borders with Iraqi forces and conducted special assassination ops against the regime's enemies in Europe and the Middle East.

An unintended consequence of the U.S.-led invasion of Iraq was to give Khomeini and the Iranian mullahs a golden opportunity to exploit the chaos in post-Saddam Iraq in furtherance of their goal of installing an Islamic regime there and making it a satellite state. Saddam Hussein had a lot of faults, but he knew who his real enemies were.

In the 1990s Ahmadinejad went into academia. Part-time, anyway. He was a zealot still trying to purify the universities, and founded Ansar-e Hezbollah (Followers of the Party of God), the members of which wore black clothes and hoods, sort of a Muslim Ku Klux Klan, and attacked student gatherings and demonstrations, beating up students and other opponents of the regime with chains, clubs, truncheons and knives. They could talk the talk, but when the chips were down, they were thugs.

In 2003 Ahmadinejad surfaced as mayor of Tehran, where he earned the nickname of the "Iranian Taliban." In 2005, this social progressive launched his campaign for the presidency of the country. Since he had the backing of Khomeini's successor, the Ayatollah Ali Khamenei, and the election was rigged, he won handily.

I perused a few of his campaign speeches, in which he often waxed eloquent on the glory of martyrdom. "If we want to resolve today's social problems," he said, "we must return to the culture of martyrs." Now there is a prescription for social peace.

The election of 2009 was a farce. Three hours after the polls closed in a country three times larger than France, one without a single voting machine, Ahmadinejad was declared the winner with 63 percent of the vote. Apparently the ballots weren't even counted.

When I had had all I could stand, I logged off and turned off the computer.

Just my luck. Jake Grafton was pointing me toward the biggest, most vicious shark in the sea. He hadn't told me yet what he wanted me to do in Iran, and I could hardly wait.

I surveyed my comfy little office, which I got to visit so seldom anymore. Why couldn't I be in charge of something like . . . building passes?

I went downstairs to the Starbucks concessionaire for a Caffé Mocha, bought an extra one for Grafton's assistant, Robin, then strolled toward Grafton's office.

"Oh, thank you, Tommy," Robin said with a huge grin when I presented her drink.

I smiled back. After all, she might be the last normal person I'd get to smile at on planet Earth.

With that happy thought ripping through my head, I went in to see Jake Grafton, who was back from his meeting.

Grafton got right to it. "What do you think about Mahmoud Ahmadinejad?"

"A raghead Stalin."

"That isn't a politically correct remark."

I shrugged. "There are a lot of assholes in this world. He seems to be in a special, small elite group at the very tip top of the heap."

"There are a couple of guys already in Iran that you'll work with. They are illegals. You'll be attached to the American Interests Section of the Swiss embassy and will be watched. Carefully watched."

I could feel the earth spinning under me.

"What's the mission?"

"I don't know just yet. Settle in, become a good, low-level career diplomat, and I'll call you when we need you. You are going to be our ace in the hole."

"More like a deuce," I muttered. I confess, I knew he had something in mind for me or he wouldn't have made these elaborate plans for my future. Trying to get a hint, I said, "One of these days you'll call and tell me to steal Ahmadinejad's underwear, while he's wearing it."

Grafton didn't smile or look annoyed. There was no reaction at all. He should have been playing poker in Vegas.

The weeping of the chador-clad woman seated in front of Frank's window brought me out of my reverie. She was a grandmother, she said, and her sons and their wives and grandchildren lived in the States. She wanted to join them, if only for a visit. Of course, she would never return to Iran, would be swallowed up in the churning sea of Middle Eastern immigrants in New York and never be heard from again.

"The mullahs are finished in Iran," Abdullaziz Nasr Qomi said. "Everyone hates them. They are rich, we are poor. All the oil money goes to the government and the mullahs, and none of it reaches us. The mullahs are living very well, though . . ." He continued, giving me his view of the world in which he lived.

Frank was concentrating on the weeping woman. He looked as if he were ready to go through the little gate and put his arms around her shoulders. He was murmuring comforting words.

He was very fluent in Farsi, could do all the dialects so well he could fool the natives. I certainly couldn't. Frank was in his forties, a career case officer, and no doubt a damn good one. Only fluent speakers could read body language, the subtle hints given by intonation and hesitations, appreciate the choice of words, understand what was meant but not being said. Fluent speakers do better at sorting truth from lies. If only the Company had more guys and gals like Frank Caldwell!

Yet he had spent six years in Istanbul at the embassy visa window, denying visas to Iranians and trying to recruit spies. Now he was in the heart of the beast, still at it. He reminded me of the guy in charge of the candy store who never, ever, said yes.

Abdullaziz Nasr Qomi finished his discourse on the state of the Iranian nation, such as it is, and stopped speaking. I forced myself to focus on him. What I saw was a stolid peasant with one leg and work-hardened hands who needed a chance. Just a chance at life, which had dealt him shitty cards so far.

I took a deep breath and looked at the form in front of me. A tourist visa. I got my pen out of my shirt pocket and flipped to the endorsement area on the back, where we were told to always mark the NO box. I marked YES.

"I am going to recommend approval of this tourist visa, for a period of one month," I told Qomi, who was obviously shocked. He had been told he was wasting his time, but he came anyway. Hell, he knew he was going to die when he marched across that minefield, and yet he lived.

Life isn't rational.

He grinned at me, displaying yellow, broken teeth. No dentist had ever seen the inside of his mouth.

"Check back in two weeks," I said. "Bring your passport."

Qomi couldn't believe his good fortune. He dropped the crutch. He reached for my hand to pump it, then realized he didn't have the visa yet.

"Two weeks," I repeated.

He got up and arranged the crutch, then pegged off up the stairs. As the grandmother sobbed, I got busy writing up the reasons why the United States of America should give a tourist visa to one Abdullaziz Nasr Qomi. "Mr. Qomi has an incredible love for his native Iran—the land, the people, the culture, the whole enchilada—and he loathes America. His family had to beg him to visit his brother, a concrete finisher in the bowels of Queens who is in poor health, and his brother's family, including a daughter who plans to marry during Qomi's visit. I have absolutely no doubt Mr. Qomi will return to the bosom of his extended family in and around"—I had to check for the name of his village, which I inserted here—"prior to the expiration of his visitor's visa."

I looked at my screed. One big lie, but . . . ho-hum. The United States was certainly big enough to swallow Mr. Qomi whole.

I signed my name with a flourish as Frank Caldwell finished with the sobbing grandmother who wanted to go to America. The answer, of course, was no. She was going to die here in Iran, in the third-world squalor of the Islamic Republic, and by God that was that.

As the black chador disappeared up the stairs, Caldwell said to me in an accusatory tone, "I thought I heard you tell that last man that you would recommend him for a visa?"

"Yep."

"You can't do that! You've read the directives from—"

"I made the recommendation. State can grant it or not, as they choose."

"You know that guy won't come home."

"If we've got room for thirteen million illegal Mexicans, what's the big deal about one one-legged Iranian?" I dropped the visa app in the tray.

"Goddamn it, Carmellini. You can't give State the finger—"

"You oughta try it sometime, Frank. It'll make you feel better. Almost human."

"Carmellini—"

"Why do you do this, Frank? Why sit here day after day, month after month, year after year, looking at the human parade and always saying no? Why don't you go get a real job and a life?"

"Because—"

"Why?"

"I like these people. Don't you?"

I pushed the heels of my hands against my eyes until I saw stars.

"Am I the only sane man left alive?" I asked aloud.

After a last glance at Frank, who was still staring at me, I pushed the button to flash the light upstairs, summoning my next victim.

CHAPTER FOUR

The evening after he returned from Israel, Jake and Callie Grafton entertained one of Callie's faculty colleagues from Georgetown University, where she taught in the language department. Professor Aurang Azari and his wife were Iranians. A year or so after the fall of the shah, he and his wife had left Iran to study in England. They had met and married at Oxford, and upon graduation, he scored a teaching position there. Four years ago he secured a position in the mathematics department at Georgetown.

Azari was of medium size, in his early fifties, Jake knew, and was not a man who would stand out in a crowd. His wife was much like him in size and demeanor, almost a female twin.

In the last few years, Professor Azari had become an authority on Iran's nuclear program. Regularly quoted in the press, he also did op-ed pieces for the big newspapers and had even written a book about Iran's nuclear program. None of this would be possible, of course, without a private intelligence network inside Iran, a network made up of enemies of the regime.

The CIA had attempted to recruit the professor several times and had been rebuffed each time. Grafton thought that Azari and his friends had probably belonged to the Mojahedin-e Khalq, the People's Holy Warriors, who first supported Khomeini and the mullahs, then became their enemies. The MEK attracted Marxists, intellectuals and the educated, all of whom the fundamentalists feared. Stealing a page from Lenin, after the Islamic Revolution Khomeini and his disciples arrested, tortured, interrogated and executed many of their political enemies. Some of the survivors, who were scientists and technicians, were recruited into Iran's nuclear program. They—Grafton thought—were probably Azari's sources, his spies.

Foreign intelligence services, including the CIA, are usually bottom feeders, vacuuming up the gossip of laborers and low-level functionaries. Azari's sources delivered gold. That their reports got from Iran to Azari said a lot about the inefficiency of the Islamic Revolutionary Guard security service. Any large classified program had leaks, but Iran's was a sieve. Still, the CIA had had no success generating the kind of intelligence that Azari obviously had access to.

Naturally, Azari knew about the Israeli attack on the Syrian reactor, even though not a word about it had appeared in the Washington or New York newspapers.

"What do they think about that in Iran?" Jake asked innocently at the dinner table.

"They're worried men," Azari said. "They might be next, and they know it."

"One would suspect so," Grafton replied thoughtfully.

When it became obvious that was Azari's only comment, Callie asked her guests what they thought of fundamental Islam. "I know you are both Muslims," she said, "but I am curious, as I know most Americans are. Are the fundamentalists representative of the Islamic mainstream? What do you think?"

Mrs. Azari deferred to her husband, as apparently she always did. He said, "Fundamentalist Islam is the last gasp of a traditional way of life that is rapidly dying. One writer, Edward Shirley, called the Islamic Revolution in Iran 'a male scream against the gradual, irreversible liberation of women and the Westernization of the Muslim home.' He was right."

Later, after dinner, Jake asked the professor to come to his study. He shut the door behind them and said, "I don't want to insult you, but would you like a drink?"

A guilty look flitted across the professor's face. "A little wine would be welcome," he admitted. "I developed a taste for it in England."

Jake removed a bottle of French wine from a cabinet and handed it to Azari, who inspected the bottle and approved. When both men were seated and sipping on a glass of wine, Grafton said, "I work for the American government, Professor, and I want to take this opportunity to ask you for your help."

The professor was taken aback. "What branch?" he asked abruptly.

"Intelligence," Grafton said. "CIA."

"Your agency has approached me before. I told your Mr. Spadafore—"

"I'm aware of that," Grafton said. He removed a sheet of paper from a desk drawer and passed it to the professor, who put on his glasses and scrutinized it.

"You recognize those numbers, of course," Jake said.

Azari said nothing, merely sat holding the paper in his hands.

"Those are the prime numbers that you and your Iranian contact use for your encryption code," Jake said. "We have been reading every message your contact sends you about the Iranian nuclear program for years. All of them. As you know, they are encrypted and buried in large photo files."

"We?"

"The National Security Agency. NSA." Jake took a sip of wine. "If we can read them, one wonders if the Iranians can."

"They can't," Azari said and placed the paper on Jake's desk. Grafton reached for it, put it back in the drawer and closed the drawer.

"They don't have the sophisticated computer programs that your NSA apparently has," Azari added.

"One hopes," said the admiral.

"One does," Azari admitted.

"We are running out of time," Grafton said. "Your articles on Iran's nuclear program have stirred up the people who run the U.S. government. Indeed, I hear tomorrow the *Post* is running another of your op-ed pieces."

Azari acknowledged that was the case. "Obviously you have friends in the newspaper business."

"My friend tells me the article claims that Iran will have three operational nuclear warheads within a year."

The professor nodded.

"Is that true?" Grafton asked.

"My contact has been truthful," Azari said stoutly. "I took raw facts and made a prediction, and I stand behind it. Ahmadinejad is enriching uranium to make nuclear weapons. That is the bald truth."

"When Ahmadinejad has the weapons, what is he going to do with them?"

Azari scrutinized Grafton's face.

He was still framing his answer when Grafton said, "The American government is requesting your help, and the help of your friends, in answering that question. We will need concrete assistance in Iran, and your friends are in a position to give it."

"They do not want to help the CIA. I have told your agency that before. Your Mr. Spadafore—"

Jake silenced him with a gesture. "We have reached a crossroads. You and your friends have successfully convinced the decision-makers in the United

States government that the Iranian government is up to something. Now you must take the next step. You must help us prove that the Ahmadinejad administration is indeed manufacturing weapons, and if it is, what it intends to do with them."

Azari was in no hurry to answer. Apparently Grafton had not impressed him. Writing op-ed pieces that ratted on the Iranian government was one thing, but helping the Great Satan screw Ahmadinejad and the jihadists was something else.

Finally he said, "Do you know what they would do to me if they thought I was actively helping their enemies?"

"Aren't you doing that now?" Grafton shot back. "Revealing state secrets is not exactly a misdemeanor."

Azari took a deep breath and exhaled slowly. He was perspiring slightly despite the cool temperature of the room. He looked around. "Is it safe to talk here?"

Grafton smiled wryly. He thought it a tad late for that question, but he said, "I swept the place for bugs when I came home from work this afternoon. We will need the names and addresses of your agents so that we can contact them directly."

"I—I must think about this," Azari said. He placed the half-full wineglass on the desk.

Jake Grafton eyed the professor without warmth. "You have risked a great deal to alert the West to the danger of the Islamic government of Iran arming itself with nuclear weapons. If your friends have been telling you the truth, the danger grows with each passing day. The time has come to cross the river and help those most threatened by the mullahs' ambitions."

"Your logic is impeccable," the professor acknowledged, "but still . . . I have made promises to my friends in Iran, and I must weigh those promises against the danger."

"One suspects there is insufficient time to consult with them," Jake said.

"I don't see how I could."

"We will talk again tomorrow," Jake Grafton said and rose from his chair.

"Tomorrow I have a morning television talk show, two radio interviews and an interview with a newsmagazine reporter."

"Then the day after," Grafton said, leaving no room for argument. "Time is slipping through our fingers, Professor. The truth is, we are flat running out of it."

The next morning Sal Molina found Jake Grafton in his office at Langley reading a newspaper. Grafton's assistant, Robin, admitted the president's aide and closed the door behind him. The admiral had a television in his office, and it was tuned to a network morning show.

"Read Azari's article yet?" Molina asked as he dropped into a chair.

"Several times," Jake Grafton said and nodded at the coffeepot in the corner. Molina shook his head.

Just then Professor Azari appeared on the television screen with the male and female hosts of the show. They gave him puff questions, and he repeated the gist of his article that had appeared in the morning *Post*. The interview lasted about seven minutes.

When it was over, Grafton turned off the television.

"So how was the Middle East?" Molina asked.

"Warming up."

"So's Washington. Professor Azari's certainly doing all he can to help raise the temperature." Molina waved his own copy of the *Post*. "Where is he getting all this information?"

"Professor Azari's Iranian contact sends him encrypted e-mail."

"We read his mail?"

"Of course. The NSA looks at everything he sends and receives. He and his correspondents use a fairly sophisticated encryption system that apparently they designed themselves. The messages are buried in the pixels of a photograph or work of art that they e-mail each other. We can crack it, but it's doubtful if the Iranian security people can. I suspect they haven't even tried."

Molina was intrigued. "How long has the NSA been reading his stuff?"

"For years. We have everything his Iranian network has sent him."

"Then you know all about Iran's nuclear program," Molina said, slightly stunned.

"No. The agency knows what Azari's contact has been sending him. Where all this stuff that the contact sends comes from, whether it's truth or fiction, we don't know. We have a staff comparing Azari's facility info with satellite photography. Some of it matches up perfectly, some of it roughly matches, and some of it doesn't match at all."

"So he has another source. Or sources."

"Apparently."

"But—"

"Sal, Azari has been writing articles and op-ed pieces for years. He's even written a book. He writes about tunnels in mountains, technical data, the location of missile factories, the names of the men in charge, the quantities and storage locations of low-enriched uranium and highly enriched uranium . . . We can verify some of it. The rest of it—we don't know if it's truth or lies. Today he made a prediction, three warheads within twelve months. How he arrived at those numbers I have no idea."

"I'm in over my head," Sal Molina said. "Gimme some light."

Jake Grafton shifted his weight in his chair while he arranged his thoughts.

"As I said, he's been revealing Iranian state secrets for years." Jake picked up a copy of Azari's book from his credenza and tossed it on the edge of the desk within reach of Molina. "Doesn't it strike you as strange that he's still alive? Ahmadinejad used to help track down and assassinate enemies of the regime. The people in Tehran haven't forgotten how to do it."

Molina blinked three or four times. "I never looked at it that way," he admitted.

"Azari is working for the mullahs, whether he knows it or not. He's still alive because the rulers of Iran think he's an asset."

Molina picked up the newspaper and opened it to Azari's article. "You are saying the Iranians wanted us to read this?"

"Probably."

"Why?"

"There are several possible reasons. The one I like the best is this one: Ahmadinejad realized that keeping the Iranian weapons program a secret was impossible. Inevitably, there were going to be leaks. So he used Azari to put bad information out there with the good in the hope that his enemies would be unable to separate the wheat from the chaff."

"Can we?"

"Not yet."

"So how close is Iran to the bomb?"

"The only thing we know for sure is that we don't know."

Molina threw up his hands. He picked up a pencil from Grafton's desk, twirled it for a moment, scratched his head with the eraser, then threw it at the wall. It fell behind a bookcase. "So what are you going to do about the good professor?"

"I'm going to sign him up to work for me, so we can get access to his Iranian network. And I'm going to have a man in Iran check on some of this information to see what is true and what isn't."

"You're going to make Azari a double agent?"

"Going to give it a try," Grafton said and sighed. "Of course, the shit could pretend to do as we say but warn the Iranians. If that happens, I'll kill him."

Molina's jaw dropped. "You wouldn't do that," he said.

Grafton didn't say a word.

"You wouldn't do that," Molina repeated.

"Oh, of course not," Grafton replied.

Sal Molina took a deep breath, then let it all out slowly. "The Israelis are running out of patience. Their ambassador told the president that the government of Israel is under extreme pressure to act now, before Iran can put warheads on missiles."

Grafton scratched his head.

"What kind of a network do the Israelis have in Iran?" Molina asked.

"They have a few agents there. Every now and then they tell us something we didn't know, but I wouldn't bet real money that they're showing us all their cards."

"Do we show them all of ours?"

"Most of them, anyway."

"What do they think of Azari's information?"

"I haven't asked them."

Molina seemed content to move on. "If those nuclear facilities are bombed, a lot of radiation is going into the atmosphere. It'll fall out all over the place. A lot of people are going to be poisoned." He thought about that, then added, "If there is any uranium there."

"The mullahs put a lot of their facilities around Tehran for just that reason," Grafton remarked.

"It didn't work," Molina shot back. "I don't think the Israelis give a damn about radiation contamination in Iran. Staying alive is the Israeli problem, not saving Iranians." He tapped on the desk with a finger, then traced a small circle with a fingertip while staring at the wall with unseeing eyes.

"The longer we wait to attack," Grafton said, breaking the silence, "the more enriched uranium the Iranians will have. They continue to harden their facilities. In other words, the longer we wait, the worse the contamination will be and the less likely it is that a conventional attack will do enough damage to halt their weapons program. The window for military action is sliding closed. The Iranians know that, and have dragged out the diplomatic process for precisely that reason."

Molina's eyes snapped into focus on Grafton's face. "The president doesn't have a political consensus. Until he gets one, the United States is not taking military action against Iran. Nor will we help Israel do it. And the president isn't going to get a consensus until you prove beyond a reasonable doubt what Ahmadinejad plans to do with his missiles and warheads."

When I finished my workday at the embassy annex, I walked out onto the bustling streets of Tehran and drew in a refreshing lungful of heavily polluted air. Ah, yes, the great outdoors for me!

Taking in the sights and sounds and listening to the roar of endless traffic, I strolled the three blocks to my hotel—actually a nice hotel designed, built and run by a European chain—and walked through the lobby. Yep, the secret police guy was sitting in his usual chair, in his usual rumpled trousers, dirty shirt and worn jacket. I didn't know if he was an employee of the MOIS— Ministry of Intelligence and Security—or the intelligence arm of the Revolutionary Guard, the mullahs' Gestapo, nor did I care. His job was keeping tabs on us diplomats. Since I had been in Iran, I had made him and his pals work at keeping track of me.

Housekeeping had tidied up my small room, which was bugged. I had amused myself one evening a couple of weeks ago by searching the place. I found three bugs that were hardwired in place. Yesterday I put switches on all three of the wires, so I could turn the bugs on and off whenever I chose. But I left them on, at least for now. If the Iranians wanted to listen to me snore, fart and take a whiz, so be it.

As I mentioned, I only sweated for Uncle Sam four hours a day at the annex, leaving the rest of the day open for clandestine activities. Unfortunately, up to now there hadn't been any of those. In case there ever were, I kept myself busy learning the town. I had strolled through and perused the collections in almost every museum in Tehran, seen all the religious sites that were open to non-Muslims and looked at all the big public stuff, like railroad stations, bus stations, luxurty hotels and the like. No doubt these expeditions were enlightening for my MOIS tails, on those occasions when they bothered to follow. Sometimes they did, sometimes they didn't.

This afternoon I changed into my running gear, paused at the door to breathe deeply of filtered, conditioned air, then took the elevator down.

I walked through the lobby without glancing at the watcher and went out the wide double doors onto the street. Left today, I decided, just for variety; I made the turn and started jogging. After a mile I picked up the pace. When I crossed at street corners I usually glanced around for traffic . . . and to see if anyone was jogging along behind me. Tonight no one was. The first week I had about given heart attacks to two guys in street clothes who tried to match my pace. They had used cars the second week, but with Tehran traffic being what it is, I generally made better time than the automobiles could, and soon they lost sight of me. These days they usually didn't bother trying to follow.

As I ran, I thought back to my last interview with Jake Grafton. We were sitting in his office at Langley, just the two of us, and little shafts of spring sunshine streamed through the double-paned security windows and played on the floor and furniture. Outside, the leaves on the trees danced in the breeze, so the sun's rays came and went, almost as if they were alive.

"Azari has been publishing the information collected by his network for several years now, airing Iran's deepest secrets in America for anyone with a dollar and a half to buy a Sunday newspaper," Grafton said. "His activities could not have escaped the attention of Iranian security."

I sat there thinking about that. After several deep breaths, I said, "Why don't you tell me all of it?"

He looked me over one more time, then rose out of his chair. "Come on," he said. We went all the way down to the basement of the building, Grafton leading the way, until we entered a large room with four big tables, the kind they hold church dinners on. They were covered with paper.

Grafton started at the table nearest the door. "Here is a copy of Azari's book, published last year"—he held it up—"and here are his three op-ed pieces for the Sunday papers." He displayed them. "About three years ago we cracked the crypto code he and his agent in Tehran use to communicate. Here are their messages." He let me examine them. They were lying on the table, arranged in chronological order. "Twenty-seven of them, so far," Grafton murmured.

"Finally, here are the facts as the book sets them forth. Factories, locations, missile sites, names of officials, all of it." All this was arranged on a large chart, with every entry numbered, so it could be cross-referenced. The references were piles of paper that covered the surface of the other tables, each pile numbered. Someone had spent a lot of time constructing the chart and checking every reference.

I began examining the chart, looking for the source of various information. Before long, I began to realize that a lot of the facts Grafton had on the chart had never been mentioned by Azari's Tehran agent.

"How much of his tale is true?" I asked.

Grafton parked his heinie on the edge of one table. "Ahmadinejad and the boys may be pulling a Saddam Hussein, trying to make us think they are a more formidable threat than they are. The benefits to that approach are the same for them as they were for Saddam. Israel and the West must treat them gingerly, with respect."

I knew he was speaking the truth. When a security service learns that there is a spy network at work in their territory, they have two choices: roll up the network by arresting everyone, or use it to feed lies to their enemies.

"Or," he said, watching the expression on my face, "the reverse might be true. They could be a lot farther along the road to the bomb than Azari's network says they are. The advantage to this ploy is that Iran's enemies continue to dither, thinking they have time to work the problem, when in truth time is running out. Your job is to find out which is the case. Is Iran all bluster, or are they a Trojan horse?"

The people who were going to help me do all this heavy spying, Grafton told me, were the survivors of an organization that had been decimated by Revolutionary Guard security. The members had been imprisoned, interrogated, tortured and executed by the dozens. The survivors, this little cabal of traitors, were the ears of Azari's network.

I swallowed hard and said, "If the network is in the government's pocket, after I make contact with Azari's agent, Iranian security will know about me."

"Yes," he said, staring at me.

I stood like a statue marshaling my thoughts.

Grafton lifted his butt off the edge of the table and moved to his chart, which he examined with one hand in his pocket and the other on his chin.

"You know," I said conversationally, "that a few years ago I was blackmailed into joining the Company. The guy who helped me steal the Peabody diamond spilled his guts. It was the CIA or prison. Right now I wish to hell I had given the government the finger and done my time in the joint."

A shadow of a grin played across the admiral's features. "The road not taken . . . Right this very minute you might have been picking up loose diamonds on the French Riviera."

"Something like that," I admitted.

"Azari's network has been penetrated, Tommy. You can bet your life on it."

"Sounds to me as if Azari is Ahmadinejad's man in Washington."

Grafton nodded.

"You want me to go to Iran anyway."

"We have to know the truth about those weapons. And if they are making bombs, what are they going to do with them?"

There are moments when I would like to strangle him . . . slowly . . . and that was one of them. I flexed my fingers.

"To beat hell out of the obvious, if this goes bad I'm going to be in a real tight crack. Want me to just swim home, or am I supposed to chew a suicide pill?"

He examined my face carefully, then said, "Somebody has to do this, Tommy, and you're the best I've got."

I threw up my hands in frustration.

The admiral smiled, which irritated me more than a little.

I thought about things for a while. About religious fanatics who tortured and murdered their enemies. Some people think that death is the worst thing that can happen to them, but they are fools. There are *many* things worse. Much worse.

"If they catch me and toss me in some dungeon for Ahmadinejad or his disciples to carve on when they have a little time, I want you to get me out or kill me."

"Tommy, I—"

I cut him off and steamrolled on. "I'm not talking to Jake Grafton, CIA spook dude. I don't give a shit about the statutes or the rules and regulations of the fucking CIA. I'm talking to Jake Grafton, human being. I want your word on it. If you can't get me out, kill me."

Those gray eyes of his were locked onto mine. He nodded. "Okay," he said softly. "You have my word."

As I ran through Tehran this evening, I thought about all this—lies and bombs and life and death.

Professor Aurang Azari dropped by the Grafton condo in Rosslyn, across the Potomac from the university, around seven in the evening. Jake took him into the den and closed the door.

He poured each of them a glass of white French wine; then they sat on the couch.

"I haven't had a chance to run your proposal by my network," the professor said. "However, after serious reflection, I believe they will approve us cooperating with your government for the greater good of everyone."

Jake Grafton nodded and tried the wine, which was delicious.

"We agreed, some years ago, that we would not assist any intelligence agency," Azari continued, "but obviously, things have changed since then."

Jake let him talk. Azari went through the members of his network one by one, naming them and the position each held in the Iranian government or with a contractor or subcontractor that was working on a nuclear project. Grafton made a few cryptic notes, but mainly he listened.

When Azari finally ran down, Grafton asked, "Do you trust these people?"

"Oh, yes. They do not believe in the regime or its goals. Of that I am absolutely certain."

Grafton reached for the wine bottle and refilled Azari's glass. "Tell me how your network works," he said.

"None of them know the others are supplying information. They each send or deliver their information to Rostram, who sends it to me."

"Rostram?"

"A code name. He is the only person in Iran who knows all the members of the net."

"He sends you information via the encoded pictures?"

"Yes."

"I have a man in Iran that I want you to put in contact with Rostram. Once he and Rostram are holding hands, we'll go from there."

They discussed the mechanics of setting up the meet. Once that was done, Azari had more questions. "Is the United States going to invade Iran?"

"Really, Professor!" Jake let his surprise show. "I am just an officer in a small government agency. Those decisions don't get made in my office, nor are we informed ahead of time. We read the newspapers with everyone else."

Azari studied his shoes. "I guess I really want to know if the United States is going to do anything at all to solve the problem of nuclear weapons in the hands of these madmen, or if you are just going to click your tongues softly and shake your heads sadly."

"As I said—" Grafton began, stopping when Azari raised his hand.

"I don't want the members of my network to suffer for your foolishness," Azari said. "They have suffered enough. More than enough. We have avoided giving direct aid to foreign intelligence services because most of them are incompetent. The CIA also has that reputation in Iran."

Grafton scratched his forehead and didn't reply.

"I tell you now, Admiral Grafton, if your man betrays Rostram, through incompetence or stupidity or for any other reason, he won't be coming home again."

"I'll pass that happy thought on to him."

"Inspire him," Azari said.

"Yes," said Jake Grafton thoughtfully. He emptied the rest of the wine into Azari's glass.

CHAPTER FIVE

Every morning when I arrived for work, I entered the little soundproof booth that I had built when I arrived in country. The wizards at Langley said it would defeat any bugs that the Iranians had planted in the building, or the Swiss. Once inside, I set up the satellite telephone, plugged it into the lead that ran to the small dish antenna on the roof—I had also installed that— and typed in the encryption code that I had memorized before I left the States.

Today I soon had Jake Grafton on the line.

We chatted a little bit about this and that, then he told me that I was on-stage. Azari's Iranian contact would contact me within the next few days.

"Tell me about this guy," I prompted.

"Don't know much to tell. Code name Rostram. Could be anybody. He'll introduce himself with that name."

It was a short conversation. After I said good-bye and broke the connection, I sat in my little plastic womb contemplating my navel. Azari's Iranian contact now knew my name, or soon would, knew I was an officer in the CIA and would be looking for me. If Azari was indeed under the control of the MOIS, they would soon know what he knew.

I felt like the guy who wrote a letter to the Devil informing Him that his soul was for sale.

These ruminations didn't get me anywhere, so I crawled out of the booth, tucked it in the corner, and went along the hallway to the Pit. Frank Caldwell was there, swilling coffee. As usual, he wanted to chat a while in Farsi to improve my grammar and diction. Today I wasn't in the mood. I stayed in English, and he switched back.

"You look cheerful this morning," he said. His medium-length hair was turning fashionably gray at the tips, and he wasn't carrying any extra weight. He looked, I thought, like a model in a Cabela's fishing catalog.

I tried to smile.

"Can't let the world get you down, Tommy. Keep your chin up."

A snotty remark almost leaped from my lips, but I managed to stifle it. I pushed the button to summon the first supplicant of the day.

Habib Sultani adjusted the large, heavy binoculars on the stand in front of him and turned the focus knob. He stared through the lens, trying to estimate how far he could see. Then he took his eyes away from the binoculars and once more surveyed the shore, sea and sky. It was a high, hazy day, with excellent visibility, yet the sky and sea seemed to merge out there somewhere, just fade into each other without a definite horizon.

Sultani was standing on a bluff on a promontory that jutted out into the Strait of Hormuz, which was about thirty nautical miles wide at this point. On both sides of the promontory, sand beaches marked the sea's edge, but below the bluff there were rocks. If one listened carefully, one could hear the steady pounding of the long rollers being pushed through the Gulf of Oman from the Arabian Sea.

To his right, almost immediately below, in a small natural harbor formed by several large rocks, were three gunboats of the Revolutionary Guard. They were manned, with engines idling, their coxswains holding them in place. Each boat carried a Russian-made 37 mm gun mounted amidships.

Sultani glanced at the boats, then put his eyes back to the binoculars.

Yes, he could see ships in the strait. There was a loaded oil tanker off to his right, heading south, from right to left, after rounding the tip of Oman, which was on a peninsula that jutted out from the Arabian landmass. The tanker would pass about twenty miles out, eight miles beyond the twelve-mile limit for Iran's territorial waters. Near the tanker was a warship—he could tell by the superstructure. That ship, of course, was American. Probably a destroyer or guided missile frigate. He scanned the binoculars. If there were other warships out there, they were hidden in the haze.

To his left Sultani saw an empty tanker heading north. He continued to scan. He knew that somewhere in the Gulf of Oman was an aircraft carrier, the USS *United States*. He knew because behind him three technicians were monitoring the UHF radio frequencies that the Americans used to talk to their planes when they were close to the carrier. English words and numbers were pouring out of the loudspeaker, profaning the Islamic Republic. Still, the American carrier could be anywhere. It was the technician with a radio direction finder who said they were to the southwest.

"I can hear the controller on the ship quite plainly," the technician said. "The radio is line-of-sight. They cannot be over the curvature of the earth. But all the tactical channels are encrypted—all we can hear is a buzz."

"How far to the ship?"

"Not far. We are about fifty meters above the water, and so is their antenna. A hundred miles, perhaps a hundred and twenty. Not much more."

It would be terrific if the Americans would bring their floating airfield into the Strait of Hormuz on their way to the Persian Gulf, Sultani thought. They rarely did that, however, and didn't appear to be doing it today.

Nearby sat a portable radar control van, or trailer, since it was usually pulled behind a truck. Sultani backed away from the binoculars and glanced at the white van festooned with antennas. On the other side of the van sat the dish, which was mounted on a large trailer that was still attached to the tractor that pulled it. Beyond it two diesel-powered generators snored steadily. Cables connecting all this gear together ran everywhere, seemingly hopelessly tangled.

"General," Sultani said to the uniformed man beside him as he gestured to the binoculars. Everyone wanted to look; it was only human.

He was walking toward the van when the door opened and his nephew Ghasem came out and strode quickly toward him. "There are twelve planes aloft over the carrier," Ghasem reported, "which is one hundred ten nautical miles away."

Habib Sultani nodded his understanding. The Americans were doing military exercises, practicing, dropping bombs on floating objects, just as they often did.

Sultani led the way back to the van and through the door, with Ghasem at his heels.

The U.S. Navy F/A-18s were spread out in loose tactical formation, in two sections, flying at 12,000 feet. The lead's wingman was a hundred feet out to his right and stepped slightly down and aft. Number Three was a thousand feet away to the leader's left and three or four hundred feet aft. Her wing-man was stepped out to her left and back slightly. This formation allowed each pilot to scan his instruments occasionally and stay updated on the nav problem without worrying about running into a comrade.

Lieutenant Commander Harry Lampert was the leader. He had his plane on autopilot as he studied the radar display of the strait ahead. The ships there showed up nicely on the radar screen. He played with several displays, then checked his ECM gear. In his ears was the bass tone of a search radar, which the tactical display showed was ahead and to his right, in Iran.

He glanced around, checking the position of his wingman, Sidney "Goose" Inglehart, and the other section, led by Lieutenant Betsy "Chicago" O'Hare. The pilots were all veterans. All except Number Four, Betsy's wingman, Lieutenant (junior grade) Jackson L. "Hillbilly" Jones, the nautical pride of Wildcat, West Virginia. "Billy" Jones—predictably, his nickname was often shortened—was on his first cruise, and this was only his second flight into the strait.

As Lampert adjusted his fanny in his ejection seat, he got a call on the encrypted radio. "War Ace Leader, this is Black Eagle. We had some Iranian gunboat activity earlier this morning, then again about an hour ago."

"Roger that," Lampert replied. "We were briefed." Black Eagle was an E-2 Hawkeye that was high above and well behind him. The Hawkeye, a twin-engine turboprop, carried a very capable area search radar and more ECM gear than could be packed into a tactical aircraft. The tactical coordinator in the Hawkeye would keep him informed.

I just hope the Iranians aren't up to something nasty today, Lampert thought to himself.

Ahh . . . nothing will happen.

Sultani looked over the shoulder of the radar operator at the screen. He saw the blips that were Lampert's four Hornets began to separate from the single spot of light as they came up the gulf. "Send the boats," he told the military aide at his elbow. The man, a colonel, picked up the telephone. The wire had been run to this site just two days ago.

At the airbase at Bandar-e Abbas, one hundred nautical miles away, two SU-30 fighters were on five-minute alert, with the pilots in the cockpits, ready to start engines. Sultani looked at his watch. They could be here within twenty minutes. Their arrival should be a nice surprise for the Americans, *if* the Sukhoi pilots obeyed orders and left their radars turned off. The F-18s' fuel state should be down significantly by then.

This might work, Sultani told himself. He found his nephew Ghasem looking at him. He made eye contact, nodded affirmatively and stepped outside. Nestled in the shade of a tree was a table that contained a computer. Wires led away in all directions to antennas spotted up and down the coast and at four sites inland. Two men were there, monitoring the signals coming in from the various sites.

The senior man, a Russian in a white shirt and dark trousers, turned toward Sultani when he saw him approach.

"Is your equipment working properly?" the Iranian asked.

"Yes. Quite satisfactory," the Russian replied and glanced at Ghasem, who was two paces behind his uncle.

"A flight of four American fighters is coming up the Gulf," Sultani said. "Our fighters are thirty minutes away. After the American planes pass us, I am going to have the gunboats sortie. They can make a run on that tanker there." He pointed to a tanker far away, just visible against the haze that obscured the horizon.

The Russian looked in the indicated direction, held his hand to shade his eyes, then turned back to Sultani. "This may be interesting," he said with a grin.

In the cockpit of his F/A-18 Hornet, Harry Lampert could see mountain peaks to his right poking up through the haze. They were about a hundred miles away, he guessed, in Iran. To his left, on the Arabian Peninsula, he saw several lower peaks, probably six thousand feet in elevation, but they were far away, indistinct, barely visible in the yellow sky. Yes, the sky over Arabia was yellow . . . Perhaps the sun reflecting from the sand and rock and packed earth of that desert hellhole upon the dust and dirt suspended in the atmosphere. Whatever, the yellowish tint to the sky extended up, up, up. Lampert thought the air over Arabia must be laden with dust well into the stratosphere.

He turned back to the business at hand, checked his radar, then his wingmen, listened to that steady beep as the Iranian radar beam swept him every few seconds, turned the plane slightly to stay in the center of the channel through the Strait of Hormuz. Causing an international incident by violating foreign airspace would not be career-enhancing.

In the Number Four plane in Lampert's flight, Hillbilly Jones was also looking at the yellow sky over Arabia. Dirt in the air, he thought. He wondered what that dirt was doing to the engines as they sucked it in. Nothing good, that's for sure.

Hillbilly wasn't worried about navigation or even paying much attention to the location of the flight. The senior guys could worry about that. All he had to do was follow Number Three, Chicago O'Hare, wherever she went. In the unlikely event Chicago got lost, he would be, too, but probably she would stay found, and so would he. All in all, being a junior officer was pretty simple.

Ol' Chicago's plane was suspended in this goo, as were the other two away to the right. They looked sort of like fish lying there motionless in the sky. They were all moving, of course, but only the relative motion could be seen, and with good formation pilots, there was damn little of that. They looked, he thought, as if they were painted upon that featureless, hazy backdrop.

Hillbilly Jones made a mental note to say that when he wrote a letter to his girlfriend this evening. She was studying for a master's in English lit and liked it when he described how stuff looked.

He sighed and tried to rearrange his testicles so the parachute harness didn't cut him so much.

The undecked open gunboats were about fifty feet long and were driven by two powerful V8 engines; they were capable of forty knots in relatively calm water. Amidships, three men stood by the 37 mm, one to optically aim and fire, the other two to load magazines as necessary. Eight other men armed with AK-47s rode forward. Their job, if the captain ordered action, was to sweep people from the decks of the victim ship while the 37 mm tore at her guts. The gunboats were cheap and effective patrol boats. Or pirate boats, depending on one's political persuasion.

Out of the harbor, the three boats set up in a left echelon formation. Soon they had worked up to twenty-five knots and were on course to intercept the tanker that Sultani had pointed out to the Russian technician, a tanker that was barely visible on the horizon to the men in the gunboat.

The captain of the lead boat, whose name was Omar, kept increasing speed as he found his boat was manageable in the swell. He got to thirty knots, decided the ride was rough enough, then backed off a few hundred RPMs on his engines. The boat pounded the swells, and the unmuffled engines sang loudly behind him. Standing at the helm with his knees bent, the sea wind streaming his hair and filling his nostrils with that clean salt smell,

Omar felt as if he had died and entered Paradise. He concentrated on holding the tanker on a constant angle of bearing, not letting it drift toward the bow or stern.

"The boats are out," the Black Eagle controller told Harry Lampert. "They are behind you about sixty miles, three of them, apparently on their way to intercept a tanker. Your orders are to provide cover for the tanker."

The standing rules of engagement under which the U.S. Navy operated said that the Iranians would not be allowed to stop shipping in international waters. On the other hand, the rules also said not to fire at an Iranian boat, ship or airplane unless fired upon. The rules went on for six pages and read as if they had been written by lawyers, which was the truth of it. Like policemen who had only seconds to make life-or-death decisions, the naval officers who had to deal with these confrontations knew that their superiors would scrutinize their actions at their leisure. Fitness reports would be written and, if necessary, courts-martial convened.

Harry Lampert wasn't thinking about any of that right now. He had the tanker headed south and the nearby destroyer on radar and began descending and accelerating. When he was twenty-five miles out, he saw the tanker's wake, then the destroyer's. The tanker was a leviathan, making about twelve knots, carrying every gallon of crude oil the captain could get in her. Even as he watched, he saw the destroyer turn to cross the tanker's wake to the east side, and he saw her wake grow longer. She was accelerating.

Lampert stopped his descent at five thousand feet and motored on inbound, doing about four hundred knots. The wakes of the gunboats came into view at ten miles.

Harry concentrated on the gunboats as he closed and flew directly over them. He extended out and set his planes up in a loose circle around the tanker. All the while the gunboats came steadily on.

Lampert's radio was ominously silent. The radar operator could see everything Lampert could see, so there was no need for chatter. The radar picture was data-linked to the carrier, where the battle group commander, Rear Admiral Stanley Bryant, and his staff could also see it. The admiral was in radio contact with Black Eagle and the destroyer that was now on the east, or gunboat, side of the tanker, whose wake was straight as a string as she plowed her way southward.

The admiral was the man on the spot. Did Iran want a confrontation, or did they want war? How far was the Iranian commander willing to go?

How many chances could the admiral take with the action right beside a tanker loaded with crude oil?

The minutes passed as the gunboats crossed the twenty miles of ocean between the shore and the ships. The Hornets made more leisurely turns around the ships. The pilots had their engines throttled back to maximum endurance airspeed to save fuel.

Going round and round, watching the boats closing on the tanker . . . Harry Lampert felt helpless and frustrated. What were the Iranians up to?

In the radar van on the bluff, Habib Sultani glanced at the radar screen, then his watch, and said to the general sitting beside the telephone that connected directly to the airbase, "Launch the fighters." The general picked up the telephone.

When they were about four miles from the ships, well into international waters, two of the gunboats changed course. The lead kept going toward the laden tanker, but number three turned south for the empty tanker coming up the strait. The second gunboat altered course to intercept the destroyer.

A half minute later the Black Eagle controller said, "War Ace Leader, remind the gunboats of your presence."

"Roger that," Harry Lampert said. He continued, "Betsy, stay high as cover. Goose, come with me."

Goose was Lampert's wingman, and he gave his lead a mike click in response. Unsaid was the implicit order for Hillbilly Jones, Chicago's wingman, to stay with his lead.

Lampert reduced throttle and lowered his nose as he completed his turn. This time he would go right over the lead gunboat at fifty feet.

In the lead gunboat, Omar saw the two F/A-18s out of the corner of his eye. They looked funny, so he turned his head to see. They were very low and moving extremely fast. A cone of gray light seemed to trail each airplane. Although he didn't know it, the Hornets were supersonic, and the gray cone was vapor condensing in the visible shock wave behind each plane.

In only a heartbeat the lead plane went over Omar's boat, and the shock wave nearly ruptured his eardrums. The shock wave of the second plane, which passed fifty yards in front of his boat, so closely followed the first that it was difficult to distinguish the two. The booms of the Hornets' passing were the loudest things Omar and his crewmen had ever heard, and they were followed by the howl of four jet engines in afterburner, a howl that rapidly dropped in volume as the two fighters raced away at nearly a thousand feet per second.

Omar had his orders. He stayed on course for the tanker, now about a mile and a half away. Considering the tanker's speed, he would be alongside in about two minutes. In front of him, the men were shouting at each other and pointing at the fighters. One of them turned and pumped his fist at Omar. He shouted something, something lost on the wind. Then Omar realized what he had said. "God is Great!"

Ah, yes.

Harry Lampert came out of burner and did a four-G, 180-degree turn, then headed back toward the gunboats, which were rapidly closing with the tanker.

Worried that he might panic the tanker's captain with a masthead pass, he elected to pass the tanker on a parallel heading about a half mile away, which proved to be outside the gunboats. Lampert got on the radio to Black Eagle, which was patching his comments straight through to the admiral in the TFCC, the Tactical Flag Command Center.

The second gunboat was charging directly toward the destroyer, which was doing about half the speed of the boat, on a collision course. Even as Harry looked that way, the gunboat turned at the last possible instant and went roaring down the side of the gray warship into her wake.

The third gunboat was still on course for the tanker to the south, and was still several miles away.

On the bluff overlooking the strait, Habib Sultani watched the action through his binoculars. He saw the low pass by the Hornets, saw the boat charging the destroyer, and he heard the buzzsaw sound of encrypted chatter on the radio. The Americans were getting excited.

"Where are the Sukhois?" he asked.

"They are airborne. Estimated arrival in ten minutes," was the answer.

"Radio the gunboat leader and tell him to get in against the tanker and shout for it to stop. Have him shoot into the water ahead of it."

The Hawkeye radar operator picked up the skinpaints of the Sukhoi fighters coming south along the coast from Bandar-e Abbas. They had been running low, partially masked by the peaks of the coastal mountains, but the Black Eagle controller had them now. He informed War Ace Leader of the closing fighters.

Harry Lampert was face-to-face with the tiger, and the news in his headset that Iranian fighters were just minutes away didn't improve the situation. Suddenly he wanted to be upstairs, facing the fighters. The destroyer could deal with the gunboats near it.

"Chicago, come on down and fly around these boats. If they shoot at the tanker, sink them. We're coming back upstairs."

"Wilco," said Chicago O'Hare and dropped her nose.

Out on her wing, Hillbilly Jones was in an information-overload condition. The radio chatter was coming thick and fast, enemy fighters were inbound, he got only glimpses of the tanker and gunboats below, and Chicago was diving toward the sea. He eased closer to her, now only fifty feet away, and concentrated on staying on her wing; someone else was going to have to run the war.

O'Hare and Jones were descending through two thousand feet when their ECM threat indicators lit up. The inbound Sukhois had turned on their radar and were probing for them.

Oh man, what now? Jones thought.

Harry Lampert couldn't enter the twelve-mile exclusion zone of Iran's territorial waters. He was checking his location, Black Eagle was relaying the admiral's reminder, and his threat indicator was lighting up like a Christmas tree. If all that wasn't enough, when he glanced down, he saw two waterspouts ahead of the tanker. Hell, that gunboat was firing warning shots!

Harry keyed the mike and relayed that information to Black Eagle, then asked for and received permission to fire a warning shot of his own. O'Hare had heard the transmissions, of course, but to make sure she understood, he said on the radio, "Chicago, put a burst in front of the lead boat."

"Wilco," said Betsy O'Hare. She was one tough fighter pilot, a Naval Academy grad, and she didn't dither. She flipped on her master armament switch, selected guns, then adjusted her flight path so the rounds would impact a hundred yards or so in front of the leading gunboat, which was paralleling the tanker's course, about a hundred yards to port. The gunboat had throttled back and seemed to be roughly matching the speed of the tanker. She would come in off the gunboat's port beam, at enough of an angle that her 20 mm cannon shells wouldn't hit the tanker if they ricocheted off the water.

Being human, she wondered what the Iranians manning those 37 mm guns were going to think about cannon shells in front of them. Since that was an unknown, she kept her speed fairly high, almost four hundred knots, as she closed, still descending. A short burst would be good enough. Let them see the muzzle blast.

Her wingman, Hillbilly Jones, was listening to all of the radio chatter—the Sukhois were coming in supersonic—and the audio from the ECM threat indicator, which was giving him audible cues on every Iranian radar out there, while the blue ocean and hazy sky changed places as Chicago maneuvered. His flying was getting ragged; he was behind the curve. It was all he could do to hang on to his flight lead. The thought that a safe course might be to break off so that he could fly his own airplane while observing this goat rope from a comfortable altitude never even crossed his mind.

He saw Chicago's gun vomit a burst, but she didn't pull up immediately, which surprised him. He had anticipated the pull-up, started pulling himself, so now he had to jam his nose down, steepen his descent to get back into position. The Gs and flying sensations had thoroughly disoriented him; the hazy sky without a discernible horizon didn't help. His only attitude reference was his leader. The radar altimeter sounded a warning, but in the cacophony of sound assaulting his ears, he didn't even notice.

O'Hare kept descending for a second, probably thinking about a low pass. When she did pull up, it surprised Hillbilly again; he was late matching her maneuver, and his sink rate was greater. He yo-yoed down toward the water. And hit it.

An object striking water at 415 knots reacts as if it had struck concrete. Even though it had struck the ocean a glancing blow, Hillbilly Jones' Hornet disintegrated on impact, killing him instantly. The pieces traveled along for almost a half mile as they decelerated, making a rolling, continuous splash. Fuel and tiny pieces rained down on the gunboat and tanker as they steamed into the cloud.

Chicago O'Hare was the first American pilot to realize what had happened.

She looked back as she climbed, saw the cloud of pieces and fuel and the roiled water and scanned for her wingman, who was nowhere in sight. She keyed her mike. "Shit, I think Hillbilly just went into the drink."

Harry Lampert had his hands full. The incoming Sukhois had him and Goose locked up for missile shots; the wailing ECM audio told him that, as did the flashing MISSILE light on the panel in front of him.

Now, on top of everything, he had a plane in the water. Did the Iranians shoot it down?

He had several decisions to make, and he had only seconds to do it. Should he turn on his ALQ-199, thereby defeating the Sukhois' radars and electronically hiding his plane, or should he leave it off? *Guess wrong and you die, Harry.*

He couldn't yet see the Sukhois, but he had them on radar. They were at thirty miles and closing.

"Gadget off, Goose," he said over the air.

"Roger."

"Chicago, did you see any flak?"

"That's a negative. Looks like Billy went in when I pulled out from my shooting pass."

Scanning for the approaching fighters, Harry asked, "Parachute?"

"Don't see one," was the reply.

"Don't let the gunboats get near the wreckage," Lampert told O'Hare, talking loudly over his ECM. Suddenly infuriated, he reached with his left hand and turned off the ECM audio. Enough of that shit!

He checked his armament panel. Still set up for guns. He flipped the switch for heat. Now the Sidewinders on his wingtips were hot. He bore-sighted the incoming Sukhois and headed right at them. If they launched a missile at him, at least he'd see the flame as the engine lit off. He turned the last fifteen degrees toward the approaching Iranian fighters.

Chicago O'Hare saw Omar's gunboat slow and turn back into the area where the remnants of Hillbilly's plane had impacted. She didn't hesitate. Nose down, she steadied out, glanced at the ball to ensure it was centered and fired a nice two-second burst into the water in front of the boat. It turned away.

She was coming back for another pass when the destroyer's bow gun began firing. Splashes landed in the wake of the gunboat, one after another, getting closer. Now the second gunboat was taking splashes in its wake.

The two gunboats within range of the destroyer were maneuvering wildly. Yet their crews did not open fire. To the south, the third gunboat was still at least a mile from the empty tanker, still heading toward it.

Suddenly, probably in response to a radio call, all three gunboats turned as one and headed back to Iran.

Harry Lampert and his wingman still had their troubles. As they closed the Sukhois, the MISSILE light in both cockpits continued to flash. To make matters worse, now Harry saw that he was getting a launch indication of an SA-20 surface-to-air missile from Iran.

So was Goose, and he said so.

Another decision to be made: Was there a missile in the air, or were the Iranians faking it to provoke an American reaction?

"Leave the gadget off," Harry said again. "These guys are just jerking us around."

Now the Sukhois were beginning to grow in his windshield. Quickly. The fighters were coming together at a combined speed of twelve hundred knots, the Sukhois still supersonic.

Harry raised his nose a trifle, and they went by so quickly that he didn't see a single detail, just a blur.

"Right turn," he roared into the radio microphone in his oxygen mask. He whipped his plane around in a six-G pull and, coming out of it, locked the Sukhois up with his radar. He didn't have a radar-guided missile aboard, but the Sukhoi drivers didn't know that. Turnabout is fair play.

But the Sukhois were only making one pass. They made a long, gentle high-speed turn that carried them almost into Oman, then headed off to the north as they slowed to subsonic speed.

With the gunboats returning to base and an American destroyer sitting on the slowly settling wreckage of Hillbilly Jones' Hornet—and presumably searching for whatever was left of Hillbilly—there was nothing for Lampert's Hornets to do but return to the carrier. The admiral already had another flight of four Hornets on the way up the strait to cover this tanker, which was still steaming steadily south toward the Gulf of Oman, the Arabian Sea, then the Indian Ocean, on her way to America or Japan or Singapore or Europe or India or China with a load of crude to keep the wheels turning.

———

"Well?" Habib Sultani asked the Russian technician at the equipment under the tree. The Russian pulled off his earphones, leaned back in his chair and lit a cigarette.

"They never turned them on," he said.

Disappointed, Sultani walked away with Ghasem at his side. "Too bad," he muttered. "I was hoping they would use an ALQ-199."

"So it didn't work," Ghasem said.

"It was always a long shot."

"You could have shot a missile at them—they would have turned it on then. Afterward, you could claim the launch was a mistake."

"Would you have done that?"

Ghasem smiled. "No. The international situation is too tense. Ahmadine-jad is in discussions with the French and Russians, and they would be outraged."

His uncle nodded. "If we want to be a nuclear power, we must show the world we can be trusted, that our armed forces will always obey the civilian government. Accidents with missiles and bombs cannot be explained away."

As they walked toward the car that had brought them to this site, Ghasem asked, "Why is it, Uncle, that you want me to spend so much time with you?"

"Your cousin Khurram is something of a fool. You know that."

"But I am a scholar. That is what I want to do with my life."

His uncle stopped and looked him in the eyes. "In the days that come I may need someone beside me with brains and good judgment, someone I trust. We cannot always choose our path. Sometimes Allah puts us where we are needed."

"I understand," Ghasem said, nodding.

Together they walked on toward the waiting car.

CHAPTER SIX

When I left the embassy the following evening, I picked up a tail. Actually, two of them, working as a team. I made no attempt to lose them; I went to my hotel.

Before I donned my running duds, I inspected them carefully, especially the shoes. Putting a beacon in a shoe would be an easy way to keep track of me. Apparently the MOIS or IRGC hadn't yet gotten around to that, but they might, whenever the spirit moved them.

I put on my running clothes and went back out onto the street. My two tails were still there, still dressed in street clothes.

I began jogging, warming up, working up a sweat. No matter how many times you have been followed, every time it happens your mind starts racing. These guys tried to follow me by running, but they weren't in shape, and soon I saw them no more. Did that mean no one was following me now, or was I the subject of a more sophisticated surveillance, and the followers just wanted me to think I had shaken loose?

And why today? Why right after Jake Grafton talked to Professor Azari?

The problem with the spy business is that nothing can be taken at face value.

I ran six miles and ended up back at the hotel. After a short walk to cool down, I went in, got a shower and headed for the dining room.

The next day I again talked to Grafton on the encrypted satellite telephone. "Rostram and Azari have exchanged e-mails," he said. "Azari advised him to cooperate. He didn't tell him to—he advised him. Don't know if that nuance is important, but it implies volumes."

"Okay."

"Be careful, Tommy!"

"Right."

That evening no one followed me when I ran. Go figure.

Just in case, I ran to the central bazaar and ducked into one of the myriad of alleys lined by booths. Three turns later, I came out the south side of the bazaar amid a nice crowd. As soon as I could, I began jogging again.

Now you may think I am some kind of exercise nut, but there was method in my madness. The faster the rabbit, the more difficult he is to follow. Sure, every now and then the security apparatus could mount a major effort to keep me under surveillance, but I had been running every night for a month, and if they had used their manpower that way, they had nothing to show for it. I was betting—hoping, actually—that if they had tried it, they had given up on me now.

Of course, there was always last night. Why last night, and not tonight?

What game were they playing?

If I stayed in this business long enough, I was going to wind up a jibbering idiot.

William Wilkins took Jake Grafton with him when he went to the White House to brief the president and National Security Adviser Jurgen Schulz. Sal Molina met the two CIA officers and escorted them to the Oval Office, where the president and Schulz were deep in conversation. Molina closed the door behind him and dropped into a chair near the door.

After everyone shook hands and found a chair, Wilkins got right to it. He briefed them on the incident in the Strait of Hormuz and let them read the Op Immediate message from the task force commander.

"So we lost an F/A-18 and pilot?"

"Yes."

"A provocation," the president said softly.

"Or an attempt to make the Americans turn on their ALQ-199s," Jake Grafton said.

"Did they?"

"The admiral was instructed to report it if they did. He didn't mention it."

Wilkins removed some satellite photos from his briefcase and spread them on the president's desk. "Iran is planning a missile test," he said. "They are moving three ships into the Indian Ocean, a destroyer and two small civilian ships with large radar arrays, and they are positioning missiles on launchers at their test site in the desert."

"They've tested missiles before," Schulz remarked.

The president picked up a photo, looked at it, then passed it to Schulz and reached for another. "When?"

"Soon. Within days, we think. They have at least one long-range missile on a launcher, a thing they call the Shahab-3. There are also four intermediate-range missiles, Shahab-2s, and four short-range ones, Shahab-1s. As Dr. Schulz noted, they have shot missiles before, but never nine at once."

"President Ahmadinejad has a trip planned next week," Schulz inter-jected. "He's going to Indonesia, the most populous Muslim nation on the planet, and Malaysia. He'll massage the leadership, take their temperature, and talk directly to the masses to gin up some grassroots support. One sus-pects the missile shoot will go off while he's abroad, so he can play the role of the modern Saladin."

"How accurate are the missiles?" the president asked.

"These things are derivations of the old Soviet Scud missiles. The Scuds were short range and wildly inaccurate, but an adequate delivery vehicle for a nuclear warhead. With conventional explosives in the warheads, the Syrians were lucky to hit Israel with the things. From Iran . . ."

"Have the Iranians updated the guidance systems?" Schulz asked pointedly.

"Probably," Wilkins said, "but we have no hard evidence."

"Another guess," Schulz said, his disgust evident.

"Dr. Schulz—" Wilkins began, but the president cut him off with a gesture.

"What is the range of the Shahab-3?" the president said.

"About twelve hundred miles. Yes, it will reach Israel. And Iraq, and the oil facilities throughout the region, and our air bases in Arabia. It will even reach our bases in Turkey."

"Terrific," the president muttered.

"The Patriot system that we have supplied to Israel is designed to knock these things down," Jurgen Schulz noted.

Wilkins glanced at Jake. "Admiral?"

"A nuclear warhead can be designed to detonate if the delivery missile changes course and speed unexpectedly, which would happen if it is hit by a Patriot missile," Jake said. "It can also be designed to be ejected from the de-livery vehicle so that it free-falls to a preset altitude before it detonates, thereby maximizing damage to surface installations. Destroy the buildings, kill all the people, and so on. And let's not kid ourselves—the Patriot system is de-signed for close-in missile defense. Patriot is a last-ditch defense weapon, and it is not perfect—no weapons system is. Some percentage of Patriot's targets will always escape destruction."

The silence that followed that statement was broken when the president said to Schulz, "We better start talking to the Israelis."

"We are talking to them."

"Talk harder."

"Do you intend to brief the congressional leadership about this?" Molina asked.

The president mulled it over. "Jurgen, why don't you go over to the Hill today and see the chairman of the House and Senate committees? I don't want to blindside them on this."

Schulz frowned. "Congressman Luvara has been stating publicly that he can't see why we should worry about Iran getting the bomb when the Israelis have it."

"If he makes a crack like that to you," the president said, "suggest that he plan to spend his next vacation in Tel Aviv. Maybe when he's sitting on Ahmadinejad's bull's-eye he'll see the problem."

"What he's really questioning is our commitment to Israel," Schulz shot back.

"I know that," the president said. He leaned back in his chair and rubbed his forehead. "The issue is larger than that, though. Will we honor our commitments to all our allies—Britain, France, Germany, Japan, Australia, Saudi Arabia *and* Israel?"

"Taiwan," Sal Molina interjected.

"And South Korea," the president said heavily. "Well, Luvara is a problem for another day."

He leaned forward, folded his forearms on his desk and scrutinized the faces of the men before him. "The hell of it is that Ahmadinejad knows beyond a shadow of a doubt that the United States will not let him wipe Israel off the face of the earth and get away with it."

"Does he know it?" Shulz asked.

"Well, by God," the president said, "pack your toothbrush, Jurgen. You can take him a letter from me. I'll tell it to him in plain English. You can even give him a Farsi translation."

"Will he believe it?" Sal Molina asked.

"That's not the right question," Jake Grafton said flatly. "Even if he believes it, will that knowledge deter him?"

———

Tehran was Ghasem's city. He had spent his life there and loved every square meter, including the spectacular view of the Alborz Mountains to the north, the sights and smells and press of people in the bazaar, the palaces, art museums, mosques, churches, parks, synagogues and temples, and the myriad of cheap apartment buildings and the perpetual traffic jams and endless crush of people, all fifteen or twenty million of them—no one knew for sure. What everyone did know was that the Persian natives had been joined by ethnic and linguistic minorities from all over Western Asia, including Assyrians, Lurs, Gilaks, Kurds, Turkmen, Arabs, Armenians, Talysh, Sikhs, Romas, Syrians and Lebanese, to name just a few. The latest people to join the mix were refugees from Iraq and Afghanistan.

The majority of Tehranis were followers of Shia Islam, but the rest covered the entire religious spectrum, from the Armenian Apostolic Church and the Assyrian Church of the East to Zoroastrianism, and everything in between, including Sunni Islam, Hinduism, Buddhism and Sufism, or Mystic Islam, the religion of the legendary Whirling Dervishes.

This religious soup was the intellectual food for Dr. Israr Murad, an elderly scholar who lectured on an irregular basis at the University of Tehran. Today Ghasem glanced at his watch as he parked his car, locked it, then trotted across campus. He opened the door and slipped into the back of the lecture hall just as Dr. Murad was making his final remarks.

When the students had left the lecture hall, Ghasem went forward to help Dr. Murad gather his notes. Murad was in his early eighties; he was still mentally active, yet arthritis and heart ailments had slowed him down. He sat and watched Ghasem pack the last of his notes in his leather briefcase.

"It went well?" Ghasem asked.

"Aii," the old man said, and made a gesture. "They ask the same questions that their fathers asked, and their fathers before them. If only they would think up new questions . . ."

"Their minds work in predictable ways," Ghasem murmured.

"And religions give predictable answers." The old man sighed and levered himself erect. "Did you bring the car?"

"Yes, Grandfather."

It had been Dr. Murad's car, but when he had decided he was no longer capable of driving it safely, he had given it to Ghasem.

When they were walking in the heat toward the automobile, Dr. Murad held on to the younger man's shoulders. He seemed lost in thought. Halfway there he signaled a pause and stood swaying, waiting . . . for his heart to stop hammering futilely, Ghasem thought. There was a bench just steps away, so

Ghasem eased the old man over to it and helped him seat himself. Then he sat beside him.

"I have a question," Ghasem said and waited for his grandfather to nod an acknowledgment.

"I heard Uncle Habib make a remark that I have been thinking about ever since. He said Iran is surrounded by enemies of God. By that he meant American armed forces. Still, in light of our conversations, I have been thinking, and wondering. Can God have mortal enemies, enemies of flesh and blood?"

The old man smiled wanly. "What do you think?" he asked.

"He could have such enemies only if He tolerates them."

"If He wishes to have them?"

"Yes."

Dr. Murad smiled again, then said, "Your god is large and powerful. Habib's is small and impotent."

"Habib Sultani doesn't see it that way."

"Indeed," the professor acknowledged. "Many men have an extraordinary ability to ignore the obvious."

Ghasem took a deep breath, then said, "So we are once again back to the core question: Is Islam a religion or a political ideology?"

"Unfortunately," answered the old man, "it is both. I say unfortunately, because Islam cannot survive in the world as a political ideology. The jihadists cannot win. If martyrdom is the fate of all true believers, then Islam will perish with them. Islam can be the faith of the dead or the faith of the living, but it cannot be both."

Automatically, Ghasem glanced around to see if anyone overheard. No one had. He took a deep breath and exhaled slowly. His grandfather was under suspicion—well, he had been under suspicion since the Islamic Revolution. The revolutionaries had closed the universities for three years, lectured professors and students on what they could teach and jailed, tortured and interrogated those who didn't toe the line of fundamental Islam. True, there were many other religions in Iran, but the official state religion was Shia Islam—Khomeini's version—and woe to the man or woman who didn't understand that and bow down. A wrong word, a gesture, a facial expression—anything could ignite the Revolutionary Guard, who roamed the campus in black uniforms, carrying weapons.

Dr. Murad gestured. "Help me up," he said. Ghasem did so, and they resumed their journey toward Ghasem's automobile.

"There is an Islamic professor in Germany," Ghasem said, "who said that the Prophet, may he rest in peace, is fiction. That he never existed. What do you think of that argument?"

"Muhammad's was the most documented life of any of the prophets," Murad said slowly, measuring his words. "Thousands of pages, thousands of facts. One suspects there was such a man, but by all accounts he was illiterate. He dictated his revelations to a scribe. The assumption has always been that the scribe was merely a scrivener who wrote down the Prophet's words verbatim. And yet the Prophet dictated the most sublime piece of literature ever written in Arabic. The language inspires and soars, it is beautiful and majestic and grand. Indeed, the language of the Koran became the Arabic that everyone wanted to speak. That scribe . . ."

"God told Muhammad what to say."

"Or the scribe took the ruminations of an illiterate, charismatic tribal chief and founded a religion."

"You should be working on your book," Ghasem said, "instead of wasting your strength on lectures."

"I don't lecture; I just talk," his grandfather said. "The students do not want to hear or think about the problems with Islam, and you know it. They have the perfect religion; they wish to hear about the strange beliefs and practices of infidels and pagans."

Since he taught comparative religion, Murad was under constant, intense scrutiny. He had survived by refusing to discuss Islam at all and discussing other religions as if they were voodoo practiced by illiterate natives starving on an isle in the sea's middle. Still, his classrooms were packed, and Revolutionary Guards were ever present, listening. Even discussing other religions was a dangerous game: Converting to Christianity was a capital offense in Iran, and if any of his students did it, Murad, the scholar, would be implicated.

A moment passed before Dr. Murad said, "I have almost finished the book."

Now Ghasem stopped short and looked at the old man's face. "When last we spoke, you said you were at least two years away."

"Your cousin Khurram was there when you asked, if you will recall."

Ghasem thought about it. "I remember."

"I do not want Khurram reading it. Nor discussing it."

Ghasem nodded. Khurram was very conventional, without a mote of intellectual curiosity. He was a chip flowing along on the fundamental Islamic stream that had ruled Iran since the fall of the shah.

"Nor your uncle Habib Sultani." The professor paused, then added, "Why my daughter Noora wanted to marry him is one of life's mysteries."

"You gave your consent."

"I did. Sometimes I wonder if Noora wishes I had refused." Dr. Murad sighed. "I want *you* to read the manuscript," he continued, returning to the subject abruptly. "Show it to no one, make no notes. Read it . . . and tell me what you think."

"Yes, Grandfather."

"I have made no copies. The one you will have is the only one."

Ghasem nodded.

They came to the car. When Ghasem had the old man seated in the right seat, the windows open and the car crawling through traffic, Dr. Murad said, "A few more days, and it will be finished. Read it quickly. My heart is acting up again. My time is drawing to a close."

After he dropped his grandfather at his house and helped the valet get him comfortable in a chair, Ghasem drove to the building where he lived. He shared a tiny apartment with a friend from the university, Mostafa Abtahi.

A licensed civil engineer, Abtahi had found a job at a printing firm that sold maps to tourists. He spent his days hunched over a drawing table updating maps of Tehran and the Iranian road system. His ambition, which he discussed endlessly with his friend Ghasem, was to go to America and get rich. Several months ago he had written to the American State Department requesting an American visa, and he was still awaiting a reply.

Tonight, as he and Ghasem shared a meager dinner—all they could afford—Abtahi launched into his favorite subject.

"My older brother has been in America for five years," he said, as if this tidbit were really news. He had told Ghasem everything he knew about his older brother a dozen times. "He owns an automobile repair shop in New Jersey. When I get there he will hire me, and together we will repair automobiles."

"What kind of automobiles?" Ghasem asked, to humor his friend.

"Taxicabs, mostly. Farrukh repairs a lot of taxicabs that are driven around New York by Iranians, Iraqis, Lebanese, Palestinians, Syrians, Saudis—men from all over the Middle East. They come to him because he speaks Farsi and Arabic and doesn't cheat them too much. Some garages install used parts in customers' cars and charge them for new ones, but Farrukh doesn't do—"

"Why America?" Ghasem asked. He had heard about the car repair business many times before. "Why travel halfway around the world to live in a nation of infidels?"

"Ah, in America they are rich. The people may be infidels, but they are from all over the earth and they go there and make lots of money. In America, people willing to work hard *can* get rich. Farrukh sees rich people everywhere. The houses, the cars, the boats—"

"There is more to life than money."

"True," Abtani agreed, scraping the last morsel from his bowl, "and a person who has money can afford to enjoy all those extra things."

"When you get to America, will you join a mosque?"

"Of course. The one Farrukh belongs to. He says it is a good place."

"Are the members supporting jihad?"

Abtani eyed his friend, then said frankly, "No."

"The Americans are fighting Muslims in Iraq and Afghanistan. Does that bother you?"

"That is not my fight."

"What do you think of jihad?"

"I am not a holy warrior, and I do not want to be one. I think martyrs are fools." He thrust out his lower jaw belligerently. "*That* is what I think. I want to find a good woman, get married, have children, have grandchildren, feed them all they want to eat, grow old and enjoy the life that Allah gave me." He made a chopping gesture. "Allah made the world without my help, and I think He could handle the infidels, if He wished. He could snap his fingers and transport them all to hell or Paradise, if He wished. But apparently He does not so wish. I will live as my parents lived and trust in His mercy."

"Perhaps that is the best way," Ghasem said thoughtfully.

"I will go to America," Abtani said stubbornly. "As soon as they send me a visa."

Like the president of the United States, Mahmoud Ahmadinejad used a trusted aide to keep close tabs on the intelligence community, both the MOIS and the Qods Force of the IRGC. Amazingly, in male-dominated, fundamentalist Iran, his aide was a woman, Hazra al-Rashid—not her real name but a *nom de guerre*. She had gotten her start during the Revolution ratting on her fellow university students, then torturing them. Her methods quickly got out of control, even for a third-world sewer like Iran, so she changed her name and was transferred to another prison. There she became a protégé of Ahmadinejad—ten years her senior—who was also earning points for Paradise by rooting out heretics and potential political enemies. He reined in her wildest impulses (which meant some prisoners lived a little longer) and drained off some of her sexual energy. They were made for each other.

Today, in the privacy of the presidential office, she told Ahmadinejad about the CIA's approach to Professor Azari. "He has suggested that Rostram cooperate with the CIA's spy in Tehran."

As usual for women employed by the government in postrevolutionary Iran, Hazra was wearing a black chador and a black scarf that covered her neck and the top of her head. Only her face and hands showed.

"Who is the CIA's spy?" Ahmadinejad asked.

"One of the new officers in the American Interests Section of the Swiss embassy. We have suspected him since he arrived, but so far he has done nothing."

The thing about the chador, Ahmadinejad mused, was that it hid everything. Intended by the mullahs to prevent male temptation by completely shrouding a woman's figure, it had just the opposite effect. Now everything was left to the imagination; women became mysterious figures who raised sexual tension wherever they appeared, even old women, the crippled, the lame and the grossly overweight.

"The American is named Carmellini," Hazra said. "He is a tall, fit man who runs at least five miles a day."

Instead of a sexless society where believers thought only pure thoughts, Iran had become the most sexually charged nation on the planet. The men thought about sex every time they saw a woman, fantasized about having sex with her and, even when she passed from view, obsessed about sex like a hormone-drenched teenage male. *We are going to have to do something about chadors,* Ahamdinejad mused. Even as he entertained the thought, he knew that course was politically impossible, as long as the Party of God remained in power.

"We are going to have one of our agents make contact with Azari," Hazra said. "We must know precisely what he told the CIA."

Mahmoud Ahmadinejad turned Hazra around, so she was facing away from him. Then he began lifting the hem of her chador.

Ahh yes, she wasn't wearing anything under the black sack. But then, she never did. He also liked the fact that she shaved her legs in the European style.

"We must confirm that the CIA believes Azari is telling the truth," Hazra said as Ahmadinejad pushed her gently down onto the desk and began stroking her buttocks and back. She spread her legs slightly, wanting him to stroke her vagina. She was already wet, ready for him. Ah, now she felt his hand.

"If they didn't believe him," she continued, "one doubts that they would want to talk to Rostram."

"You have done well, my beloved," Mahmoud Ahmadinejad said as he thrust his penis into her.

I was going to ruin my lungs if I kept running every evening. This evening the crap in the air hid the Alborz Mountains to the north.

I walked the last few blocks back to the hotel, trying to cool off. Occasionally I coughed, hacking up the goop from my lungs.

A block from the hotel I heard someone say my name. "Tommy Carmellini." I turned, looking for the speaker . . . a skinny kid leaning against a building smoking a cigarette. He looked about eighteen. Smooth cheeks, medium-length hair, grungy trousers and a long-sleeve shirt and sweater.

I turned and walked toward him. "Those cancer sticks will kill you," I said conversationally.

"I'm Rostram," he said and took another nervous drag on his butt. I thought I heard a trace of a British accent.

I glanced right and left to see who was watching us. No one, apparently. I took another good look. Someone was jerking me around.

"And I'm the fucking Wizard of Oz," I said, turning away.

"Hey," he said. "Hey." He stepped after me and tugged at my sleeve. "Don't bugger this up, you bloody Yank. I'm Rostram."

"Okay," I said. "You picked a rotten place for a meet."

"We must meet somewhere," he said, sucking on that weed, "and no one is watching you. You're clean tonight. Let's go across the street to the park and sit down."

I didn't know what to think. I had been expecting some fifty-something bureaucrat or scientist who hated the regime, and instead I got this kid.

We jaywalked and didn't get run over. Found a bench in the park. I sat on it, and the kid perched on the back. He lit another cigarette and blew smoke around. He was smoking Marlboros, I noticed, and he smoked like a beginner, nervously, very aware of the weed. I wondered where he got the damn things. His eyes were constantly moving, but at least some of the time he was sizing me up.

Then he made a gesture, reached up to brush some hair back off his forehead, and the revelation hit me like a hammer. This was no boy! Rostram was a woman!

I looked at my shoes, scanned the passersby, then looked at him again. Yep, almost no Adam's apple, really clean cheeks, slender fingers and just the faintest hint of a chest.

Oh, man! The one thing everyone in the world agreed upon was that the Islamic fundamentalists were super-protective of their women. It wasn't enough that I was a spy in the house of the saved. Oh, no. That goddamn Jake Grafton had sent me here to hook up with some Muslim traitor babe.

I sat there trying to keep my temper from going thermonuclear as I let the reality of the situation sink in.

"So how did you meet your pen pal?" I asked finally, when Rostram had smoked her weed about down to the filter.

"Pen pal?"

"The guy in America you correspond with."

"Oh," she said. "He was a professor at Oxford when I was there."

"How old are you, anyway?"

"Twenty-five."

"Does your daddy know you're out running around in men's clothes, smoking cigarettes and talking to foreign spies?"

She flipped her cigarette away and gave me The Look.

"You had me fooled there for a while," I told her.

"What tipped you off?"

"That thing you did with your hair. It's a woman's gesture."

"Not my stride?"

"Nope. Fooled me there."

She got out her Marlboros and kicked one out of the pack. Stuck it in her mouth and lit it like an English schoolboy who was pretty damn cool and ditching school and didn't care who knew it.

"So how did you get into treason, anyway?" I asked, just to make conversation.

"My pen pal asked for my help. I agreed to do it because I loathe the fanatics who are running this country."

"Passing military secrets to foreign spies strikes me as a bit more than a political protest."

"These fools are about to start World War III."

"They catch you, you won't live to see it."

"I know that. That's why I've been watching you for two days, checking to see if anyone is watching you. They aren't."

"Or you just haven't seen them."

"You're clean, Carmellini."

"What's your real name?"

"I'm not going to tell you. Rostram is enough."

I nodded and looked casually around. No one seemed to be paying any attention to us, but that may have been only window dressing. For all I knew we were being filmed for a starring role on the six o'clock evening news. I could see the headlines now: AMERICAN SPY SEDUCES ISLAMIC WOMAN.

"Why are you in Iran spying on us?" she asked.

I tried the old Carmellini charm, which had apparently worked fairly well for dear old Dad or I wouldn't be here. "Well, I had a choice. Several choices, actually. My boss wanted me to do this gig, but I could have gone back to Iraq for another tour of tracking down roadside bombers, or I could have resigned from the Company and joined my brother-in-law in his bagel business. Or I could have taken a banana boat to South America and become a beach bum until the money ran out or I ruined my liver, whichever came first."

She was eyeing me while I ran my mouth, wondering if any of this was true.

"You worry a lot, do you?" she murmured. She was playing with the cigarette pack.

"All the time. Don't you?"

"So what is it you want from me?" she asked. Her eyes darted around again, then lit on me. This was one nervous woman.

"Are you nervous because we're doing a little treason, because I'm an infidel, or because you're out and about with a strange man?"

"A bloody headshrinker," she said disgustedly. "Let's get to it. What do you want?"

"Who do you get your information from?"

"You want names?"

"Names and where they work."

"Get their names from Azari. He set up the network, and he made promises to them."

"Do these people know that you are a woman?"

She dropped the cigarette from suddenly numb fingers and stared at me with big eyes. "No," she whispered.

"How do you get your information?"

"Dead drops."

I tried to keep a straight face. If that was true, she had only Azari's word that there even was a network. Nor could she verify any of the names Azari gave Grafton. Anyone could service drops, including the MOIS.

"We practice good security," she said, almost as if she were trying to sell me. Or herself.

I rubbed my face with my hands to restore circulation. I was up to my eyeballs in it this time. There was absolutely no doubt in my criminal mind that the Iranian government controlled Rostram and Azari and the flow of information to the West. I would have bet my life on that. Then it occurred to me that I probably already had.

"Go home," I said and waved my hand in dismissal.

"Don't you want to set up another meet?"

"I'll find you if I do."

"But you don't—"

"Get the hell outta here."

She started to say something else, thought better of it and left. I watched her go.

Well, she had the stride right, anyway. She walked like a guy.

I went straight to the embassy, crawled into my soundproof booth and called Jake Grafton. "Rostram is a woman," I told him when we finally got connected and the crypto gear had timed in. "Not only that, she doesn't know who supplies the information she transmits to Azari. She picks it up from dead drops."

"Oh, great," Grafton said disgustedly. "Does she know she's working for the Iranian government?"

"I doubt it. She thinks she's doing a noble thing."

"Who is she, anyway?"

"She refused to give a name. She says she's twenty-five and studied under Azari at Oxford. She's maybe five-five, dark hair, trim, boyish figure. How many of those girls could there be?"

"I'll get you a name."

"What's my next move?"

"If you're up for it, find out who is servicing the dead drops. Use the guys in country."

"Okay. What then?"

"I'll think of something, Tommy."

I called Jake Grafton back twelve hours later, in the middle of my workday.

"I talked to the Brits," he said. "They think her name might be Davar Ghobadi. If so, her father is the president and CEO of a big construction company that is building a lot of Ahmadinejad's hardened factories and launch sites. Her uncle is Habib Sultani, the minister of defense."

"So she's somebody."

"With a capital *S*," he said. "She was also a math wizard at Oxford. One of the British profs said a brain like hers comes along once in a generation."

"If I hang around her, the powers that be are going to get antsy."

"The Iranians have gone to a lot of trouble to sell us some lies," Grafton said. "The only possible reason to do that is to hide the truth, whatever that is. Let's see how far they can be pushed."

"Truth is rare, these days," I remarked.

"Priced that way, too," the admiral observed.

The booming of thunder woke Davar Ghobadi in the middle of the night. Her room was in the attic, tucked up here under the eaves. The room was chilly, and she could hear the rain drumming on the eaves of the old house quite plainly.

Too plainly. She opened her eyes and, as lightning flashed, saw that her window was open. The curtains were dancing in the breeze coming though the opening.

She threw back the blanket, got out of her small bed and walked past her desk and the big table covered with her father's blueprints to the window. Hadn't she shut it before she went to bed?

She paused a moment in the darkness, listening to the wind and rain in the trees and looking out at the neighborhood, which was composed of monstrous old houses on big lots on the hills on the north side of Tehran. In the early part of the century rich people and foreigners had built these houses, trying to escape the noise and traffic of the city center. They had succeeded. This neighborhood was an oasis in a third-world sea.

Davar shivered, then pulled the window closed.

She turned—and a gloved hand was clapped over her mouth as she was seized roughly.

Panic swelled, and she tried to struggle against the overwhelming strength that imprisoned her. She could taste the leather of the glove on the hand over her mouth. Recovering from her momentary terror, she ceased struggling . . . and felt the pressure of the hand over her mouth lessen.

"I didn't think you were a screamer." A male voice, whispering in English. American English.

She recognized the voice. It was that spy, Carmellini.

She saw him in a lightning flash, dressed all in black, towering above her, a shadowy, damp presence, his strength still immobilizing her.

Now the hand over her mouth came away.

"Is there anyone else on this floor?"

"No."

"Can we be overheard?"

"I don't think so."

He released her from his grasp and retreated, a dark shape in a darker room. When the lightning flashed and the thunder boomed again, she saw that he had taken off the black hood that covered his head, and he was smiling.

"Sorry to drop in on you like this, but getting a date in this town is just impossible."

Finding the Ghobadi house in the toniest neighborhood of Tehran with the help of a GPS hadn't been difficult. Deciding which room to enter had been dicier, and I finally settled on the attic. My night vision goggles, which used both starlight and infrared, helped ensure I wasn't going to stumble onto a guard in the yard or climb through a window onto an occupied bed.

She was wearing only shorts and a T-shirt, and Muslim or not, she didn't seem embarrassed by my presence. I remarked on that as she lit a cigarette and puffed nervously.

"I had a boyfriend," she told me by way of explanation. "When I was in England. He was from Oklahoma."

"Uh-huh."

"I should have married him."

"Why didn't you?"

"My mother was ill. When I got my degree, I came home to take care of her. She died last year."

While she was talking, I was scoping out the room, which was large. Apparently she had most of the attic, or all of it. Large tables held blueprints. I looked them over with my penlight while she told me about mullahs, life in Iran and the life she had had in England.

"What are these?"

"Construction projects my father's company is building."

"Why do you have them?"

"I check the math for him. Sometimes his engineers make mistakes."

"And you don't?"

"Not with numbers."

"May I photograph these?" I asked.

"If you wish," she said. She seemed to have no problem betraying the mullahs.

She segued right into politics and nuclear weapons while I rigged blankets over the windows, the one I had entered and another on the opposite side of the room, then turned on every light in the place.

Old-time spies used Minox cameras, but my agency had gone digital. I got out my Sony Cyber-shot, which was perfect for this use; just lay the document flat, focus and click.

"Are you married?" she asked.

I shot her a glance. She was trying to look nonchalant, and failing. "This year all the foreign spies are single."

"Do you have a girlfriend?"

"I'm temporarily between," I muttered as I repositioned blueprints.

"In England I had many boyfriends," she said and slowly peeled off the T-shirt.

Uh-oh! It wasn't enough I was in a Muslim woman's bedroom photographing state secrets; now she was stripping down to her birthday suit.

I stopped taking pictures and took the memory card out of the camera. Meanwhile Davar was removing the shorts. Well, she was a woman, all right.

I dug in my backpack and got out the satellite burst transmitter. Somehow I managed to get the camera card in it, got the thing turned on and stuck it outside on the window ledge, all the while watching Davar pose on the back of a chair. I wasn't nervous—I was terrified.

"Do you Iranians still stone sex fiends to death?" I asked her.

"You can kiss me if you wish," she said and arched her back to display her breasts better.

"Tell me about this guy from Oklahoma." I checked my watch. Another sixty seconds or so on the burst transmitter, which would erase the camera card after the transmission, then I was out of here.

"He wanted me to marry him."

"Why didn't you?"

"I had to return to Iran. I've told you that."

"Write him a letter," I said as I went around the room turning off lights. "Tell him you changed your mind. Women have the right, you know." When the place was as dark as it was going to get, I pulled on my backpack.

I ran into her in front of the window. She wrapped her arms around me.

I thought, *What the heck?* and gave her a long kiss. Her lips and tongue tasted delicious. She pressed her naked body against me.

"Write him a letter," I said huskily, pushing her away.

I pulled the blanket down and pulled on my night vision goggles. No one in sight. I retrieved the burst transmitter from the window ledge, then eased out the window and felt for the handholds I had used to climb up.

Davar Ghobadi stood at the window until Tommy Carmellini reached the ground and disappeared into the night. One instant he was there, then he was gone, swallowed by the darkness.

She went back to bed, but sleep wouldn't come.

Her thoughts were still tumbling about—Tommy Carmellini, Iran, mullahs, nuclear weapons, Ghasem, Azari—when she finally drifted off to sleep.

CHAPTER SEVEN

G hasem's uncle Habib Sultani was a harried man. His afternoon interview with President Mahmoud Ahmadinejad did not go well. The president had just publicly reissued his call for the dissolution of Israel, peacefully or violently, which had boosted his and Iran's status in the Muslim world to giddy new heights, as he had intended, and had caused temblors to once again rock Western capitals. Today Ahmadinejad was suffused with enthusiasm over reports of his speech from Arabia, Syria, Libya, Yemen and certain quarters in Palestine, Jordan, Egypt and Pakistan. His face seemed to glow.

"We play a dangerous game," Sultani said bluntly to the exultant president when they were alone. "The Israelis and Americans know about our missiles. They know of their capabilities and their location. They know the design and location of the reactors to the precise inch. They could destroy the reactors and all our nuclear facilities aboveground with impunity, as they did the Syrian reactor. Our antiaircraft defenses are no better than the Syrians'."

Ahmadinejad did not appreciate hearing the bald truth. He was a man who believed firmly in Allah and himself, although there were some who privately said that the order was reversed. "The Americans are great cowards," he declared, and not for the first time. "They have announced to the world that they do not believe we have a weapons program. Yet they know that we are enriching uranium, and they know that an attack will release large quantities of radioactivity. They fret about poisoning the earth and wring their hands like old women."

"The possibility of radioactive contamination didn't stop the Israelis," Sultani noted.

"Ah, yes, the Jews," Ahmadinejad said. "Infidels without scruples."

The irony of Ahmadinejad's comment did not escape Sultani, who had yet to observe a scruple in the president of Iran.

Mahmoud Ahmadinejad spoke as if God were whispering in his ear. "The godless Americans will do nothing—nothing—and they will not provide assistance to the Israelis. Without American airborne tanker assets, Iran is out of range of Israeli bombers."

Once again Sultani was left to contemplate the carnage caused by the incompetence of the American CIA, which had agreed with the publicly issued National Intelligence Estimate that said Iran had discontinued its nuclear weapons program. He knew that the separation of weapons-grade plutonium from enriched uranium had never stopped—in fact, the man in charge of that effort worked for him. He also knew that the nation possessed enough plutonium to manufacture twelve bombs, and that the stockpile was growing at several kilos per month. Never, he thought, in the history of the world had a foreign intelligence estimate been seized upon with such glee.

What he didn't know was that Ahmadinejad and Hazra al-Rashid had been playing two hands at once. Perfectly willing to have the world believe they were manufacturing nuclear weapons, they had used the Azari connection to let the world think they were several years away from operational warheads, when in reality Iran was much closer.

"We have tricked those fools," Ahmadinejad had chortled.

Or they have tricked us, Sultani thought then, although he didn't make that remark aloud.

Now, this afternoon, he advised the president that his attempt to get an assessment of how the Americans' latest electronic magic was performed had failed. "The American fighters refused to take the bait," he said in summation.

"We must put more pressure on the Russians," Ahmadinejad said. "Those liars! The promises they made, the lies they told . . . *They* know the Americans' secrets and are not sharing with us."

Back in his roost at the Defense Ministry, Sultani rubbed his chin and tried to envision how Iran could gain access to one of the Americans' magic boxes, which he knew were in their frontline warplanes, those carrier jets that flew boldly up and down the Persian Gulf with impunity. *We could always shoot one down,* he thought. *Or arrange a midair collision, so that one crashes and we are first to gain access to the wreckage.* He thought about the crash of the F-18. The pieces of the airplane were still out there in the Strait of Hormuz, which was deep, with swift tidal currents—and, of course, it had crashed beyond the territorial limits. If there was a magic black box somewhere on the floor of that strait, Iran lacked the technology to find it. No, that box was beyond reach, although there were plenty of others.

The real issue, he well knew, was the vulnerability of Iran's nuclear program to a conventional air attack. The Iranians had spent over twenty billion dollars moving the entire weapons program underground. Entire underground cities had been created to house the enrichment facilities, the manufacture of neutron generators, the bomb plant itself and the missile factories. Only the reactors were still aboveground: unfortunately, they could not be moved. Everything else, including the spent fuel that was being enriched, was buried deep in bombproof tunnels bored into solid granite. Or built under the city of Tehran itself.

The real question, Sultani decided, was when the enemies' window of opportunity would close. At what point would an attack be futile, pointless, unable to stop Iran's march to the bomb?

He removed the files holding the plans for the tunnels and the overview of the program from a safe behind his desk and spread them out so that he could study them. The conversion of uranium from yellowcake, a solid, into a gas, uranium hexafluoride (UF6), was proceeding nicely at Isfahan. This was a major industrial operation, and it took place underground. But if the facility were attacked with conventional weapons, would the underground factory be able to sustain operations? This required a calculation of how much damage the bombs might inflict on the hardened site. Of course, any breach of the tanks containing the radioactive gas would cause serious contamination. Perhaps the entire cavern would be unusable. Certainly the radiation would kill everyone there.

Still, the off-site stockpile of UF6 was adequate and growing by the day. That stockpile was held in four locations, all inside tunnels carved into mountains.

The next step in the process was to raise the concentration of the U-235 isotope in the UF6 from its natural level of .7 percent to between 3 percent and 5 percent by the use of centrifuges. The product the centrifuges produced was called low-enriched uranium, or LEU. The cascade centrifuges at Natanz were 160 feet underground. This process took approximately 70 percent of the time and effort necessary to get to the final product, which was highly enriched uranium, HEU, containing weapons-grade concentrations of over 90 percent U-235.

Of course, even if Natanz was destroyed, Iran also had a laser enrichment facility and a heavy water facility, all hardened.

The detonator and warhead factories were also deeply underground.

All these facilities were protected by Russian S-300 antiaircraft systems, which fired the SA-20 surface-to-air missile at attacking planes. In Syria, this system failed to detect the inbound Israeli bombers.

Habib Sultani carefully studied the LEU and HEU production levels.

Finally he sighed and began arranging the materials back in his file.

Two weeks, he decided. In two weeks Iran would have enough HEU to manufacture twelve warheads. Regardless of what happened after that, bomb assembly could continue deep within the earth. If the Israelis or Americans attacked before that, they would of course do some damage, release some radioactivity, and delay the production of U-235. However, Sultani concluded, the time when they could shut down the program with conventional weapons had already passed.

There was nothing short of nuclear war that the Israelis and Americans could do to prevent Iran from becoming a nuclear power.

Twelve nuclear warheads, mounted on missiles hidden in deep tunnels in solid granite mountains. The missiles could be run out of their tunnels and fired in minutes.

Twelve warheads should satisfy Ahmadinejad, Sultani thought.

Callie was in bed Saturday night when Jake heard his doorbell ring. He padded to the front door and peered through the peephole. Sal Molina was standing there.

Grafton unlocked the door, held it open and said, "Come in, come in."

"Can a man get a drink around here?" Molina asked.

"If he has plain tastes and isn't a connoisseur of the finer things in life."

"I've been accused of a lot of things," Molina said with a sigh, "but no one ever called me a connoisseur."

As they walked toward the kitchen, Molina muttered, "You alone?"

"Callie is in bed. Name your poison."

"Bourbon. It's not just for breakfast anymore."

Callie came out in a robe and said hello, then made her excuses and went back to bed. Settled in Grafton's den with the door closed, Molina said, "I was on my way home and thought maybe you could tell me something that would make me sleep better."

"I doubt it, but ask away."

"You've been at the CIA . . . what? Three years?"

"About."

"What's your assessment of the agency?"

"I'm not going to trash my boss."

"This is off the record. I want an honest opinion, if there is such a thing inside the Beltway."

Jake Grafton took his time answering. He sipped his drink—he was having bourbon, too—then said, "The Company is a large, fossilized bureaucracy. Most of the people there are mediocre, at best. A serious number are incompetent. Most case officers don't speak the language of their subject countries. No one reads the area newspapers. The analysts' reports are often treacle—all they do is look at satellite photography and radio intercepts. Human intelligence is not high on the priority list and hasn't been for a generation. A lot of the agency's people are working their way to retirement by doing nothing that makes waves—most bureaucracies are like that. This one is no different." He turned over a hand. "How much more do you want?"

Molina made a face. "That's enough, I guess." He worked on his drink. "How likely are we to find out what Iran is going to do with its nuke warheads, which the agency says it isn't building?"

"The agency said it has no hard evidence Iran is building nuclear warheads," Grafton said, correcting Molina. "The turtle has pulled its head into its shell."

"What about these op-ed pieces Professor Azari has been writing? They're full of facts and figures. He's making us look like total idiots."

"Azari has been getting info from a private spy network in Iran. Some of his information is verifiable, some of it isn't. I suspect some of his people are government double agents."

"Does Azari realize that's a possibility?"

"He suspects it, I imagine. Hell, he may be on Ahmadinejad's payroll."

"Is Iranian security reading these messages, too?"

Jake Grafton considered his answer carefully. "I doubt if they have cryptographers sophisticated enough and computer programs powerful enough to break the code. They might have the contact in their pocket, of course, and have gotten the key from her. Or from Azari."

"Her?"

"*Her.* The Iranians read the American press, so they must know about Azari and his articles, and they must have penetrated his network."

"You have a man in Iran, don't you?"

"Yes. Tommy Carmellini."

"What's he doing?"

"Trying to find out the truth about their nuke program."

Sal Molina took a healthy swig of his drink, then sat processing Grafton's remarks. He changed the subject. "The generals think they have the factory pinpointed that is making the EDs that Iran is sending to Iraq." EDs were explosive devices—bombs. "They want to launch a commando raid against the factory. What's your assessment?"

"Now isn't the time to stir up the Iranians," the admiral said. "Not with Tommy trying to gain access to government buildings. Can we wait a while?"

"Wait, wait, wait. That's hard for generals and politicians to do. Everyone is getting damn tired of waiting. Our kids are getting killed and maimed in Iraq and the press is full of stories about Iranian nukes."

"Waiting is difficult for Americans," Jake Grafton agreed, "but timing is everything in life."

"The waiting for this is over." Sal Molina attacked his drink again. After a bit he said, "Does Carmellini have a chance?"

"If I didn't think so I wouldn't have sent him over there," Jake replied.

Ten minutes later, when Jake escorted Molina to the door, he asked, "Did you get anything to make you sleep better?"

"Hell, no. I never do when I talk to you."

"I'll send you some intelligence assessments in the morning. They're good bedtime reading."

"Send me something on the Russians. Those bastards are good copy."

Grafton pursed his lips in thought, then said softly, "The Russians will be in the catbird seat if the Middle East explodes, won't they?"

"With all their oil and gas, Russia will become the new Saudi Arabia," Sal Molina said sourly. "Russia will quickly become the richest nation on the planet, and Vladimir Putin will be the most powerful man on earth."

Molina walked out Grafton's door and headed for the elevator.

The Mossad's Joe Mottaki was full of information when he and I finally got into the little soundproof security booth I had built in the basement of the embassy annex. It was about the size of a telephone booth, so we were cramped.

Mottaki had a job with the firm that cleaned the embassy, and he came around every other day or so. He was a little guy, looked every inch a Persian, spoke Farsi like a native and fairly decent Arabic. The first time I met him he told me he had been born in Egypt. He refused to tell me any more about himself.

"Davar Ghobadi is single," he told me today. "No lovers or suitors that we know about. She has spent the last two days talking to a variety of people all over Tehran, all apparently friends of hers. Don't know the subjects, but the conversations were serious and long."

"Um." I wondered if she had told everyone in town that she was talking to an American spy, but even if she had, what could I do about it? "What about Ahmadinejad's political opposition?"

"They are unhappy. Most of the people in this country are poor as dirt, yet Ahmadinejad and the mullahs are squandering tens of billions of petro-dollars on the nuclear program. Even if the program was for peaceful pur-poses and they gave electricity away to everyone in the country who wanted it, that wouldn't justify the expenditures. People also need clean water, roads, hospitals, sewers, schools—in short, everything."

"Is Ahmadinejad in danger of a political revolt?"

Mottaki shrugged. "Who can say? The opposition does what it can un-der the gaze of the mullahs. Believe me, all is not well at the Parliament building."

We talked for an hour about names and personalities. I was learning a lot, but I wondered if any of it meant anything.

When we had beat the hell out of that topic, I told Joe that Davar had told me she used dead drops. "It would be nice to find one and aim a camera at it. See who services it."

"I have exactly three people," Joe said, "counting me. Your two chaps make five. Still, only five men . . ."

"Do the best you can."

"What if she lied to you?"

"Well . . ."

"We can't prove a negative."

"Watch her carefully for a couple more days. See if you can catch her at a drop."

"We'll have to really stick to her."

I'm such a hard-ass. I didn't say anything.

"Okay," he said forlornly.

"Someone needs to write a new Koran."

Ghasem stared at his grandfather with his jaw agape. One didn't hear blasphemy very often in Iran these days.

"Of course," Dr. Murad continued, "hardly anyone ever reads the old one. If they did, they'd discover how little theology is really in it."

They were sitting in the garden outside his grandfather's house, where the old man was feeding the birds, a pastime that consisted of tossing birdseed on the ground and seeing how close the birds would come to his feet to get it. Since the professor had been doing this for years, the answer was, very close.

"God spoke to Muhammad, may he rest in peace, and he gave us the Koran," Ghasem said. "He was the last prophet."

"God could speak to someone else. You or me, for instance. Anyone."

"Why did He choose Muhammad?"

"Aah, a very good question. My students are afraid to ask questions, afraid of being accused of blaspheming. The fear of being unorthodox is one of the major problems facing Muslims."

"All religions control their adherents, to a greater or lesser degree," Ghasem retorted.

"Indeed. Social and political control is one of religion's major functions. Without control, religions would not have proven so popular through the ages." The old man dropped more seed just beyond his shoes. The birds went for it fearlessly.

"Why Muhammad?" Ghasem repeated.

"He had the standing in society, the charisma, the ego, to found an empire, to make people follow him, to lead them to military victory. Yet no one would have followed him unless he claimed he had a mandate from God."

"God spoke to him," the young man replied, "and he obeyed."

"Megalomaniacs and the mentally ill often tell us they hear God's voice," the professor shot back. "Muhammad could have been either." He shrugged. "Or both."

Ghasem waited for lightning to strike the old man dead. When he realized it wasn't going to happen right there and then, he exhaled.

The manuscript was heavy in his hands. It was wrapped in paper, tied with a string, and was several inches thick.

"Islam is a fundamental religion," Israr Murad mused as he watched the bravest bird peck tiny seeds near his right shoe. "It was a tool to create a nation. All who didn't follow Muhammad were the enemy. For many Muslims, that distinction is quite real even today. They see the world as us versus them. Nor can they imagine a legitimate secular government to which they owe obedience. Muhammad ruled by divine right; he was God's anointed. Baldly, the Muslims are stuck in the seventh century while the rest of the world has evolved, has grown tolerant of different people, different religions and different ways of life. Only through tolerance can different people live under a secular government that rises and falls based on political issues that have nothing to do with religion. Islam is the most intolerant major religion on the planet."

"All religions have problems," Ghasem said thoughtfully. "At the core, each must be accepted by faith."

"Yes. Faith."

"One must surrender to God."

"Yes."

"Do you believe, Grandfather?"

"In what? In the Koran? In the Christian Bible? Judaism? Hinduism? Buddhism? What?"

"In God."

The old man thought about that. *After a lifetime of scholarship and contemplation,* Ghasem thought, *he has to think about the most basic question.* With a jolt he recalled his grandfather once remarking that by trying to learn everything, a scholar risked knowing nothing at all.

"I don't know," the old man confessed, his voice barely audible. He thought about that for a moment more, then tried to straighten up in his chair. He couldn't. Age had bent him like a twig. "All religions today share a common problem," he whispered. The professor gestured toward the manuscript, which caused much fluttering among the birds near his feet. "Read," he said. "It's all in there. A lifetime of work and thought. I put it all down."

Ghasem was young—he couldn't help himself. "What is the common problem?"

"The god that they worship is too small."

Hyman Fineberg met General Darma at a small estate well outside Jakarta. The general's limo had picked him up in town, and the driver, the general's son, let him off in front of the house. He wandered around back and found the general sitting alone by a swimming pool, in a swimming suit and short-sleeve shirt, drinking beer.

The general offered Fineberg one, and he accepted.

"I think your day is next Thursday," Darma said. "He will arrive on Wednesday, meet with the president that afternoon and evening, then attend a state banquet. On Thursday morning at eleven he has a meeting scheduled with a group of religious leaders. It was scheduled then to give him a few hours to rest and recover from the banquet."

"Thursday afternoon?"

"Another audience with the president, then a press conference."

"But the morning?"

"The limo will be waiting in front of the hotel. I can pull the security people away, so when he and his bodyguards come down in the elevator, they will be alone."

Hyman Fineberg took a sip of cold beer and considered. He had spent the last two weeks as a guest in that hotel and knew every inch of it. Darma knew that, of course. What Darma didn't know, Fineberg hoped, was that two other Mossad agents had also been in the hotel, watching his back.

They drank beer and talked about how it would be. "You cannot use explosives," Darma said. "Can't blow up the hotel. Too many casualties. No poison gas, nothing exotic."

"I understand." Indeed Fineberg did. He had his instructions from Tel Aviv; they wanted Ahmadinejad dead, but no innocent people. On the other hand, he reflected, Tel Aviv was prepared to swallow a lot if in the end they could see Ahmadinejad's head on a platter.

"This . . . incident . . . will not cause you too much grief, will it?" Fineberg asked.

General Syafi'i Darma considered his answer. When he spoke, Fineberg watched his eyes. "There will be questions—after all, I am the director of Indonesian security. I will be contrite. The Mossad's reputation is well known. It is possible, however, that for political reasons the president may ask me for my resignation. If so, I will go quietly. I have had a long military career, and whatever happens, I will have a comfortable retirement. Due to your generosity, very comfortable." Darma smiled.

Fineberg smiled back. Unfortunately only one side of his mouth worked as it should.

Yes indeed, the Israeli thought. The little fat bastard might be contemplating a double-cross.

"Please keep in mind," Hyman Fineberg said pleasantly, "that if my government gets the slightest suspicion that you took our money and betrayed us, your future will become problematic."

"Don't threaten me," Darma snapped.

"I beg your pardon, General. I do not mean to demean or insult you. I merely mentioned a fact of life, one of which I am sure you are well aware. A faux pas on my part, no doubt. Accept my apology, please."

"I keep my promises."

Fineberg smiled broadly, which made his face look even more lopsided. "And I keep mine."

That evening Ghasem went to his uncle's home to visit with his cousin Davar in her room in the attic. She spent her time here doing mathematics, playing with her computer, and calculating costs and materials for her father. Stacks of his blueprints and specifications were neatly arranged on a table in one corner.

"Why don't you go out?" Ghasem asked her for the thousandth time. "Go to the university? Meet your old friends? Why don't you get a life?"

She eyed him, then ignored his comments, also as usual. The truth was she did go out, and often, and talked to a wide variety of people. Some of them were giving her material to pass on to Azari in America, some were just people she liked being around, and some were people she thought had something important to say about where Iran was and where it should go in the future. These people were men and women. Ahmadinejad and the mullahs didn't understand the power of women. They forced them back into chadors and manteaus, but the women were the impetus that was going to someday overthrow the mullahs, or so Davar hoped.

"Did you see Grandfather today?" she asked her cousin.

"Yes." Ghasem threw himself into the only stuffed chair in the room. He stared at his toes. "His health is failing."

"He will be free soon," she remarked.

"Free?" Ghasem wasn't sure what she meant.

"Death is the only way you can escape the clutches of the government," she said.

Ghasem rolled his eyes and sagged back into the chair. Davar had spent three years at Oxford, and although she never said it, she had obviously loved England. She came home transformed, as British as Prince Charlie. She had arrived home three years ago this past July. Her father, who should have wanted more for her, thought her presence a godsend. At his request she did all the calculations necessary for his huge construction projects, which he got because he wholeheartedly supported the regime.

Ghasem straightened slightly and looked at his cousin. She wasn't a pretty woman. Sort of plain, actually. Also brilliant, well educated, and widely read. Not many men would appreciate such a wife, but there were a few that might. There were even rare ones who would treasure her. She would never meet them, he thought, nor they her. If he or her father brought such a man to meet her, she would refuse to see him.

"Not the manteau thing again?" Ghasem said disgustedly. Manteaus, or ripoushes, were loose-fitting, full-length coats that covered the wearer from neck to ankles. Those worn in summer were made of light cloth; those for winter were much heavier. They were plain or discreetly patterned, usually muted pastel colors.

"I loathe the things," she said. "They are a symbol of all that is wrong in Iran, all that is wrong with this religion. Allah wants me to wear a chador or manteau? I don't think so."

"You will become an old maid, never marry, be childless . . . Have you ever thought about the future, about what will happen when your father dies?"

"I'll come live with you."

"Better think of something else," Ghasem shot back. "I *do* intend to marry, when I find the right woman, and my wife, whoever she turns out to be, might not appreciate having a maiden cousin as a permanent boarder."

Davar said nothing. She became even more engrossed in a set of blueprints. Ghasem rose from his chair and looked over her shoulder. These were blueprints for a large underground city. The regime had worked diligently for years to get all nuclear weapons and missile fabrication activities completely underground.

"Which tunnel is that?"

"The executive bunker," she said. "The galleries are over a hundred meters below the surface. If the Israelis or Americans attack with conventional or nuclear weapons, the Supreme Leader, President Ahmadinejad, and the key mullahs and parliamentary supporters will ride out the hostilities in this bunker. They could stay down there, cut off from the world, for years before their supplies ran out."

"What about the people on the surface?"

"In a nuclear war, anyone without a bunker ticket is going to be cremated alive or die of radiation poisoning, either fast or slow."

"While the mullahs will be safe below," Ghasem mused, "urging us martyrs on to glory."

"Something like that," Davar muttered. She made a note on a sheet of paper and continued to stare at the blueprints.

Realizing the conversation had reached a dead end, Ghasem left, closing the door behind him.

When the door latched, Davar stood and took a deep breath. She went to the window and gazed out. Across the rooftops she could glimpse the mountains' snow-covered peaks and the clouds building on the windward side.

The chador was loathsome, to be sure, and the manteau only a little less so, but they weren't very high on her list of things she hated about life in Iran. Shia Islam—the way it permeated every nook and cranny of life—was perhaps first on her list. Then there was the status of women. Oh, women could and did have careers, but in Muslim society they were strictly second-class citizens.

Then there was her father, who thought Khomeini was sent by the Prophet to straighten things out here in Iran. He was arrogant and small-minded, with a nose for which way the wind was blowing. After the Islamic Revolution he landed lucrative government contracts and became even richer. Her father was precisely what was wrong with Iran, Davar thought.

If her mother had been gone when she graduated from Oxford, she would have married that American boy who followed her around like a shadow and gone with him back to Tulsa. Her mother had still been alive, though, only dying last year. So she had made her choice. She kissed the boy, told him good-bye, donned her manteau and flew home.

Remembering her mother, she rubbed her forehead.

At least there were no more tears.

Then there was her younger brother, Khurram, whom Davar loathed. A devout Muslim and member of a volunteer paramilitary branch of the Revolutionary Guard called Basij, he believed in the revolution with all his heart and soul, and tried to make the rest of the world believe as he did. He was always getting in fights with people who criticized the revolution, the government or the president. No scholar, he was lazy and self-righteous, his sole virtue his love for fighting.

Oh, how she would love to get out of this house. Out of Iran. Out, out, out.

Unfortunately, death was the only escape.

Davar glanced at the plans for the executive bunker. Those fools . . . Carmellini had photographed these blueprints, she knew, so at least the Americans knew where Ahmadinejad and the mullahs were going to hide.

She had lied to him. Told him all her information came from dead drops, when in truth there was only one drop. Much of her material came from the people she knew and talked to, the young professionals who made Ahmadinejad's nuclear program possible. If Carmellini knew their names and he was tortured, they were as good as dead.

And yet . . . the truth was, they were all doomed. Death would come soon for a great many Iranians, she thought, and she knew she was one of them.

"Okay," George Washington Hosein said and handed me a folded sheet of paper, which I pocketed. G. W. was our illegal in charge in the heart of the beast. "The names on that paper are the people we know she had been meeting. There are some others, but I don't know their names. Those four are prominent critics of the government. It's a wonder that they're still above-ground and breathing."

"She figured out she's being tailed?"

"If she knows we're following her, she doesn't seem to care. Nobody else is tailing her. She isn't taking any precautions. Takes her car and goes wher-ever."

"How about you and Ahmad and Joe's guys? You got tails?"

"Clean as new pennies. Not a soul is interested in us."

We were in the main bazaar, and Hosein was again selling fruit and veg-gies from his stand. He had to keep up appearances. I paid him for a pear and automatically rubbed it on my sleeve without thinking.

"Don't you dare eat that without washing it," he whispered fiercely. "They'll have to hammer a cork up your ass to keep you from shitting your-self to death. This is a non-toilet-paper country, Tommy. Use your goddamn head."

I felt foolish. After all, I spend half my life in the third world. I acknowl-edged the point and inspected the apples.

"So what do you think?" I asked.

G. W. glanced around to see if anyone was listening to us. "I think Davar is skating on damn thin ice," he muttered.

CHAPTER EIGHT

The ScanEagle drones arrived over the southern part of the Iranian city of Tabriz in midafternoon. There were two of them; one went into an orbit at nine thousand feet above the ground, the other ten thousand. They were very small, weighing just forty pounds each, with a wingspan of about ten feet, and if they were detected by Iranian radar, there was no Iranian response. The Iranian radars were indeed sweeping—black boxes in the drones detected every pulse—yet the skinpaint returns were very small, easy to overlook on the Iranians' air traffic control scopes, if they were displayed at all. Usually returns this small were classified as static and automatically eliminated from the presentation.

Both ScanEagles contained a variety of sensors, the size, type and sensitivity limited only by their small carrying capacity. Today one broadcast an encrypted television camera signal to a satellite in geosynchronous orbit; the other sent an infrared picture.

The area of interest was a large, low, flat-roofed building, a factory, in the southern suburbs of the city. The cameras watched as the workers left for the evening and the parking lot emptied. The watchmen on their hourly hikes around the building were picked up by the sensors, and their routes and times carefully noted and compared to past observations.

The people doing the comparing were sitting in a command and control center at Balad Air Force Base in Iraq. The data the ScanEagles were broadcasting was painstakingly compared to the database, which had been compiled in evening and nightly observations by drones every evening for the last two weeks.

Two colonels conferred, then went to the general, who was standing behind the monitors looking at the raw video.

"Everything is the same as it was," one of the colonels said. "Nothing out of the ordinary."

"Have we heard from our guy on the ground?"

"Yes, sir. He said the right code words."

"Then it's a go," the general said.

"Yes, sir."

"Launch 'em."

"Yes, sir."

The general walked over to an encrypted satellite telephone and placed a call to the duty officer in the War Room of the Pentagon.

It was nearly midnight in Tabriz when three Russian-made Mi-24 Hind helicopters swept across the rooftops of the city and landed in the parking lot of the factory. Six soldiers in Iranian uniforms, armed with AK-47s, jumped from each helo. As the members of one squad took up defensive positions around the building, an officer led the other two to the main entrance.

The guard there looked at them in bewilderment.

He was summarily disarmed, handcuffed and led away. The officer opened the door, and the troops trotted through it.

On the other side of the world it was midday Sunday. In the War Room of the Pentagon, the president's right-hand man, Sal Molina, shifted uncomfortably in a padded chair. He was surrounded by six generals, four army and two marine, and one civilian, Jake Grafton, who wore a sports coat and white shirt but not a tie.

"Who is leading this expedition?" Molina asked.

"Captain Runyon Paczkowski, U.S. Army," he was told.

Molina just shook his head. "An O-3. Really!"

"Yes. Really," said the army four-star who served as the deputy chief of staff.

Molina eyed the bemedaled general and said, "Oh."

Grafton sagged an inch or so down into his seat. He knew Molina well enough to recognize the warning. He watched the ScanEagle feeds being presented on big screens in front of the pit, behind the podium and desk where two duty officers were seated before a bank of phones and computer screens. The natural light picture was nothing but a collection of spots from lights on the ground. The infrared picture, however, was quite good.

Due to the magnification of the lens, it was as if the viewers were hanging about five hundred feet over the factory. Jake could see the bright spots of helo exhaust, the warm people moving around and the cold, black streets leading to the factory. Empty streets . . . He consciously crossed his fingers, hoping the streets stayed empty.

"I'd like to know," the army four-star said, "why we didn't just bomb this damn factory and be done with it. Why are we putting boots on the ground, risking our men?"

"We've been through all that," Molina said with finality.

The senior marine four-star weighed in. "We bought all those damn B-1s for the Air Force, two billion dollars each, and they can't even use one to bomb a factory in Iran making EDs to kill our kids?"

"This isn't Korea or Vietnam," Molina said testily. "We're trying to save GIs' lives without goading Iran into a declaration of war."

"Well, by God," the army general declared, "you'd better take a good look around, Molina. Iran is fighting a war with *us*. They know it and the troops know it. 'Death to America!' How many times does that asshole Ahmadinejad have to shout it before you start listening?"

"I didn't come over here to listen to your insubordination, General," Molina shot back. Silence greeted that sally.

Jake watched as two soldiers carried what appeared to be boxes from a helo into the factory. Those boxes, he knew, contained demolition charges to ignite the explosives in the factory. Since they lacked certain knowledge of the munitions available inside, the troops had brought their own.

Sal Molina was still stewing. Sometimes people in uniform affected him that way. "I seem to recall that just last week the army asked the administration for more tanks in the next fiscal year," Molina said. "Tanks don't kill terrorists. Neither do F-35s or F-22s or attack submarines. I know you Pentagon boys like your toys, but you keep asking for crap to fight World War II all over again. This is another *century*, gentlemen; WW II and the Trojan War are ancient history. Get over it."

"We need—"

Molina wasn't in the mood. He gestured at the screens in the front of the room. "Drones! We have to contract for drone services because the army and marines don't have the organization or supply system to operate them. The air force doesn't really want them, insists they be flown by rated pilots, not enlisted men—but there ain't no glory for drone pilots, no medals, no parades."

Sal Molina smacked his hand down on the arm of his chair. "The brass running the American armed forces had better figure out how to fight twenty-first-century wars—*the wars we have right now*—or we are going to get some new generals pretty damned quick."

He sprang from his chair and snarled at Grafton. "Call me and tell me how Captain Paczkowski's little adventure turns out." Then he stalked from the room.

Captain Runyon Paczkowski was in the middle of his adventure, and he didn't think of it as small. In fact, it was the biggest adventure of his life. He was leading a military raid into a foreign country, and his men were wearing that country's uniforms. All their lives were very much on the line; if they were caught, they would be shot as spies.

It was damned heady stuff for a twenty-eight-year-old graduate of Texas A&M, and he felt his responsibility keenly. He also felt the weight of his superiors' expectations; they believed that he could successfully blow up this Iranian bomb factory and bring his men back. They wouldn't have given him the job if they didn't think he could do it—and by God, he could!

In one ear he was listening to the tactical net, the net his noncoms were on. In the other ear he listened to the frequency that allowed the Tactical Operations Center in Balad to talk to him. The TOC, which was also monitoring the feeds from the ScanEagles overhead, would give him the first warning if real Iranian troops put in an appearance.

Inside the factory his men were busy placing demolition charges around the machinery and in the stockpiles of completed roadside bombs awaiting shipment to Iraq and Afghanistan. Paczkowski strode into the office. Two of his troopers were hurriedly packing every sheet of paper they could find into boxes. One of them already had the only computer unplugged and was wrapping it in bubble wrap, which he had brought along just in case he got this opportunity. The monitor and keyboard he left on the desk.

"Hurry up," Captain Pac muttered, but his men didn't need encouragement. They were working as quickly as possible.

"We have a visitor." He heard these words in his left ear. Sounded like the pilot of the lead helo, who was still strapped in with engines turning. "Police."

"Fry?" Paczkowski said on the tac net.

"I'm on it, Captain."

Fortunately Warrant Officer Fry, the Special Forces team's second in command, was a fluent Farsi speaker.

"Rodriquez?"

"Got him covered, boss."

Paczkowski checked his watch. The men had another two minutes before they were scheduled to leave.

The two cleaning out the office grabbed their bundles and headed for the front door of the factory. Another two sergeants came in and picked up boxes of paper. The enlisted men on the team were all sergeants and, as Paczkowski well knew, were probably capable of running this mission without him; they were that good.

One box of documents remained, so the captain called another sergeant in to get it. The captain needed both hands free to make calls on the two networks.

When his men inside had their charges placed and the fuses running, Paczkowski joined them at the door. Fry was still talking to the police.

Paczkowski now had a decision to make, one that he hadn't planned for. Should he lead his men to the helos and get aboard while Fry talked to the police, or should he give Fry a moment or two longer to get rid of them? Or should he have the cops taken down?

He knew that he had two other men watching the cops. If the policemen made the slightest move to harm Fry, or to detain him, the troopers would kill them both on the spot.

He keyed the radio to talk to the TOC. "Sixty more seconds." Then he keyed the tac net. "Sixty seconds, and if the cops are not leaving, drop them."

He got mike clicks in reply as he checked the second hand on his watch.

Captain Pac stared through the door at the two cops like a wolf watching sheep. He was perfectly willing to kill the two Iranian cops—he could clearly see that there were just two. He had seen the results of roadside bombs up close and personal, had seen men with arms and legs blown off, had seen men killed. These two weren't responsible for that carnage, but this was their country and they were in the way, so if they didn't leave they were going to have to take the fall.

Without thinking, Captain Pac pulled the .45 automatic from the holster strapped to his thigh. He kept it pointed down, at the ground. Fortunately Fry had turned so he was facing the factory, which meant he had maneuvered the cops into turning their backs on the building.

Pac glanced one last time at his watch. Ten more seconds. Fry had crossed his hands in front of his chest and shifted his weight to one foot. Very good. Fry was one cool customer.

"Five . . . four . . . three . . . two . . . one," Paczkowski muttered, then motioned to his men and walked through the door. He headed straight for Fry, who looked completely relaxed and nonchalant.

When Pac was fifteen feet from the cops, one of them saw the troops trotting toward the chopper and turned quickly to look at the factory.

Pac already had his pistol up at arm's length. He fired once, dropping that cop, then shifted and shot the other one, who was trying to turn and draw his pistol at the same time.

"Let's put them in the police car," he shouted at Fry, "then drive it over by the building."

"Looks like more police heading your way," said a voice over the radio. "Two minutes, maybe."

One of the cops was still alive. Fry shot him again; then Fry and Captain Pac loaded the Iranians into the car. Fry drove it over to the building as the rest of the team piled onto the choppers. The one in front was filled first, so it lifted into a hover amid a spray of loose gravel, turned left ninety degrees, then accelerated as it climbed. The second one, with Warrant Officer Fry aboard, went as Paczkowski ran for the last one. He was barely aboard when he felt it lift from the gravel.

As the chopper went over the street, he saw another police car coming around the corner of the factory.

Runyon Paczkowski dug into the backpack he had left aboard the chopper and pulled out a radio transmitter. He turned it on, waited for a green light, then checked the frequency.

The chopper was about a mile from the factory, flying at two hundred feet above the city, when Pac lifted the red shield that guarded the detonator button and pushed it. He glanced out of the open chopper door, looking back the way they had come. Sure enough, the factory was going up in a huge ball of fire. Lord, it looked like half of Tabriz was exploding!

Sergeant Rodriquez eased his head out, too, and pounded Paczkowski on the back.

In the War Room of the Pentagon, Jake Grafton and the generals watched the ScanEagle feed of the factory going up. Less than a minute after the detonation, the heat from the explosions wiped out the infrared picture. The light from the blast and ensuing fires showed nicely on the natural-light television video. Then something, smoke, probably, obscured the picture. The smoke was warm, so the infrared picture merely glowed.

After a minute or so the drone pilots had their birds into clear air, and the sensors refocused. The initial blast seemed to have leveled the factory, but the rubble was now afire and burning intensely.

The generals shook hands all around, then got up and left. Jake stayed in his seat and called Sal Molina on his cell. "They got it."

"Everyone okay?"

"I think so. They're on their way back to Iraq. Got some mountain passes to get through, but the weather is acceptable."

"Call me tomorrow when you get a copy of the debrief."

"Yessir."

Jake leaned back in his chair and rubbed his forehead. The three Hind helicopters had an hour to fly before they crossed the Iraq-Iran border. Once in Iraq, they would refuel on the ground.

The army had pulled out all the stops to make this commando raid happen—yet if the Iranians acted quickly, they could still catch the helicopters carrying the troops. Too bad Paczkowski had to blow the factory immediately. It would have been much better if the timers on the demolition charges had detonated the bombs an hour from now, when the choppers were safely in Iraq.

Jake Grafton well knew the burdens of command, and he appreciated the risk Paczkowski had decided to run. The mission came first, so he had detonated the charges rather than take the chance the police would find and disarm them. If the Iranians shot the choppers down, the surviving Special Forces solders and helicopter crews would just have to fight their way out of Iran or die trying. But that bomb factory would be history.

"Twenty-first century or not," Jake Grafton said aloud, although the duty officers twelve rows down couldn't hear him, "we still need good soldiers."

WHAT HAS THE GOVERNMENT DONE WITH $200 BILLION IN OIL REVENUES? the headline screamed in the Tehran newspaper. I thought that an excellent question. Iran had been living on its oil revenues, and now that the price of oil had dropped almost a hundred dollars a barrel, the flow of cash was greatly diminished. The government was hurting for the cash to fund the social programs that kept the population alive. The mullahs, of course, were paid government salaries, so they didn't share in the common man's pain.

The average Ahmad had plenty of pain. The inflation rate was 25 percent, with the price of food rising 35 percent in the previous month alone. Unemployment was rampant, and it was impossible to finance real property, machinery or inventory purchases.

The Parliament was at loggerheads with Ahmadinejad, who wanted to end state subsidies on fuel, electricity and water, and enforce the sales tax. Clearly, the natives were getting restless.

"So whaddaya think?" I asked my expert, Frank Caldwell. We were on a break from disappointing supplicants anxious to leave the Islamic Republic, sipping coffee and trading newspaper sections.

"This place reminds me of a boiler with the safety valve wired shut," Frank replied.

"It's all the fault of the Great Satan," I said and turned the page of my newspaper.

"Gotta blame somebody," Frank agreed. "Certainly this mess couldn't be the fault of God's Elect."

After work I spent the afternoon in a carpet museum broadening my mind, then walked a while, people-watching and taking in the scene. I wondered if I was going to get any cooperation from Davar Ghobadi. She certainly wasn't a loyal fan of the regime, and she also had a bunch of friends who weren't. Or was all that just an act? Musing along these lines, I coughed up the worst of the lung crud and went back to the hotel for a shower.

The hotel used magnetic cards for keys. I inserted mine, the light turned green, and in I went. As the door swung shut behind me, I stopped dead. Davar Ghobadi was sitting in the soft chair beside the bed wearing nothing but a short nightie and smoking a cigarette.

I took a quick look right and left. Nope. She was the only one.

Before she could say anything, I held my hand up to silence her. I went over behind the television, pulled the handful of wires and cables up where I could see them and found the on-off switch I had installed to silence the IRGC's bugs. I flipped it off, then tucked the wires back where they belonged.

I turned around to face her. "How'd you get in here?"

She held up a door card.

"Where'd you get it?"

"A friend of mine works here." She stretched out a leg and pointed her bare toes, then pulled it back.

"Are you aware of the fact that this hotel is under twenty-four hour surveillance by the IRGC? That every room in the hotel is bugged?"

"Didn't you just turn the bugs off?"

"Yes, but—"

"See, I have faith in you, Tommy Carmellini." She had some trouble getting her tongue around my last name, but she did it. "Besides, the IRGC toadies have been watching me come and go, here and there and everywhere, for years, and they've said nothing. They're watching you infidel suit-and-tie spies."

The drapes on the window were open, and she would be visible from a building across the street. I walked over and closed them, which made the room darker.

"What do you want?" I asked curtly as I sat down on the footstool. She was putting us both in a lot of danger, and I resented it. Putting me in danger, anyway. How much danger she was really in was something to speculate about, and I tried to do that just now as I watched her blow smoke rings like a fifteen-year old teenybopper.

"You," she said, which didn't surprise me. After all . . .

She dropped her butt in the water glass she had been using as an ashtray and came over to me. She arranged herself on my lap. Her skin was smooth and silky. I tried not to touch her, but that didn't work. I wrapped my right arm around her to keep her from falling off my legs.

"How old are you again?" I asked.

"Twenty-five," she whispered. She put her lips on mine. It was like being kissed by a butterfly.

Finally she broke contact, moved her face away an inch or so. I found myself looking deep into two big brown eyes. "Don't you like me?" she asked.

"You're a very forward young lady."

"This is the way they do it in England."

"We aren't in England."

"I bloody well wish we were."

"And I'm not your Oklahoma boyfriend." I made her stand up and pushed her toward her chair.

She didn't pout, just went, and sat facing me with her knees together and her elbows on them.

"Tell me about this dead drop you use."

"No."

"Has it occurred to you that it may well be serviced by a government security agency?"

I could see the astonishment in her face. So the answer was no, it had indeed never occurred to her.

"That you and Azari may simply be conduits to tell the story the Iranian government wants the world to hear?"

"Azari recruited me. We devised our communication system. He and I alone."

"So you send Azari pictures from time to time. The Iranian government must know he's spilling secrets all over infidel America, and you are the only art lover he knows. Or maybe he has one or two art devotees sending him e-mails. So why haven't the holy warriors questioned you?"

She arose and walked slowly around the room. In that nightie she looked pretty good, let me tell you. After a moment, she turned to face me. "You are intimating that we are being controlled by the government."

"No. I am stating it flat out. The Iranian government is probably controlling you and Azari."

She made a noise with her lips and went back to the chair.

"Tell you what. Why don't you put your clothes back on and get the hell out of here so I can take a shower and go to dinner?"

She grabbed her clothes and went to the bathroom. In less than a minute she was back. I held out a cell phone. "For you," I said.

She just looked, refusing to touch.

"This one the government doesn't know about," I explained. "You can call me on it by just pushing the 'one' button. If you change your mind and want to tell me what you know, or want to help me find out what is really going on in this country, push that button."

She pocketed the phone and stepped right up to me. The top of her head was just below my chin. "I am a woman," she said.

I wrapped her up and gave her a real kiss. She gave it right back.

"You sure are," I said when we finally broke for air.

Then I opened the door and gently nudged her through it. I closed the door behind her and put the chain on.

CHAPTER **NINE**

The destruction of the Tabriz bomb factory by American commandos was even more of a media nonevent than the destruction of the Syrian nuclear reactor the previous May. Not a single drop of ink on newsprint anywhere on the planet recorded the event, nor a single syllable on broadcast media. The fact that the factory had exploded did make the Internet, but in answer to inquiries, the government of Mahmoud Ahmadinejad said that the factory in question had been manufacturing fertilizer and had had a minor fire in the middle of the night. The American government was asked no questions, so didn't need to lie.

The irony of his position had President Ahmadinejad in high dudgeon at the cabinet meeting the morning after the raid. Since Iran had repeatedly and publicly denied manufacturing roadside bombs and supplying them to Iraqi and Afghan holy warriors to murder and maim their domestic enemies and American troops, Ahmadinejad found it impossible to complain about a commando raid, an act of war, which resulted in the destruction of an officially nonexistent factory.

He did, however, find it very satisfying to tongue-lash the minister of defense, Habib Sultani. "The glorious armed forces of the Islamic Republic have been humiliated," the president shouted, his voice filling the cabinet room. "American commandos sneaked across the border undetected and unmolested, sabotaged a vital munitions supplier, destroyed it so thoroughly that nothing was left this morning but a smoking hole, and made a clean escape. The air force radars failed to detect the helicopters on ingress or egress, no fighters scrambled, not a single shot was fired at the godless villains."

Habib Sultani almost said, "Makes you wonder whose side God is on," but he didn't. That remark would have driven Ahmadinejad right over the edge. What he did say was, "You may have my resignation, if you wish."

Ahmadinejad was tempted—Sultani could see it in his face. Yet Sultani's departure would not make the armed forces more capable or efficient, nor would it stimulate the Americans to behave themselves. As Ahmadinejad saw it, Iran had to cooperate with the holy warriors if it hoped to have any influence with them, and influence with them was more important than the good graces of the Americans and Europeans, who were, after all, on the other side of the world. "The holy warriors are right here, or just down the road," he had once remarked. The hard fact that in this small world the Americans and Europeans were also "just down the road" was something the president chose to ignore.

The mottled red in Ahmadinejad's face faded by degrees. While this transformation was occurring, not a word was spoken in the cabinet room. Most of those present looked at their hands or focused their eyes on the wall—or infinity, which was visible from here. Several shuffled through the papers they had brought with them.

When the president was again in control of himself, he went to the next item on the agenda, which was the economy. Foreign goods were scarce, and inflation was rampant. Critics said that the lack of foreign goods in the shops and stores was due in large part to the international sanctions foreign governments had placed on Iranian banks and international trade due to Ahmadinejad's nuclear ambitions, and the inflation was due to the government's easy credit policies, low interest rates and subsidized gasoline prices. The president saw it differently. Today he began outlining new government initiatives to address these problems.

When the meeting was over, Ahmadinejad signaled to Sultani to remain as the other ministers filed out. When they were alone, he asked, "Why were the Americans not detected?"

"Three helicopters—one witness said two, one said four—flew very low to and from Tabriz. They probably flew too low for the radars to detect, and it is possible they used the Americans' secret technology, this ALQ-199, to hide the machines."

"The Bushehr reactor—it is surrounded by troops," Ahmadinejad mused.

"Troops, and layers of radar defenses directing antiaircraft artillery and missiles. Still, with the ALQ-199, the Israelis penetrated a similar protective cocoon to bomb the Syrian reactor."

"We don't protect the processing facility," Ahmadinejad said. The processing facility was the place where enriched uranium was refined into weapons-grade plutonium.

Sultani cocked his head. "The decision was made several years ago to disguise that facility, to keep it hidden. If the enemy doesn't know where to find it, it will be safe."

"If they don't know."

"Yes, sir."

"What if they do know?"

"Then they could attack it with commandos or with an air raid."

Mahmoud Ahmadinejad tapped his fingernails on the table as he mulled the problem. "The Americans could bomb the reactor today with a B-1 stealth bomber, and we wouldn't see the aircraft on radar, isn't that correct?"

"It is," Sultani acknowledged.

"So the only airplanes the technology protects are conventional airplanes, such as those flown by the Israelis, who don't have stealth bombers."

Sultani nodded.

"To preserve the peace, the Americans would send the Israelis to do their dirty work." The expression on Ahmadinejad's face was not benign. "We *must* learn the Americans' secret."

Sultani nodded again. "Our best hope is the Russians. They have an extensive intelligence network in America. They will buy or steal the secrets and pass them to us."

"The Russians," Ahmadinejad said with a sneer. "They are as bad as the Americans. Infidels, criminals, assassins, cheats . . . They have wanted access to a warm ocean for four centuries and would do anything necessary to get it. They would topple this government and enslave the Iranian people if they could. Don't ever forget that."

He rapped once on the table, then continued. "We need to know how to see American and Israeli planes so that we can defend ourselves. Iran *must* protect itself from its enemies. The events last night proved that beyond any doubt."

The president of Iran took a deep breath and exhaled. "Get that technology any way you can."

They discussed other matters for a few moments. When they finished, as the president gathered up his papers, Sultani asked, "Have you ever wondered if we are on the winning side?"

"We are on God's side," Ahmadinejad declared. "The Devil has arrayed his forces against us, but the way to Paradise is always there, always open for us. All we need is the courage to fight God's battles."

As he rode back to the Defense Ministry, Habib Sultani reflected on Ahmadinejad's last comment. The president was not a man given to speaking in metaphors. The way to Paradise? What way was he referring to?

Despite the heat, Sultani felt a sudden chill.

Herman Strader stood in front of the huge covered bazaar in central Tehran and looked around without enthusiasm. Beside him his wife, Suzanne, was haggling with a bearded man with a huge nose over the purchase of a leather handbag.

Herman, a building contractor back home in Bridgeport, Connecticut, had been eyeing the buildings around town ever since he and his wife arrived with the tour group three days ago. Half the town looked as if it had been ruthlessly demolished during the last thirty years and rebuilt by graduates of the Joseph Stalin School of Architecture. Wretched blocks of apartments, hideous office buildings . . . it wasn't a pretty picture. Unfortunately, the old half of the city, still standing, wasn't much better.

Oh well, Herman reflected as he reached for a cigar, then remembered where he was, Suzanne was having fun. Of all the places on the planet they could have gone on vacation, she had opted for a church group tour of this third-world bunghole. Herman eyed the lady now. Having a wife who got religion late in life was not easy, and Herman felt a little sorry for himself. Hell, they could be vacationing on the French Riviera, or touring Greece, or eating their way down the boot of Italy, but the churchies voted for mysterious, romantic Persia.

Herman Strader sighed and pulled a map of the city from his hip pocket. He and Suzanne had slipped away from the rest of the thumpers for a few hours of walking, and now he was ready to make a beeline back to the hotel.

Suzanne was in the final stages of negotiations for that purse as Herman unfolded the map, then turned it around because he thought he had it upside down. He decided he had it right the first time. He turned it around again and began studying the squiggles and lines.

In the afternoons when he finished his work at the mapmakers, Mustafa Abtahi liked to walk the streets of Tehran. After his hours at the drawing board, he thought the geometry of the streets had a certain beauty. His employer had a map of New York City, and when he had a few minutes, he liked to study it, comparing it to the hodgepodge of streets that formed this ancient city. New York was much newer, of course—thousands of years newer. It would be so wonderful to actually see it, to walk the streets, to hear all the languages spoken around him, to see the beautiful women and tall buildings and smell the smells . . .

Dreaming these thoughts, he almost bumped into a couple standing on a street corner. As he started to apologize, he saw that they were studying a map. A map of Tehran. One of *his* maps.

Now he took them in. Western dress, a couple in their fifties, perhaps, a man with a plain, strong face and a striking woman. Not beautiful, but with a strong, clear face, a face to match the man's. They were a nice couple. Now they smiled at him and said something in a strange language.

He started to speak, tried to understand.

The realization struck him with the impact of a fist. They were speaking English! This was an opportunity to try out *his* English, which he had acquired three years ago during a monthlong visit by his brother who lived in New Jersey.

"I am Mustafa Abtahi," he said, the first two words in English.

He said it so fast his listeners looked blank. He said it again, slowly, and when he saw no comprehension moved right along. "Where you from?"

Now they understood. The light in their faces was wondrous to behold. "America," they said in unison. Then they smiled.

"I will be an American," declared Mustafa Abtahi with joy in his heart. "When my visa comes. I take the plane. Fly." Their faces looked puzzled. "Fly," Abtahi shouted and stuck his arms out and pretended to be an airplane.

Herman Strader looked at the medium-sized, swarthy, bearded man with an unruly head of black hair spouting barely recognizable English and waving his arms and wondered if this was one of those fundamentalist throat-slitters he had been warned about back in Bridgeport.

Iran, birthplace of taxi drivers! Of all the places on God's green earth—

Suzanne chattered with the man—she could actually understand his gibberish—and huddled with him over the map.

They finished with the map, and Suzanne listened intently to the maniac. "His name is Mustafa Abtahi," she reported. More gibberish. "He is awaiting his visa to America." Blah, blah, blah. "He has a brother in New Jersey. Hoboken."

She jabbered a while with Mustafa, then finally turned to her husband. "I need a pen and some paper."

"What on earth for?" Herman Strader asked his wife.

"I am getting his address. I want to send him some English-language in- structional tapes."

Herman knew better than to argue. He gave his wife one of his business cards and a pen. She started to write on one, then realized she had two. She gave one to the Iranian as her husband watched in horror.

God Almighty—they were going to have terrorist cells turning up at their door asking for donations!

Suzanne talked all the time she worked on getting the Iranian's address. She gave him a warm smile and returned Herman's pen.

After handshakes all around, Herman grabbed his wife's arm and es- caped the presence of Mustafa Abtahi.

"Are you nuts?" he demanded when they were safely away and marching along the sidewalk. "That guy might be bin Laden's brother-in-law."

"My mother's father came to America from Slovakia when he was twenty- three years old," Suzanne said, "without a dollar in his pockets, speaking not a word of English, with nothing but the clothes on his back. I don't want to hear any more bull from you."

Herman Strader pulled out his cigar, paused to light the damn thing and blow smoke around, then took his wife's arm and marched on. "Yes, dear," he said contritely.

The thing about women, he reflected, *is that sometimes they are right.*

"What do you think of this purse?" Suzanne asked. "Was ten dollars too much?"

"Look on the bottom," Herman advised. "It was probably made in China."

His aunt told Ghasem that his grandfather was in the garden. "He had a bad night," she said.

Ghasem went through the house and into the garden. Dr. Israr Murad was seated in a wooden chair, watching the birds. They had brought him out in a wheelchair, which was sitting empty a few feet away. Apparently he had asked to be moved to the wooden chair. He didn't look up at Ghasem's approach. He only looked when Ghasem squatted so that his face was on a plane with his grandfather and said, "Good morning, sir."

Now the old man saw him, and his face brightened. "Ah, Ghasem, my wise one." His voice was a whisper, barely audible. Ghasem sat on the ground. The birds fluttered around, then again went after the seeds, ignoring him.

"Your birds are very tame."

"I suppose so."

They sat silently watching the birds as the minutes passed. Ghasem had been too busy to start on the manuscript, and he didn't want to say that, although he had decided to tell the truth if the old man asked. He didn't. Ghasem wondered if he had forgotten the manuscript.

Finally Ghasem broke the silence with a question. "Is there an afterlife, a Paradise?"

Dr. Murad seemed to consider the question. He tried once to straighten up, then quit trying. Finally he said softly, "I hope so."

Ghasem couldn't resist. "I see you are avoiding the question."

This comment caused the old man to smile. "Since man realized that he was mortal, he has wished for an afterlife. Dreamed of it. Prayed for it. The prophets all promised it. If they didn't, no one listened to them and they are forgotten by history."

"And you, what do you believe?"

He took a deep breath and exhaled. "I do not know. A lifetime of study and contemplation, and I realize I know nothing. Or, at any rate, very little. I want there to be an afterlife. I want to see your grandmother again. I want to see my parents, my brother who died so long ago . . . I can see their faces sometimes, but I get them mixed up, get the wrong person with the wrong face. Sometimes I am thinking about my wife and the face is my mother's, and when I see my brother I think he is my father. My head is all mixed up." He rubbed his forehead with two fingers, closed his eyes for a moment.

When he opened them, he put his hand back in his lap and said, "Life is a miracle. That is the only true thing I know. Everything springs from that one hard fact. When you take a religion that has lasted, one that has appealed to people for many generations, and boil it down, render it to a nubbin, all you get is two things. You should love God."

Dr. Murad paused. "Love God, but how? Ahh . . ."

He rubbed his forehead again, shifted his weight in his chair.

"And the second thing?" Ghasem asked when he began to fear the old man had lost his train of thought.

"Be kind, compassionate, merciful to your fellow man. There are all manner of ways of saying it, but they all amount to the same thing. Do unto others as you would have them do unto you. Love thy neighbor as thyself. Judge not, that you be not judged. Treat everyone as if he were a true believer." He sighed and fell silent.

Finally he said, "Everything else is just details."

He dribbled out some birdseed from the small sack in his lap. After a while his eyes closed, and he slept.

Ghasem crept away.

When the U.S. national security adviser, Jurgen Schulz, arrived at the Mehrabad airport, I was there to meet him. Normally the senior person at the American Interests Section would have been there to meet him, or if he or she was in the hospital dying or recently dead, the number two would go.

Amazingly, the message that arrived yesterday instructed the senior State person, our chargé d'affaires, Eliza Marie Ortiz, to send me, the lowly Carmellini, to carry the great man's luggage.

Ortiz showed me the message. "You," she said.

Accustomed as I am to cheerfully obeying orders without question or bitching, I passed up the morning jog that day, put on clean underwear and a clean shirt and drove the State Department's heap out to the airport. I flashed my diplomatic passport at a heavy-lidded, overweight guard with big lips and a scraggly beard, parked in the diplomat section of the parking lot and wandered into the terminal as jet engines whined and roared and growled their usual insane symphony.

The plane was late. Some Iranian government types, with armed guards circling, waited near the gate. Finally the plane arrived, and people started filing off, first class first, of course. There was a little confusion when they decided some roly-poly guy was the NSA, but I recognized Schulz right off. I gave him the Hi sign, and he nodded at me. Through the interpreter, I was directed to rescue his luggage and take it through the diplomatic line at customs/immigration. With his check slips in hand, I wandered off to baggage claim while the diplomats shook hands. I kept my eye on them, and they marched out and climbed into a stretch limo. Looked like a Chrysler 300.

When I had Schulz's two bags, I put them in the car and drove off, carefully—because Iran's drivers are maniacs—and headed for the hotel.

Up in his room, with his bags on the bed, I started looking for bugs. The electronic kind. Found three. Didn't move them. I was standing at the window with my hands in my pockets when Schulz came in.

"Tommy Carmellini," I said and shook hands.

I handed him a note that told him the room was bugged. He read the note, nodded and pocketed it.

I asked him about his flight; we chatted amiably, and he said to pick him up in the morning at ten. He had an appointment with Ahmadinejad, he said, and wanted me to come along and take notes.

"Sure."

I left him there to fight jet lag all by himself.

The next morning when I knocked on his door, he was ready to go. "Where can we talk?" he asked as we walked down the hallway.

"We think the annex is safe, but there's always a chance. The best place would be a park, on the way to your appointment."

So that is what we did. I pulled over; we got out and walked away from the traffic.

"I had a little talk with your boss before I left," he said. "He wanted you to see this building, to go to the interview with Ahmadinejad."

"I figured."

"Do you need me to do anything?" he asked.

"Ignore me, let me tag along and pretend to be your aide. That'll do."

He made a face, then nodded curtly and headed back for the car with me following him. We went to the embassy annex, I parked and we headed up-stairs. I dropped him at Ortiz's office and hung around in the hallway. Sure enough, in thirty minutes Schulz came out with Ortiz.

She looked me over. I had only met her a couple of times, and of course she knew I was CIA, although that was never discussed. We were in the belly of the beast, so to speak. She was in her midforties, trim and prematurely gray. I knew she had come up through the State Department ranks and was here in Tehran because she was a hot rising star. At that moment I would have given even money that she wished she weren't.

With a sigh, she led off. We had a limo waiting, and I got to ride facing forward and listen to Ortiz tell Schulz about Ahmadinejad. She actually thought there was a serious underground opposition to the mullahs, who had picked Ahmadinejad and rigged two elections to get him in.

"But does he need the mullahs now?" Schulz asked.

"More than ever," she said. "Political opposition to the regime is crystalliz-ing. The main opponents call themselves the National Council of Resistance. They have organized open demonstrations here in the capital. A thousand women marched some months ago and were attacked by MOIS agents. Still, a thousand women, parading for equal rights, in Iran . . . And this ferment is not just in the capital—it's in the provinces, too. Perhaps more so there than here."

The ministry was a huge, colorless mausoleum obviously copied from some Moscow masterpiece. Officials met us at the front door and escorted us inside. The chargé was recognized, and the three of us were led through long hallways and rode upstairs in an elevator made in France. Uniformed armed guards, IRGC, were stationed all over, standing in front of doorways and at intersections of hallways. I didn't see any security cameras or IR sensors, no laser alarms, none of that.

There was a little crowd waiting in Ahmadinejad's office. Schulz and I were the only two clean-shaven men there. Ahmadinejad was wearing a sports coat without a tie. Iranians, I knew, didn't do ties these days. Too Western.

He was a little shorter than I thought he would be, but full of machismo and obviously the leader of the pack. Some of the mullahs had turbans wrapped around their heads, but several didn't. Universally, they ignored our chargé, since there was a man present who outranked her in the enemy government. I wondered how she got anyone in this town to pay any attention to her. To put up with this bullshit on a regular basis—well, I thought she was a tough, classy lady.

As Schulz talked, through an interpreter, I surveyed the mullahs, putting faces to names. Then I saw three guys standing in the back that I recognized from their photographs. They were certainly not mullahs. One was Brigadier General Dr. Seyyed Ali Hosseini-Tash, the head of the weapons of mass destruction program. Another was Major Larijani, chief enforcer for the Ministry of Intelligence and Security. Beside him was his boss.

In the back of the room was a woman in a chador, with a black headscarf. I glanced at her several times to make sure. Yep, it was Hazra al-Rashid, the spymaster. I had never seen her in the flesh, but I had seen a couple of poor photos. She always wore a chador. All the mullahs and generals seemed to be ignoring her. It was as if she weren't even there.

As the introductions ended, I whipped out a pad and pencil and began making notes in my bastard, law-student shorthand, notes that only I could read.

Schulz started with a little speech about the United States' concern that Iran was manufacturing nuclear warheads. He paused every few sentences for the translator to convert his English into Farsi, which allowed me to stay with him. I glanced at Ahmadinejad a time or two, just to see how he was taking all this.

His face was impassive. I couldn't read it.

Ahmadinejad didn't bother repeating his government's public assertion that they weren't making weapons, merely developing nuclear power.

When Schulz had said everything he wanted to say, he removed an envelope from a breast pocket. "The president of the United States sent me here to personally deliver this letter to you, President Ahmadinejad," he said and handed it to the man.

Ahmadinejad took the envelope and tapped it several times on one hand as he thought. "I will read it, and my government will consider the contents," he said, glancing at the mullahs and generals.

That was pretty much it. After a little milling around, we left, with Schulz following Ortiz.

As we rode away in the limo, I took a last good look at the ministry. Yep, it could be done. If necessary, I could get in there and root through the safe behind Ahmadinejad's desk—and, if I had enough time, the locked cabinets in the outer offices.

I would need a diversion to occupy the guards, who I knew would be there twenty-four hours a day. As we rode through the streets in the back of the limo and Schulz and Ortiz chattered, I began thinking about what kind of diversion was possible, and about the equipment I would need.

The next day the Iranians invited us back to the president's office. Thanks to Jake Grafton, I got to go along. I was still noodling about how to create a diversion if I needed one.

Of course I was preoccupied as Jurgen Schulz, Eliza Ortiz and I rode through the streets to the ministry. Schulz and Ortiz conferred in low tones; I paid no attention. I was looking at the streets, the power poles, the wires, a helicopter motoring across the city, thinking about how a clandestine entry could be physically accomplished, how I could stay in there for four or five hours and escape afterward with my hide intact.

The hallways were literally full of soldiers, all armed, who stood shoulder to shoulder along each side of the passageway. Each and every one of them looked us over as we went by. Most of their attention was devoted to Ms. Ortiz, who walked with her head erect and pretended not to notice them. The whole experience was something akin to visual rape.

The president's office was packed with men. The only woman was Hazra al-Rashid, a black ghost tucked into a corner. She reminded me of the Wicked Witch of the West, but as I recall, the witch was better dressed. There were a lot of beards and fashionably grizzled faces; it looked like an actors' try-out for the part of Rutherford B. Hayes in an upcoming movie. Lots of turbans, too.

Mahmoud Ahmadinejad was standing in front of his desk, and he wasn't standing still. He moved nervously from foot to foot; his face was sweaty, his movements jerky. Even his hands were in constant motion as we filed in. The guy looked like he'd had a handful of uppers for breakfast.

Ol' Mahmoud skipped the social pleasantries and got right down to it. He waved the letter and said loudly, "This is an ultimatum, a threat. If I had known that the Great Satan—the embodiment of evil and cruelty against mankind—was going to threaten me in my own office, I would have refused to see you."

The translator did this in English for us as Ahmadinejad wiped a hand across his face and shifted his weight from foot to foot.

"Our nuclear program is designed for peaceful purposes, yet the Islamic Republic of Iran is surrounded by enemies. Never in history has a nation had a more righteous reason to gird itself for an onslaught by the forces of Satan."

He was spouting Farsi, and I was getting most of this, and the translator rendered a faithful translation in English, which allowed me to get the gist in shorthand. Sometimes translators try to tone down more strident politicians. This one knew better. We were going to have to take it neat.

Ahmadinejad took off next on the Jews, on Zionism, on the malignancy of Israel and its supporters around the globe. The stuff was downright vituperative, and he ended with this: "The Zionists control the banks in Europe, the parliaments, the allocation of capital—and they control the American government, which treats us with contempt." He waved the letter at his audience and at Schulz. So far he had ignored Ortiz, but that changed almost immediately.

"Your president treats us with contempt, as if we were foolish children. We are not children. We know an insult when it is thrown in our faces. You insult us when you send a woman as your representative, a woman who refuses to wear a chador, a woman who parades in Western dress that is an insult to every Muslim."

A murmur went through his audience. I didn't bother glancing at them. I scribbled on.

"You insult us with your threats. Now I say to you, tell your president that his threats didn't work. If we are attacked by the Zionists, we will destroy them. We will bury Israel. We will defend ourselves before Allah and man against the attacks of Satan, and no power on earth can prevent it."

There was more, but I'll spare you. Still, I was a little surprised when he got to his peroration. "America is a living fossil, a godless imperialist that interferes with our commerce and prevents us from selling our goods internationally. America's day is done. Over. Finished. America will soon be groveling in the dirt and begging for mercy from the true believers, who will show no mercy."

A rumble of approval came from those behind us and to either side who were listening to this rant, and it grew in volume and intensity as he continued. "Death to the spies and provocateurs and saboteurs. Death to all those who sneak across our borders in the dark of night and murder Iranians. Death to all those who oppose the will of Allah. Death to their friends, death to all infidels. *Death to America!*"

As the audience cheered, Ahmadinejad threw the president's letter on the floor and stepped on it.

"Be gone," he said over the noise to Schulz, "and take this shameless woman with you." He made a shooing motion with his hand.

We went.

We were in the car, creeping through traffic, when Eliza Ortiz swabbed her forehead with a hankie. "When you get back to Washington," she said to Schulz, "talk to the people at State. I want another assignment, and sooner rather than later."

"I talked to them before I left," Schulz shot back. "The reason you are here is because you are the best they have."

So I wasn't the only person that heard that lie. I kept that comment to myself, though.

Schulz had more to say. "We can't let the prejudices of third-world dictators decide the careers of our diplomats. Can't and won't."

"Ahmadinejad is just . . . impossible," Ortiz said. "All of them are. They are chauvinists, xenophobes, homophobes . . . ignorant, self-righteous, ranting prigs, and . . ." She ran out of words there.

"Assholes," I put in.

Startled, Ortiz and Schulz looked at me as if I had just cut a stinky wet one. I smiled broadly.

"Yes," Ortiz said, nodding her concurrence. "That is the perfect word to describe them." She turned back to Schulz. "I have had enough. The whole crowd is going straight to hell, and, personally, I think that is precisely where they ought to be. I want another assignment."

"I'll see what I can do," Schulz assured her.

"I'd like another assignment, too," I said brightly. "Assistant visa officer at our embassy in Paris would be just perfect. I've been here for six weeks saying no, and I'm getting pretty good at it. As it happens, I know a couple of women in France, and—"

I shut up because Schulz and Ortiz were both staring at me as if I had three eyes. It's such a bother when the help don't know their place.

CHAPTER TEN

We followed Davar to a drop," G. W. Hosein told me when I stopped by his cart to buy a pear. "It was sheer dumb luck. Joe saw her reach into an upright pipe, part of an old fence. She took out a piece of trash, reached in again and got something, then stuffed the trash back in and walked on. Couldn't have taken more than ten seconds. By some miracle Joe was in the right place at the right time."

"Where is this drop?" I asked as I squeezed pears, looking for one that was ripe, but not too.

He told me the location. "It's a nice drop," G. W. admitted. "It's on the edge of a little park, really just bare dirt, and hard to observe due to the way the buildings and trees are situated around it."

"You and Joe use your people to set up around-the-clock surveillance. I want a photo of the person who services it."

Another customer came to the cart, so G. W. nodded at me and I left, without a pear. Better luck next time.

The sun had been up only an hour, yet desert heat had already begun to build. The sky was cloudless, and there was little wind, less than predicted. When one schedules an event weeks in advance, one never knows about the weather.

Perhaps Allah has taken a hand, Habib Sultani thought.

Sultani and his nephew Ghasem stood on a small rise a quarter mile away from a launcher that contained the largest missile to be fired today, a Shahab-3. The launcher had raised the missile into a vertical position. Since the sun was at their backs and reflecting off the stark, white-painted surface, it looked, Ghasem thought, somewhat like the finger of God.

Missiles were normally painted in a neutral, two-tone camouflage scheme to make them more difficult to see as they rode around on their launchers, but this one was painted white so that cameras could more easily follow its flight. Staring at the thing, Sultani thought it looked proud against the browns and yellows of the desert.

Sultani focused the large binoculars on the stand as he listened to the countdown on the radio that sat on the small table behind him. Then he turned and surveyed the crowd, noting who was there. Various technicians manned movie and television cameras to his right and left. A flock of Revolutionary Guard generals with binoculars dangling from straps around their necks stood around making small talk. The general in charge of the Ministry of Intelligence and Security stood somewhat apart, with Major Larijani, his chief enforcer, at his side. They were holding a private conversation.

Brigadier General Dr. Seyyed Ali Hosseini-Tash, in charge of the WMD program, stood, arms crossed, talking to no one.

The tension rose as the moment approached. Sultani turned back to his binoculars and looked again at the upright missile.

Ghasem seemed to sense his mood. "It will work as it should, Uncle," he said softly, so only Sultani could hear.

Ahh, faithful, loyal, brilliant Ghasem.

"The ships downrange are in position," Ghasem continued. "The ship with the bad radar has it working again. The airplanes are almost in position. The radar station on the coast is in telephone communication. All is in readiness."

"Very good. And the Americans?"

"Their carrier is a hundred miles away from the target area."

Close, but not too close, Sultani thought. *Of course, the Americans know we are going to launch these missiles and are observing. They will get an eyeful.*

"Even the sun is at the proper angle," Ghasem added.

"Thank the sun," Sultani said as the radio announcer said there was one minute to go.

Sultani heard only the whisper of the breeze in his ears as he stared at the missile.

The first glimmer of fire from the exhausts came precisely when the announcer said it would.

The fire grew rapidly to a focused flame, almost as bright as the sun. The wave of sound washed over them, a deep booming thunder, forcing Sultani to momentarily abandon the binoculars.

His eyes refocused in time to see the missile rising above the launcher, accelerating against the hazy shape of the distant mountains. Then it was above the mountains into the deep blue of the sky, the sun full upon it.

"Go," he heard Ghasem shout.

The missile accelerated as it raced into the sky. The sound was dropping in intensity, which was welcome. Then, twenty seconds after liftoff, when it was very high and its exhaust a brilliant baby sun, the missile began to tilt to the southeast.

Sultani grabbed the binoculars on his chest and raised them to his eyes. He had a moment of trouble locating the missile, then he had it. He thumbed the focus knob, bringing it into sharp relief.

He watched the missile through the binoculars until all he could see in the southeastern sky was a dot of moving light. Then, finally, even that disappeared.

The sound was still audible, though, a whisper now. Then it, too, faded.

Ghasem smiled broadly.

Dr. Hosseini-Tash approached Sultani. "Minister, we need to talk," he said.

Habib Sultani nodded, and the two men walked away from the group for a private conversation.

Ghasem was looking at the now empty launcher, watching the crew prepare it to be driven away, when he felt someone at his elbow. It was Major Larijani. He didn't bother to introduce himself but said, "I understand your grandfather has written a book."

Ghasem looked blank. Then he said, "When he was young?"

"No. He has just finished it."

Ghasem looked Larijani full in the face. "What is it about?"

"I think you know."

Ghasem focused on the man's eyes. "I know nothing about it," he said. "Perhaps you should talk to him."

"Oh, I shall. I shall."

As the CIA had predicted, the Iranians fired nine missiles that day. All were successfully launched and raced away over the horizon. The Shahab-3 flew 1,150 miles and missed its target by twenty miles. The others flew shorter distances and hit closer to their aiming points, with the closest being a short-range missile that missed by only four miles.

The Iranians kept that information to themselves. Sultani didn't mention it that evening when he had a press conference in the ministry to announce the tests, and President Ahmadinejad didn't mention it at his airport press conference in Jakarta, Indonesia, when he arrived. He did make a point of explaining to the press that the missiles that were tested did not contain warheads. The ones in Iran's military inventory, however, contained conventional explosive warheads.

After Amadinejad made his statement, a reporter asked, "Do you expect the Israelis and Americans to attack Iran?"

"Of course not," the president responded. He knew how to tell the big lie, and he wanted to reassure the Indonesians that all was well. God's soldier had it well in hand. "Any talk about such an attack is complete foolishness, a joke. Iran's nuclear program is for the peaceful production of electric power. We have explained that again and again." He couldn't resist adding, "Even the American CIA has said we do not have a nuclear weapons program."

Jurgen Schulz returned to Washington just in time to get the news. He went straight to the White House and was ushered into the Oval Office.

"Tell me about your trip," the president said.

"I gave Ahmadinejad the letter. The next morning the chargé and I went back to his office, and he denounced the letter as an ultimatum. Threw a duck-fit, ranted about Zionist imperialism and the sovereignty of the Islamic Republic, which was protected by God. He also made some interesting predictions about the future of America, which is, as you are well aware, the enemy of God."

"I see," the president muttered.

"Never had an experience like that before," Schulz admitted. "How Eliza Ortiz puts up with that crap is beyond me. By the way, she wants a transfer. The Holy Joes over there treat her badly. As for me, I couldn't wait to get the hell outta there."

"Umm," the president said.

That evening a small delegation of the senior House and Senate leaders called on the president at the White House. They had telephoned and asked for an appointment and had been given this hour.

When they arrived, they found the president and Jurgen Schulz huddled with the chairman of the Joint Chiefs, Admiral Howard Young. The three ceased their conversation when the senators and representatives were shown in.

After the social pleasantries, a White House staffer briefed the group on the events of the day. Almost everything she had to say had already been on the television networks and the Internet, and the congresspeople knew most of it. If they were learning anything new, they never let on.

"We want to know," the senator who headed the Joint Committee on Foreign Affairs said to the president, "how the administration plans to react to Iran's missile tests."

"Our policy hasn't changed," the president said. "We are carefully monitoring events in Iran."

"Oh, don't give me that. Nine missiles? An eleven-hundred-mile shot? They never did *that* before."

Congressman Luvara weighed in. "I'm very concerned that the administration is going to take steps that will escalate into a war with Iran, and even worse, send a billion Muslims all over the world rampaging on some kind of suicidal jihad."

Another congressman, who represented a district on the Upper East Side in New York City, ignored Luvara. "I'm concerned that the administration is going to dither and wring its hands while the Iranians launch a bunch of missiles with nuclear warheads at Israel."

Another senator asked, "What precisely is going on in Iran? Are they or are they not manufacturing nuclear weapons?"

Dr. Schulz tried to field that one. "The CIA—" he said and was rudely cut off by three of Congress' finest speaking at once.

"We don't want to hear about the damn CIA." "Those idiots!" "Damn keyhole peepers listening to cell phone conversations—what the hell do they know?"

"Gentlemen, gentlemen," the president said, trying to calm them down. The two ladies in the group visibly stiffened. "And ladies," he added, unapologetically. "Iran has had a missile program for years. Everyone in this room has been briefed on it on a regular basis. This nation and our allies have done everything short of a physical blockade to prevent the Iranians from enriching uranium. At first they denied they were doing it, then they lied about it, repeatedly, and finally they admitted what we knew to be the truth. They have a major enrichment program. They have publicly refused to stop doing it.

"Today the Iranians thumbed their nose at the world and shot off nine obsolete missiles. The situation has not changed since yesterday or last month. They continue to enrich uranium, they continue to tell lies, and we continue to try to find out what the heck it is they are really doing, and pull every diplomatic string we can get hold of to convince them to stop."

"Just as we did with Saddam Hussein," one of the ladies remarked.

"Before we went to war," Congressman Luvara added.

The meeting went downhill from there. Twenty minutes later, after the congressional delegation had left, the president and national security adviser resumed their conversation with Admiral Young. The president had a large world globe mounted on a stand, and the three of them consulted it as they talked. The president spun the globe idly, then stopped it to stare at the Middle East.

Jake and Callie Grafton watched the news of the missile tests in their kitchen on a small television that sat on the counter near the toaster. They saw Ahmadinejad's press conference and a conference at the Defense Ministry in Tehran. Habib Sultani didn't think the possibility of an attack by Israel or the United States was a joke. He said, "We will retaliate to any attack by launching missiles at Tel Aviv."

"That's about as plain as he could say it," Grafton murmured.

"These tests," Sultani said, "demonstrate our resolve and might against enemies who in recent weeks have threatened Iran with harsh language."

"Harsh language . . ." Callie muttered.

Jake Grafton snapped off the television.

"Are they or are they not making nuclear warheads in Iran?" Callie asked.

"Probably," Jake Grafton said. "You read Azari's book. He made a pretty stong case. He had a lot of detailed information on the Iranian reactors, the enrichment plant at Natanz with the cascade centrifuges, the laser enrichment facility near Lashkar Ab'ad, the heavy water production plant in Arak, the work on the components of the neutron initiators—he told me more about bomb production than any sane man would want to know."

"Why did they shoot nine missiles today?"

"To prove that they could," Grafton said. "The missiles were obsolete. They have better stuff. They shot these off so Ahmadinejad could strut in the Far East, get some allies for his jihad. A few years back a renegade Ukranian sold Iran and China six cruise missiles each. The Iranians have reverse-engineered theirs and now have about nine hundred of the damn things. They have a range of about eighteen hundred miles and can carry a two-hundred-kiloton warhead. They are making these things at a site tunneled into a mountain at Parchin."

He sipped beer, then continued. "They also got some help from the North Koreans with their ballistic missiles. The ones they are building are called the Ghadar-101 and 110. These things will reach out for eleven hundred to eighteen hundred miles. They build the components, including the warheads, in tunnels buried under mountains. For example, the Hormuz tunnel outside of Tehran is a small city a hundred and sixty-five feet underground."

"So a conventional attack won't touch them."

"That's right. Won't touch the nuclear program either. It's also underground."

"Jake, nuclear warheads on ballistic missiles controlled by religious fanatics—it really worries me. The mullahs in Iran are not rational men."

There it was in a nutshell, Jake thought. Deterrence rested on the assumption that both parties wouldn't risk their entire nation to destroy another—mutually assured destruction, or MAD. That theory had worked ever since Ethel and Julius Rosenberg stole nuclear secrets from the Americans and gave them to the Soviets, who promptly made their own bombs.

"I think Ahmadinejad and Osama bin Laden are a lot alike," Callie added. "They are both avowed enemies of Israel and the United States—and the secular civilization of the infidels."

"There's a huge difference," Jake replied thoughtfully. "Bin Laden is hiding somewhere in a cave or mud hut, and Ahmadinejad is running a nation with enough oil money to fund some serious weapons."

"What is he planning to do with them?" Callie mused. After a bit, she said, "You sent Tommy to Iran, didn't you?"

Grafton nodded.

"He has a lot of faith in you," she remarked.

Remembering his promise to Tommy, Jake Grafton said softly, "Yes, he does."

Over in the White House, the president of the United States was having a bad moment as he dressed for bed. He had survived twenty years in politics by making decisions on the best information available, then forgetting about them and marching on to the next one. Agonizing over past choices was not one of his vices. However, sweating future decisions was, and tonight he was doing just that.

If Iran shot nuclear-armed missiles at Israel, would he order a massive retaliation?

Could he order the nuking of Iran?

If Ahmadinejad and the mullahs jerked the nuclear genie out of the bottle, the blame would be on their heads. The president took no comfort from that fact.

Even if those madmen pulled the trigger, *should* he nuke Iran?

He turned out the light and welcomed the darkness. He sat on the edge of the bed, completely alone, thinking about life and death, nuclear weapons and the murder of millions.

The president of Iran, Mahmoud Ahmadinejad, awoke in the hour before dawn in the presidential suite on the top floor of the Hilton Hotel in Jakarta and couldn't get back to sleep. A servant made him tea. The large sitting room was furnished with stuffed chairs facing a window with a magnificent view, so he sat in one and stared out.

The servant put the tea tray beside him, poured a cup and withdrew.

Ahmadinejad took a sip, then another.

He had come to the Far East to test the waters, to determine the anti-Western fervor of the governments and the masses. The governments of Indonesia and Malaysia were courteous—after all, he was the president of an Islamic republic—and listened politely. The people, they said, first and foremost, wanted jobs that fed their families. Both these nations were firmly tied to the economies of the United States, Japan, Australia, New Zealand and China.

The masses were more emotional. The religious ties to their fellow Muslims, even if they were Shiites, had a powerful pull. When Ahmadinejad extolled the virtues of an Islamic state in private to a group of mullahs during his last visit, he got an enthusiastic response. The idea in the abstract always got an enthusiastic response, wherever in the Muslim world he trotted it out. Yet when Ahmadinejad said a few words about the glories of martyrdom to the same group, they squirmed uncomfortably. Still, the news of the successful missile tests had raised his stature with both governments and mullahs.

He had anticipated their attitudes and reactions before he came. He had come, in the fine old phrase of the British, "to show the flag."

The crunch came last night, after the news of the missile tests had charged the atmosphere, when he had a private audience with the president of Indonesia. "Are you building nuclear warheads for your missiles?" the Indonesian chief executive asked point-blank.

Ahmadinejad took his time answering, then gave a response he had thought about and prepared for weeks. "Obviously I cannot discuss military secrets. As I have said many times, our nuclear program is for peaceful power purposes. Still, if the life of the nation is threatened, we will take all necessary steps to defend ourselves against the forces of Satan. You may rely upon it."

"Do you anticipate an attack upon Iran?"

"They would be fools to attack us. I believe they are foolish, but not such big fools as that. On the other hand, in 1989 the Americans shot down an airliner on its way to Mecca, murdering the pilgrims. They are animals, capable of any atrocity."

Ahmadinejad firmly believed that USS *Vincennes* had fired its missile on the orders of the criminal American government, intending to murder the Muslims aboard for political reasons. All non-Muslims, in his view, were animals, engaged in corruption of the spirit and the flesh. The fact that the Islamic government of Iran had funded, directed and orchestrated terrorist activities throughout the world since coming to power—indeed, he himself had been a holy warrior—did not change his view. He was fighting for God, and the infidels were fighting for the Devil.

The president of Indonesia had been a diplomat for a long time and was not so easily fobbed off. "Is the life of Iran being threatened?"

"They have said some harsh things about us," Ahmadinejad said lamely. He certainly didn't want to discuss the recent commando raid on the munitions plant. "The Israelis attacked the Syrians, as you know, and they might attack us. It will be as God wills it."

"Indeed," the Indonesian said, then added a phrase rarely heard in Iran. "Most things are."

This morning, sipping tea, Ahmadinejad thought again about the USS *Vincennes'* shoot-down of a Mecca-bound airliner. Ayatollah Khomeini knew that it had been deliberate, a brutal statement that Iran would not be allowed to win its war with Iraq. Iran could not yet compete on the battlefield. Khomeini had ended the Iran-Iraq war and directed an all-out effort to manufacture nuclear weapons and missile delivery systems, an epic effort that had almost borne fruit.

Soon.

Very soon.

The problem had always been the Iranian masses, who wanted what the Indonesians wanted—material prosperity. The corruption of the decadent West had done its work in Iran as well as here.

Well, the true believers had fought their enemies in Iran and prevailed. They controlled the oil money, the media and the military.

"Augh," he muttered. *Forget the past. Concentrate on the future. The glory is within reach.*

The world is changed by great events, which sweep away the decadence and decay. Martyrs make great events. And what event could be greater than a nation joined in glorious martyrdom against the forces of Satan? The example of a nation standing together in the glory of Allah, smiting the Devil's disciples, would unite Muslims throughout the world in jihad. On that glorious day Allah would take a hand and Paradise would be won.

Mahmoud Ahmadinejad knew the final victory was close. It was his destiny.

He smiled and helped himself to more tea.

It was the middle of the night in the Sea of Japan when the task force rendezvoused with a supply ship and a tanker out of Yokosuka. The wind was blowing fairly steady at twenty knots, and the seas were running about eight feet from trough to crest. Low clouds hit the starlight, made the night black as the pit.

In this maelstrom of wind and water, the ships queued up and joined on either side of the supply ship. Red and white floodlights high on the masts and superstructures lit the decks and the sailors in life jackets manhandling lines and moving pallets of supplies with forklifts. As the ships bucked and lunged into the swells, food and machine parts, soft drinks and ice cream, toilet paper and mail were high-lined across the yawning chasms.

The nonnuclear ships joined on the tanker, two by two. Lines were shot across the gaps, and soon hoses linked the ships together. The warships began topping off their bunkers with NSFO, Navy Standard Fuel Oil. When each ship had its share of oil, the hoses went back to the tanker and the ship steamed ahead, making room for the next ship in line. Finally, the aircraft carrier came alongside to top off her jet fuel tanks.

The guided missile cruiser, USS *Hue City*, took her turn at the supply ship, but since she was nuclear powered, she skipped the tanker.

The tightly choreographed underway replenishment took almost three hours. When each ship of the task force had everything it needed, the formation turned and set a course southward that would take it through the China Sea to the Strait of Malacca, and from there to the Indian Ocean.

On the other side of the world, in Mayport, Florida, another guided missile cruiser, USS *Guilford Courthouse*, was getting under way. On that clear early summer morning, the crew had said hasty good-byes to their wives, children and lovers standing on the pier. Those people shouted at the sailors aboard ship and waved little American flags while a hastily summoned band near the head of the pier belted out Sousa marches. Three tugs eased the long gray ship away from her berth.

Two piers down, two destroyers were also getting under way.

Soon the three ships joined up outside the harbor. With the cruiser in the middle of the loose formation, they turned their bows eastward into the great Atlantic and began working up to thirty knots. Their screws churned the blue water into great white rivers of foam as the ships raced east with bones in their teeth. Little puffy clouds appeared in the sky ahead and cast shadows on the water. Soon the low, flat shore of Florida sank into the sea behind, and the three ships were alone on the restless ocean with only the clouds and eternal wind for company.

CHAPTER ELEVEN

The Russian-made T-54 tank was already in the square in front of the Hilton Hotel in Jakarta when four other tanks arrived. It was parked across the square from the hotel and sat with the turret hatch open and the engine idling. Inside, Hyman Fineberg sat at the gunner's station sipping hot coffee. Ari Zameret was in the driver's seat. Up top, in the commander's chair, sat Ivan Davidov, who was wearing the uniform of a captain in the Indonesian army. Beside him on top of the turret sat a 12.7 mm DShK machine gun on a swivel mount; a belt of ammo led from the can to the breech, and a round was chambered. Fineberg had an armor-piercing round in the chamber of the big 100 mm gun.

The other four tanks took positions on the corners of the square. As they did so, Davidov said to Fineberg, "You didn't brief us on tanks."

Fineberg grunted.

Davidoff continued, "Man, something is going down. I don't think Darma is an honest man."

Sure enough, before long an officer, a captain, came striding over to talk to Davidov.

"I was told there were to be only four tanks here this morning," the captain said, looking up at Davidov, who was trying his best to look bored and sleepy.

"We've been here since midnight on the specific orders of General Darma," Davidoff said. He wiped his face with a hand and yawned. "If you have other orders for us . . ." Davidov left it hanging there, implying he and his crew were ready to leave immediately if the other officer wanted to take the responsibility of overriding the general's orders.

The captain on the ground obviously didn't want to run afoul of the general.

Davidov decided to play another card. "We were told we would be the only tank here."

"Maybe that was the plan," the captain said, "but we got our orders two hours ago and moved out as quickly as we could."

Davidov merely nodded.

"They told us to stay off the grass," the captain said, gesturing at the huge manicured park replete with trees and flowers that formed the setting for the hotel. "We'll be on the corners," he said, meaning the corners of the parking lot, and turned and walked away.

At the gunner's station, Hyman Fineberg again put his eye to the telescopic sight. He used the knob to run it across the top floor of the Hilton. The crosshairs tracked nicely. Nope, every window had the curtains drawn. The structure that housed the presidential suite occupied half the top floor, and opened onto a patio that contained a pool. That patio formed half the roof of the main building. One could see it from three sides, but from this angle, one couldn't see much.

Ah, if only Mahmoud Ahmadinejad would step onto that patio with a cup of tea. If he did, Hyman Fineberg would be delighted to see if he could cut him in half with a 100 mm shell.

He took his eye from the sight and looked again at his watch. Three of the shooters were just off the lobby, in the room behind the front desk. The desk clerk was bound and gagged in one corner. The fourth man, named Moshe, was behind the desk, casually keeping an eye on the elevator that serviced only the penthouses on the top floor.

"Turn up the radio," Fineberg told Ari Zameret. "If this new tanker gets on the horn to headquarters, we have another problem."

Inside the Hilton, Moshe looked at his watch. Still fifty-seven minutes before Ahmadinejad's limo was due to arrive to take him to his appointment with the local Islamic clergy. He pursed his lips and whistled silently as he played with the reservation computer on the desk below the countertop. A Japanese man came out of the regular elevator and crossed toward the desk.

"May I help you, sir?"

"I wish to check out."

Moshe was all business. "Your room number, please?"

The minutes crept past, and the radio in the tank remained silent. Of course, Fineberg thought, that captain could be calling headquarters on his cell phone. He used the periscope to examine each tank in turn, ensuring he knew their precise locations. Each had shut down its engine, which he thought was a good sign. If they restarted their engines, however . . .

Automatically he checked the cannon shells on the tray. All HE. "Ari, come change out these shells. I want AP instead of HE."

"Yes, sir."

In the Hilton, Moshe was checking out an Australian couple when his telephone rang. He picked up the instrument from its cradle and tucked it between his shoulder and his ear. "Front desk," he said.

"Red, red, red. Soldiers are getting out of a bus in back and going into the basement. They are armed. I thought I saw the general."

"Roger."

Moshe hung up and said to the couple at the counter, "Please wait a moment. I'll be right back." He stepped into the room behind him and said, "Red. Soldiers are coming in the basement in back."

One of the men tossed Moshe an Uzi.

Fineberg's cell phone rang, and he answered.

"Red, red, red. Soldiers going into the back of the hotel. Looks like Darma's with them. They came in a bus."

"It's blown. Let's try to get our guys out of there."

Behind the hotel in a car parked in a service area, the man who made the call reached behind him and pulled an AT-4 light antitank weapon from under a blanket on the backseat. He stepped out of the car, pulled the telescoping tube to full extension, aimed the weapon at the bus and pulled the trigger. The 84 mm warhead shot across the hundred yards that separated the car from the bus and hit it dead center. The explosion knocked down the two soldiers standing at the front of the bus.

The man who fired the antitank rocket dropped the empty tube and

pulled an M-16 from the backseat. He opened up on the soldiers in semiauto-
matic aimed fire. He dropped them both before they could find cover. By now
a hot fire was burning in the middle of the bus, giving off a lot of smoke.

General Syafi'i Darma found Ahmadinejad in the presidential suite dressing for his daily appointments. He was admitted by one of Ahmadinejad's
security team, who carried a pistol in his hand even though Darma was in
uniform.

Darma delivered the message in a rush. "The security ministry has uncovered an assassination plot aimed at Your Excellency. The assassins are in
the lobby."

As Ahmadinejad stared, Darma turned and motioned with an arm, directing a squad of soldiers to enter the suite. All were armed with assault
rifles. They arranged themselves in front of every window and the sliding
glass door that led to the huge patio and pool. Two men went out onto the
patio and looked toward the street twenty-four floors below. Two more soldiers carried a light machine gun out onto the patio and set it up on a tripod. Men carrying ammo boxes followed them. In less than a minute, the
gun was in position to shoot down any helicopter that might approach the
building.

While all this was going on, Ahmadinejad asked, "Who are these assassins?"

"Israelis, we believe," said General Darma. He started in on a convoluted
tale of how he and his men uncovered the plot to murder the president of Iran,
but Ahmadinejad turned away, apparently uninterested.

Israelis!

"They're going in. Start engines," came the command over the tank's radio.

Hyman Fineberg swung the turret until the optical sight of the 100 mm
gun rested on the side of the tank to his right. He pulled the trigger, and as
the tank recoiled, the armor-piercing round blew up the target tank.

"Reload," he roared as he spun the turret, and Davidoff, who had anticipated him and dropped down into the turret, slammed another round home.

Fineberg settled the crosshairs on the tank to his left across the square,
which was facing him almost head on. He lowered the crosshairs to rest on the
forward right tread wheel and pulled the trigger. The tank rocked under the
impact.

Davidoff opened the breech, the spent shell was ejected and he slammed home another round.

The four Israelis in the lobby managed to get out just as soldiers came rushing in from the stairwell. One of the Israelis paused in the door and triggered a burst at the first three soldiers he saw in order to slow them. Then he let the door slam shut and followed the others along the hallway past the administrative offices toward the employees' entrance on the side of the building.

Moshe opened the door a crack and looked out. Soldiers in uniform, at least a dozen, were running to take cover behind cars.

"Grenades," he said to the men behind him. Each took a grenade from his pocket and pulled the pin.

"We are going to have to fight our way out. I'll open the door, you throw the grenades, then we go. Now!"

He banged the door open, and the grenades sailed through. Someone outside fired a short burst into the doorway, which tagged one of the men. He took two bullets in the chest and one in the neck. He fell, bleeding profusely.

Moshe and the other two charged through the door with Uzis blazing just as the grenades exploded. Moshe was shot as he ran; then the man who had blown the bus shot three of the Indonesian soldiers, turning them around to face this new threat.

Bullets spanged into cars and skipped off pavement and tore at flesh. Another Israeli went down. The survivor ran like the wind.

With the door to the patio open, the sounds of small-arms fire, grenade explosions and 100 mm tank gunnery washed into the presidential suite. Ahmadinejad strode out onto the patio and found himself looking down into the parking lot in back of the building, far below.

He was the first one to spot a tank coming at a good clip around the corner of the building, diesel smoke pouring from its exhaust.

Someone was standing in the turret, and he opened up with the swivel-mounted machine gun.

Almost at the same instant, the barrel of the tank's big gun swung toward the hotel and a belch of fire and smoke erupted. Through his feet, Ahmadinejad felt the building absorb the blow of the huge shell at point-blank range. What he couldn't see was the carnage the shell caused among the eight soldiers who were in the hallway off the lobby trying to get out of the employees' entrance. That outside door was obliterated, and bricks rained down into the yawning chasm the shell's explosion had caused.

From his perch high above, Ahmadinejad saw a man running on the asphalt jump onto the back of the tank, then clamber up onto the turret and disappear inside as the tank accelerated away from the hotel and vanished under the foliage of a stand of trees.

When the tank reappeared in a small clear area, it was going quickly. Even as Ahmadinejad watched, the turret spun, steadied up and belched forth another shell. The concussion of the report was surprisingly loud.

The Iranian looked to see what the gunner had fired at . . . and saw a tank to his left that had just cleared the edge of the building stopped and on fire, with a great greasy cloud of black smoke roiling aloft.

The fleeing tank accelerated away from the hotel across grass and flower beds, disappearing momentarily under the foliage of the lush tropical trees that dotted the grounds.

Ahmadinejad turned to find himself looking at General Darma, who was intently watching the scene below. Darma had thought Hyman Fineberg and three other men were going to be in the lobby—and had discovered that at least one tank was involved. The smoke from the burning bus wafted skyward. Two of the tanks in front of the hotel had been destroyed; the crews were presumably dead. Syafi'i Darma felt a bit overwhelmed.

He wondered about helicopters. Maybe Fineberg had a helicopter. He scanned the sky, looking . . .

The sky was empty. He looked again for the tank that had been shooting and realized that, although it was going away from the hotel at almost 25 mph, the turret was turned this way, backward, and the 100 mm gun was elevated. Pointing at him.

He screamed and pushed Ahmadinejad sideways onto the patio just as fire flashed at the muzzle of the gun.

Both men felt the supersonic wash of the huge shell passing just inches over their heads. The boom of the report came a second later.

Then the tank turned onto the main road leading into the city and was lost amid the surrounding buildings.

Both men got slowly to their feet.

"They escaped," Ahmadinejad roared and pointed in the general direction in which the tank had disappeared. "You incompetent fool—they *escaped*! They'll try again. They'll burn this hotel to the ground with us in it if you don't get them." He gave the general a push toward the door, still shouting, "Go *find* them! *Arrest* them! *Kill* them, you incompetent fool, *before they kill us!*"

Of course, Ahmadinejad was wrong. Spectacularly wrong. If Hyman Fineberg could have gotten permission from his superiors to burn the hotel down with Ahmadinejad in residence, he would have done it, but the Israeli government would never approve such a plan. They wouldn't even approve a plan that endangered any significant number of bystanders. This abortion was the best Fineberg could do in light of his instructions. As he rode the tank along the road toward the waiting escape cars, Hyman Fineberg consoled himself with the thought that the plan would have worked . . .

It would have worked, bad as it was, if General Darma hadn't betrayed them.

The Zionists almost killed me!

Yet their assassination attempt failed. Obviously Allah has other plans for me. Allah knows the depth of my commitment to jihad and wants me to have the glory of martyrdom and taste the pleasures of Paradise.

The Israelis or Americans may try again to kill me, but since I am under Allah's protection, they will not succeed.

Oh Allah, hear me. I am only one man, a mortal man, yet I wish to serve you as have the prophets and martyrs before me. I want to unite the believers in a holy war against the infidels, a final battle in which the forces of Satan shall be once and for all time destroyed, totally defeated, never to rise again. The believers shall proclaim your glory in every corner of the earth, on the land and the sea, in the great places and the small, in the plains and the mountains, in the deserts and forests. Woe to the unbelievers, who shall be utterly defeated.

I, Mahmoud Ahmadinejad, pray that you help me do this thing. Help me to serve you. Let me be the agent of your triumph.

CHAPTER **TWELVE**

Ghasem checked his cell phone when he returned home from the desert. Davar had called and left a message.

He listened to it. "Grandfather has been arrested and taken to the headquarters of the MOIS for questioning."

Ghasem's hands trembled as he called his cousin. "It's me," he said.

"They arrested Grandfather yesterday evening. They've been watching his house for days—but you knew that." Dr. Murad's house was next to the Ghobadi residence. "It's something about a book."

"What book?" Ghasem asked. After all, the MOIS might be listening to this conversation.

"Some book they think he wrote. About religion. One of them let slip that Khurram has been talking to them. Khurram thinks there is a book somewhere. After they took him away, they searched Grandfather's house."

"Did they find this book?"

"I don't know."

"Have you heard anything from him?"

"No."

"I'll go to headquarters," Ghasem said and broke the connection. It would be useless for Davar to go, or their unmarried aunt who took care of Grandfather; the secret police would ignore them. No, only a man could inquire. Sultani, Murad's son-in-law, was still down in the desert. Khurram had betrayed his grandfather. Yas Ghobadi was somewhere in a bomb factory trying to get it finished or make the systems work. Ghasem's father, Murad's son, was dead.

So Ghasem Murad went alone to the headquarters of the Ministry of Intelligence and Security, the largest, most secretive instrument of political repression remaining on the planet. Here the enemies of the regime were interrogated, imprisoned or executed. It was a fairly new building, another architectural monstrosity, with much concrete, few windows and no humanity.

His name got him past the sergeant on the desk to see someone in an office. This man had a desk and one chair, which he sat in. He was only about forty, overweight, with an unkempt short beard and protruding eyes.

"Dr. Israr Murad, the religious scholar," Ghasem said. "I understand MOIS agents arrested him yesterday and brought him here for questioning. I am his grandson. I am here to take him home."

The man picked up a telephone and called for a file. He wrote in another file while waiting. Ghasem stood impassively in front of the desk and looked over the man's head through the little, dirty window. Outside the breeze was making a tree shake. A bird sat on a limb, ignoring the wind. Ghasem tried to think of nothing but birds and trees and wind—instead of his grandfather, whose fate was in the hands of these grim, merciless men.

Eventually someone opened the door behind Ghasem and put a file on the desk of the man with protruding eyes.

"He wrote a book," the man said after a bit, glancing at Ghasem. "A book profaning the Prophet and Islam."

"Who told you this lie?" Ghassem asked, careful to keep his voice under control.

"Your cousin Khurram Ghobadi. He said he once read parts of it."

"Ah, then he knows all about it, if he is telling the truth. Why are you questioning Dr. Murad, who is an old man?"

"Dr. Murad denies the book's existence; Khurram Ghobadi swears that it exists and is blasphemy. We want this book. If indeed it does contain blasphemy, if it mocks the Prophet or Islam or the Islamic Republic, then the man who wrote it will receive the proper punishment."

Ghasem was unimpressed. "Until you find it, if it exists, it seems to me that you might as well release Dr. Murad. He is an old man in poor health and isn't going anywhere. If you do find a blasphemous book and can prove Dr. Murad wrote it, you will know precisely where to find him, eh?"

"I know where to find him now."

"Perhaps you are unaware that Dr. Murad's son-in-law, and Khurram's uncle, is General Habib Sultani. He should be back in Tehran tomorrow. No doubt he will come to see you, demanding Murad's release."

"What do you know of this book?"

"Absolutely nothing. I do not believe there is a book. I suspect Khurram is lying to you for reasons of his own. If you have met him, you are well aware that he is stupid, vindictive and venal. Since he was very small he has been a paranoid cretin who likes to invent lies and tell them on others. Allah knows that he has told his share about me."

"Wait in the hall. When I have something to tell you about Murad, I will know where to find you."

So Ghasem found a place on a bench in the hallway with nine other people who were also waiting.

His grandfather was in the bowels of this building—somewhere in here—being interrogated. Ghasem harbored no illusions. Since the dawn of the human experience, interrogation in Iran had meant physical abuse and torture. Iran had had one tyrant after another since the first farmer planted a seed; the tyrants' men pursued their enemies in the dark, foul places that never saw the light of day.

Israr Murad would not tell them about his book—of that Ghasem was certain, because Ghasem had read the book. It was Murad's life's work, a vision of man and his relationship to God that made the religious writings of the last three millennia seem small and dated. Murad's vision took Ghasem's breath away, filled him with awe. Perhaps the first people who heard Moses and Jesus and Muhammad had felt that way, overpowered by the vision and eloquence of the prophets. Murad's vision shattered myths and embraced life, all of life, from the simplest organisms to the most complex.

The religious fanatics who ran Iran, with their tiny, closed minds, would think the work blasphemous. Ghasem knew that as well as he knew his own name. Of course, so would Davar's brother, Khurram, who was a member of the Basij, the volunteer, plainclothes paramilitary task force that operated under the wing of the Revolutionary Guard. In addition to indoctrination camps touting the glories of Islam and visits to martyrs' cemeteries and religious shrines, the Basij volunteers rode buses to prodemocracy or antiregime demonstrations and attacked the demonstrators with bicycle chains, truncheons and knives. In short, they were facist thugs. Khurram fit them like a hand fits a glove.

Ghasem wondered if even now, as he sat in this corridor while the night crept on, the MOIS or Basij thugs were searching his apartment. If so, they would not find the book. It was hidden in his uncle Habib Sultani's office. He had secreted it on his last visit, just in case.

He figured that anyone rooting out blasphemy would think twice before tackling the office of the minister of defense.

Khurram—that stupid, evil man. Selling his own grandfather to the MOIS . . .

Footsteps echoed in the hallway, the naked lightbulb overhead stayed on, and the hands of his watch marched slowly and relentless on into the night.

"The Mossad's assassination attempt failed," William S. Wilkins told the president. "Our contact in Tel Aviv reports that the Indonesian general they bribed betrayed them."

The president's face was a mask. The Israelis hadn't told the Americans about the attempt until it had failed, so what was there to say?

CIA Director Wilkins, National Security Adviser Schulz, Sal Molina and Jake Grafton were sitting in the Oval Office in front of the president's desk.

"So where do we go from here?" the president said.

Wilkins spoke up. "Admiral Grafton has a plan."

Jake removed a small metal box from his briefcase and placed it on the edge of the president's desk. "This is an ALQ-198, the first generation of the new active stealth technology. To the best of our knowledge, the Iranians don't know that the planes in service now have the ALQ-199 installed, which uses completely different protocols and algorithms. I propose to give this box to the Iranians."

The president rubbed his chin as he eyed the box, then Jake Grafton. "Why?"

"If and when they get nuclear weapons, we're going to have to go after them. If they think they have an edge, and don't, we'll have an advantage. They'll rely heavily on their air defense system, and we can defeat it."

Schulz took a deep breath, let it out slowly.

"Dr. Schulz," the president prompted.

"If they think they can shoot down any American or Israeli airplanes that cross into Iran, they may be emboldened to try something they wouldn't have."

"Such as . . ."

"Shoot missiles at Israel and the U.S. task forces in the area. Maybe lob one or two at our bases in Arabia and Iraq."

The president reached for the box and examined it. Finally he set it on the desk in front of him. "Admiral?"

"The Iranians know we have stealth technology that protects conventional planes. They saw it in action when the Israelis bombed the Syrian reactor. They continue to manufacture enriched uranium and test missiles. Obviously they believe a conventional attack by us will not hinder their quest for nuclear weapons. It is in our best interests for them to believe that they have the antidote to a conventional attack by us and our allies. If they believe they have the problem solved, they will stop looking for other solutions."

"Mr. Wilkins. Your thoughts."

"I believe Jake is right," the CIA director said. "If we have to attack, we need every advantage we can get."

"Sal."

Molina looked at his hands, hunched his shoulders forward, then looked the president squarely in the eye. "Ahmadinejad told you how it is. Sooner or later, we are going to have to attack and destroy those missiles and enrichment facilities."

"I don't want to do that," the president shot back. "There is a large block in Congress, not to mention the think tanks and pundits, who are convinced we are just going to have to learn to live with a nuclear Iran." He rubbed his forehead, then muttered, "Maybe they're right."

Sal Molina didn't hesitate. "If they shoot missiles at Israel and our armed forces, what then?"

"That's a different problem," the president admitted. "I just told that son of a bitch what will happen if he does that."

"And you have his answer on your desk."

"The question in my mind," Schulz said slowly, "is this: Does giving the Iranians this box make it more likely that Ahmadinejad will pull the trigger?"

"Wrong question," Jake Grafton said in the silence that followed. "We should ask ourselves this: If Ahmadinejad pulls the trigger, will the presence of this box in Iran make it more likely that our armed forces can successfully destroy their nuclear capability? My answer to that is yes."

No one had anything else to say.

The president rose from his chair and went to the window. He stood looking out for a moment, then turned to face them. "A nuclear attack on an American ally or U.S. forces will require a military response. We will have no other political options. Literally, we will have no choice, none at all." He paused and took a deep breath, then exhaled.

"I feel like a condemned man walking a plank at the point of a pirate's sword while sharks circle in the water below. The Iranians have lied and prevaricated and stonewalled and threatened, and continued to enrich uranium to weapons grade. They have flaunted their missiles in the world's face. All of our diplomatic efforts have been futile. I think that son of a bitch Ahmadinejad has already made up his mind, and nothing we can do or say will change it. Give him the box."

"Israr Murad is dead."

The man with the protruding eyes was standing in front of Ghasem, who was still seated in a crude wooden chair in the hallway of MOIS headquarters. Only two other chairs were still occupied. Ghasem stared up at him, unwilling to believe the words.

"He's dead," the man said. "Come back in the morning and we will give you his body for burial." The man turned away and disappeared along the hallway.

Ghasem forced himself to his feet. He looked at his watch. Ten minutes after 3:00 A.M.

He walked slowly out of the building, trying to get his emotions in check.

He didn't go to his apartment but to his uncle Yas's home. He parked and used his key, went up the narrow staircase to the top, not bothering to turn on lights, then on up, all the way to the attic, where he knocked on Davar's door.

After a minute, she opened it.

"He's dead," Ghasem said and went inside. His cousin closed the door. The room was dark, with no lights. "The MOIS beat or tortured him until he died. I can pick up his body in the morning, they said."

"Why?" she asked.

"A book. He wrote a book. Khurram must have read some of it and reported him to the MOIS. Said it was blasphemous."

They sat in the darkness, silent, with their thoughts.

"Do they have the book?" she said.

"No. I have it. He would have denied writing it. If they could get their hands on it, they would destroy it. It was his life's work."

"What do you want to do?"

"It must be published in the West," he replied, his voice cracking. "He would have wanted that. Future generations will read it." Tears were leaking down his cheeks. He wiped them away angrily. "Murder. Stupidity. Religious fanaticism. What kind of people are we?"

"How will you get it out of Iran?"

"I don't know."

Davar sat silently, weighing the next step. Her cousin knew nothing of her espionage. Nor of the American agent who had photographed her father's construction plans, the plans for the hardened weapons sites and executive bunker.

"My scanner is too small," she said. "A whole book . . ."

"It is a handwritten manuscript. I will scan it at the ministry," Ghasem said. "Use the computers there to put it on a DVD."

"They will catch you," she said scornfully. "The computer will remember everything. The hard drive will retain it even if you try to erase it."

"I have the manuscript hidden in Uncle Habib's office. I cannot leave it there. If it is found there, Habib Sultani will be ruined."

"*You* will be ruined," she shot back. "They will execute you. Or beat you to death, as they did Grandfather."

He had no reply.

After a moment she asked, "Why do you help Uncle? Why do you help them make nuclear weapons to murder their enemies, as they did Grandfather?"

"I don't know," he said softly. "Uncle says the weapons will cause the world to respect us, will prevent the Americans from invading or bombing us."

"Do you believe that?"

"I don't know what to believe." Unable to sit for another second, he sprang from his chair. "Never, ever, did I think they would murder an old man, a scholar who was no threat to any living soul. Never!"

"I know a man," she said. "He is an American diplomat. He could take the book to the Swiss embassy and send it to America. Perhaps someone there will publish it."

"A diplomat?" Ghasem was flabbergasted. His cousin? "How do you know a diplomat?"

"He is a spy. He came to me. I have been sending information to Azari in America."

"Azari? The MEK Azari? What—"

"I met him at Oxford. He asked for my help when I got back to Iran, and I said yes."

"Azari? Wasn't he one of the men the MOIS released, banished into exile?"

"Yes. They tortured him. He hates them."

Ghasem wouldn't let it rest. "Or he agreed to help them if they spared his life."

"Don't be such a cynic! We must trust *someone*! Do you want the book removed from the country, or don't you?"

His *cousin*! A *spy*! Her brother had betrayed Grandfather, and he and Uncle Habib were building nuclear weapons for Ahmadinejad and the mullahs.

They were all doomed.

"I must think on it," he whispered, and left her there in the darkness of her prison.

He didn't mention that Davar was a spy when he talked to Habib Sultani later that morning in Sultani's office. The sun was up and shining in the window. The book was safely in his coat, the pages divided into packets and tucked into slits, which was the way he had brought it into the building last week.

The news of the old man's death at the hands of the MOIS shook Sultani badly. He slumped in his seat and closed his eyes. Finally he opened his eyes and focused again on Ghasem. "Why?"

"Khurram told them that Grandfather wrote a book, a blasphemous book. He told them he had read some pages of it at some time or other. They arrested Grandfather and took him to headquarters. I sat there last night waiting until one of them came to me and said he was dead."

"A book?"

"A book."

"Khurram."

"Yes."

"They didn't call me. Didn't consult me. Just dragged him away and interrogated him until he died."

"Yes."

"What do you know of this book?"

"Nothing." The lie was right there, ready for Ghasem to spit out, and he did so without hesitation. He respected his uncle, and yet . . .

Habib Sultani sat silently for a long time. Ghasem found he could sit no longer and walked slowly around the room, looking at this and that. The DEATH TO AMERICA sign on the wall captured his attention. He was still staring at it when he heard Sultani say, "Come. We will get his body and see to funeral arrangements."

Habib Sultani didn't talk to his nephew Khurram at the mosque. He tried to ignore him. What could he say? If Khurram was a spy for the MOIS, what might he be whispering about his uncle the defense minister?

The family had not discussed the reasons why the old man had died. Fortunately, Sultani reflected, there was not a mark on the body. If he had been beaten, the damage had been internal. More than likely, Murad's heart had simply given out.

His daughters knew that his health had been deteriorating, so they accepted his death as a natural occurrence. If they had any doubts, they did not voice them. He had died talking to the police. They left it there.

Yas Ghobadi seemed preoccupied with his construction projects. He had little to say, seemed to be merely going through the motions.

Being human, Sultani reviewed his official and private conduct over the last few months, trying to decide if there was anything he had done or said—or failed to do or say—that might be misinterpreted by the secret police. Or twisted to use against him.

The Supreme Leader controlled the MOIS. Obviously there were political tensions swirling through the upper echelons of the government—people are pretty much the same everywhere. Ahmadinejad was on a tightrope, steering the nation along a perilous course. Any miscalculation by the government could cause a major political backlash that might endanger the mullahs' grip on power. So they were worried, trying to discredit the political opposition, arresting domestic enemies, breaking up demonstrations, looking for any hints or signs of disloyalty. They were keeping the Basij busy.

One of the inherent problems with any secret police force, Sultani reflected, was that they had to find traitors and domestic enemies to justify their existence.

Whispers circulating in the government said that Ahmadinejad had been badly shaken by the Mossad's attempt on his life. Well, the Israelis wanted him dead, to be sure—but Ahmadinejad must be wondering about his domestic enemies, too. After the last election, his claim to popular support had evaporated. Perhaps, Sultani mused, the president was the driving force behind the investigation of Murad. If the mullahs ever doubted his zeal for defending the faith, Ahmadinejad was through. The MOIS report on the interrogation and death of Israr Murad would also be routed to Ahmadinejad. Would the president mention it to Sultani?

Davar held her emotions under tight control. She, too, avoided speaking to Khurram, who was busy pretending he knew nothing of the events that led to Murad's arrest and interrogation. She watched him when he wasn't looking at her . . . and saw nothing. Khurram was in his early twenties, a disappointment to his family. He preferred Basij activities to working, in his father's business or anywhere else, which was just as well, since he had few if any skills. He was, she thought, a classic sociopath, interested only in himself, whose antisocial urges were legitimatized by the religious Nazis.

Had he really betrayed his grandfather, though? Why had the MOIS officer given Ghasem his name? One possibility, she realized, was to protect the real informant, who could be anybody. Any student at the university who took an unauthorized peek at some manuscript pages . . . or Murad's housekeeper. *Secrets are difficult to keep from a nosy housekeeper,* Davar thought.

The more she thought about it, the more certain she became. She made inquiries. The housekeeper had stopped going to Grandfather's house immediately after his arrest. She hadn't been back.

Ghasem found that his emotions were not under his control. His grandfather had been a true holy man, willing to forgive anyone anything. That was clear from his writing. No doubt he would have forgiven Khurram—if he had been told that it was Khurram who had betrayed him. One suspected he was not given that information.

It was curious, Ghasem reflected, that the secret police had dropped that tidbit on him. Like his cousin Davar, he realized that the MOIS could have given him Khurram's name to protect the real traitor. Did the police hope he would attempt to take revenge?

He was tempted. Thought about killing Khurram, because in his heart of hearts he hated the lazy, sanctimonious, bullying bastard. Thought about how gratifying it would be to slowly strangle Khurram with his own two hands, crush his windpipe, watch his face turn blue, then purple, watch his eyes glaze over in death.

Yet when he tried to reconcile his rage with his grandfather's life and teachings, he couldn't.

Out of this swirling cauldron of emotions came one concrete thought. He decided to meet with Davar's spy, give him Grandfather's manuscript—and he was going to do it sooner rather than later.

When I got the call on my cell phone from Davar, I was amazed. She wanted to meet at a mountain pass north of Tehran, she told me in English. She gave me the time, 2:00 A.M., and left it at that. We had previously agreed that any meet would occur three nights after I received the call.

I got out a map and looked for this pass. Found it, and got really antsy. The road led up a canyon, through the pass and down the other side. If Davar was followed, our only options were to drive on over the mountain, so we would be on the side away from Tehran, or to hike along the ridge in one direction or the other.

The place had no easy exits, which was very bad. Did she just not realize how wrong the place was, or was I being set up? Did someone tell her to lure me out there?

I buttonholed Joe Mottaki, Israel's man in Tehran.

"I need a weapon," I said.

"I have a pistol. Nine millimeter. I can let you borrow it."

"A rifle, too, if you have one."

"The pistol holds thirteen cartridges. If you need more than that, you'll be in a war and had better shoot yourself."

The guy was a real ray of sunshine. "A rifle," I said.

So he came up with one. An old AK-47 with two magazines. I was less than thrilled. AKs are not known for their accuracy. The warriors in these parts like to shoot them from the hip, empty a whole magazine in the general direction of their enemy, spray and slay. Sometimes they get lucky—usually they don't.

I spent the afternoon contemplating my luck and listening to tourist visa pleas. Just before quitting time, Abdullaziz Nasr Qomi came carefully down the stairs, leaning on his crutch. He saw me and his face lit up. "It's been two weeks," he said. "Has my visa come?"

"Sit right there and let me check." He made himself comfortable in the visitor chair on the other side of the room divider. Fortunately my colleague Frank Caldwell was out for the day, so he didn't have to witness my treason.

I trotted upstairs and checked with the clerk. Nothing from the State Department today, and I hadn't seen anything this week.

I went downstairs to tell Qomi the bad news. "Not yet," I said. "Maybe you had better check back in two more weeks. I can't imagine it would take more than a month to get a yes or no."

He took a deep breath and glanced around the room. Then his eyes found me again. "Why would they say yes?" he asked.

I smiled. "Why would they say no?"

He had no answer to that so levered himself up and went up the stairs. I sat there alone contemplating my navel. I had disobeyed the rules when I marked the yes box on the visa app form, and in doing so had gotten Qomi's hopes up. If he was turned down—and I suspected that he would be—what was I going to tell him?

You didn't get approved for a tourist visa because you are an uneducated Islamic peasant from a third-world shithole, and we have found folks like you never, ever leave the U.S. of A. if they can get there.

While I was sitting there, someone came trooping down the stairs. I knew he was an American when I saw his shoes. Now the trousers, the shirt and jacket, and the clean-shaven white face. Behind him was an Iranian male.

"Hey," he said. "My name is Herman Strader." He shoved his passport through the window at me. "This guy is Mustafa Abtahi. He's been writing letters to the State Department in Washington asking for a visa and hasn't gotten any answers. The people upstairs said to talk to you."

I pretended to scrutinize Strader's passport. Meanwhile Herman and Mustafa arranged themselves in the only two chairs on their side of the divider. "What kind of visa?" I asked.

"Hell, I dunno. Guy wants to go to America. He's an engineer. Works for a mapmaker here in Iran. If you can get him to the States, I got a job for him in my construction company."

Three minutes later I had it all. Strader's wife, Suzanne, thought Mustafa Abtahi should get a chance at America. While Strader was talking, I looked Abtahi over. He seemed okay, no obvious deformities or diseases, so when Strader ran down, I asked him in Farsi who he knew in America. A brother in Hoboken, he said, and launched into a five-minute exposition of his brother's life and car repair business. He was voluble, well spoken and engaging. I liked him, too. Actually, I liked most of the Iranians I had met during my stay. Maybe I'd been here too long already.

Finally I stopped Abtahi's speech with an upraised palm and spoke to Strader in English. "Mr. Strader, we are not accepting immigration visa requests these days from Iranians. They have Khomeini and the mullahs to thank for that. Nor are we supposed to recommend anyone for a tourist visa unless we are absolutely certain that they will not overstay their visa."

Strader looked at me as if I had lost my mind. "Half the taxi drivers in New York are from Iran. Where in hell have you people been?"

"I don't run the government, sir; I merely work for it. Greater fools than I make all the big decisions. As I was saying, we are not supposed to recommend anyone for a tourist visa. However, if I do and Mr. Abtahi gets one, goes to America and overstays his visa, he will become an illegal alien. If the INS snags him, out he goes."

Strader made a noise with his lips and tongue.

"If you are employing him, you might get in trouble. It's a federal crime to knowingly employ an illegal alien or help him obtain false documents, such as a Social Security card or driver's license. In fact, it's a felony."

That shut him up.

I took a tourist visa app from my desk drawer. "You and your wife need to do some thinking. Here is a tourist visa application." I passed it through the hole.

He took it, nodded and stood. Abtahi had obviously been trying to follow the conversation and had gotten lost. His face mirrored his confusion.

After they left, I went down the hall to my soundproof phone booth and placed a call to Jake Grafton on the satellite telephone.

"Hey, Tommy," he said.

"Hey, boss. Got a favor to ask. I approved a tourist visa application for a guy named Abdullaziz Nasr Qomi and haven't heard back from the State Department. I doubt they're going to approve it. Could you check on that?"

"Tommy—" he began.

"This is a personal favor I'm asking, Admiral. This guy has only one leg, and he needs a chance. I want the app approved."

He hesitated for about three seconds, then said, "Spell the name."

After I did, he said, "Anything else?"

"Yeah. Guy named Mustafa Abtahi is maybe going to submit a tourist visa application." I spelled that name, too. "If he does, I'd like it approved as well."

Grafton chuckled, then the chuckle became a belly laugh. "Tommy," he said finally, "you are supposed to be a rough, tough spy guy."

"Yeah."

"Anyone else you want smuggled in? A widow, orphan, child prodigy or somebody with a weird disease?"

"Not right now."

"I'll see what I can do," he said.

CHAPTER THIRTEEN

Jake Grafton was in his office at Langley when his assistant, Robin, brought him a cassette tape. "They just brought this upstairs. Said you would want to listen to it as soon as possible."

"Thanks."

When the door closed behind her, he got out his old tape player and slipped the cassette in. This player had some miles on it, but it still worked pretty well. Even the earphones. He put them on and pushed the PLAY button.

"—ed to chat. I thought we might meet for drinks tomorrow evening." A man's voice, one Grafton recognized.

"Solzhenitsyn's, perhaps. On H Street. Do you know it?" Another man's voice, with a pronounced accent, yet easily understandable.

"Perfect. The usual time?"

"Right."

The connection was severed.

Grafton listened to the conversation two more times, then picked up the telephone and called a colleague in the FBI, Myron Emerick.

After the social preliminaries, Emerick asked, "So what can we do for you today, Admiral?"

"I want a restaurant bugged under that National Security John Doe warrant we got last week. Solzhenitsyn's on H Street."

"When?"

"Just as fast as you can get it done. Meet may be tomorrow night, 'at the usual time.' That could mean this evening, tomorrow, Friday, Saturday, Sunday noon, whatever."

"You don't want to wait until they close tonight?"

"No. Invent an excuse to close them when you get there. Leaking gas next door, whatever."

"What if 'the usual time' means someplace else?"

"Then they're just too clever for us old fudds."

"I'll get right on it."

"I'm a phone call away. If the bugs pick up that voice, call me immediately."

"I know the drill."

"Thanks, Myron."

After Jake hung up, he sat staring at the cassette. The conversation on this cassette had been picked up by a computer that sampled tens of thousands of telephone calls an hour, listening for particular voices. The voices were actually compared by voiceprints, no two of which were exactly alike. When the computer found a voiceprint it recognized, it began recording the conversation.

A similar, although smaller, computer would monitor the bugs the FBI agents were secreting all over the Solzhenitsyn restaurant. No conversations would be recorded, protecting the privacy of the diners, until the computer recognized *that* voice. The agent monitoring the computer would alert Grafton, who had to be nearby. He would need a hotel room in the neighborhood.

He called Robin in, and together they examined a map of downtown Washington.

The hotel nearest to the restaurant turned out to be right above it. Solzhenitsyn's was in the basement. Robin reserved three rooms, one for Jake and two for the FBI. Jake went home, packed clothes and managed to get to the hotel by four that afternoon. A light rain was falling from a low gray sky.

A gas company truck was parked in front of the restaurant, and the door sported a CLOSED sign. The hotel seemed to be doing business as usual, though. He left his car with the valet, gave his bag to the bellman and went inside.

The hotel was in a building that had been a bank. The lobby was huge, three stories high, and a round open safe door formed part of one wall. Patrons went through the safe door into a cocktail lounge. The check-in counter had obviously once been a teller window. The counters and floor were marble.

As Jake signed in, he asked, "I notice there is a gas company truck parked right outside. Is there a problem?"

"Routine maintenance, sir."

"Fine."

His room was on the fifth floor. He had a view of a side street and an apartment building across the street. After a few minutes of standing at the window watching Washington in the rain, he rigged up his computer, arranged his cell and encrypted satellite phone on either side, took off his shoes and sagged into the padded easy chair. Callie had given him a copy of the *Post* and *Wall Street Journal*, so he settled in with them. By seven, after sunset, he was disgusted with the state of the nation and the planet. He turned on the television, found a baseball game and ordered dinner from room service.

At nine his wife called. "Any fish yet?"

"No."

"Sounds exciting."

"I'm taking my pulse every quarter hour to ensure I'm still alive."

"Sooo . . . I don't have anything scheduled for tomorrow morning. Mind if I join you in your little love nest?"

"Take off your wedding ring, sneak in and don't let anyone see your face. Room five-oh-seven. Seriously, take a taxi and use the side entrance. The elevators are in a hallway off the lobby. Don't go into or through the lobby."

Callie chuckled. "See you in about an hour."

They were still awake at midnight, lying in bed watching raindrops on the window. A light shining on the side of the hotel made every drop visible on the glass. Apropos of nothing, Jake said, "I've had a good life, you know."

"It isn't over yet."

"I know. I'm just commenting."

"We are very lucky," she told him. "We've had each other all these years, Amy, good health, interesting jobs . . . This fish you are waiting for—has he anything to do with Iran?"

"Yes."

"You are going to have to go there one of these days, aren't you?"

"One of these days," he said and kissed her before she could say any more.

Israeli agent and embassy janitor Tom Mottaki stopped by the break room where Frank and I hung out when we weren't denying Paradise to the locals. Since he and I were the only people there just now, he showed me a photo. The camera had captured an image of a figure dressed in a chador, on an empty street, with the remnants of an iron pipe fence behind her.

"She serviced the drop."

"Man, I can't make out her face."

"Welcome to the club. That photo was taken with a little unmanned surveillance camera mounted in a tree. The camera actually took twelve pictures of her, and that's the best one."

"Terrific. Who the hell is it?"

"A woman, probably," Mottaki said, pulling the print out of my grasp. He studied it for a moment. "Maybe not."

"Okay. What did she put in there?"

From his pocket he pulled a sheaf of papers. I opened them. They were copies of government documents, reports of production of enriched plutonium. One of the documents was the plan for testing a neutron generator, the trigger for an atomic weapon. The last sheet in the pile was a timetable. I studied it. According to the timetable, if I was reading this correctly, the Iranians were still a year away from having an operational warhead.

When I finished perusing the papers, I asked Joe, "Do you have your own copies of these?"

"Yeah. The originals went back in the drop."

"I'll keep these, then, and send them to Washington."

"Okay." Joe got up and walked toward the door as I folded the papers and stuck them in my pocket. "Hazra al-Rashid always goes around in a chador," Joe said, tossing the words over his shoulder.

"She and a million or two other women in this town."

"Just a thought."

"Sure."

The Graftons ate breakfast in the hotel dining room on the top floor. The satellite phone was in its case at his feet, and his cell phone was in his pocket. Afterward, Callie headed off for her ten o'clock class at the university. Jake took a complimentary newspaper back to his room and settled in. Robin called him from the office on the encrypted phone, and three long conversations took up most of his morning.

The afternoon passed slowly when he wasn't on the telephone. Fortunately, telephone conversations took up about half the time. He looked at his watch at least every five minutes, so he took it off and put it in his pocket. The clock on the television control panel said it was a few minutes after six when he hung up for the last time.

He ordered dinner again from room service. He had finished eating and was watching the Discovery Channel when his cell phone rang. He grabbed it.

Myron Emerick. "Our guy is in the restaurant. He's got the table in the back left corner as you stand at the door. One man is having a drink with him."

"Okay. I'm on my way."

Jake put his shoes on, then his sports coat, turned off the television and picked up the satellite phone and his cell. He walked out the front entrance of the hotel and looked around.

A gas company van was parked across the street, which glistened in the lights. Everything was wet from the rain. Grafton walked to the van and tapped on the rear door.

Emerick opened it. He and two other men, technicians, were packed between two banks of equipment. There was almost no free space left, but Grafton squeezed himself in and pulled the door shut behind him. He got a cardboard box to sit on. Emerick handed him a set of headphones.

The admiral found himself listening to two men relaxing over drinks, one the voice Jake knew, the other one he didn't. Obviously these two knew each other well. They talked like old friends, sure of how their comments would be received, sure of the values and experiences they shared—and they talked in Farsi. As Jake listened to the raw audio in his left ear, an off-site translator was giving him the English translation in his right.

"Who is this guy?" Jake murmured.

Someone had already managed to photograph the two men with a small digital camera. That photo was on the computer monitor behind Jake's right shoulder. Emerick nodded toward it. "We're trying to find out," he said. One of the two techs in the truck was working the keyboard, accessing various databases.

Soon the two in the restaurant were discussing the Iranian political situation, inflation, unemployment, and the scandal du jour, the removal from office of one of Ahmadinejad's lieutenants by Parliament, which was getting restless. Then they moved on to the political situation in the entire Middle East.

They had finished with the main course and were noodling about dessert when the strange man said, "What have you heard about this Carmellini?"

"He wants Rostram's help."

Emerick caught Jake's eye. Jake nodded, and Emerick got out of the van.

The conversation continued, and after some thought, the stranger said, "Tell her no to both requests."

"I have already instructed her not to help him into any forbidden place. She will obey."

"What is it precisely that this Carmellini wants?"

"Proof that we are making nuclear weapons, and our plan for using them when they are operational."

The man snorted, then said, "There is no plan. He is looking for something that doesn't exist."

Jake took off the headset and handed it to the technician who was recording all this. The man running the other computer handed him a written note. On it was an Iranian name, and the notation *trade secretary at the UN mission*. This was the identity of the stranger.

Jake was sitting in an office in the Washington FBI complex when two agents brought in a man in handcuffs. He looked tired, depressed—and scared. His belt, tie and jacket had been taken from him, and the pockets of his trousers were pulled inside out.

"Well, well, well, Professor Azari," Grafton said acidly. "We meet again. A little espionage over dinner, eh?"

"I want a lawyer."

"So they told me. Be seated." When Azari sat, Jake nodded at the two agents, who departed.

"You think maybe you can beat this charge? Is that it?"

Avari said nothing.

"You think, *These infidel fools, they were too stupid to make a recording of our conversation.*"

Azari bit his lip.

"Once you go into the holding cells and we call a lawyer, you will be flat out of options. We will charge you with espionage and try you and probably get a conviction. You'll live out the rest of your life in a cell in a federal prison and, considering your age, probably die there. Is that what you want?"

Silence.

"Answer me," Grafton roared. He had a good roar, and it stunned Azari. "No."

"The alternative to that is that we wait on calling the lawyer and you tell me everything. Everything! If I think you have been truthful and cooperative, and you continue to cooperate, you won't need that lawyer. Life will flow on for you just as it has been. You will go home to your wife, continue to teach mathematics, be a respected member of the academic community and live a long and happy life. But you will be working for me, and only me. Do you understand?"

Azari was perspiring freely. He tried to wipe his forehead with a shirt sleeve and succeeded only in soaking the fabric.

"Am I being clear enough?" Grafton asked.

"You want me to betray them," Azari said bitterly.

"You have been pretending to betray the Islamic Republic for years, professor. Think of the lies you told, thousands of lies, millions, tons of them, and the articles, the book. When I read your scribblings, I wondered why you were still alive. A man like you who frequents public places—you would be easy to kill, and yet they let you live. I asked myself, Why is that?"

Azari simply stared at Grafton, who got out of his chair and seated himself on the edge of the desk. Azari had to look up to see his face, so he didn't. He looked at the wall.

"So easy to kill," Jake mused. "If someone shot you dead at the university one of these days, everyone would be sure the IRGC had ordered the hit, wouldn't they? Ahmadinejad or Khamenei gave the order in Iran, and you died here." He snapped his fingers, and Azari looked at him. Those gray eyes were as cold as ice in winter.

"You could try to rabbit back to Iran, of course," Grafton continued, "but your IRGC superiors would be less than pleased. Your mission here would have failed. Then they would know that *we* know. Because we would tell the newspapers that you talked. That you told us everything, even if you didn't. Would they reward you handsomely for your failure, Azari? Tell me that. Would they?"

Azari couldn't help himself. "No," he whispered.

"So you see, you really have only two options. You can go to the cells, get the best lawyer money can buy to hold your hand and go to prison for the rest of your life. Or you can cooperate with me, do as I say, and life will continue as it is. There is no third option."

He reached back, picked up the phone and pushed a button. After a few seconds he said, "You got it ready? Bring it in."

Fifteen seconds later an agent brought in a laptop. He set it on the desk. Then he pushed a key.

A voice could be heard speaking in Farsi, and the translation overlay. "What is it precisely that this Carmellini wants?"

Then Azari's answer. "Proof that we are making nuclear weapons, and our plan for using them when they become operational."

The agent stopped the replay. "You could have only gotten that information from Rostram, your agent in Iran," Grafton said softly. "I never said those words to you." Grafton leaned toward the Iranian. "Remember that prison in Tehran? The rats? The screams at night . . ."

The afternoon before I was to meet Davar, Herman and Suzanne Strader and Mustafa Abtahi came down the stairs to my monk's cell. Mr. Strader shoved Abtahi's tourist visa app through the hole. He introduced me to his wife, said, "We're leaving for home this afternoon," then got down to it.

"We came to ask you to process this application for Mr. Abtahi as a personal favor to two American taxpayers," Herman said.

"I'll send it along," I said, glancing at Mrs. Strader, who started to speak.

I held up my hand, stopping her. "Don't tell me anything you don't want repeated to my superiors or any other federal agency."

Mrs. Strader was in her fifties, I would say, but she could easily pass for ten years younger. She eyed me carefully, then said, "Thank you, young man, for that warning, but I have something to say to the United States government, and you might as well be the one to hear it."

She struck me as a woman with a mind of her own. Herman certainly didn't tell her what to think. I wondered what she thought of fundamental Islam and the subordination of women. I thought she might tell me, but she didn't.

"My grandfather went to America as a young man with only the clothes on his back. People like him, poor people, people with nothing to leave behind and everything to earn in the future, have been immigrating to America since Columbus discovered it. Say what you will about the Columbian exchange, the fact is that hundreds of millions of people live better, more productive lives today because their forefathers came to a land that valued individual freedom. Individual freedom, Mr. Carmellini, is our gift to the world. Mr. Abtahi deserves a chance to earn a place in America for himself and his children yet to come. With a little luck, he will make life better for himself, for them and for all Americans."

She eyed me, checking to see if I wished to disagree. I didn't.

She stood. "Thank you." She turned and headed back up the stairs. Herman grabbed my hand for a quick shake, then went with her.

Abtahi dropped into the chair, radiating hope. I decided to check the app to make sure everything was correct. "Passport, please."

He passed it across and sat there watching me check the numbers against the app form as if I held the threads of his life.

That evening I drove around Tehran for an hour to ensure that I wasn't being followed before I took the road I wanted, which led north toward the mountains. The houses and estates became more opulent the higher in the foothills I went. Obviously some people in Iran were doing quite well, thank you.

Finally the estates petered out, the entire megalopolis was below me, and I was climbing a rough dirt road up a wooded canyon. The road literally clung to the cliff in places. I checked my watch, saw that I had plenty of time, so I pulled over at a wide place where I could see the road behind me. It was an hour past midnight, and the road was empty.

I got out my binoculars and scanned down the canyon, making sure there were no vehicles coming. Looked up the mountainside and also saw no headlights. It looked dark as the pit up there. Then I got out a radio receiver, a bug finder, and checked the car for beacons. Nothing. The needle refused to move.

Satisfied, I drove on up to the pass. No cars there. I pulled down the other side and found a place I could run the car off the road into the brush. I parked it there and walked back to the pass.

A chilly wind was blowing at least twenty knots through that notch in the mountain, which the map had said was over ten thousand feet above sea level. East and west along the ridge I could see the muted whiteness of snow on the higher elevations, snow that had yet to melt. No snow right here, but by God, it was nearly cold enough to do it. At least the road was relatively dry.

I scrambled fifty yards or so up a steep bank, which was nearly a cliff, stepped into the trees where I would be out of the wind and sat down with the AK across my lap. The pistol was in my coat pocket. I put my backpack on the ground beside me. I had an hour to wait and fret.

I sat there listening and heard only the wind in the trees. With nothing better to do, I got out my night vision goggles and put them on. I could see jagged peaks across to the east, across the cut, jutting up several more thousand feet. It looked like the snow was lying in the crevices above the treeline and in gulleys hidden by the sun. I wasn't at the treeline at my elevation, but almost. The trees around me were low and hunkered down.

Two trucks ground up the grade from the north and disappeared down the road toward Tehran. One car came up from the city and crossed headed north.

No people, no huts, no sign of fires . . .

I wondered why we were meeting here. She was bringing someone, I hoped, who could help me gain entrance to a bomb factory. Or maybe Ahmadinejad's clerk, the guy who typed the tippy-top secrets of the Iranian regime. Or perhaps a guy who had filched Ahmadinejad's missile targeting plan.

God, I hoped it was someone important, someone worth getting this scared and cold for. I pulled my legs up to my chest to keep warm and sat there in the darkness, in that cold wind, thinking miserable thoughts.

When Azari started talking, the dam broke. He had been arrested by the IRGC, interrogated and tortured. Ahmadinejad himself had supervised the interrogation, sat in on the questioning. Of course, he was frightened and realized they could inflict more pain than he could stand, so he betrayed his friends in the MEK, told his interrogators everything.

They tortured him anyway. Beat him; threw him into a cell with no food, only water in a pan, made him lap it like a dog; tied his hands behind him so that he dirtied his trousers. Twice they used electric shocks. He had screamed.

He was sweating profusely when he told this—the words just came pouring out.

Finally, after a week, with only enough food to keep him conscious, they put a proposition to him. He could serve the Islamic Republic and live . . . or be executed.

As one might suspect, he readily agreed to do what they asked. With the proviso that if he ever betrayed them, he would die.

"So you became their slave," Grafton said.

"You sit here in America and say that so easily," Azari shot back. "What other choice did I have?"

"When you got to England, you could have called New Scotland Yard. You spent years there and never called. When you got to America, you could have looked up the FBI's telephone number in any telephone book. You didn't bother. No, Professor, you may have been pushed into this, but you sorta like it. Screwing the infidels is fun, isn't it?"

Azari remained silent, so Grafton roared, "Answer me!"

"Yes," he admitted.

"So which of your options do you like? Prison or cooperation?"

"I'll cooperate."

They talked for several hours. Azari got a restroom break midway through, and they talked on. When they finished, Grafton said, "You are going to be watched day and night. Everywhere you go, someone will be watching. Your telephones are tapped. We listen to your cell calls. We will see who you talk to and hear what you say."

Grafton came around the desk and pulled up a chair. He leaned forward so that his face was inches from Azari's. "Iran may be building nuclear weapons. If they use them on anyone, we will nuke Iran. We will turn your country into a radioactive wasteland. You are a very small chip in a very big, very dangerous game. A lot of lives are at risk, so what happens to you won't even be a footnote."

Azari was perspiring again. "I don't want to go to prison," he said.

"If you warn your case officer, by word or deed, the tiniest hint, the FBI will arrest you for espionage. I want you to believe that."

Azari's eyes widened, and he stared.

"This I promise," Jake said. "If you betray us, you'll spend the rest of your life in a cell."

After Azari was gone, Grafton and Myron Emerick listened to some of the recording of the interview. It was well after two in the morning when they shut it off.

"I hope he believed you," Emerick said.

"I hope he got the message." Jake clucked his tongue. "How many men do you have to put on him?"

"Six. And if this goes on more than a couple of weeks, it will be maybe four. You know how thin we're spread."

"Umm," Jake Grafton said. "I want you to talk to them. Someone may well ice Professor Azari."

"You think?"

"That's one of the moves on the board. If the Iranians murder him, it would appear that the stories he has been telling are true."

"Okay," Emerick said slowly.

"Remind your agents that they are not bodyguards; they are observers."

"What they are is law enforcement officers," Emerick said curtly. "If a crime happens in front of them, they will try to apprehend the perps—and prevent anyone else from being hurt."

"Fine. Just tell them not to stop a bullet to save Azari's worthless hide."

Myron Emerick stared at the admiral, then said, "Okay." Changing the subject, he asked, "How will you know if Azari squeals to his case officer?"

"The Iranians will put Davar Ghobadi against a wall and shoot her," Jake said. "They won't need her anymore."

I saw the helicopter long before I heard it. It was running without lights, but I picked it up right away with the night vision goggles while it was still ten miles or so away, several thousand feet below where I sat.

He was making big, slow oblongs. As I watched I realized he was working closer. Coming this way.

The realization that he was probably keeping a car under surveillance crystallized in my nervous mind.

Finally I saw the car, still three miles or so away, crawling up that dirt road toward the pass.

The chopper was higher now, almost at my elevation. I wondered if he could hover at this altitude.

Even if he couldn't, if he thought Davar was meeting someone up here, he could call for help, blockade the road. The road leading off the mountain to the north, too. We would be trapped up here, sure as shootin'.

Once I realized what he was up to, I got behind a tree and braced the AK against it. Selected automatic fire.

I didn't have long to wait. Within a minute, while the car was still a couple of miles down the grade, he came scooting for the pass, no doubt looking it over.

I watched him come, found that aiming the damned rifle with goggles on was difficult, to say the least. Now I could hear his engine and the rotor whop, faintly at first, but getting steadily louder as he approached. I jerked the goggles off and dropped them.

Now I saw him, a darker shape in the dark night.

He was only fifty or so yards away, right over the road, and I could see the glow of his cockpit lights when I squeezed the trigger. Holding the rifle on the cockpit as best I could and tracking the chopper as it flew from my right to left, I gave him a long burst, sprayed him good.

When I released the trigger, the machine was in a gentle descent on the north side of the ridge and the sounds of my shots were echoing around me. The helicopter kept going down, the sound fading. I was having trouble following it with my eyes—it seemed to be veering right . . . straight into a steep slope, where it crashed. I saw a flash and heard the crunch, and the engine fell silent. Flame flickered, then became brighter. I thought the chopper might explode, but several moments passed and it didn't. Just burned steadily.

I put on the night vision goggles and took a squint. The crash was at least a mile away, and the flame made it impossible to see anything near it.

I checked in the other direction. The car grinding up the hill was still a good distance away.

I gathered my stuff and began working down the steep slope to the road. I was walking south toward the edge of the cut when the car came up the hill and stopped beside me. Davar was in the passenger seat, wearing her boy's outfit.

After I took off the goggles, I opened the rear passenger door and climbed in.

"Did you people see the helicopter that was keeping an eye on you?"

"What helicopter?" Davar said, obviously shocked.

"I shot it down. It's over there on that slope, about a mile away. Someone will miss it soon, so we better do our talking and get the hell off this mountain. Why in the name of God did you pick this damn place for a meet?"

She ignored the question. The driver was looking me over, checking the AK. He was about thirty—it was hard to tell with just the panel lights illuminating them. A head of unruly hair, a nice shirt and a short beard, which was more of a fashion statement than a religious one.

"My cousin Ghasem."

"Hey," I said, reluctant to take my hand off the pistol grip of the rifle.

"He wants you to send a manuscript to America."

"You're kidding, right?"

"A manuscript," she repeated. She held up the package for my inspection.

I was underwhelmed. I had just shot down a helicopter and killed a planeload of men for a fucking *manuscript*?

"I can do that," I agreed, trying to keep the anger out of my voice. "Then what?"

They obviously hadn't thought that far ahead. Confusion reigned for ten or fifteen seconds. "Pass it to Azari," Davar said.

"That jerk may be a shill for the mullahs," I said roughly. "Someone is feeding him information he isn't getting from you. Whatever this manuscript is, you want it to see the light of day, better come up with another plan."

They started to discuss it, but I cut them off. "I'll send it to my boss—he'll figure it out. Ghasem, pull down the road a hundred meters or so and turn around. My car is there. Anything else?"

Ghasem got the car in motion.

"You wanted to see a bomb factory," Davar said. "If you deliver the manuscript to safety, Ghasem will take you there."

Oooh. Things were looking up, which always made me suspicious. I am getting so damned cynical. A friggin' manuscript, and now an offer of help! Who is running the universe this week, anyway?

Ghasem found the spot where I'd stashed my ride and began turning. Far below, coming up the grade from the north, I saw a set of headlights.

It took him three back-and-forths to get the car turned. I was sure he was going to get it stuck, but he didn't. When he had the car pointed back toward Tehran, I opened the door and got out. Held the door open and asked, "Where and when?"

He named a restaurant. Three days from now.

Davar passed me the manuscript, which was wrapped in paper and held with a string.

"See you then," I said and slammed the door.

The car drove off.

I didn't waste a minute. Got in my car and backed out. Left the headlights off and began following them down the grade. After a few hundred yards, I put the night vision goggles back on.

If they got stopped on the way down or on the road into town, I intended to bail out and abandon the car.

With each turn of the road the tension increased, if that was possible. I was sweating, my hands were so wet they were slippery, and I had on too many clothes. I didn't stop to take anything off, but I rolled down the window several inches, and the fresh air helped.

There is nothing worse than waiting for the ax to fall . . . and it doesn't. Not in this minute, or the next. Or the next. Had I been a praying man, I would have wrestled with the Lord that night.

Finally we got low enough to pass shacks and huts beside the road. Some old trucks sat in the yards. Now there were occasional vehicles on the road, more as we entered the suburbs.

With one corner of my mind I wondered about the manuscript: What could it be? Plans for a weapon, an account of Ahmadinejad's perverted love life, or perhaps the dirt on secret negotiations with the Russians?

Two hours after we left the pass, I was in the embassy looking at the manuscript. It was handwritten in Farsi by a person with tiny, crabbed handwriting, and I couldn't read a word of it.

Ten minutes later I was on the encrypted satellite phone talking to Jake Grafton.

CHAPTER FOURTEEN

Brigadier General Dr. Seyyed Hosseini-Tash was a nervous man, Ghasem thought. Today, at the long-awaited test of the neutron generator, he exuded everything but confidence. His uniform was rumpled, and, despite the pleasant temperature inside the tunnel in which they stood, the brigadier was visibly perspiring. Although he was a major general, Ghasem's uncle Habib Sultani never wore a uniform, preferring civilian clothes instead. In contrast to Hosseini-Tash, who was in charge of the weapons of mass destruction program, which of course included the manufacturing of neutron generators, Sultani appeared collected and in control.

In addition to the brass, there were two men from the president's office standing here in the tunnel, along with the MOIS enforcer, Major Larijani.

This was the official party, which stood off to one side, out of the way, while a dozen technicians in white coats, wearing radiation detectors on strings around their necks, worried and fretted over various instruments. The instruments were arranged on tables in the center of the tunnel, which ran forward about two hundred feet and ended in a rock wall. Actually the tunnel turned ninety degrees, but that opening was hidden from where the official party stood. Wires from the instruments ran along the ground to the rock face and around the corner.

Down the hidden gallery about three hundred feet was a wall. It had been hastily constructed of material that absorbed radiation. On the other side of the wall, on the tunnel floor, lay the neutron generator, surrounded by a layer of high-quality chemical explosives. The explosives were decorated with six detonators. This whole device weighed but ten pounds.

The instruments the technicians were fretting over were radiation detectors. Finally, after several hours of nail-biting tension while the technicians checked wires and voltages, the senior technician approached a still-perspiring Dr. Hosseini-Tash and told him all was ready.

"Very well," the brigadier said, glancing at Sultani and the men from the president's office. "Proceed with your test."

So this was *it*, Ghasem knew. The neutron generator would either produce enough radiation to trigger a nuclear explosion, or it wouldn't. The thing was made of beryllium and polonium-210. Refining the beryllium had required a huge industrial effort; yet even more money, billions, actually, had been spent enriching uranium sufficiently to get usable quantities of polonium and plutonium.

Ghasem took a deep breath and waited until his uncle glanced at him. His uncle raised one eyebrow, then looked away. So he was feeling the tension, too.

The whole thing was anticlimactic. One of the technicians flipped a switch, needles jumped on the dials in front of them, and other needles squiggled black ink lines on a continuous roll of paper. After a few minutes huddled with the technicians studying the lines on the paper, Hosseini-Tash turned to Sultani with a smile of relief on his face.

Ghasem thought he would hear a small pop when the conventional explosive went off, but he didn't—the thing was too well isolated under and behind millions of tons of rock.

Watching the uniformed brigadier and his uncle, who also looked relieved and proud, confer in low tones, Ghasem was well aware that this test had taken Iran one step closer to the bomb, a weapon the mullahs apparently wanted but, as Ghasem was well aware, the average poor Iranian thought was a grotesque waste of money.

Regardless of the wishes of the man in the street, the bomb was coming: The mullahs were going to get precisely what they wanted. Ghasem thought about that. Well, at least Ahmadinejad was getting what *he* wanted.

"I got your message," Sal Molina said to Jake Grafton, who was standing in the doorway to Molina's cubbyhole White House office. "Come in and sit."

Molina gestured to a chair, then realized both of his chairs were stacked with files. He grabbed a handful. Lacking anywhere else to place them, he stacked them in one corner of the room. Jake put the rest of them on top of the heap and sat.

"You're leaving for the Middle East in a few hours, aren't you?" Molina asked.

"Yes," the admiral said. "Before I left, I wanted to bring you up to date. Apparently the Iranians tested their first neutron generator ten hours ago. It'll be in tomorrow's intel summary."

"So they have enriched uranium, workable detonators and missiles to deliver warheads," Molina summarized.

Grafton nodded. "The only thing remaining is to assemble weapons, test them and mount them on missiles."

"How long?"

Grafton shrugged.

"How did you learn of this test?"

"Rostram's cousin called our man on Rostram's cell phone."

"How did he learn about it?"

"He was there, he said."

"Is Rostram going to send this news to Azari?"

"Probably."

"So how do you and Azari stand?"

"He is working for me now, and he knew he was feeding us information supplied by the Ahmadinejad administration. Rostram and the code and all of that are there as window dressing for the NSA."

"He confessed?"

Jake Grafton simply nodded.

"Is he going to write any more op-ed pieces for the newspapers?"

"I haven't decided."

Sal started to say something, then changed his mind. He leaned back in his chair and laced his fingers behind his head. "There will be no preemptive military strike on Iran."

Jake Grafton smiled as if he were amused. "Did you give a copy of that memo to the Israelis?"

"They're with us on this," Molina said. "The latest adventures with Hamas in Gaza have convinced them that they will lose the war in the court of public opinion if they strike first at Iran. Israel cannot afford to be seen as the aggressor."

Jake Grafton blinked. "Not even to save the lives of every man, woman and child in the country?" he asked.

"No preemptive strike," Molina said. He unlaced his fingers and sat up in his chair.

"Was this our idea or Israel's?"

"I don't think a postmortem on how we got here will be productive."

Grafton didn't say anything.

"After the Iranians fire their missiles, however, we will need to take out their missile manufacturing and warhead production facilities, the reactors and all the rest of it. Today the Joint Chiefs will be tasked for coming up with a plan. They're going to need all the information you can give them."

"Sal, I can't believe this. The president is actually going to let Iran fire missiles armed with nuclear warheads at Israel, or wherever in hell Ahmadinejad aims them, and only then are we going to kick Iran's butt?"

"That's about the size of it. Politically, that's the only option, and the Israelis understand that. If we attack Iran first, we will have World War III on our hands. It will be the Western world versus the Muslim world in the kind of dogfight that breeds hatred and violence that may last for centuries. We simply must let Iran fire the first shot."

"I think it was Khamenei who noted that only one missile has to get through," Jake said, "to wipe Israel and the Zionist problem off the face of the earth."

"The president promised Israel that none would get through."

"Or what? He'll publicly apologize?"

Sal Molina set his jaw.

Jake Grafton stood and nodded his head as he processed it. "You'd better tell the military to make it snappy," he muttered. "I have this feeling that the curtain is going to rise sooner rather than later."

Although he had felt calm and in complete control at the test of the neutron generator, Habib Sultani certainly didn't feel that way as he prepared himself for his first appointment with the president after he returned from his Southeast Asian diplomatic mission. Sultani felt like the world was spinning faster and faster. The successful test of the neutron generator was only a small part. The arrest and subsequent death of his father-in-law meant that someone somewhere in power had serious doubts about the Sultani family religious orthodoxy, which went hand in hand with political orthodoxy. Political and religious correctness was the only way to survive in Islamic Iran, and Sultani well knew it.

Then there was the assassination attempt on the president's life in Indonesia. According to the whispers, it had been a close call for Ahmadinejad. Assassins were waiting in the hotel lobby to murder him. A 100mm tank cannon shell had missed him by inches. The Mossad, of course—and no one on the planet thought that the Israelis wouldn't try again.

Sultani tried to push all that out of his mind. He saw himself as a servant of the nation, and he truly believed that a nuclear-armed Iran would be safe from its many enemies, including Israel, America, Russia and Iraq—and Iran was almost there.

He tried to calm himself. Made sure his clothes were presentable and went off to see the president.

Troops surrounded the palace, and four tanks. Sultani had to show his credentials four times to get into the president's wing of the palace, where he was carefully searched for weapons. After that, he was escorted along a hallway to the foyer of the president's office. Six armed mullahs were there, and they didn't take their eyes off him. After an interminable wait, he was admitted to the president's office. When the door closed behind him, they were alone in the room.

Mahmoud Ahmadinejad looked stressed and tired.

"When?" Ahmadinejad demanded, skipping the social preliminaries.

Sultani knew precisely what the president was asking. "We will have a dozen missiles with nuclear warheads two weeks after you order them into production," the defense minister said. "We have built one warhead. We can test it underground, then go into production, or we can go straight to production today."

"How long will it take to test a warhead?"

"About three or four weeks. We must transport it to the desert test site, properly instrument it, then detonate it and check all the data."

"And if it works as we believe it will, then it would take another two weeks to manufacture identical warheads and install them in the missiles?"

"Yes, sir."

Ahmadinejad rubbed his hand through his hair, then used both hands to massage his face. He took a deep breath and looked at Sultani. "You know about the Israelis' attempt to murder me in Jakarta?"

Sultani nodded.

"We are approaching a critical moment in the life of our nation. Our enemies do not want us to have these weapons to defend ourselves. The closer we come to that capability, the more dangerous the situation."

"I understand," Sultani muttered, because he thought he had to say something.

"If we test a warhead, underground or aboveground," Ahmadinejad said, almost to himself, "our enemies will of course learn about it. A nuclear explosion is impossible to conceal. And within hours, I believe, they will launch their attack. I do not believe we can safely test a warhead until we have operational missiles to defend ourselves."

"If we build a dozen warheads without testing the design," Sultani explained, "we run the risk that the design will not work as we hoped. A nuclear warhead is an extremely complex, compact machine. If we use all our beryllium and weapons-grade U-235 on a dozen faulty warheads, we will be several more years away from having truly safe, operational weapons."

Ahmadinejad wiped at his forehead and vigorously rubbed his face again. He leaned back in his chair and took his time answering.

Sultani thought at least a half minute had passed before Ahmadinejad said, "We cannot wait. The political situation does not give us that luxury. We must have warheads as soon as possible. Build them now. Once we have them, we will select one to test."

"Which missiles do you plan to have the warheads installed upon?" Sultani asked. All the missile guidance systems were preprogrammed, of course, so once the fire order was given, military crews could simply roll the transporter/launchers from the tunnels where they were housed and fire them. "Since time is a consideration, I suggest we merely select missiles aimed where you want the warheads to go, take out the conventional warheads and install nuclear ones."

"I haven't decided," Ahmadinejad told him. "I'll study the target list and let you know as soon as possible."

Both men were well aware of the logistical problems of hauling warheads and technicians all over the country to the various missile sites. That task alone would take up most of the two weeks they believed necessary to do the job. They discussed that, and the possibility that the target list had been compromised, which meant stolen by the enemy.

"Even if the enemy has the entire list," Sultani said, "we have nine hundred operational missiles. They won't know which ones carry the nuclear warheads."

"Even if they knew the precise missiles," Ahmadinejad said aloud, "they won't be able to tell one from the other, either on the ground or in the air. If we must fire our missiles, some of them will get through to their targets."

"I am worried about the accuracy of the missiles," Sultani confided. "Israel is a very small place, surrounded by Muslims, and the distance is very great."

"Allah will help us," Ahmadinejad said, in a tone that indicated he wanted no more discussion of that topic.

Ah yes, Habib Sultani thought. *Once you have done all you can, trust in God. Unfortunately, God often seems to forget about the Muslims or is too busy to give much aid.* He kept these thoughts to himself, of course.

Sultani rose to go, but Ahmadinejad motioned with his hand. "I heard the sad news about your father-in-law. Tragic. I have no doubt that he is in Paradise now."

Sultani set his jaw. The injustice of it screamed to be voiced, and on an impulse, he said, "Someone whispered to the MOIS that an aged religious scholar had written something blasphemous, and for that reason alone, he was arrested and beaten until he died."

"His heart stopped," Ahmadinejad explained. "A tragedy, as I have said, but I offer no apologies. We must defend the Prophet against the voices of the unbelievers, who seek to create doubts in the simple-minded. The one true faith is under attack from all quarters. Only by defending the faith against all enemies with every means at our disposal, with every fiber of our being, with every ounce of strength our bodies possess, can we earn glory—and Paradise."

Almost as an afterthought, he added, "Without Allah, and the glory we earn defending him, what reason is there to live? We would be like mice in the field, living meaningless lives. Through the Prophet, Allah promised Paradise. Our task is to earn it."

He signaled that the interview was over.

Sultani walked out of the office.

The incident in the Alborz Mountains had me severely worried. I figured that the MOIS and Revolutionary Guard guys were going to get stirred up when they found that a helicopter trailing Davar and Ghasem had been shot down. And they would find out—bullet holes are easy for anyone to spot.

Ghasem's invitation to a warhead factory had been the best offer I'd had since I got here, yet if the security types grabbed him and his cousin for interrogation, I could forget it.

The truth is I was just plain paranoid. Not knowing what the Iranian security forces were up to made it worse.

I expected to get arrested any minute. When that minute passed, there was another, and another.

My jitters amused me for about an hour; then I became disgusted with myself. Nerves aren't becoming in a professional thief.

Get a grip, Tommy.

Nazra al-Rashid spent no more than ten minutes at the crash site in the mountains before she became convinced the helicopter had been shot down. It had burned, of course, and the Plexiglas had melted in the conflagration, which had pretty well consumed the bodies and all the plastic in the cockpit area.

What was left was scorched metal, which displayed bullet holes quite nicely.

She turned and looked southward toward the pass. Probably when the helo came through, she thought.

As she walked back to her waiting car and driver, one of the MOIS men brought her a handful of spent cartridges and pointed toward the east side of the pass. They were 7.62×39 mm. An AK-47, of course. There were millions of those weapons in the country and more millions in surrounding countries, so that knowledge meant little.

The helo had been keeping tabs on Davar and Ghasem. Since Professor Murad had been implicated in writing a blasphemous book, the security forces had been keeping tabs on them. Then someone shot back. Who?

"Who shot down the helicopter?" al-Rashid asked the general in charge of the Revolutionary Guard as she tossed the handful of spent cartridges on his desk.

"We are not sure," he answered, paling slightly behind his frizzy beard. He had always had a problem discussing business with a woman, but Ahmadinejad had made it clear that he had no choice. Still, the whole situation rankled. Justifying himself to a woman!

"I saw a report that the Ghobadi girl was seen talking to the American spy, Tommy Carmellini. Where was he when the chopper was shot down?"

"I do not know," the general said starchily. "We were not tailing Carmellini that evening."

"Why not?" Hazra al-Rashid demanded. "Did you not see my written orders that Carmellini was to be followed around the clock?"

"Pfff," said the general. "We have not the men for an operation of that size."

Hazra had not sat down; she was still standing in front of the desk. Now she leaned forward, toward the general, putting her fists on the desk to support her weight. "You will obey my orders, General, or I'll be looking at the color of your insides. And the president can name a new man to your post, since you'll be in no condition to continue serving. Do you understand me? Around the clock."

The general was no wallflower. He hadn't gotten to the top of this gang of thugs and fanatics by taking crap from anyone. He stood now and, with his fists on the desk, leaned toward Hazra. "Don't threaten me, whore. Remember your place." His voice was rising. "This is an *Islamic* nation. I will not—"

Hazra had thrown open the office door by then, and four men came shooting through. She pointed at the general. "Take him to Evin Prison. Ward two-oh-nine. I'll be there in an hour."

The general was shouting and struggling with the four men when she walked out of the room.

Ahmad Fassihi was a secret Marxist. Also, although he was outwardly a Muslim, he believed in most of the tenets of Zoroastrianism and, through some mysterious mental process, had managed to mesh Marxism with this ancient religion. He liked Marxism because of its emphasis on providing the necessities of life for everyone; he knew little about the old German's views on religion, the "opiate of the masses," and cared less. The teachings of the prophet Zoroaster, however, spoke directly to his soul. Zoroaster spoke of the one universal and transcendental God, preached that life is a temporary state in which mortals must actively participate in the battle between truth and falsehood and taught that good thoughts, good words and good deeds are necessary to ensure happiness. Had he but known it, he was close to the beliefs of the late Israr Murad, but unlike the philosopher, he had never really devoted much thought to politics or religion.

Like people everywhere, Ahmad Fassihi ignored political and religious tenets about which he knew little, or with which he disagreed. Ahmad Fassihi was, in his heart of hearts, a practical man.

Since he had been wise enough to avoid the MEK, his natural political home, Ahmad Fassihi was still alive in postrevolutionary Iran. Yet, believing as he did, he was a Russian spy, and had been one for twenty years. He received no money for his efforts, nor had he ever asked for any. Passing Iranian military secrets to the Communists was a good deed, a stand that a moral man must make in the battle against evil. After the collapse of Communism, screwing the Islamic fundamentalists became his goal, and his activities continued as before. However, as promotions and increasing responsibilities came his way due to his engineering talents and hard work, the value of the intelligence he passed increased.

This morning Hazra al-Rashid appeared in his office with a secret envelope, one that was numbered and that he had to sign for as she stood watching across the desk. Fassihi waited until the black cloud that was al-Rashid had departed and the door to his office was firmly closed before he opened the envelope and stared at the single sheet of paper that it contained. At the top of the page in Arabic script were the words TARGETS FOR THE JIHAD MISSILES. Under the heading appeared twelve positions defined by latitude and longitude. He had no idea what places the numbers represented, nor was he curious enough to consult an atlas and find out.

His job, as head of the Iranian missile program, was to get the guidance systems of the twelve Jihad missiles previously designated by the president reprogrammed to these targets.

This target list, Ahmad Fassihi thought, was a document the Russians would like to have. He was far too careful to copy it on the old Xerox machine down the hallway—the MOIS routinely checked the drum to see what had been copied. Instead, he used a sheet of paper from a notebook to write down everything that was on the secret paper, including the title. He triple-checked the numbers to ensure he had copied them correctly, then folded and refolded the sheet into the smallest square possible and inserted it into a small cavity in the heel of his shoe.

That done, he replaced the secret paper in its important envelope and set off to give new instructions to the department that sent technicians to service the missile guidance systems.

The copy in his shoe he would place in a secret drop, one serviced by his Russian handler. With that small act, he would help the forces of truth overcome the forces of falsehood and evil.

Ahmad Fassihi felt *good* about himself.

CHAPTER **FIFTEEN**

The ready room of VFA-196, the Savage Horde, aboard USS *United States,* was packed, with an officer in every seat. The doors to the space were locked when the squadron commanding officer, Commander Harvey "the Fly" Burgholzer, walked to the podium and surveyed the crowd. Instantly the conversations stopped.

"Ladies and gentlemen, as you know, this is a classified meeting. The information you hear in this ready room is classified Top Secret and will not be discussed with or repeated to anyone outside of this space."

His audience, the officers of his squadron, well knew what classified information was, so Burgholzer continued. "One of the items of classified information is the name of our guest." He nodded toward a man seated beside the executive officer, or XO. This man was wearing a khaki shirt and khaki trousers but had no rank insignia or name tag, which meant he was a civilian. "Let's give Rear Admiral Jake Grafton a rousing Savage welcome."

As Grafton got out of his chair and made his way to the podium, carrying a small wooden box, the officers let out a tremendous, "Helloooo Asshole!"

Grafton set his box on the podium and grinned at his audience. "Thank you, thank you. It's good to be back where I am appreciated. Now, one question." He leaned an elbow on the podium and looked expectantly at the squadron skipper. "Why 'the Fly'?"

Almost as one, the junior officers roared, "He's the Fly in the Wine."

When the laughing ceased, Grafton got serious. "Folks, I want to reiterate, everything said in this room is classified. As you know, loose lips sink ships, and loose lips *will* destroy a naval career." He glanced at the faces in his audience. Apparently satisfied, he muttered, " 'Nuff said."

He opened the box and pulled out two instruments. One was merely a black box, about six inches square, and the other was an instrument with a faceplate on it that obviously was intended to be installed in the instrument panel of an airplane. He held up the instrument bearing the faceplate. "This cockpit instrument probably looks familiar," he said. "It's driven by an early version of the ALQ-199, the ALQ-198." He held up the black box for them to see, then put it back on the podium. "With your help, we are going to give this thing to the Iranians."

A murmur swept his audience.

"We're going to put the ALQ-198 in one of your planes in place of the 199, ensure it is working, then the pilot of that plane is going to jump out of it in such a way that the plane crashes in Iran."

Dead silence.

"There were several possible ways to handle this operation," Jake Grafton continued. "I believed the best way to stop tongues from wagging and keep the secret was to just tell you, the officers of this squadron, the truth, so that is what I'm doing. Any questions so far?"

One hand went up. Jake nodded at the owner of the hand, a female in a flight suit who asked, "Who do you work for, Admiral?"

"CIA."

Another question. "Why do you want the Iranians to have this box?"

Grafton tugged thoughtfully at his ear. "I'm tempted to pass on that one, but I think I'll put it this way: They don't know we have a better one, nor do they know that the better one is actually put together differently and uses different algorithms."

He pointed at another hand.

"What is the plan, sir?"

Grafton's face brightened into a smile. "Well, the first requirement is that the Iranians believe a U.S. Navy F/A-18 crashed accidentally in their territory. Second, they have to believe we don't want them to have this box. Finally, and most importantly, we have to get everyone involved back alive and in one piece." He looked thoughtful again. "I hope that your skipper and ops officer can help me put together a scenario that is realistic enough for the Iranians and yet doesn't cost us any American lives. It's a tall order, and it's going to take some guts and finesse to pull it off. By necessity, we *are* going to violate Iranian airspace. Once we have a script for our passion play, we'll run it by your battle group commander, Rear Admiral Stan

Bryant, and the folks at State. If we can get their blessing, we'll give it a go."

"Who gets to fly this puppy?" one of the junior officers asked.

"I thought I was going to," Grafton said dryly, "but my boss in Washington thought that I wasn't." That one drew a laugh. "So I've talked with the Fly, and he tells me he and your XO can come up with an equitable way to pick the lucky person. Skipper?"

Jake sat down, and Burgholzer arranged himself at the podium. "Any volunteers?" he asked.

Every hand in the room shot up.

"That's what I thought would happen," the Fly said, grinning. "Damn, you people make me proud."

The squadron ops officer was Lieutenant Commander Harry Lampert. He was about six feet tall and skinny, with a crew cut and a chiseled profile. This was, he said, "an interesting problem." He was huddled with Jake Grafton, Burgholzer and the squadron Executive Officer, the XO.

If the plane had much fuel in it when it crashed, everyone agreed, the wreckage might well be destroyed by fire. On the other hand, if the plane lacked fuel, that might give suspicious Iranian minds something to chew upon.

Then there was the issue of where the pilot would eject. If over water, the plane would have to be on autopilot to reach land. If over land, an in-country rescue situation would develop.

The best option, they decided, was for the pilot to eject over water and the plane to continue on autopilot into Iranian airspace and run out of fuel somewhere over the Iranian desert.

"Why does the pilot need to eject?" the Fly asked. "The Iranians are going to ask that question."

"It's going to be a pile of rubble," Lampert argued. "The people who examine this wreck won't be able to figure out why it crashed."

"Never underestimate your enemy's technical savvy," the XO said. "That's usually a mistake. After all, they can get Russian help any time they ask."

"How long do you need to fool them, Admiral?" Burgholzer asked Jake Grafton.

"A while," he said and smiled.

"That's what I like—a man who keeps his cards close to his vest," Burgholzer told his officers.

Eventually they had a plan, and Jake asked each of the squadron officers to sleep on it.

He was a guest that evening of Admiral Bryant in the flag mess. The two renewed an old acquaintance and, inevitably, found themselves discussing the situation in the Middle East. "Forty million barrels of oil a day come out of the Persian Gulf into the Arabian Sea," Bryant said, "on its way to ports all over the earth. That's just a smidgen less than half the earth's production. Any disruption for any significant period of time will have a huge impact on the world's economies. What happens in this corner of the world matters to everyone on the planet."

When they were alone, they discussed Jake's plan. "Should work," Bryant said. "There's a frigate stationed in the Gulf of Oman, just outside the entrance to the Strait of Hormuz. She has a helo on board. I can make sure she has that helo on alert or in the air when your guy goes out, and we can run one of ours partway up there, having him practice smoke hovers."

The admiral also decided who would need to know what was going down. He named the captain of the ship, the commander of the air wing, his chief of staff and a couple of other officers. "Tell me when you're going and I'll brief them," Bryant said.

They sliced and diced it, two professional naval aviators talking carrier aviation, then moved on to discuss mutual friends and naval matters.

For Jake Grafton, it was all very pleasant. Being at sea on a carrier again, smelling the smells, hearing the sounds, walking through the endless passageways, thinking about flying—all of it brought back pungent memories. He walked out of the flag spaces after dinner with a light step, certain that all was right with the world.

Up on the flight deck he found that the sun had set and the wind was up, a wind laden with salt and the smell of the sea. It tore at his clothes and messed up his hair as he picked his way between the tied-down planes and walked between the catapult tracks to the bow. There was a good sea running, so the bow was rising and falling at a rate that made it difficult to stand. In the darkness, the rising bow tried to throw him off his feet, and the descending bow, dropping out from under him, made him feel light.

These were old sensations, ones Jake Grafton had first known as a young man. Periodic tours on carriers through the years kept the sea and the ships fresh in his memory. *You can never go back, they say . . . but if only you could!*

After ten minutes savoring the sensual feel of the eternal wind and the ship riding the restless sea, he went below to the empty cabin he had been assigned. He undressed and lay down on the small bed, but in minutes he was thinking about the plan, about how it would go. When finally he drifted off to sleep, he found himself dreaming about it.

The ship was launching aircraft the next afternoon when Harry Lampert walked into the Mission Planning spaces with one of his pilots, a woman wearing a green Nomex flight suit. She was of slightly less than medium height, perhaps 130 pounds, with dark brown hair that she wore fairly short. She was trim and fit, solidly muscled.

"Lieutenant O'Hare, sir."

Jake Grafton was in Mission Planning looking at the latest satellite photographs of the Iranian coast. Above their heads on the flight deck, planes were being launched. The subdued, muffled howl of the jet engines at full power reached them occasionally, then disappeared as the catapults threw the planes into the sky. The thuds of catapult spears slamming into the water brakes could be felt all over the ship.

Grafton nodded at each of the junior officers and said, "Commander Burgholzer told me he thought you two could pull this off if anyone could." He handed them a single sheet of paper containing four paragraphs.

"This is the plan. We submitted it this morning to the battle group commander, who approved it and sent a message describing it to CENTCOM, the theater commander, who will undoubtedly send it on to Washington. Don't expect to hear back for a day or two." Grafton unrolled a map and spread it over the huge photo he had been studying. He had marked up the map carefully and showed them the points mentioned in the plan.

When they had run out of questions, he said, "Still want to give it a try? You can walk away right now without a backward glance."

"How'd you get into the spook business, Admiral?" Harry Lampert asked.

"Can't play golf, so none of the defense contractors would hire me."

"Tough break," said Chicago O'Hare with a grimace. She was still staring at the map, trying to visualize how it would be.

"So which of you is going to jump out of our sacrificial goat?" Grafton asked.

"How about a game of acey-deucey?" O'Hare said, glancing at Lampert. "Winner jumps."

"The hell with that," Harry Lampert shot back. "We'll do it the tried and true navy way—the senior officer will decide. And I have. I'll fly it."

"Oh, be a sport," Chicago urged.

Lampert made a rude noise with his lips and tongue as Jake Grafton chuckled.

———

Even though Grafton's operation had been approved at the highest level of the U.S. government, it took three days before the State Department gave a cautious, qualified approval, and then only after citing a classified National Security document to which none of the people in the military had access. During this time a civilian technician who had flown out to the ship swapped the ALQ-199 in one of the Horde's planes for the ALQ-198 Grafton had brought with him. Grafton had also brought a set of backup boxes with him, just in case, but they would not be used unless the first set went into the ocean and the Iranians didn't try to recover it.

Meanwhile Commander Burgholzer ordered a squadron "safety stand-down day" in which all of the pilots were required to get refresher training on the ejection seat and the ejection sequence while wearing all their flight gear. They even hung in a harness from hooks installed in the ready room overhead while finding and touching every piece of equipment attached to them. Harry Lampert and Chicago O'Hare took their turns with everyone else.

The following day the southern half of Iran was under a low pressure area that generated desert windstorms, so Grafton ordered the operation delayed for a day.

Low clouds covered the Persian Gulf and southern Iran the next day, yet after consultation with the battle group commander, Commander Burgholzer, Harry Lampert and Chicago O'Hare, Grafton said, "Do it."

The flight schedule had Lampert and O'Hare scheduled for a surface surveillance mission into the Persian Gulf. The carrier was in her usual position, where the Gulf of Oman widens to meet the Arabian Sea, about a hundred and fifty miles southeast of the mouth of the Strait of Hormuz. The E-2 Hawkeye early warning plane would be airborne, the helo detachment had two "up" helos ready to pull airmen from the ocean . . .

Jake Grafton watched Lampert and O'Hare walk across the flight deck to their planes from a perch behind the Air Boss' chair in Pri-Fly, the "tower" of the carrier. Both were in flight suits, over which they wore G-suits, which covered their legs and lower abdomen, and over that, a parachute harness and survival vest. They carried their helmets, oxygen masks and charts in a bag especially designed for that purpose.

The Boss and his assistant, the Mini-Boss, were busy monitoring the activities on the flight deck and the arrival of the planes awaiting recovery overhead, under the clouds, so they ignored Grafton, who was, as far as they knew, just another civilian.

Only the officers of the squadron, and other key officers the battle group commander had briefed, knew that Lampert's plane would not be returning. For everyone else on the ship this was another routine launch, another day at sea, another day far from home.

Grafton's attention was riveted on Harry Lampert, who preflighted his airplane and the ejection seat, then climbed into the cockpit. The plane captain helped him strap in. Lampert and the plane captain had a lively conversation, and Grafton saw the pilot grin at something the young sailor said.

Ejecting from a tactical jet was damned risky, and everyone who knew the plan was well aware of it. Especially Lampert and Grafton.

Even as Grafton watched, the squadron skipper, Burgholzer, came strolling along the deck. He paused and chatted with Chicago O'Hare, who was now in her cockpit, and then had a word or two with Harry Lampert. He casually looked over Lampert's jet—said good-bye, probably—and then walked along to speak with the pilots of the other two Savage Horde Hornets going on this launch.

After a glance at his watch, the Air Boss ordered "Start Engines" on the deck loudspeaker and the deck intercom system. Yellow-shirted plane directors twirled fingers, and jet engines came to life all over the flight deck. Out on the angle, the rescue helicopter started its engines, engaged the rotors and took off straight ahead. It would orbit to the right of the ship, ready to come to a hover over any pilot that ejected nearby.

Grafton kept an eye on Lampert's plane. If Harry had a problem with it, the operation would have to be postponed since only that plane had the ALQ-198 installed.

Would that box fool the Iranians? Would they think Lady Luck had smiled upon them, or would they smell a rat?

The flight deck ballet began. One by one the airplanes were queued up for the catapults. The E-2 Hawkeye went first on Cat Two, then a couple of S-3 tankers were shot off the waist, then the Hornets were launched. Lampert was second in the queue for Cat One. He taxied onto the catapult and cycled the controls. The cat officers today were shooting from the flight deck. Jake saw the catapult officer signal for full power, then afterburner. The cat officer returned Lampert's salute, looked toward the bow, checking everything one last time, then swept down and touched the deck. One potato, two potato . . . and the catapult fired. In less than three seconds Harry Lampert was airborne. He made a clearing turn, the gear retracted, then the flaps, and the Hornet accelerated away, between the sea and the overcast.

Jake watched O'Hare launch, then wandered out of Pri-Fly. He found himself going down the ladder toward the flag spaces—TFCC, the Tactical Flag Command Center. The admiral would be there. It was there that the message that Lampert had ejected would quickly arrive. The rescue helicopter the admiral had ordered to practice open sea rescues in a clear area would be immediately vectored northwest, and the frigate would be directed to launch her chopper.

Jake Grafton felt nervous. He hoped to heaven he hadn't sent Harry Lampert to his death. As he thought about that, he realized he hadn't even asked Lampert if he was married. Or had any kids. Of course, even single people had parents and brothers and sisters.

Maybe, Grafton decided, he was better off not knowing.

He was only a few steps into the flag spaces when one of the sailors said to him, "Sir, this is a secure space. You aren't cleared to be in here."

Jake opened his mouth to speak—and found himself face-to-face with Admiral Bryant, who took in the situation at a glance. "He's with me," the admiral told the sailor. He grabbed Jake by the arm and steered him into TFCC.

Harry Lampert was a hundred miles northwest of *United States* flying on autopilot at twenty thousand feet when he opened the fuel dumps. Jake Grafton wanted this plane to penetrate about fifty to seventy-five miles into Iran and crash due to fuel exhaustion, which would maximize the chances that the black box that was the ALQ-198 would survive the crash. He didn't want it to fly until the Iranians managed to shoot it out of the sky.

As he jettisoned fuel he nudged the stick to the left, and the plane settled into a fifteen-degree angle-of-bank turn. Chicago O'Hare was glued out there on his right wing.

Harry checked his moving map display and compared the information it gave him to the picture his radar presented. He had the radar in the surface search mode. The coastline of Iran was quite distinct, and behind it, lots of land return. The left hairpin of the Strait of Hormuz, and beyond it the Persian Gulf, appeared on his scope as black ribbons of no return. The coastlines were quite distinct ribbons of light. Since the plane was still turning, the land disappeared off the scope.

The sea immediately below was empty of ships. He had been watching this area for the last fifty miles. The nearest ship was twenty miles northwest, going into the strait.

Lampert was more than a little nervous. Grafton hadn't asked, and he hadn't volunteered the fact that he had never ejected from an airplane. Let's face it; most naval aviators never have to jump. Minimizing the necessity to bail out is what aviation safety is all about.

He was going to have to jump, descend into the sea, get into his little one-man life raft, then wait for the help from the carrier to arrive. It would take perhaps half an hour or more for the helo to make the trip to his area; then it had to find him, one man in a tiny raft in the great wide sea. If he was injured going out, or the chute failed to deploy properly, or his survival vest failed to inflate, or he couldn't get the life raft to deploy or was too banged up to get into it, things could get dicey. In fact, there were about a thousand things that could go wrong, and all of them were bad.

Still, Harry reminded himself, this was no different from the chance he took every time he climbed into one of these flying war machines. Naval aviation was a risky business. Things could go to hell damn quickly: A guy might have to pull the handle and jettison the airplane just any ol' time. The odds were pretty good that it wouldn't happen, but luck was such a fickle bitch . . .

As the fuel in his tanks streamed out into the atmosphere, Harry Lampert thought about his wife and son. He and Stella had waited for years to have a kid, and finally Stella said the waiting was over. She wanted the baby now, before she got too old, before their parents were too old to come visit and enjoy their grandchild.

With two thousand pounds of fuel remaining, Harry Lampert secured the dump valve and steadied the plane heading 350. Pointed it at Iran. Then he turned off his airplane's transponder.

He glanced right, and Chicago O'Hare gave him a thumbs-up. He flashed her one right back. He eased his butt back in the seat and straightened his spine, put his head back in the headrest.

With the coast just tickling the fifty-mile range line on the radar display, Harry Lampert whispered, "I love you, Stella," took a deep breath of oxygen and used both hands to pull the ejection handle above his head and bring the face curtain down over his face.

A tremendous force hit him in the ass and he was up and out and the wind blast was tearing at him. He kept his elbows in tight. He heard the drogue chute come out and felt the seat stabilize. He had a ways to fall before the main chute opened.

"Black Eagle, Black Eagle, this is War Ace Three Oh One," Chicago O'Hare said over the radio. "Mayday. War Ace Three Oh Five has just ejected. He went out a hundred and two miles from the ship on the three-four-nine radial. Did you copy?"

The controller repeated the numbers. "I have no emergency squawk," he added. "Are you certain about the location?"

"Yep. Vector the angel," O'Hare replied.

She consciously dropped back from the Hornet flying along without a pilot so she could watch the falling seat with Harry Lampert aboard heading toward the cloud deck below. The tops, she knew, were about ten thousand, and the base about a thousand feet above the sea. Harry's chute should open at thirteen thousand, and if she dove, she should see it. But she didn't leave the now pilotless jet, and in seconds, she lost the seat in the vastness of the sky.

She had her orders. "Make sure that plane goes to Iran," Jake Grafton had said. "Or into the water. Nowhere else. Shoot it down if you have to."

Her armament switch was in READY; the gun was selected and charged. She added a little throttle to close the distance to War Ace 305. The autopilot was holding it steady as a rock.

So far so good.

As she flew along, the Black Eagle controller began questioning her. The controller, a woman, had no idea that this was a scripted scenario, and she wanted to know if O'Hare had the chute in sight.

"No. I've lost sight. Do you have the angel headed this way?"

"Yes. Why did the pilot eject?"

"Not sure," Chicago said, "and, for some reason, my transponder is acting up." She turned it off.

The controller let that go by . . . for now. "Can you get underneath the clouds and find the pilot in the water?" she asked.

"I'm going down now." She wasn't, but she didn't think the Iranians would know that if they were listening, and they probably were. Grafton said they monitored these freqs, and he should damn well know.

She was thirty miles from the coast when War Ace 305 began the gentlest of right turns, into her.

O'Hare gently eased her left wing under the right wing of the other plane and held it there. She didn't want it to make contact—but to allow the air slipping between the two wings to exert upward pressure on the right wing of the other plane, and that was what happened. War Ace 305 returned to level flight. The heading change had been about ten degrees.

She could live with that, she decided. She moved several yards aft and sat monitoring the empty jet's flightpath.

Lampert's ejection from War Ace 305 would have caused the transponder in his aircraft to began broadcasting an emergency code, had the transponder been turned on. The emergency code would have been picked up by the radar in the airborne E-2 Hawkeye and by the big search radars aboard the carrier and the guided missile frigate only fifty miles southeast of the place where Lampert would enter the ocean. Since Harry had secured the transponder before his ejection—after all, the Iranians could receive the transponder codes on their radars, too—and there was no transponder code, some hurried radio exchanges between the Hawkeye and the frigate occurred before the frigate began the launch sequence for her ready helo. A long ten minutes would pass before the chopper was airborne, yet this bird would reach Lampert before the angel from the carrier. If he was on the surface of the sea and hadn't been pulled under by his chute. And if the chopper could find him.

In *United States'* flag portion of the Combat Direction Center, Jake Grafton saw and heard the news of the ejection, and heard the communications that diverted a flight of Hornets from their scheduled mission to the site of the ejection to search for the survivor. Air Ops also ordered the angel helo on deck scrambled and talked to the CDC aboard the frigate on one of the ship-to-ship voice circuits.

All this took less than a minute, almost a reflex action.

Harry Lampert's parachute opened with an audible bang and his ejection seat fell away toward the cloud deck, which was right under his boots. He inspected the chute, which looked blessedly full of air and intact.

Then he fell into the clouds.

Chicago O'Hare's nudge of the pilotless Hornet seemed to work. The wings stayed level as it closed with the Iranian coast. The Black Eagle controller came back on the radio, informing her that her transponder was malfunctioning and asking for a location. O'Hare turned the volume on the radio down as low as it would go and ignored it.

She watched the coastline march down her radar display toward the apex. Fifteen miles, ten, five . . . She could hear the deep beep of an Iranian search radar as it swept her plane periodically.

At two miles her ECM warnings lit up. A fire control radar was looking.

Chicago turned on her ALQ-199. This black box should fool the Iranian radars and protect both planes until War Ace 305 ran out of gas.

The fire control radar failed to achieve a lock. After a moment it went off the air. The search radar continued to sweep. The two Hornets crossed the coast and continued northwest into Iran.

When he came out of the clouds, Harry Lampert was unsure of his height above the water. He took off his oxygen mask and threw it away, then deployed his seat pan, which fell on a lanyard until it dangled about twenty feet below his feet. His life raft fell out of the seat pan, inflated and hung below it. He got a firm grip on the parachute riser release fittings on his harness and watched the life raft. It would hit the water first, signaling him he had twenty feet to go until he went in.

He realized he could see whitecaps, then swells, then the life raft splashed, and he had time to draw exactly one breath before he went under.

He was still underwater when he toggled the riser releases. The emergency life vest on his harness inflated, squeezing him like an anaconda. In seconds he felt himself bobbing to the surface.

The chute was still in the air, within a foot or two of the water, safely downwind. Lampert spit water and gagged and tried to draw a breath. He didn't see the parachute go into the ocean.

He was floating with his head well out of the water, still wearing his helmet. He began looking for the seat pan and life raft. Not finding either due to the height of the swells, he felt around for the lanyard and started pulling. Eventually the seat pan, then the life raft, appeared in front of him.

Now to get in the damned thing. He tried pushing it under him and working himself over it. Fell off twice. *This was always so easy in the pool during refresher survival training,* he thought.

The third time was the charm.

He was sitting in the thing, wet and cold and happy, when he heard the first jet. Now he needed his flares. He fumbled in his survival vest until he found one, lit it and shouted as orange smoke began pouring out. The jets were running under the clouds and apparently didn't see him.

Two minutes later they were back, working on a different track, when one of them peeled away from the formation and came diving toward him. He waved the flare, which was spewing a tremendous amount of smoke.

The two jets set up an orbit over Harry, and it was only then that he remembered his survival radio, which was in his vest. He tossed the flare into the water, got out the radio, turned it on and squeezed the transmit button.

"Hey, this is War Ace Three Oh Five," he shouted into the thing.

"Hey yourself, shipmate. We saw your smoke and decided to drop in. A helo is on the way. You okay?"

"Yeah yeah yeah. I'm okay." Actually he was shivering uncontrollably and felt his first twinge of nausea, but he wasn't going to say that. He was so very happy.

"You sit right there and behave yourself while we get on the horn to the guys on the big boat. Okay?"

"Yeah yeah yeah." Harry Lampert sat in his tiny life raft, with his ass partially submerged, shivering and smiling. Life was good, he decided. And he wasn't parting with his anytime soon. Yeah! He vowed then and there to buy a bottle of the best whiskey he could find for the guys and gals in the parachute shop. Yeah!

He raised his helmet visor so he could see better and waved at the circling jets.

The Iranian search radar was still beeping in Chicago's ears when War Ace 305 ran out of gas. It was 110 miles deep into Iran. Chicago realized the fire had gone out when the plane began to decelerate and its nose came down.

It seemed to find a new equilibrium as it descended, something like eight degrees nose down. The wings stayed level.

She was in a level turn by then, watching the descending jet fall away.

Chicago O'Hare leveled out heading back the way she had come and got on the radio. She sent a prearranged code over the two-way, secure Link 16 to Black Eagle and the carrier, where it would reach Jake Grafton.

War Ace 305 came out of the clouds several thousand feet above the desert floor. The autopilot had disengaged, and the plane was in a shallow left turn, its nose about eight degrees down. It was still in that attitude when it met the earth and began sliding along. The plane shed a cloud of pieces as the wreck decelerated. Finally the largest piece, the engines and the remainder of the airframe, came to rest and the remainder settled to the ground. The dust cloud drifted away on the wind and dissipated.

Chicago O'Hare was twenty miles from the coast when she saw the two MiG-29s at least five thousand feet above her and to her right. They were crossing from right to left, heading generally east.

Uh-oh!

She advanced her throttles from cruise to full military power. Her airspeed began to build. The jets crossed in front of her, and then the nearest one began a left turn. *He's looking me over*, she thought. The second one turned behind the first.

Chicago O'Hare didn't want to engage either of them, but trying to run away was probably begging to get shot down, and that had no appeal whatsoever.

In for a penny, in for a pound, she thought and slammed the throttles forward into burner while she pulled up and into the wingman. She was wearing a joint helmet-mounted cueing system (JHMCS) today, so she designated them both as targets. The F/A-18 used a hands on throttle and stick (HOTAS) system for managing the plane's armament, so she didn't even have to take her hands off the stick or throttle to arm the AIM-9Xs, the Super Sidewinders, she carried on the wingtips. These employed a focal-plane array seeker and a thrust-vectoring tail control package, so they were fire-and-forget short-range dogfight weapons with the capability of turning square corners.

Chicago turned into the lead, which meant the wingman was out on her right. She got a tone in her ears: Her right 'winder was locked onto the wingman.

The Iranian wasn't a good fighter pilot. He continued as if she weren't there, following his leader. Maybe she wouldn't have to shoot.

Perhaps he hasn't looked to see what I'm doing. Perhaps he thinks his leader will take care of me.

But right in front of her the leader was pulling Gs, turning hard, trying to get his nose around toward her.

At a push of a switch, the missile designated for the leader came alive, locking on. She pulled the trigger, and it left in a flash of fire. She turned hard into the wingman, who was proceeding straight ahead, obviously not into the fight.

The safe thing to do was to just zap him, but maybe he wasn't a real threat.

Even as that thought went through her mind, she saw the flash as the Sidewinder she had fired impacted the leader.

Chicago O'Hare rolled down and into the wingman, pulling smoothly right up to five Gs, and kept going until her nose was vertical, pointed straight down. Only then did she ease off on the G. Her burners were still lit, so the airspeed built quickly.

Then the clouds surrounded her and she came out of burner and off the throttle and began pulling for all she was worth. Passing fifteen thousand, six Gs. ALQ-199 flashing green. Now that Iranian was trying for a radar lock, but it wasn't happening for him.

She pumped off some flares from her chaff box, just in case the guy behind her triggered a heat-seeking missile into the clouds, and kept the G on until her nose was back to the horizon. She was down to four thousand feet, still in the clouds.

Weren't there some mountains on this coast?

She pulled hard and rocketed back up toward ten thousand. There she stabilized and began an eighty-degree turn toward the coast.

As the coast went under her nose she broke out of the clouds, which seemed to be dissipating. No Iranians in sight. She came out of burner, checked her fuel, turned on her transponder and called Black Eagle on an encrypted frequency.

"I need Texaco," she said. "Send him toward me."

"And where are you?"

She gave the controller her position. He didn't say a word.

After a last look behind her, she pulled off a glove and used it to wipe the perspiration from her face. Too bad about that MiG, but . . .

"Black Eagle, War Ace Three Oh One. Did they find my playmate?"

The helo pilot had Harry Lampert pop another smoke so he could see the wind direction and get a good idea of its velocity as he made his approach. Lampert lowered his helmet visor to keep spray raised by rotor wash out of his eyes. The pilot circled to approach him into the wind, then came into a hover over him. The horse collar was already in the water.

Lampert grabbed for it and fell out of his raft. He managed to get the thing around him and give a thumbs-up to the man in the door. He felt himself being pulled out of the water. The rhythmic pounding of the rotor wash reminded him that he was completely alive.

The winch raised him up beside the helo's door; then the operator grabbed his parachute harness with both hands, pulled him in and relayed that to the pilot on the ICS.

"We have him," the pilot told the controller in the E-2 Hawkeye, and she relayed the news to Chicago O'Hare in War Ace 301.

CHAPTER SIXTEEN

Three days after the F/A-18 Hornet crashed in Iran, President Mahmoud Ahmadinejad announced at a news conference that Iranian fighters had destroyed an American navy fighter over Iran. While print reporters scribbled furiously and cameras rolled, Ahmadinejad motioned to two men behind him. They whisked away a large cloth, revealing what appeared to be a panel from an airplane wearing the U.S. Navy's low-viz paint scheme. On the panel were the words, USS UNITED STATES, and a squadron number, VFA-196. The panel, irregular in shape, was dented, and one side appeared to be torn, as if a piece had been ripped off.

Ahmadinejad entertained his audience with an account of how this airplane had illegally and provocatively penetrated Iranian airspace and been intercepted. After a short air battle, he said, it was shot down.

"Where is the pilot?" one of the international reporters shouted, and was ignored.

Other pieces of the plane were produced, a half dozen, with the largest being the tail hook. It took four men to carry it into the room. The shank of the hook was slightly bent, and the whole thing was dirty.

The president regaled the reporters for another twenty minutes with some aerial fiction, and then he turned serious. "This airplane was obviously in Iranian airspace to spy upon the Islamic Republic." He continued in this vein. Its presence was a serious breach of international law, and the government of Iran expected an abject and humble apology from the Great Satan.

The story shot around the world at the speed of light. In Washington a

Pentagon spokesperson told the press that the matter was under investigation. She added, "If there has been an inadvertent penetration of Iranian airspace, of course we will apologize. However, until the investigation is complete, I am unable to say what the facts are. I seriously doubt that anyone intended to violate the sovereignty of Iran. We are querying the USS *United States* battle group commander. We will have an announcement in due course."

At Naval Air Station Oceana, the home of VFA-196, the pilots' spouses and significant others had already been notified that the squadron had lost a plane and the pilot was safe. Press inquiries were rebuffed by the Oceana public affairs office.

In Tehran, the chargé, Eliza Marie Ortiz, trooped over to the Foreign Ministry and offered an official apology for the inadvertent violation of Iranian airspace and requested that the wreckage of the U.S. Navy plane found in Iran be returned to the U.S. authorities. The request, which was in writing, was taken under advisement.

The Iranian government showed the document to the press, but the story died anyway. The Iranians had some airplane pieces and a far-fetched tale of how they got them. No living pilot or dead body was produced. The U.S. Navy wasn't talking. The public went on to other things. After all, the news from the Middle East was always bad.

Two days later Janos Ilin, of the Russian SVR, stood in the desert looking at the Hornet's wreckage from a distance of about fifty feet. He was certainly no expert on airplane crashes, but this one looked remarkably intact. It seemed to have struck the ground in a flat attitude, skipped and plowed along shedding bits and pieces, then went up a little hill and got airborne again. On the other side of the hill the nose hit hard, almost crushing it; then the thing turned ninety degrees and skidded sideways to a stop. The remains of the crushed belly tank could just be seen about two hundred yards away.

Two of the men Ilin had brought with him did indeed specialize in the examination of crashed planes, and they began poking and prodding the wreck as the Iranians conducted their own examination. There were a dozen or more Iranian air force technicians, armed with a variety of tools and test equipment. The workers were supervised by at least a half dozen officers, who conferred, moved to another portion of the wreck and conferred again.

Habib Sultani and his nephew Ghasem stood beside Ilin, watching the entire evolution.

The most obvious thing about the plane was the shattered canopy and the missing ejection seat. The next thing Ilin noticed was that there were no bullet or cannon holes in it that he could see. Or holes made by shrapnel.

He turned so he could look back up the path the airplane had plowed as it decelerated, a path that pointed almost straight east. Not a trace of fire.

The airplane didn't burn.

He looked at the wings. One of them had been nearly wrenched away from the fuselage and was bent at an angle.

There was no fuel in the plane when it crashed.

Ilin sighed and got out his cigarettes. He lit one and took a deep drag. The smoke from the cigarette zipped away on the stiff breeze.

"Would you like to inspect more closely?" Ghasem asked.

"No, thank you. This is close enough. Where is the pilot?"

"Not here," Ghasem said abruptly.

"Obviously. The ejection seat is missing. Is he still running around out here in this desert, or do you people have him in custody?"

Ghasem said nothing.

"How far are we from the ocean?" Ilin asked.

Ghasem knew the answer to this one. "One hundred and sixty kilometers."

Ilin nodded and puffed on his cigarette. He was on his third one when the two Russian experts came over to him. "No fuel in the plane. The engines were only windmilling when it struck. They are essentially intact."

"Why did the plane crash?"

"The pilot ejected. Without a pilot . . ."

Ilin frowned at the man. "Why did the pilot eject?"

"I don't know. It doesn't seem to have any battle damage, no sign of fire, no airframe failure that might have occurred in the air. Perhaps the pilot got lost and ran out of fuel. Perhaps he had a total electrical failure, although we saw no obvious damage to the electrical system in our quick inspection. The ejection seat may have malfunctioned and simply blew him out of the plane. There are a lot of possibilities, including an oxygen system failure. If we had a hangar and a couple of months, we could probably eliminate many of them."

"How about the box?"

"It's still in there. Should we take it out?"

Ilin deferred to Sultani, who of course said yes. The Russians went back with an assortment of hand tools. Meanwhile, the Iranian technicians began working to remove one of the Sidewinder missiles, the one nearest Ilin, from the tip of the twisted wing.

Ilin turned and strolled away from the plane. He was standing at a comfortable hundred feet when the rocket motor of the Sidewinder ignited and it shot out across the desert floor like a snake with its tail on fire.

The men around the wingtip were screaming in agony when the missile struck a rock some distance away and exploded. After a long moment dirt and shrapnel began raining down, gently.

One of the technicians seemed to have been burned to death, Ilin gathered, and several were badly injured. Ilin's Russian techs, who were working adjacent to the fuselage equipment bay, were unhurt.

Janos Ilin lit another cigarette.

It was after lunch, and the wounded and dead had been taken away in a truck, when the technicians came over to where Ilin sat on a folding chair. One of them was carrying a black box in his hands, one about six inches on each side, with a variety of wires protruding from it.

"We will need several days to identify where all the wires that were connected to this box led to."

Ilin handed the box to Sultani.

"By all means," Sultani said, cradling the box in his hands. He looked pleased. "By all means."

As Sultani stood examining his prize, the technician lit a cigarette and paused beside Ilin, who was still contemplating the plane.

"Too bad about the radar," the technician said. The nose cone was crushed and the radar inside severely smashed. "Still," he added, "it would be nice to have the waveguides, the navigation/attack computer and some of the other bits."

Without even glancing at the Iranians, Ilin said, "Take off anything you want."

Ghasem supervised the loading of the dead man and the wounded after the Sidewinder missile ignited as the technicians attempted to remove it from the wingtip. The crashed airplane was interesting, but he had other things on his mind. Even the agony of the burned didn't engage him intellectually.

The fact that his cousin was passing Top Secret data about the weapons program to a former professor of hers who was now in America had come as a shock. Yet he had always known Davar had a mind of her own. They had discussed her choice for hours the other evening on their way to and from the meet with the American spy, Carmellini. Conflicted as he was about his government's decision to spend billions of precious oil dollars on nuclear weapons, Ghasem found he was unable to condemn her. She wanted the world to know what the mullahs were doing, and that seemed logical. These mullahs with their secrets . . .

And their fears and hatreds, one of which had killed Grandfather. Today in the desert, Ghasem found himself thinking about Grandfather's manuscript, about the grace of the ideas it contained and about the kind, gentle man who was murdered by the secret police.

He also found himself surreptitiously watching his uncle Habib Sultani. What did he think? In his heart of hearts, did he believe Ahmadinejad's diatribes about the glory of martyrdom? Did he really believe Iran, this poor third-world country, needed nuclear weapons?

Ghasem's plan to get Tommy Carmellini into the warhead manufacturing facility was simplicity itself, which convinced him he could probably get away with it. He was going to disguise Carmellini as an official visitor and squire him around.

Contrary to what one might think, the facility did indeed have official visitors, and in the past Ghasem had indeed played tour guide for them. The visitors were from North Korea, China and Germany. The Koreans and Chinese were the experts, having built bombs of their own, and were there with the knowledge and consent of their governments. While the Federal Republic of Germany certainly didn't condone nuclear warhead manufacturing, some enterprising Germans had built a nice business evading the ban on machine-tool sales to Iran.

In fact, next month a Venezuelean official was coming to look over the whole operation. President Ahmadinejad took his political allies where he found them.

Thinking it over, Ghasem decided that Carmellini would do best as a German. He would be an employee of the last company that had sent a man to take measurements and offer expert advice.

"You'll be Herr Reinicke," Ghasem told me at a restaurant in one of the blue-collar districts in the southern part of the city. "Tomorrow."

"Let me see if I have this right. We are just going to walk in, you'll give me the tour, and we'll walk out?"

"Yes."

"Oh, man." My chosen field is burglary, and there are plenty of reasons for that, not the least of which is that it fits my twisted personality. This proposal was about as far from burglary as a man could get: We were going to go onstage and do it in plain sight.

"I was followed this evening," I told Ghasem. "There were at least four of them, maybe more. I had a devil of a time getting loose. Seems as if they sent the best they had, this time."

Ghasem said nothing.

"Are they following you?" I asked. I had checked the outside of the restaurant carefully for watchers before I entered—now was certainly not the hour for me to be seen by the Islamic Gestapo hanging around with Ghasem, the aide to the minister of defense. I saw no one, but that meant little. If they were really working at it, I had little hope of detecting a passive surveillance. And, of course, there was Ghasem, who I doubted was knowledgeable enough to spot a good tail, and way too ignorant to ditch one.

"What will happen to you if they catch us?" I asked.

Ghasem shrugged. "I'll be spared the indignities of old age."

I tried to keep a straight face, but it was difficult.

He looked at me through narrowed eyes. "Are you trying to back out?"

"Believe me," I said, "if I could get out of this, I would. Now walk me through the day. How will it go?"

When I left the restaurant two hours later, I had a new respect for Ghasem. He was either an extremely with-it, competent young man with a king-sized set of gonads, or he was setting me up big-time. One thing was certain: He knew more about nuclear warhead design than anyone I had ever met. According to him, the plant we were visiting, in the Hormuz tunnel complex in the foothills of the Alborz Mountains, northeast of Tehran, had sufficient plutonium on hand to construct *twelve* warheads. This was *four times* more warheads than Azari said they were making. Also, they weren't months from having warheads, they were "almost finished." Two or three weeks, he said. Ahmadinejad had ordered the warheads into production. In two or three weeks Iran would have operational nuclear-armed missiles.

I went straight to the embassy, set up the portable telephone booth and called Jake Grafton on the satellite phone.

The secret police pounded on the door at two in the morning. Ghasem opened it, and six of them came storming in. MOIS officers took Ghasem and his roommate, Mustafa Abtahi, to separate cars in the front of the building to question them while two officers remained behind to search every square inch of the apartment.

"The manuscript. We want it. Where is it?"

"What manuscript?"

"Don't take us for fools. The manuscript that Professor Murad wrote. We know you have it. Where have you hidden it?"

And so it went. Ghasem stuck to his story. He knew nothing about a manuscript, had never seen it, had talked to no one about it.

While he was telling the officers these lies, Ghasem was wondering what Mustafa Abtahi was saying. After all, the manuscript had been in the apartment and Abtahi had probably seen it. He might not have known what it was, but he had probably seen the bundle of paper tied up with strings.

So it went. After forty minutes of this, the officers who had been questioning Ghasem went to question Mustafa, and the officers who had been grilling Mustafa came to question Ghasem. Fortunately they didn't start pounding on the two men. That would come some night in the future.

Then, suddenly, the interrogation was over. The men upstairs came down, the officers shoved the suspects out of the cars, and the six of them drove away.

Ghasem and Mustafa watched the cars disappear, stood for a moment trying to calm down, then went back upstairs. Their apartment was trashed. Everything movable was piled in the middle of the floor.

They worked for an hour putting things back together, then lay down on their mattresses and tried to sleep. Ghasem didn't mention the manuscript. Nor did Mustafa. Both men knew that if either had acknowledged the past presence of a manuscript, they would right now be on their way to prison. Neither of them had, so no discussion was needed.

Ghasem picked me up on a street corner in downtown Tehran. I had been followed from the hotel and worked hard getting clean. Went to the bazaar, went into and out of four buildings, caught a taxi, abandoned it at a light and caught another. There had been at least four of them on foot with two cars carrying backup guys.

They were really serious about following me, and I was worried. Why now? Did they know that I was talking to Ghasem?

Lots of questions, and no answers. Every day I spent with Ghasem and managed to telephone Jake Grafton was gold. I was convinced he was telling me the truth, yet so far I didn't have anything that would convince the skeptics back in the States, who had been burned once too often.

As I dodged Iranian agents, I wondered why everyone had decided to lie to the CIA. Seemed like a good idea to me, but still . . . everyone?

Pollution this morning was terrible, so bad I couldn't even see the Alborz Mountains to the north. Ghasem glided by in an older BMW, right on time. He circled the block while I watched to see if anyone was following him. Apparently not. Of course, if they had a beacon on his car they wouldn't need to follow him.

The second time he stopped, and I climbed in. We were on our way. He started to speak, and I held up my hand. From my backpack I removed a radio receiver. I used it to carefully pace through all the possible frequencies I thought a beacon might be on. Then I tried to check to see if there were bugs in the car transmitting.

Again, apparently not.

"Okay," I told Ghasem. "We're clean, I think."

Ghasem nodded and checked his rearview mirror again. He, too, was worried. When you turn spy, you have a lot to worry about. "Ahmadinejad gave the order a couple of days ago to put warheads in production," he said. "Today you will see them being manufactured."

My mouth made a little round O.

"Ahmadinejad had two goals for the nuclear program," Ghasem continued as we rode along, "and they have both been met. He wanted to put it underground, and he wanted it under military control. Nuclear weapons production is housed in the Hormuz Tunnel, which we will visit today. Missile manufacture occurs at the Parchin complex, the largest tunnel system in Iran, which is under the Khojir region in the mountains just east of Tehran."

"How about testing one, just to see if it'll go bang?"

He shrugged. "Ahmadinejad elected not to test a warhead, so the warheads will go into the missiles, which have been programmed and are ready to launch."

We talked about missiles for a bit, and when we had exhausted that subject, Ghasem said, "The leadership has also constructed a hardened city for themselves under the Abbas Abad district of Tehran. The entrance is through a religious center, the Mosalla Prayer Grounds. The chosen can get to it quickly from Parliament and the government ministries. This bunker is built to withstand a direct hit from a nuclear device."

Fortunately I had photographed the blueprints of all of these bunkers and sent them by burst transmission to a satellite, which re-sent them to NSA.

"I always wondered," I mused aloud, "who the fortunate souls will be: those aboveground who die immediately, or the bunker rats who crawl out, eventually, into a nuclear wasteland?"

"That is a question," Ghasem acknowledged.

"Where are the operational missiles kept?"

Ghasem grinned. "You are a spy, aren't you?"

"You thought I might not be?"

"The regime has some very clever officers."

"I was wondering if you were one," I said, eyeing him.

Ghasem flashed that grin again. "The missiles are spotted all over western and southern Iran. They occasionally move during the night by transport, going from one hardened storage site to another. There are twenty-five sites. Unfortunately, to launch one, it must be pulled from its storage site, which is like a railroad tunnel, and placed in the open. The launcher is placed in launching position, the missile is unstrapped from the launcher, power is applied, the gyros and other systems are started and checked, then the missile is fired. All this can be done rather quickly."

"How quickly is rather quickly?"

"Twenty to thirty minutes."

"How many operational missiles are there?"

"Hundreds. Perhaps as many as nine hundred—I do not know the exact number. It changes weekly."

"But the regime will have only a dozen warheads?"

"At first. Over time that number will increase to at least a hundred. The technicians will go to the various storage sites throughout the country to install the new warheads. The missiles will not be moved."

"Targeting for the missiles—how does that work? Are they preprogrammed, and how long does it take to change a target?"

"The guidance systems are preprogrammed on the ballistic missiles, the Ghadars. Those programs are complex and changing them involves computers. The task requires technical experts and takes hours. The cruise missiles are also preprogrammed, but a good technician can change the target in perhaps half an hour, if he has all the correct targeting data, such as its position and distance and so forth. Still, the easiest way to target the nuclear warheads is to simply install them on preprogrammed missiles, all of which have been checked by the ministry's experts. That way we don't have to rely on technicians in the field, who might make errors."

My mouth was dry, yet my palms were sweating. We were in the suburbs when I had Ghasem pull over and stop. I heaved my breakfast, then climbed back into the car. Amazingly, I felt better.

"Have you seen a target list?" I asked. "Or a list of missiles that will get the warheads?"

"No."

Ghasem was looking at me, cool as snow in January. "Are you okay?" he said.

"Little touch of something," I told him. "Let's go and get this over with."

He put the car in motion again.

"You sure I won't be searched?"

"Neither of us will."

"That's good. I have a couple of cameras on me, and I'll be taking photos."

"Not obviously, I hope."

"Nope. I'm a sneaky bastard."

We stopped talking then and rode silently toward our doom. I worked on getting control of my stomach and my game face in place. When you are wall-climbing, cracking a safe or picking a lock, you don't have to worry about your face, so all this was relatively new to me. One thing I knew for sure—I didn't like it. Still, I figured I could get through this unless someone who had seen me in the president's office recognized me. Then I would be in a world of hurt.

So there we were, two spies in the house of love, when we pulled up to the gate in a chain-link fence. Squads of armed soldiers lolled about, here and there, all clad in sloppy green uniforms and sporting AK-47s. Ghasem spouted Farsi at the guard—I got most of it—and displayed his pass, which I later learned bore the signature of his uncle, the minister of defense.

The card did the trick. The guard gave Ghasem a sloppy, kiss-my-ass salute and we were on our way. A quarter of a mile later we arrived at the entrance to the underground complex. Ghasem parked, and we walked over to the entrance.

I snapped some photos with the camera in my lapel. Digital photography has advanced so far that every person in the developed world has a tiny camera embedded in their cell phone. This was the same technology, without the phone.

This being the third world, there were no plastic IDs with photographs and embedded magnetic strips, nor were there any computers to read them. Security consisted of four soldiers—officers, I assumed—who sat around a folding table at the entrance. They, too, looked at Ghasem's card and listened to him introduce me. Herr Reinicke. One of the soldiers was eyeing me, so I met his eyes, rolled the dice and asked, "*Sprechen Sie Deutsch?*"

He gave me a blank look.

We walked into the tunnel and boarded an electric trolley, which set off on a journey into the mountain. Ghasem gave our destination to the trolley operator. The caverns were huge, at least twenty-five feet high. I asked Ghasem about that, and he said they had to be large to get the rock-drilling and earth-moving machinery in and out.

We rode for at least eight minutes. As we approached an intersection, the trolleyman pointed left or right, and a man stationed there threw a manual switch, changing the track.

Arranged here and there were large curtains hanging from the ceiling, radiation curtains. There was just room in the curtains for the trolley to get by. Due to the constant change of direction, I assumed the curtains were reasonably effective in trapping radiation.

When we got to the end of the trolley line, we went into a dressing room, where we donned one piece antiradiation suits, complete with gloves, helmets and radiation-absorbent badges. Ghasem knew the guards, who didn't even ask to see his pass. Nor did they ask him about me. On the overhead were four surveillance cameras, silent sentinels. I wondered where the camera control room was.

As I dressed, I took some photos with the camera in my Dick Tracy watch. We were just about ready to go when an officer I had seen before walked in. He knew Ghasem, who addressed him as Major Larijani. I remembered him, a glowering, bearded asshole. This guy had been in the president's office when Ahmadinejad did his rant. I half turned, so Larijani didn't get a full face of me, and didn't waste any time pulling on the head covering. Larijani talked to Ghasem about a manuscript. Being smarter than the average bunny, I immediately jumped to the conclusion that the manuscript in question was the one Ghasem and Davar had given to me. And baby, it was gone, on its way to America.

Ghasem told Larijani he knew nothing about it, and after a minute or so, Larijani let it go.

After passage through an air dam, Ghasem and I found ourselves on the personnel side of the manufacturing facility. A radioactivity barrier stood between us and the plutonium. Over a dozen people in suits were working at control stations, manipulating large machine tools and conveyor systems. Monitors mounted all over the place allowed them to see precisely what the tools were doing. As Ghasem and I watched, they maneuvered plutonium into a press.

"In the press," Ghasem whispered, "the plutonium will be shaped into half of a warhead. Ultimately the halves will be assembled around a neutron generator trigger and control unit and pressed together. Then the warhead is coated in beryllium, which has the unique property of reflecting neutrons back into the warhead, helping the plutonium go critical and enhancing the explosion. In short, the beryllium coating allows us to build a warhead with less plutonium. Finally, the entire warhead is coated in lead to prevent radiation leakage."

Some people were taking notice of their visitors, so Ghasem began an earnest discussion of how the computer remotely controlled the various tools. I inspected everything and tried to act as if I knew something about all this. Our conversation was conducted in English, of course. Ghasem knew no German, and I suspected none of the Iranians did either. I knew just enough to order a beer in Munich and ask for a kiss. Other than casual interest, no one paid us much attention. No one, that is, except the surveillance cameras.

After a thorough inspection of the remote controls, Ghasem led me along the partition to where I could see into the bay. Eight warheads completely assembled and coated in beryllium and lead lay on pallets under the hydraulic arms that moved them about. I peeled back the cuff of my glove and took a photo with my watch.

"Only four more to go," Ghasem said.

"I've seen enough," I said. "Let's get the hell outta here."

So we did. Larijani was nowhere in sight as we took off our radiation coveralls and turned in our radiation badges.

He was sitting in the front of the tunnel when we got off the trolley, though. He motioned to Ghasem that he wanted to talk, so Ghasem wandered over. I took a few more steps and stood looking over the parking area and the distant mountains while Ghasem and Larijani chewed the fat. I couldn't hear the conversation.

This whole visit had been too easy, which worried me. The conviction grew and grew that they knew who I was, that they were making it possible for me to get information to pass on to Washington. Yet what could I do about it?

The tension mounted with every passing second. Several people came and went, and every one of them glanced into my face. No beard, pale skin, taller than average, I was going to attract attention. I didn't smile. Tried to not look stressed either. Bored was my game this morning, and I worked at it.

Finally Ghasem came walking over and we strolled to the car. When I glanced back, Larijani was talking to the soldiers at the desk.

I was so relieved to get out of there that I almost went to sleep on the way back to town. I came fully alert when we ran across a demonstration that blocked one of the main thoroughfares. Hundreds of people were chanting and waving signs while at least fifty heavily armed security troops watched. It was difficult to see much from our vantage point, but when I saw another busload of troops arrive, I pointed them out to Ghasem, who began backing our ride into a small park, where he turned around and drove around trees and over the grass and dirt until we got to a street going the other way. We passed a bus full of young men going the other way.

"Basij," Ghasem said. "Thugs. They will attack the demonstrators."

"Great country," I remarked.

"Isn't it?" he shot back.

CHAPTER SEVENTEEN

The news that Iran was a mere two weeks away from atomic weapons struck those movers and shakers inside the Beltway who were cleared to hear it with the impact of a bunker-buster.

"Prove it to me," National Security Adviser Jurgen Schulz roared at Jake Grafton in the Cabinet Room of the White House. Also gathered around the table were the president, Sal Molina, the secretary of state, the chairman of the Joint Chiefs, the secretary of defense, and William Wilkins, the director of the CIA. Behind them a collection of high-ranking aides stood with notebooks and pens, ready to turn decisions into action.

Jake had already given a DVD to the multimedia person, and now he glanced at the appropriate wall and twirled his fingers. In less than a minute a screen dropped down from the overhead and the people in attendance were looking at the photos from Tommy Carmellini's watch camera.

"There are eight nuclear warheads in this photo, sir," Jake Grafton said, "hot off the assembly line and ready to be installed in missiles. Our man in Tehran believes they will have four more within a day or two, and all twelve will be installed in operational missiles within two weeks from yesterday."

"Where was this photo taken?" the SecDef wanted to know.

"In the factory where the warheads are assembled, a tunnel under the Hormuz Mountains near Tehran."

"The photo is genuine," Wilkins said heavily. He was in no mood to put up with people who wanted to split hairs and quibble, rather than face facts.

The president cut to the chase. "When the missiles are armed with these warheads, what are the Iranians going to do with them?"

No one had an answer to that question.

"It sounds as if the consequences of our sins are arriving all at once," the president said lightly. No one in the room cracked a smile.

"Obviously," he continued, "the Iranians' options range from doing nothing—highly unlikely—to threatening their neighbors—more likely—to immediately launching some of those missiles at the people they like the least, which would be us and the Israelis. The last option seems insane, improbable and highly unlikely, and yet one suspects Ahmadinejad and the holy warriors are capable of it."

"If they do—" the secretary of defense began.

The president cut him off. "I have made an executive decision, for better or for worse, and this is the time to tell you of it. I am not going to order the use of nuclear weapons against Iran, regardless of whom they shoot missiles at or whom they kill. We will respond with conventional weapons only. And we will not attack first; the Iranians get the first shot."

Dead silence followed that remark, broken only when Jake Grafton asked the president directly, "Have you shared that tidbit with our troops in Iraq and Arabia, or with the Israelis?"

The president stared at Grafton, then looked around the room at the faces looking back at him. "If we attack first, the political damage will lead to a *century* of warfare in the Middle East, which has something like fifty percent of the world's oil. The economies of the United States, Europe and Japan will be severely impaired. Quite simply, a first strike on Iran will inaugurate a war between Islam and the West that will not end until every last Muslim is dead. Gentlemen, I am not going to go there."

"If American soldiers are killed with nuclear weapons and you fail to retaliate, the American people will eat you alive," Grafton said softly. "You'll be impeached."

"I am aware of that," the president shot back. He was obviously irritated that Jake Grafton was talking when he should be listening, yet he had to respond.

With Grafton silent, the president paused, collected himself, then continued. "I have thought long and hard about nuclear retaliation. Iran is not the Soviet Union, nor is it modern Russia. Iran is controlled by a collection of religious fanatics who want to be somebody. They rant, bluster and threaten, and the world ignores them. We will elevate them to the status of a worthy enemy if we overreact. Overreaction and underreaction would both be grave mistakes, ones we will not make."

When he paused, no one in the room had a word to say.

The president again surveyed the faces, then went on. "It is my hope and prayer that the Iranian government will not attempt to use nuclear weapons on anyone. However, in the event that they do, we must be ready to do whatever is required to shoot down the missiles and prevent them from employing nuclear weapons in the future."

The president looked at his watch, then rose from his chair. "Sal," he said, "keep me advised." Then he walked out of the room.

Shortly after that, the meeting broke up. The chairman of the Joint Chiefs waggled his finger at Grafton. "You come over to the Pentagon as soon as you can. We're going to need your help."

"Yes, sir."

Sal Molina buttonholed Grafton and his boss, William Wilkins, before they could get out of the room. "You didn't need to make that crack, Jake."

Wilkins wasn't in the mood. "Someone around here needs to remind everyone, and I mean *everyone*, that the Iranians are playing for keeps. The survival of Israel is at stake. Millions of lives are on the block. *Millions!* And some thousands of those people are American servicemen."

"The president is aware of the risks," Molina shot back.

"He'd damn well better be," Wilkins retorted grimly, "because however the worm turns, he's going to have to live with it."

"We all are," Grafton muttered. He stepped around Molina and headed for the door.

Fifteen minutes later, when the president and Sal Molina were alone in the Oval Office, Molina wanted to apologize for Jake Grafton's comments. The president waved him off. "Oh, I don't mind Grafton. He's our mine canary. He doesn't give a damn if we fire him this afternoon, so he calls it the way he sees it."

"He's not a team player," Sal said.

"We've got enough team players," the president said sourly, fingering some of the mementos on his desk. "What we need are some original thinkers." He eyed Molina. "We can't keep doing business as usual in the twenty-first century. You see that, don't you? We spend billions on ships and planes and tanks that are essentially useless against stateless guerrillas and terrorists, who are the people we will be in conflict with for generations."

The president abandoned the toys and dropped into his chair. "Jake

Grafton is a damn smart warrior who swings a very sharp sword. I want him on my side."

After I sent off the photos from the weapons factory and called in my report, my life became more focused. Grafton wanted to chat every few hours. Zipped into that portable security telephone booth, I felt like the interior of a frankfurter.

"Tommy," he said, "I hate to have to ask you to do this, but I must. I want the target list of those dozen nuke missiles."

"Why don't you Google it?" I shot back.

"Also, if possible, I want to know the types of missile they are putting the nukes on and their launch locations."

"All I can do is try, boss. But how do we know Ahmadinejad and the mullahs are going to do anything?"

"We don't know."

"Ahmadinejad may simply call a press conference, strut and rant for a while and dare anyone to knock the chip off his shoulder."

"He might," Grafton acknowledged.

"And he might have bigger ideas," I admitted.

"If he *is* going to pull the trigger," Jake Grafton said, "I suspect he will complicate our problem by launching everything they have that will fly. Anything you can tell us that will help us identify the hot birds will help."

"I couldn't get that information even if I could charm Ahmadinejad into marrying me."

"Talk to Rostram's cousin. See if he has any more rabbits in his hat."

"Yo. Rabbits."

"And the sooner the better."

I tried to salute, but there wasn't room in that damn zip-up plastic bag.

I got out of the bag, put the satellite phone away and went in search of Frank Caldwell.

"Hey, Frank, do you still have that motorcycle?"

"Yep," he said smugly. "It's perfect for riding around town. I get over fifty miles to the gallon."

"I need to borrow it."

"Say what?"

"I need a bike that the MOIS hasn't seen before. If anything happens to it, the Company will buy it from you and you can get another."

He eyed me without enthusiasm. Although Frank was a case officer, he rarely if ever got his hands dirty. He still hadn't forgiven me for recommending two tourist visas to the States, either. It was as if he'd caught me cheating at cards. He agreed with ill grace.

"Terrific," I said with comradely warmth. "Let's go take a look at it."

He had it parked behind the annex and locked with a chain through the wheels. The thing was made in Japan and had a 500 cc motor. New five to ten years ago, it was still in reasonable shape. Tires had been replaced recently. Two helmets were locked onto the back of it.

"Great," I said as I looked it over. "Now how about riding it down to the central train station, park it and lock it up, then take a taxi back here and give me the keys?"

He tried to wheedle some information out of me about how I intended to use his ride, but I just shrugged it off. Caldwell didn't need to know.

After he left, I got my spy cell phone from my trouser pocket. I kept it set on vibrate so I would get a cheap thrill when and if Rostram/Davar called. Hoping the Iranian Gestapo hadn't yet glommed onto our numbers, I gave her a ring.

When she answered, I said, "Hey, Hot Lips, I need to see you," then instantly regretted my flippant choice of words. This wasn't a woman you could flirt with. Hell, this wasn't a country you could flirt *in*.

"Tonight, if possible," I added.

"Yes," she said.

"Be in front of the Armenian Church of St. Thaddeus at seven. Do you know it?"

"Near the main bazaar?"

"That's it."

"See you then, lover," she said and hung up.

I have known a few women in my time, and even fallen pretty hard for a couple of them, but this one had me flummoxed. Davar seemed to be ready, willing and able, but that sort of killed the fun, somehow. Then there was the fact that this whole country was going to go straight to hell in about thirteen days, more or less. Bedding my Iranian contact didn't seem smart. Or ethical. Or . . .

Maybe I was overthinking this. "Eat, drink and be merry, for tomorrow we shall die." Who said that? Lions or Christians?

When Frank returned he gave me the keys and told me precisely where he had parked his ride.

"Anyone follow you?" I asked.

A startled look crossed Frank's face. He hadn't thought to check for tails. "No one ever follows me," he said lamely.

"Must be all that clean living," I remarked as I pocketed his keys.

After work, I set off to shake any and all tails. I headed for my hotel, just to see who might be following.

I was getting really antsy. All the political posturing, ranting, slogans and billions of dollars spent on bombs had led to this moment. Expectations had been created and promises made. I felt as if we were all passengers on a runaway train with the Devil in the cab. When the crash came, it was going to be bad. Really bad.

I knew the nukes were going on the missiles and Iran was going to be a nuclear power in two weeks, and if I knew it, the security forces knew it, and would become more and more paranoid, which meant they would be watching us foreign spies with commendable zeal.

Sure enough, I picked up a couple of tails soon after I left the embassy annex. One was walking behind me, and the other was on the other side of the street. A block from the hotel, I unexpectedly threaded my way through traffic to cross the street and go along a sidestreet. This maneuver almost got the man behind me run over; the other guy was on his cell phone, no doubt summoning help. Which meant, to me, that these guys were serious this afternoon. Someone had lit a fire under these people.

I ignored my tails and headed for the central train station, walking briskly.

The day was hot, so I took off my sports coat and carried it over my shoulder. Somehow the women in chadors and manteaus managed to keep from passing out from heatstroke, which amazed me.

The neighborhood around the train station was not the best. A lot of homeless people lived here on the streets, some straight from the village. They came to the capital to find a better job and a better life and lived catch as catch can. I could only hope Frank's motorcycle was where he left it.

I went into the station and found it packed with humanity, as usual. I circled the room once, then ducked out a side door. Sure enough, Frank's bike was chained to a rack with a couple dozen other motorcycles.

Working as quickly as I could, I unlocked it, wrapped the chain around my waist, put on a helmet and my coat, climbed aboard and fired it up. Went zipping off into traffic.

In the mirror I saw one of my tails run up to the rack where the bike had been. He was on his cell phone.

I threaded my way through traffic, detoured to the sidewalk twice and let that bike roll. Unless they were on motorcycles or in a helicopter, no one was going to follow me. Of course, they could alert every cop and paramilitary gun toter in town to look for me, so I needed to stage a disappearance. This proved relatively easy. I rode to a park I knew, kept going right into the place and parked the bike in the shade under a tree, where it couldn't be easily seen from the boulevard. Then I checked the bike for a beacon—there wasn't one—and sat down to wait.

At the appointed time I rode up to the Armenian Church near the main bazaar. Traffic was nearly bumper to bumper, but I made good time weaving through the mess. Davar was standing near the fence, waiting. She was dressed as a woman tonight, wearing a powder-blue ankle-length manteau and a darker blue scarf.

Stopped by the curb, I waved to her. She walked hesitantly over to the bike, looking it over. I handed her a helmet. "C'mon," I urged.

She didn't say a word, just clamped the lid on and seated herself sidesaddle, with both legs on the left side. Her right hand went around my waist.

Satisfied, I popped the clutch and let the bike roll.

When we had cleared the bazaar traffic and were actually riding normally, off the main boulevards, I took her back to my park.

There, with her standing beside the tree I had spent part of the afternoon under, I told her what I wanted.

My assertion that the regime was installing a dozen warheads on missiles stunned her. "My information is that the regime was at least a year, perhaps two, from having operational weapons. That is what I told Azari."

"You were lied to."

"Where did you learn about these warheads?"

"Your cousin Ghasem. Didn't he tell you?"

"No." After a bit, she asked, "So how are you going to get the information you want?"

"I don't know. I need to talk to Ghasem. Perhaps he can help me. Will you set up a meet?"

She nodded, then looked around the park as if seeing it for the first time. "So, they were using me. I passed lies to Azari, and he publicized them in America."

"That's the way it looks," I admitted.

"Does Azari know they were lies?"

"Yes."

She stood there silently watching the dusk creep over us and the lights of the city come on. Finally she said, "Let's go. We've been here long enough."

"Where are we going?" I asked as I climbed on the bike.

"To a party."

"You do parties in Iran?"

"Of course," Davar said and gave a little giggle. I figured she had picked up her giggle in England, but maybe women everywhere did them. I couldn't have been more than four or five years older than she was, yet it felt like a generation.

With her behind me sitting sidesaddle, I piloted us through traffic, which wasn't bad that time of night, following her directions.

I confess, I was curious about her. She was smart, competent and very much a woman.

We wound up in North Tehran in a neighborhood similar to Davar's, definitely upper middle class. She knocked on the door, and a young man opened it. The hallway behind him was dark. Davar murmured to him, then seized my hand and led me along the hallway to a door. When she opened it, I heard music and laughter and saw subdued lights below, in the basement. It was American music, a pop singer wailing in English, although I didn't recognize the tune. Too out of date, I guess. Down the stairs we went, two pilgrims looking to escape the grimness of revolutionary Iran.

We had plenty of company. The basement was packed with young people, all talking at once, loudly, or dancing to the music or smoking foul dark cigarillos. Little red lights made the tobacco haze glow and illuminated the dancers. I stood there in amazement, looking at the women, who were wearing miniskirts, net stockings and high heels. Breasts thrust against tight blouses . . . hair swaying with the music . . . American music, most of it. Pop tunes.

I felt as if I had gone through a portal into the twilight zone. This is *Iran?* Beam me up, Scotty.

Davar appeared at my elbow. The manteau and scarf were gone, her skirt ended a couple of inches above her knees, and she had put on a pair of high heels, which lifted her eyes closer to mine and did something subtly wonderful to her figure. Seeing the look on my face, she laughed.

She led me around and introduced me to some of the attendees. She whispered what they did. Several were university professors, one was a lawyer, one of the women was a doctor, several people were engineers, and three or four were employed by the government doing this and that.

One couple was smoking hash in a corner—I could smell it, and I'm sure Davar could. She pretended she didn't. "Who are they?" I asked.

"The man is a judge," she said and pressed herself against me. "Let's dance."

We did, for almost an hour. Fast, slow, whatever, we gyrated, swayed and tangoed. As I said, the majority of the tunes were American, with a smattering of English and French and a few singers that Davar whispered were Iranian. I wondered if Ahmadinejad had ever heard one of those Iranian chanteuses; maybe he listened every night. When someone put on a hip-hop tune, I led Davar off the floor.

She made a tiny motion with her head, so I followed her up the stairs. The same guy was still in the hallway. The whole scene reminded me of a Prohibition speakeasy. What the party-hearty crowd downstairs was going to do if the Islamic Gestapo arrived with sirens blaring and guns out, if they ever did, was a bit beyond my powers of prediction.

We took another set of stairs upward. She opened a door, inspected a room, then pulled me in. She closed the door, then wrapped her arms around my neck, glued her body to mine and planted her lips on my mouth.

"Whoa," I managed when she came up for air. "Just whoa."

"Come on, big guy," she whispered. "Give me what I want."

"And what is that?"

"Guess."

"Affection, sex, love, respect? This ain't the way to any of those things."

She pulled back far enough to look into my eyes. "How much time do you think we have, Tommy? How much time do you think *I* have?"

Well, she had me there.

I was still supporting her weight, so I carried her over to the bed and deposited her gently. Then I kissed her the way I thought she should be kissed.

When the technicians got the first warhead installed in a missile, a Ghadar-110 ballistic missile with an 1,850-mile range, Habib Sultani informed the president, Mahmoud Ahmadinejad, who of course wanted to go look. The official party went that evening in four vehicles. They were accompanied by armed troops in four more vehicles, just in case. Ghasem rode with his uncle Habib Sultani in the third vehicle. The general in charge of the weapons of mass destruction program, Brigadier General Dr. Seyyed Ali Hosseini-Tash, and his senior aide rode with them.

Hosseini-Tash was feeling mighty good. He had accomplished his goal;

under his direction thousands of technicians and scientists had designed and built a facility to enrich uranium to weapons grade, designed and constructed a trigger and designed and constructed a warhead. It was, he told Sultani and Ghasem, the biggest engineering project in the history of Iran, and he had pulled it off.

Sultani asked about testing a weapon underground, and that sobered Hosseini-Tash. Having the damned things go bang with the oomph they were supposed to have was, after all, the real final hurdle. Until the weapons passed the test, Hosseini-Tash's head was still on the block.

Hosseini-Tash's aide, a bearded, turbaned math freak, began a long, technical explanation about why a test wasn't necessary. He even discussed some of the key calculations as they rode through the darkness of the evening to the missile factory in the Parchin complex under the mountains east of Tehran.

After the troops in the lead vehicle had paused for a brief discussion with the guard officer on duty, all the vehicles were waved on through.

Ghasem watched Ahmadinejad stride away, accompanied by the officer in charge of the missile plant, who had been waiting. Soon they were in the tunnel, which drifted straight back into the mountain. The bombproof doors were closed, and access was by a smaller door, which stood open, in one corner of the larger one. Ghasem knew that the larger door was only opened when large objects needed to be moved into or out of the tunnel, such as a missile on its transporter.

Indeed, there they were, ballistic missiles riding transporters, dozens of them. They were arranged two abreast in the large tunnel, and others were parked in galleries that ran off at right angles. Seeing them here under the lights, within the security of the tunnel, painted and polished and gleaming, with the national flag on their tails, was heady stuff.

The sight seemed to straighten Habib Sultani, Ghasem noticed, and added an inch or two to Ahmadinejad's erect stance. All these advanced weapons, waiting, ready . . .

The second gallery on the left was the one the officer led the party to. Soon they were standing in front of a Ghadar-110 missile with the panels that normally covered the warhead removed, exposing it. With the missile on the transporter, the warhead area was at least twelve feet off the ground, so the official party clambered up on a scaffold. There wasn't room for Ghasem, who stayed on the ground. Consequently he didn't hear much of what was said by the missile expert to Ahmadinejad and Sultani and Hosseini-Tash and the other officials, who had packed the scaffold platform.

Troops were arranged along the walls of the gallery, and they stood loosely with their AK-47s across their chests, watching the official party and looking bored. No doubt they had been trotted into position to impress Ahmadinejad, if he noticed.

Ghasem wondered what Tommy Carmellini would say if he were here, looking at the military might of Iran.

Of course, Ghasem wondered what Ahmadinejad and the other officials of the government intended to do with these nuclear weapons. He had assumed that film crews would be here, filming Ahmadinejad's inspection, but there were none. If Ahmadinejad was going to make a major announcement to the press, there should be film crews, Ghasem thought.

Why have the weapons if the leaders weren't going to announce the reality and demand the respect of the nation's enemies?

Nuclear weapons were worthless unless your enemies knew you had them. Even Israel, which pretended it lacked such weapons, made sure the Arab states were well aware that they lived in a nuclear shadow.

Now Israel lived there, too, as did the American armed forces scattered around the Persian Gulf. And at sea.

The officials on the platform were huddled around Ahmadinejad, who was telling them something. He spoke so low that Ghasem could not hear his words, nor any of the other observers and soldiers near him.

"This afternoon before we began this inspection trip, I spoke to the Supreme Leader," Mahmoud Ahmadinejad said. "The decision has been made. Iran will become a martyr nation. We will strike a blow for Allah that will resound throughout the world, a blow that will win glory for the Iranian nation and a place in Paradise for every Iranian.

"We have it in our power! *Here* are the missiles that we will use to destroy Israel and the concentrations of American forces that surround us. When the believers see our power, they will rally around us, unite and destroy the infidel dogs wherever they can be found."

His listeners stood with mouths agape. They had been expecting some serious saber rattling, but not *this*! Not a nuclear strike against the Great Satan or its ally, Israel. To shake one's fist at a lion is a political statement, but to stick one's head in its mouth goes beyond politics.

In the silence that followed Ahmadinejad's statement, a lone voice said, "If we initiate a nuclear war, the Americans and Israelis will kill us all. They will launch a hundred missiles at us for every one we shoot. Iran will cease to exist. The Islamic Republic will have committed suicide."

Habib Sultani looked to see who had spoken. It was one of the two missile technicians, one wearing a white coat.

He looked Ahmadinejad right in the face and continued, "Jihad is for those who wish to be martyrs. Most Iranians have no wish to die like that. I—"

He got no further. Ahmadinejad cut him off with a roar. "*No more!* The decision has been *made*. You will serve your nation and Allah or we will execute you as a traitor! Do you hear me? You *and* your family will be *shot*. Which will it be? A traitor's hell or a martyr's Paradise?"

General Hosseini-Tash said nothing on the trip back to Tehran, nor did Habib Sultani. The strained silence was almost more than Ghasem could bear, but he kept his mouth shut, as did the math nerd. Ghasem figured he would hear whatever it was that his uncle thought when his uncle felt the time was right.

General Hosseini-Tash and his aide got out of the car at the WMD ministry, and the driver took Sultani to his. The driver stopped in the underground parking area that was used by the most senior officials. Sultani got out, followed by Ghasem. As the car pulled away, Ghasem spoke, only to be motioned into silence by his uncle.

"Later," he said. He went to his car and motioned for Ghasem to climb in, and together they rode up the ramp and out into the streets of Tehran, now emptying for the night.

Sultani drove to a park, locked the car and walked away across the grass with Ghasem following.

"They listen to everything," Sultani explained. "The office, the car, the house—there is almost no place that witch Hazra al-Rashid isn't listening. No place." Then he told Ghasem of Ahmadinejad's statement.

Ghasem stood transfixed, unable to speak as the horror washed over him. Israel and America would transform Iran into a radioactive wasteland. This city, this nation, these people—all would cease to exist. Everyone not killed by the initial blasts, or the fires, would succumb to radiation poisoning. Everyone would die. *Everyone.* So the Supreme Leader and Mahmoud Ahmadinejad and a few chosen mullahs could earn a gold-plated ticket to Paradise.

When he again became aware of his surroundings, Ghasem saw that his uncle Habib was sitting in the dirt with his head in his hands.

———

Once a year the university faculty got together at a formal dinner. Callie Grafton always went, and since he was in town just now, Jake went with her. He dutifully shook hands and tried to remember names and listened politely to whatever anyone had to say. Since he was getting a little deaf, he missed some of it, but he tried to smile at the right times and laugh when everyone else did.

"You could get a hearing aid," Callie whispered, eyeing him askance.

"I can hear you just fine."

"You can not. You are merely getting better at reading lips."

Before Jake could reply to that, Callie spotted her department head and led him in that direction.

After the cocktail hour, everyone went into the dining room—this affair was being held at a hotel—and looked for their names on the round tables, each of which seated ten people.

After the greetings by the president of the university and the dean of the faculty, waiters brought around salads. The waiter who placed a salad in front of Jake muttered, "Admiral Grafton?"

"Yes." Jake glanced up. A young man in his twenties, clean-shaven and trim.

"This is for you," the waiter said and passed him a letter-sized envelope. "I'm to tell you that it's from a Mr. Ilin."

Jake reached for the waiter's arm, detaining him. "Who gave you this?"

"A man this afternoon. I didn't know him. He paid me twenty bucks to deliver this envelope to you. I didn't think you'd mind."

Jake nodded and let the waiter go. He looked at both sides of the envelope: His name was typed on one side; the other side was blank. Made of cheap paper, the envelope was thin, containing no more than one or two sheets of paper, and sealed. He examined the seal. Apparently intact.

Jake stuck the envelope in an inside coat pocket and took a long hard look at the people around his table. All were colleagues of Callie in the language department, or their spouses. No one seemed very interested in him.

When he could stand it no longer, Jake excused himself and went to the men's room. In a stall he opened the envelope. It contained one sheet of paper, which seemed to be a copy of an original. On the top was something in Arabic script. Then twelve pairs of numbers. Obviously latitude and longitude coordinates.

He recognized none of the positions. He put the sheet of paper back in the envelope and replaced the envelope in his coat.

Jake and Callie got home to their flat in Rosslyn about ten thirty. He went straight to the office and pulled out an atlas. He was plotting coordinates when Callie came in.

She watched him for a moment and said, "Was that what was in the envelope?"

"Yes. The waiter said a Mr. Ilin wanted me to have it."

Callie had met Janos Ilin, a Russian high in the SVR, holding a rank equivalent to lieutenant general. He wasn't the type of man one forgets. "Surely he didn't give it to the waiter?" she said distractedly.

"Oh, no. Someone who works for him delivered it and used his name."

"What is it?"

He handed it to her. Although she was a linguist, she couldn't read the script at the top.

"At first glance," he said, "I thought it might be the locations of Iran's nuclear-armed missiles, but it couldn't be. Two of the locations are Tel Aviv; the others are locations of American military bases in Iraq, Qatar and Kuwait. One of the locations is Baghdad International. Then there is this one."

He pointed at the map.

She compared the location of his finger with the numbers on the sheet. "There's some kind of mistake," she said finally. "This couldn't be a target list. That location is right in the heart of Tehran."

"There's no mistake," Jake Grafton muttered.

"The government of Iran is going to launch a missile to wipe out their own capital?" Callie asked skeptically.

"Looks like it," her husband said.

"Oh, that list is something else. It isn't what you think."

Jake Grafton didn't reply.

The room was quiet, and I could hear Davar's heart beating. She had a strong, lazy heart.

"I hate the fundamentalists," she whispered, apropos of nothing.

"When this is over, you gotta get the hell out of this country," I told her. "One way or another."

"There is no way out."

"Remember that guy from Oklahoma." I got out of bed and began dressing. "He's out there somewhere, and he's got a life to offer you. A *life*."

"What about you?"

"I don't have a life for myself, much less a woman. The kid from Oklahoma. He's the one."

"Have you ever been to Oklahoma?"

"Yeah."

"So what's it like?"

"It's flat. Rolls a little here and there, but mainly it's flat. Despite the flatness, good people live there. A person can live any way he or she wishes in Oklahoma, and the law leaves you alone. They've made the leap to toilet paper—you'll like it."

I sat down on the bed. She was lying atop the sheets, her head on the pillow. In the light that came through the window I could just make out her features.

She sat up, reached into her tiny purse for her cigarettes and matches and lit one. After she blew out a cloud of smoke, she said, "After the MOIS beat Grandfather to death, Ghasem became a different person. I always knew they were capable of any crime, but perhaps he didn't. Or if he did, he refused to think about it."

She made a gesture of irritation, got out of bed and began dressing. The cigarette dangled from her lips, and smoke curled up around her head.

"The Supreme Leader says the MOIS and the Qods Force work for him," she said, "and he will ensure they obey God's laws. So they beat an old man to death, a scholar and philosopher who did no one any harm."

She pulled on her skirt, worked it around her hips into position and fumbled with the top button. Ash from her cigarette fell to the carpet, and she ignored it. I couldn't help noticing that she had a really nice set of legs. Actually, everything was very nice. Trim, taut, athletic . . . perfect.

"There is a serious problem with people who think they are doing God's work," she said bitterly. "Once moral ambiguity is eliminated, every human equation evaluates to infinity. Without moral ambiguity, people become capable of anything—any arrogance, any conceit, any gross stupidity."

Still naked from the waist up, she took a drag on the cigarette and blew smoke around while she eyed me. "Any crime, any atrocity. Mass murder? Nuclear war? Believe me, our holy men are perfectly capable of pulling the trigger."

CHAPTER EIGHTEEN

Georgetown had several dozen funky restaurants, and Professor Azari liked most of them. Small and intimate, they had an ambience he found pleasant; the staff always had a smile and kind word, and if he ordered carefully, the food was usually excellent. A man could ask for no more.

Today he sat outdoors in a small courtyard at a table in the shade of a tree. This was, he supposed, one of his favorite restaurants, and he amused himself by tabulating the ones he liked the best. He ordered a salad with a flavor he thought would be unique. The waitress, who had served him for years, had prevailed upon him to try it, so he had thrown caution to the winds and said yes.

With the salad he ordered a dry white wine. He marveled at the exquisite taste of it and took the tiniest sips he could, to make it last.

When a man he knew came in and sat across the room, Azari ignored him. He finished the wine before the salad and gave in to temptation—he ordered another glass. The salad, when it came, was indeed superb.

He had finished his meal and paid the bill and was sipping a cup of coffee when the man he knew rose from the table where he had lunched and departed. Azari rose, too, smiled at the waitress and made his way out.

The man was walking up the street. Azari followed him, half a block behind. After two blocks, the man paused to read a historical sign on a building—one of many such signs in Georgetown—and Azari caught up with him. He, too, paused in front of the sign.

"The CIA has bought it. Iran is at least a year away from operational nuclear weapons," Azari said. "The man who talks to me is named Grafton.

THE DISCIPLE — 207

He says various people high in the government still refuse to believe there is a weapons program. However, the government is trying to formulate a policy, in the event the CIA is right."

"Who in the government?"

"He did not say. 'Highly placed people' was the phrase he used."

"Very well," the man said. He turned and walked away.

Azari turned toward the university, which was five blocks away in another direction. A block from the university a man sitting in a car rolled down the window and motioned to him. He got into the passenger seat.

"You did well," Jake Grafton told him.

"You got it, then?"

Grafton nodded.

"How did you know he would want to talk to me?"

"Just a hunch."

"How do you know he didn't follow me toward the university, to see if I talked to anyone?"

Grafton picked up a walkie-talkie from the seat beside him. "We're keeping an eye on him. You're clean."

"You people are watching me day and night," Azari said accusingly.

Jake Grafton's voice hardened. "This isn't a gentleman's game we're playing, Professor. Lives are on the line, including yours. Keep that fact firmly in mind."

Grafton eyed Azari, then continued. "Better be on your way. Wouldn't want you late for class."

The professor got out of the vehicle, closed the door firmly to ensure it latched, then walked on toward the main entrance of the university. He didn't look behind him.

I was unlocking the bike in front of the party house when Davar's cell phone rang. She listened a moment, glanced at me and muttered something into the instrument that I didn't catch.

She turned off the phone and said, "Ghasem wants to talk to you. I suggested that we meet him at the metro station at Azadi Square."

"Okay."

Was the MOIS listening to these cell conversations? Were they watching any of us? Were they incompetent, or were they giving us enough rope to hang ourselves? I wondered how much more time we had.

I rode along thinking about a wall and a blindfold and a firing squad. Of course, this far east of Europe firing squads were probably obsolete; in these climes some holy warrior would merely put a pistol against your skull and pull the trigger.

Perhaps I should cut and run right now.

I was mulling the possibilities when I realized Davar was talking about the people at the party as she rode along behind me. She was speaking loudly, so I would hear. One of the lawyers, a woman, was a women's rights activist and a political force to be reckoned with. She had been arrested several times for political reasons and had led a campaign to prevent the legislature from passing a proposal that would have allowed a husband to take a second wife without the permission of the first wife.

On she chattered, detailing the careers, prospects and political aspirations of many of the prominent young people of Tehran, most of whom she knew, and all of whom she admired.

"Iran is not a nation of religious fanatics out to murder anyone who doesn't believe as they do. Iran is a nation of young people, seventy percent of whom are under thirty-five years of age, trying to find their place in the world and make a contribution. Someday we will defeat the fundamentalists. Then this nation will bloom and take its rightful place in the world."

I had no answer to that. It looked to me as if the God Squad had a pretty firm grip on things around here. They were arresting people for political protests and convicting them of treason, executing women by hanging and stoning . . . All in all, the place looked like I imagined Nazi Germany looked in the 1930s, complete with goon squads and Gestapo. They even had a dictator with a direct telephone line to God. All they needed to do to make Iran perfect was to declare war on the rest of the human race, and it looked to me as if Ahmadinejad just might do it.

I didn't say any of this to Davar, of course. I didn't have the heart.

In the Pentagon the plans for conventional strikes on Iran's nuclear facilities were coming together slowly. There were a lot of problems, as Jake Grafton expected. The reactors were easy to hit, but the uranium processing facilities, the bomb factory and the missile factories were all underground. Many of the key facilities were under Tehran. The distances involved meant that all the strike planes, including navy planes launched from aircraft carriers, would have to be refueled, some of them twice, a few three times. Tanker assets would have to come from all over the world.

And since it was assumed that Iran would be launching cruise missiles, some of them armed with nuclear warheads, a lot of fighters would need to be in the air to shoot them down and protect the strike birds from Iranian fighters.

Ballistic missiles that flew up and out of the atmosphere, then reentered on a steep dive to their targets, were an entirely different problem. Fighter aircraft lacked the weapons to knock them down.

The officer in charge of the planning was an air force major general, Stewart Heth, and he had officers from all the American armed forces to help him. He had the targets laid out on one wall chart, aircraft required on another and weapons on a third chart. A fourth chart showed assets, where they were located and the missions they would be assigned to. Staff officers were busy measuring distances and calculating times. Others were examining satellite reconnaissance photos and computing GPS coordinates.

Today Jake Grafton found General Heth huddled with two army Special Forces officers, one a general and the other a colonel. Heth looked up at Jake when he saw him and motioned him to join them.

"We have problems," Heth said after he had introduced Jake to the army officers. "There is no way we can crack some of these bunkers. We're going to have to put boots on the ground and blow the bunkers from the inside. All the centrifuges, the laser separation facility, the heavy water plant, all of that stuff is at least a hundred and sixty-five feet under bedrock."

"Opposition?" Jake murmured as he looked at the chart on the table in front of them, a chart with the locations annotated.

"Lots of it, and if they are going to launch nukes, the guard troops will be on full alert. The only way we have a chance is to target the troops on guard, blow them to holy hell and put the Spec Forces guys right into the smoking craters before they have time to regroup. And they will regroup. Here around Tehran are several armored divisions and a couple of infantry divisions. These guys aren't the Wermacht, but there are so many they'll be tough to handle."

"If their leadership is even halfway competent," the Special Forces general agreed. "To be brutally honest, I don't know if we can do it with paratroops or Special Forces. We may need armored columns punching in from Iraq. Battles are won with firepower."

"Casualties?"

"I would expect to lose at least half my troops," said the Spec Forces general. "Maybe more. The real problem is that our guys will have limited firepower, and once they go through what they have, it's going to get really exciting. Air support will have to come from a thousand miles away, and I don't care what anybody says, that's too far."

"Extraction?"

"We were discussing that. After the teams do their mission, they would have to egress to an airport where we can actually pick them up. And flying transports in will be a whole other problem."

Jake spent a few more minutes with them, then left to go look at the large map of Iran posted on the wall. Iran was a damn big place, about three times the size of France. Over a hundred million people lived there. A lot of it was inhospitable deserts and mountains, much like Arizona, so most of the people were crammed into urban centers where they tried to earn a living.

In 1980 the military had tried to rescue American hostages held in the U.S. embassy in Tehran. They had flown helicopters north through the desert; the mission failed when one of the helos crashed trying to land in a cloud of dust and dirt. Iran was huge and inhospitable, yet the American military had learned a lot about desert operations since 1980.

Jake was standing there scrutinizing the map when he felt someone at his elbow. He turned. Sal Molina.

"I saw that list you sent over this morning. 'Jihad missiles,' no less. You didn't make that crap up, did you?"

"Food for thought, eh?"

"Come clean. Where'd you get that list?"

"It happened just as I set it out in the cover memo."

Molina stood looking around at the charts and maps. "Israel," he murmured, "Baghdad, Doha, Kuwait, and—this is the part that I find unbelievable—Tehran." He was silent for a moment. "So what do you think?" he asked finally.

Grafton took a deep breath. "We really have two problems here. One is the ballistic and cruise missiles that get launched. The other is the people who ordered them launched."

Sal thought a little bit about that. "Okay," he finally said.

"Some of the missiles are going to get into the air unless we do a first strike, which your boss ruled out. We need a layered defense, a defense in depth, to try to knock down as many of those missiles as possible before they reach their targets."

"I'm with you."

"We won't get them all."

Sal Molina didn't respond.

Grafton continued. "Uranium enrichment, bomb and missile factories aren't a threat in and of themselves. It's the people who build bombs that are the problem. Taking out those facilities will require an invasion of Iran. I doubt that the president will approve it, even if the Iranians wipe Israel off the face of the earth."

"Go on."

"What we need to do," the admiral said, "is cut off the head of the dragon."

"A *coup d'état?*"

"Something like that, yes."

"America has tried those before, once in Iran, I believe. They don't work very well."

"You'll like the idea a lot better after you talk to General Heth."

"Can it be done?"

"I think so," Jake Grafton said and tapped his finger on the map, way up near the top, on Tehran. "Iran has a vibrant young population and a political opposition that the regime has tried to sit on. All they need is a chance."

I spotted Ghasem in front of the metro station. He seemed to be alone, a twenty-something guy, obviously middle class, with a short beard and trimmed hair.

We rode past him once, looking for the tails. There were plenty of people around at that time of night, yet all seemed to be going somewhere. No one was standing around, watching other people or pretending to read a newspaper or book.

I assumed that if Ghasem thought he was being watched, he wouldn't stand there like a store dummy waiting for us.

I stopped in front of him on our next circuit of the block, and Davar got off the back of the bike. "I can get home from here," she said as she pulled off her helmet. Ghasem stared at his cousin; apparently he had never seen her on a motorcycle or wearing a helmet. Davar helped Ghasem don the helmet and fasten the strap under his chin. As he climbed on the bike, she smiled at me.

I winked at her, then eased the clutch out. I figured the park was as good a place as any, so I rode in that direction.

There weren't many people there, which was fine with me. I parked the bike and killed the engine. We both dismounted and took off the helmets.

Ghasem looked tired and under a lot of stress. Well, hell, welcome to the wonderful world of treason.

"What is this all about?" I asked.

His Adam's apple bobbed up and down several times before he spoke. "Today," he said, "Ahmadinejad told the top ministers that when the warheads are installed, he wants to launch the missiles at his enemies. Iran will become a martyr nation."

He didn't look like he was pulling my leg, but still, what if this was just a ploy to goad America and its friends into attacking Iran?

"A martyr nation," I said slowly. "What does that mean to you?"

"That the Supreme Leader and the mullahs will launch a nuclear strike, and Iran will die under massive retaliation. What else could it mean?"

I told him I didn't know.

After a moment he continued, a man talking aloud to himself. "The other possibility is that they will use the twelve warheads on us, the Iranians, detonate them over Tehran, Shiraz, Isfahan . . . all the cities—then blame the Americans or Jews." He took a deep breath, then exhaled explosively. "They are capable of that, I think. As long as they thought the will of Allah was being done . . ."

I didn't try to figure it out. What I needed to do was get this information to Jake Grafton. I fingered the cell phone in my pocket. Unencrypted, but it was doubtful if the Iranians were listening. They might be, but I didn't think so.

Then there was the encrypted satellite phone at the embassy. All we had to do was get there and sneak Ghasem in without the usual government watchers getting a gander at his face. Of course, I could go alone, but that meant leaving Ghasem somewhere, and no doubt there were a million questions I should ask. I just hadn't thought of them yet.

Eenie meenie minie moe . . . I pulled the cell phone from my pocket and dialed the number for Jake Grafton.

He answered on the fourth ring. "Yes, Tommy."

After I repeated what Ghasem had said, I handed the telephone to him. The Iranian went through it in greater detail, then listened a while to Grafton.

Finally he handed the telephone back to me. "They will undoubtedly install the warheads on missiles spread around the country," Grafton said. "We need the location of those missiles, Tommy. That's your job."

I muttered a good-bye, snapped the phone shut and smiled at Ghasem. He was my ticket.

————

When Jake Grafton came home from work, he handed a bundle to Callie.

"What is this?" she asked, weighing it in her hands.

"A manuscript. A man in Tehran gave it to Tommy Carmellini, who sent it to me via the diplomatic mail."

She carefully unwrapped the manuscript and stared at Israr Murad's handwriting on the first page. "I can't read this," she said.

"I was hoping you might take it to the university's language department, see if anyone there can read it. Have them translate a few pages, give me some idea of what's in it."

Callie nodded. "I can do that." She loosened the string holding the manuscript together and reverentially turned the loose pages. The fine, cramped script ran on and on. *The miracle of the human mind*, she thought, for she had always been in love with words and language and books. It wasn't really the words she loved, she thought now, but the ideas that they captured and held tightly, until another human found and read them. This passing of ideas across the abysses of time and distance was the miracle, she knew, the greatest triumph of the mind of man in the history of the earth.

His triumph or his curse.

What, she wondered, could be in this manuscript? Love, hate, or dry, unemotional facts?

"Tommy thought this book important?" she said now, absently, as she rubbed her fingertips across the page, caressing it.

"Yes," her husband murmured, unwilling to say more.

Habib Sultani was torn between two loyalties. He was an Iranian through and through, a patriot who loved his country and its people, and he was a Muslim who believed in Allah and Paradise and obeying the teachings of the Prophet, may he rest in peace. Still, he knew the power of the infidels. Israel, America and Great Britain were nuclear powers and perfectly capable of meeting fire with fire. Then there was Russia, the wolf to the north, which professed friendship, yet would swallow Iran whole if Putin thought he saw an opportunity.

Sultani thought Ahmadinejad was on a course that would destroy the nation, sacrifice it on the altar of jihad. He spent a long twenty-four hours meditating upon it and gave voice to his fears the following day when he saw Ahmadinejad. It was before a large meeting was to begin. The Supreme Leader, Ayatollah Ali Khamenei, was also there. By reputation, Khamenei was a shallow lightweight who represented the clergy, the mullahs, and fiercely defended their privileges.

"The decision has been made by the Supreme Leader," Ahmadinejad said to Sultani, frowning as he did so, "and there is nothing we can do about it. Our legal duty and religious duty are clear. We must all obey." Then he brushed on by Sultani.

The minister of defense looked around the room, which contained the senior military commanders and the heads of the MOIS, the Islamic Republican Guard, and the Qods Force. He also saw Hazra al-Rashid in the back of the room, wearing her black chador, the uniform of female government employees.

The people Sultani didn't see were civilian politicians, senior members of Parliament or the civilian ministers of the government.

Ahmadinejad got the meeting under way. It quickly became clear that President Ahmadinejad and Ayatollah Khamenei were taking the nation in the direction they wanted it to go, and there were to be no arguments or foot-dragging.

General Hosseini-Tash was the man of the hour. He reported how the nuclear warheads were even now being transported to selected missile sites for installation, which would be completed in twelve days, by the end of the month. The technicians were on site, and they had the tools they needed; Hosseini-Tash swore that the job would be done and the nuclear missiles ready to launch at the designated hour.

All the missiles would be ready, the general in charge of the missile force reported. A massive effort had been made. All the transporters and missiles had been checked once again. Approximately 90 percent were operational, which the general thought quite good, and trained crews manned every one. He glared at his audience, inviting someone to make a disparaging comment, but no one did. After all, the nation had over a thousand missiles. Nine hundred operational missiles should be enough to accomplish any military mission.

When Sultani nodded at them, the heads of the army and the Islamic Revolutionary Guards stood and reported that they were ready to do battle with any foreign invaders. The general in charge of the air force announced he was ready to launch his fighters to intercept and shoot down any intruders.

What no one discussed, Sultani thought wryly, was the chances of all these troops and Revolutionary Guards and air force ground crews surviving if America or Israel retaliated with nuclear weapons. He courageously decided to make that point, and stood.

Ahmadinejad recognized him. "Supreme Leader, Mr. President," Habib Sultani began. "Our soldiers and airmen and revolutionary guards have no shelters or protective clothing in the event our enemies launch nuclear missiles at us in a counterstrike. Our civilian population will also be defenseless. It is quite conceivable that within twenty-four hours of launching our missiles, ninety percent of our population will be dead. That is over *ninety million people*, men, women, the elderly, children—all dead of the initial blasts or massive doses of radioactivity. We do not even have public showers so that survivors can wash the radioactive dust and dirt from their clothes. We don't have masks to distribute so that people will not breathe lethal dust into their lungs. We do not have—"

"*Enough!*" Ahmadinejad roared. "If the infidels murder innocent people Allah will take them to Paradise. All of them, each and every one. The blood of martyrs is holy, glorious beyond description, and will unite believers worldwide in a jihad that will wipe the nonbelievers and their filth from the face of the earth. The final triumph of the Prophet is at hand, if only we have the courage to seize the moment."

Ahmadinejad went on, shouting and gesturing and demanding that everyone do his duty and stand upright before Allah.

Habib Sultani sank into his seat.

Hazra al-Rashid met him at the door when the meeting broke up. She escorted him to a small room off the conference room and was sitting there with him, silently, when Ahmadinejad came in.

"General Sultani," the president began, his tone much different than it had been when Sultani had spoken at the meeting. "I understand your concerns. Yet the decision to proceed had been made at the very highest level, by the Supreme Leader. Each of us must do our duty. I come to you, a loyal Iranian, and ask you to put aside any private reservations and do your duty with all your heart and soul."

So I am not to be immediately shot, Sultani thought. *I have earned a reprieve. No doubt a brief one.*

"I am a loyal Iranian soldier," he said.

"Which is precisely why I am speaking to you," Ahmadinejad said, using all his charisma and charm. "In a war there are always casualties. Those we must accept as we do our best to prevail upon Iran's—and God's—enemies. With nuclear weapons we can and must strike them a blow from which the Zionists and the Great Satan will never recover. We must light the fire of holy war in the heart of every believer. If we can achieve *that*—and the

Supreme Leader and I believe it is within our grasp—we will set the people of the world on the path that leads to Allah's kingdom on earth. That was the task the Prophet set before us. That is the highest and best use of our lives."

"I understand," Sultani said.

"Good. We need your help. The forces of Satan are well armed and aggressive. They will do their best to serve the Devil by defeating us." He paused, then placed his face inches from Sultani, uncomfortably close. "We have successfully fooled them so far. It has been a great deception, and our triumph will soon be plain. But that was merely one battle. Allah requires us to try to win the war for the souls of all mankind. That is our duty. And Allah will reward each and every one of us who does his duty."

Ahmadinejad drew back, scrutinized Sultani's face. Seemingly satisfied, he turned and left the room. Hazra al-Rashid followed him, leaving Sultani alone with his thoughts and his conscience.

CHAPTER NINETEEN

The Pentagon briefer, an air force major who wore an impeccably tailored uniform, pointed at the screen with a small penlight that emitted a red light. "Ladies and gentlemen, we are here today to do a preplanning brief. We will try to outline the military problem as we, the staff of the Joint Chiefs, believe it to be."

No one had any comments, so the major continued smoothly, "We have identified twenty-five missile sites using satellite imagery. They are all located near a small population center, all have a military presence—ranging from a little to a lot—and all are underground, in what appear to be drift tunnels bored into cliffs." Using the penlight, he pointed them out. "They are spread out over an eleven-hundred-mile arc that runs along the western and southern sides of Iran. These locations were obviously chosen for geological reasons, but siting them too deep into Iran would have given the enemy too much warning when the missiles were launched. Conversely, placing the sites too near the frontier would have made them easier to attack with air strikes or commandos."

On the image projected on the screen, each site was depicted with a letter of the alphabet, starting with *A*.

"If you look closely," the major continued, "you will see a ballistic missile sitting on its tractor-trailer launcher outside Tunnel Hotel." The red light rested momentarily on the missile. "Each tunnel contains missiles, anywhere from one to fifty or more, and we believe all are on launchers. When the order comes to shoot them, the transporters are simply run out of the tunnel into the desert, a hydraulic ramp on each lifts the missile into a launching position, and when the systems are running and checked out, it is fired. It's the old Soviet system, simple, reliable and—for a strategic offensive weapon—reasonably fast. Ballistic missiles will be launched from a vertical position, the cruise missiles from approximately thirty degrees of elevation. We estimate that a missile could be pulled from the tunnel and launched within twenty minutes."

Jake Grafton looked around at the other thirty or so people listening to the brief. In the front row, beside General Heth, sat the president and Sal Molina. Arranged down the row and onto the next one were flag officers, including the entire Joint Chiefs and the heads of some major commands, including the U.S. Central Command, into whose jurisdiction Iran fell.

The briefer motored on, discussing missile guidance systems. The old Soviet missiles used gyro-based guidance systems, and the limiting factor on the speed with which the missile could be launched was the time required for the gyro to spin up to operating speed and be properly aligned. Gyros were wildly inaccurate—some of the Scud missiles fired from Iraq during the 1991 Gulf War had missed Israel. Iranian missiles were thought to have updated guidance systems, perhaps an inertial nav system or even GPS, the global positioning system, either of which would dramatically improve their accuracy.

"The military problem is quite simple," the briefer said. "For political reasons we must wait until at least one missile is in the air, and then react as best we can. Since we don't know the Iranian launch schedule, one assumes that they will get more than one missile in the air before we manage to destroy the ones still on the ground."

"There will be a lot more than one missile in the air," General Heth said heavily. He spoke directly to the briefer. "Tell these folks how we think they are going to do it."

"The limitation on the Iranians' ability to launch a cloud of missiles has always been the number of trained technicians they have," the briefer explained. "We believe it takes about eight men to fire one missile. If each site has five eight-man crews, that is a thousand trained technicians. That many, we believe, is about the practical limit. Analysis of the living quarters around these sites supports that.

"Our best guess is that they will roll out five missiles, each with its own crew, and fire all five. Then the technicians will go back into the tunnel and bring out five more. That implies a maximum launch rate of about two hundred fifty missiles per hour."

There was more, a lot more, in the general overview, which didn't go into details. Fifteen minutes into the briefing, the president asked to see a certain map again, one that had been displayed early in the brief. In a moment it filled the giant screen behind the briefer.

On this map were displayed the targets the CIA believed the Iranians wished to hit, almost fifty targets. The twenty-five suspected launch sites were depicted. Connecting the launch sites and possible targets were hundreds of black lines, lines generated by a computer based on probabilities, such as range of missile, terrain, flight time, defensive reaction time and a half-dozen other factors. No one suggested the map was accurate: It was merely a prediction.

"The whole purpose of their attack," said William Wilkins, the CIA director, "*if* they attack, is to fire up Muslims worldwide and put Iran in the driver's seat for World War III. They have to sell their story worldwide, and they don't want doubts."

"This may sound ridiculous," the president replied, "but we don't want to wind up on the short end of the political stick either. If only a few cruise missiles squirt out of Iran and we whack them hard, believe me, the Iranians and Al Jazeera will say we attacked first, and the Iranians launched a few in self-defense."

General Heth weighed in. "Mr. President, if everything goes perfectly, and in war it never does, there is no way we can smack all those missile sites before the second salvo. We took a hard look at the Special Forces option, which was inserting Green Berets near enough to the launch sites that they could launch antitank weapons at the tunnel entrances and effectively shut them down. Unfortunately, every one of those sites is guarded. We think there are perhaps five sites where we can insert teams that have a reasonable chance of surviving until missile launch. Five! Believe me, a cloud of missiles is going to come out of Iran." General Heth gestured at the map on the wall.

The president stared at the map, which was certainly an impressive piece of work. General Heth filled the silence. "We can't keep forty planes airborne over Iran until Ahmadinejad gives the launch order. Our forces must be outside Iranian airspace. A lot of them will be on the ground when the first missile is rolled out, which creates another problem. If we launch then, on first rollout, the Iranians may not shoot, and our birds will run out of fuel and have to be landed. Then they'll do it."

Sal Molina muttered to the president, "This is what has the Israelis in a tizzy. We must shoot down the missiles in the air."

The chairman of the Joint Chiefs spoke up. "One nuke detonating anywhere in the Middle East, such as over an airbase in Saudi Arabia, will change the world as we know it. I want everyone in this room to understand: If one single nuclear weapon detonates over Israel, Iraq, Kuwait, Qatar, Dubai, Saudi Arabia, our task forces in the Arabian Sea—anywhere—life on this planet will never be the same. We are playing a game for all the marbles, with the collective lives of our nation and our allies all on the line. And the lives of millions of human beings."

In the silence that followed, someone said, "I don't believe there is a chance in a million that they will launch a nuclear weapon. No sane man would initiate nuclear war."

The president didn't bother to reply to that. He motioned for General Heth to continue the briefing. Everyone else thought this was a "What if" exercise, but the president didn't. He had received a Top Secret memo this morning relating the facts of Tommy Carmellini's telephone call.

Of course, Jake reflected, maybe the president didn't believe Ghasem's warning. Jake didn't even know if he believed it himself. No doubt the National Security Council would have a fiery debate later today on the value of the intelligence. The experts would debate the credibility of the message, the history of the source, the lack of confirmation from other sources—in short, all of the factors one had to consider when weighing intel.

Intelligence came from many sources. Some people believed that a trained ear could discern which bits of noise were true and which weren't. Unfortunately, we humans tend to give more weight to information we expect to hear than news that we don't. Yet even if Ghasem's message was labeled a lie, an Iranian attack on Israel and American assets within range of its missiles was a serious possibility.

"What we are going to have to do," General Heth said, "is try to cut down the number of missiles that get launched. It will take hours for them to launch everything in their inventory. While they are hard at it, there are some things we can do." The briefer then took over, referring to the map with a red dot pointer.

Ten minutes later, when the briefing broke up, Sal Molina stood and motioned to Jake Grafton. He waited in the back of the room until Molina came over.

"The president wants to hear your plan for slaying the dragon," Molina said. "As you predicted, the president isn't going to approve invading Iran for any reason under the sun. The army and air force say they can't destroy those deep bunkers without adequate forces on the ground. They are talking armored brigades that can be heavily reinforced, and that ain't gonna happen."

After the crowd filed out, there were only a half-dozen people in the large briefing room. The president sat in the same chair he had occupied for two hours, seemingly quite comfortable. Near him sat the National Security Adviser, Jurgen Schulz, William Wilkins, General Heth, and the chairman of the Joint Chiefs. Sal Molina dropped into a chair on the end. Jake Grafton started to sit down beside him, but the president motioned him up. "I saw the memo that Wilkins sent to the White House this morning, and the copy of the document that was attached. Will you explain to these gentlemen what was in it?"

Every eye in the place went to Grafton's face. "We just acquired a list we believe to be the target list for Iran's nuclear missiles," he said. "A dozen locations are on it. One of them is Tehran."

"They are going to nuke their own capital?" the chairman asked, his face expressing his doubt.

"Yes, sir," Jake replied.

Schulz turned to Wilkins. "Where'd this hot tip come from? How reliable is it?"

"I'm not going to share any of that," the director of the CIA said frankly. "Grafton received it, and we discussed it thoroughly. We think this information is genuine, and we are not going to open that assessment to debate. I said precisely that in the memo to the president that he just mentioned."

In the silence that followed that remark, the president motioned for Jake Grafton to continue. "President Ahmadinejad wants to lead a holy war against Western civilization," the admiral said. "He recently remarked to his chief lieutenants that Iran must be a martyr nation. That implies, to me, that he is willing to sacrifice tens of millions of Iranian lives to smite his enemies. Still, being a victim isn't going to get him where he wants to go. Victimhood didn't do it for Saddam Hussein, and it won't do it for Mahmoud Ahmadinejad. He must position himself as a leader who went forth boldly on a jihad to slay Israel and America, the Great Satan. Then the millions of dead Iranians will be seen as casualties in a holy war—martyrs—and Ahmadinejad will be the leader to rally around."

"But he isn't going to wait for us to retaliate and nuke Tehran?" Schulz said.

"No," Jake Grafton said. "He obviously believes that if you want something done, you'll get better results if you do it yourself."

"After all," the president interjected, "just because we said we'd retaliate to a nuclear attack on our allies doesn't mean we'd really do it. I can see Ahmadinejad musing on this and asking himself, Why take the chance? Jake, give us the target list."

Grafton used his pointer. "Two ballistic missiles are targeted at Tel Aviv. If they aren't shot down, they will hit in Israel, Palestine, Jordan, Syria, Lebanon or Egypt. We are talking air bursts of one or two hundred kilotons.

"Moving right along, Baghdad International is on the list, as well as Balad, Mosul, Al Asad, and Tallil airbases in Iraq. In Kuwait, they have targeted Al

Jaber Air Base, Camp Arifjan and Kuwait International Airport. In Qatar, it's Al Udeid Air Base. And, saving the best for last, Tehran."

"Admiral Grafton," the chairman said, "Ahmadinejad must assume he will survive a nuclear exchange."

"Oh, yes, sir. He plans on being very much alive when the fallout settles or blows away." Jake aimed a red laser pointer at the satellite photo of Tehran hanging on the wall at the side of the room. "He's going to ride it out with his chosen lieutenants here, inside a bunker two hundred feet underground."

The president rose from his chair and shook out his trouser legs. "General Heth, I appreciate all the work that went into the plans that were briefed this morning. Much of that can be used. However, we are not going to invade Iran. If that means their hardened nuclear sites remain intact, so be it. We are going to shoot down any missiles that they launch—and unfortunately we are going to have to let them launch some, to prove to the world that they struck first—and then we are going to decapitate the Iranian government. That's it. That's all we are going to do."

He looked from face to face.

"I am putting Admiral Grafton in charge of the entire effort. I want everyone in and out of uniform to report to him. He will brief me on the plan. If it becomes necessary to alter it for political reasons I will order him to do so, and we'll go from there. Any questions?"

"Political reasons?" the chairman murmured.

"The Israelis are demanding a first strike—I'm trying to talk them out of it," the president said. "I can plead and beg and twist arms, but with the Israelis, there is a very real limit. The life of every Israeli is on the line. I spent an hour last night with the Israeli ambassador. He asked me what I'd do if the missiles were in Havana and were going to be launched at America."

No one else had any other comments. The president walked out, with Sal Molina trailing him.

Jurgen Schulz studied Grafton's face. "Did you know that was coming?"

"No. And I didn't ask for it." Grafton rubbed his forehead and eyes, then said, "Well, gentlemen, we've been told what to do. Let's figure out how we're going to do it."

I was going to work every morning, trying to pretend that I didn't know jack about the Iranian mullahs' plans to declare war on civilization in order to rid the world of unbelievers. I knew things were winding up to the breaking point here in Tehran—I could feel it in the air—and I was stuck in the middle. So were Davar and Ghasem and the folks at the Swiss embassy, not to mention all the other spies and tourists and naive Iranians who lived in this third-world hellhole.

The prospect of being caught in the middle of a nuclear war has a remarkable cleansing effect on the mind. Survival bubbles right to the top as your number one priority; everything else fades into insignificance. You stop worrying about your waistline, your job and how your IRA is doing.

I would have been hunting for a hole to hide in with all the fervor of a rat running from a rabid cat had it not been for Jake Grafton. "Give me the locations of the nuke missiles," he said. Being a flesh-and-blood human, I was tempted to blow him off, tell him that I would send him a postcard from Rome or Buenos Aires, Cape Town or Timbuktu.

Of course, my only possible source of information that hot was Ghasem Murad, who was spending his days at the Defense Ministry. He said he'd help, of course, but he wasn't around. I thought about trying to put some pressure on his cousin Davar, but all she wanted to do was curl up in a quiet place with me.

Ol' Ghasem knew what I wanted, and he knew the stakes—literally, the survival of the Iranian people—so I was waiting for him to call, which on a good day is one of my least favorite things to do, and on bad days is torture. If I ever get the job of running hell, I'll put a telephone in every cell and tell the inhabitants that they can leave when it rings. But it would never ring. Ever.

I was musing along these lines one morning as I opened the diplomatic mail, and there it was—a tourist visa for one Abdullaziz Nasr Qomi. I dug through the envelope . . . and found another, one for Mostafa Abtahi.

So Jake Grafton came through. Good on 'im.

What if, before they left for America, Ahmadinejad shot off his missiles and Israel or America retaliated? These two guys who never had a chance would be cremated alive or have their hides burned off or be poisoned by radiation. All because they were still here, still trapped in this fascist shithole.

I put the visas in my pocket, locked everything up and headed for the stairs. I had both their addresses, so why not deliver the visas?

I went after Qomi first. The map I had in the government sedan suggested that the street he lived on might be in a workingman's slum on the southwest corner of town. Only one way to find out. I got the car in motion and threaded it into traffic.

I drove along for a while before I remembered the MOIS. What if they were following along? Well, they had seen Qomi enter the embassy, so . . .

On the other hand, maybe they didn't know why he went there. Maybe if they found out that he had actually scored a tourist visa, they would take his passport and visa away from him, send some suicidal jihadist to America in his place. That possibility was, I reflected, probably one reason State was in no hurry to give these damn tourist visas out to sheet-heads. Thank you, bin Laden.

I pulled over when traffic allowed and checked the radio frequency band for beacons. Apparently, no.

I had to park the car on the edge of what I hoped was the right neighborhood and go walking. The streets narrowed and the pavement ended. The houses were huts, jammed together. Most of them lacked electricity.

I found Qomi's place, finally, after talking to four people. Needless to say, he wasn't there. I settled down to wait. And wait. And wait.

If I hadn't been so fixated on nuclear war, on what this neighborhood was going to look like in ashes, maybe I would have given up, written him a note or something. But I didn't.

It was in the hour before dusk that he appeared, walking slowly on his crutch. He was dirty, and his clothes were, too. He had obviously spent the day at manual labor.

He saw me and paused. Stood staring. Finally started my way, walking as fast as he could.

"Meester Carmala," he said. "Meester Carmala."

"I have your visa," I told him in Farsi. "When can you leave?"

"You have it?"

I pulled it from my pocket and showed it to him. It was in English and Farsi, so he could read some of it, anyway. He bent down, afraid to touch. When he stood up, he was beaming. A smile split his face almost in half.

"When can you leave?"

A variety of emotions played across his face. He jerked his head, then led the way into his hut. One rude bed, a wooden-frame chair, a teapot, a little chemical heater and some clothes carefully folded on a small table. That was it. The toilet facilities, such as they were, were out back.

I took charge. "Your passport."

He produced it from a pocket of his trousers. No use leaving that around for someone to steal.

I opened it, examined the photo. Yep, it was him, all right. I shoved the clothes out of the way and used the table, peeled the protective paper off the visa and glued it to a page in his passport.

Luggage? I looked around. There was nothing.

"A bag. Luggage. Something for your clothes?"

Qomi slowly lowered himself onto the bed. He bit his lip and shook his head.

"You have money for an airline ticket, don't you?"

He shook his head, once.

I waved the passport at him. "You were going to sell this?"

He refused to look at me. Lowered his gaze to his hands.

I stood there feeling like a fool. All day I had been waiting, walking the neighborhood, looking at abject poverty in the fourth richest oil-producing nation on the planet. No fucking trickle-down around here, by God. The mullahs were latching on to every single petrodollar and squandering it on reactors and missiles and warheads.

"Well, you're going," I said to Qomi. "Get up, let's go. Anything you want to take with you to America, better put it in your pockets."

He stared at me. "Get up," I roared in English. Then Farsi.

I must have looked like a madman standing there, waving that damn passport.

He amazed me. It began to sink in. *America*. He got up, balancing himself while he looked quickly around. He took a small photo that he had jammed in a crack in the wall over the heater, put it in a trouser pocket, then started for the door. I followed him.

At the Grand Bazaar I purchased him two sets of clothes and a small carry-on bag to carry the set that wasn't on his back. We dickered with a shoe merchant over one shoe. He insisted we take a pair, which we did, for half price. Qomi put on the shoe he needed, and we threw the other away. Then we drove out to the airport and parked.

I got Qomi a reservation on Turkish Airways to Istanbul, then London, and United to New York. I put the tab on my spy American Express credit card. As I was signing the invoice, it finally hit Qomi that he was going and I was sending him. He began sobbing.

We spent the night in the airport terminal. I bought food, and we ate in a lounge. He snuffled a while, then slept. I walked around, looking, wondering when all this was going to be obliterated. If all these people I was looking at were going to be dead next week. The men, the women, the kids, the Revolutionary Guards with their submachine guns, infidels and faithful, sinners and saints, rich and poor, every last one of them.

At ten o'clock the next morning I shook Qomi's hand, pressed a hundred-dollar bill into his hand and shoved him toward the security line.

"I can't pay you back," he said.

"Life isn't about payback. Find a woman, have some kids, be a good dad."

He pumped my hand one more time, then got in line. After he was through the pat-down, he disappeared through the door.

I waited until his plane was taxiing out before I turned to go.

My cell phone rang as I was hiking out of the terminal. It was Jake Grafton. "You get those visas?" he asked.

"Yeah. Thanks."

"Your voice sounds funny," he said.

"Yeah. Thanks, Admiral. I owe you."

On the way to my hotel I stopped at the mapmakers' shop where Mostafa Abtahi worked. He was hunched over a drawing table in the back of the shop; I saw him as I walked past the racks of maps on display. A clerk asked me what I wanted in Farsi, and I pointed at Abtahi, who turned, saw me and came charging toward the counter.

I pulled the little envelope from my pocket and said, "Have your passport on you?"

"*The visa?*" he whispered.

"Yes."

He whipped the passport out and handed it to me. "Ghasem said you'd come through, oh, yes. He told me I was going to America, oh, yes. I didn't believe him, but he said it would happen, oh, yessss!"

I stood there frozen, staring at him. "Ghasem?"

"Ghasem Murad," he said, as if I were an idiot. "He and I share an apartment. Every night we talk about my dream of going to America. Ghasem said you were a good man, that my dream would come true."

Although there are billions of people, it's really a small world. Tiny, in fact. I wondered what else my buddy Ghasem had told Mostafa Abtahi about me.

The clerk was standing there watching, openmouthed. Abtahi noticed him now and hit him on the shoulder as he shouted, "I am going to *America!*"

While they gabbled at full throttle, I glued the visa into the passport and shoved it at Abtahi. "The sooner the better," I said. "Go as soon as you can."

The future newest American looked at me quizzically.

"Damn country is filling up fast," I explained. "Hurry on over while there is still some American Dream left to get."

Hazra al-Rashid worked hard at staying informed about the activities of foreign spies in Iran. With over fifty thousand employees, the MOIS had sufficient manpower to keep tabs on most of the foreign visitors, many of whom, Hazra believed, were spies.

Foreign diplomats got the full treatment, since all of them were spies. Their comings and goings and contacts were observed and reported and logged.

This American, Tommy Carmellini, had her stumped. Since he had arrived in Tehran, he had disappeared for hours at a time, on several occasions for as many as twenty-four hours. Slippery as an eel, he was undoubtedly an active spy milking information from traitors.

Yet, according to the MOIS daily reports, just two days ago he spent a day in a working-class slum in the southwestern section of town, met a one-legged laborer who had lived there for six years while working on residential construction projects—nothing for the government—then accompanied him to the airport, bought him a ticket to America and waited with him until he left. Abdullaziz Nasr Qomi. A nobody. His dossier made that crystal clear. He had lost that leg in the Iraqi war and had been doing common labor ever since. Attended mosque occasionally. Never worked in the defense construction industry. Qomi had an American tourist visa in his passport when he presented it at the airport. Carmellini had undoubtedly delivered it. Why? What could Qomi have done for the Americans that they would reward him with a visa?

Then Carmellini had gone to the Islamic mapmaker's shop and delivered an American tourist visa to Mostafa Abtahi, who was the roommate of Ghasem Murad, the grandson of the deceased scholar, nephew of Habib Sultani, the defense minister, and cousin of Davar Ghobadi, al-Rashid's conduit for passing misinformation to the CIA via Professor Azari in America. Abtahi was going to America, too.

Due to his relationship with Murad, Abtahi was a much more interesting person than Qomi. Abtahi could be a spy, a conduit from Ghasem Murad to Carmellini. Was he? What secrets had he passed?

Al-Rashid knew precisely how to find out. With a telephone call, she could have Abtahi picked up and interrogated by the MOIS. She could even assist in the interrogation. She knew from long experience that Abtahi would eventually admit all of his crimes against the Islamic Republic. He might resist at first, but he would talk. They all did.

But was that the right move at this time?

The day of reckoning was eight days away. On that date, Zionism would be smashed a fatal blow, and Iran would be catapulted into a leadership position in a worldwide jihad against the infidels.

Hazra al-Rashid rose from her desk and went to the window of her office, from which she could see the skyline of Tehran.

Assuming that Carmellini had learned everything that Ghasem Murad knew, which was everything that Habib Sultani knew, and had passed it to the CIA, would the spymasters in America believe it? The missiles, warheads, the targets, the date of launching . . .

Iran was but eight days away from seizing a leadership position in the Islamic world, one that would make her a major power and give her leaders a prominent voice in remaking life on planet Earth.

For the last few years the spymasters in Washington had received an impressive river of intelligence that said Iran was years away from being a nuclear power. The simple fact was that Iran's nuclear program was too big to hide. Too many people of doubtful loyalty were involved; the truth would eventually leak out. So al-Rashid had done what Churchill recommended during World War II, given the truth a bodyguard of lies.

Humans, al-Rashid knew from hard experience, tend to believe those bits of data that support their political and religious views and prejudices, their framework for making sense of the physical and spiritual world, and tend to reject all data that don't fit into the framework. This was a universal human trait.

If she went after Tommy Carmellini now, Hazra al-Rashid thought, she might give him instant credibility and force Washington to reevaluate whatever information he had been passing.

That didn't strike Hazra al-Rashid as a wise move. Not just now.

On the other hand, hearing what Mostafa Abtahi knew from his own lips might give her information she did not have and provide some clarity to the intelligence picture.

Hazra al-Rashid picked up the telephone and asked for the number two man in the MOIS.

CHAPTER **TWENTY**

Four MOIS agents came for Mostafa Abtahi at two in the morning. They found his passport, examined the American tourist visa, then hand-cuffed him and settled in to search the apartment. They trashed it as Ghasem Murad dressed, then watched. He knew better than to try to leave or to object. He merely stood and watched, expressionless, as he tried not to think about what was in store for his friend Abtahi.

Arresting people for political reasons was an old story, as old as kings and dictators and tyrants, yet that made it no easier to endure. Ghasem watched as Abtahi bit his lip to keep tears from leaking out.

Ghasem also bit his lip. He well knew that this might be the last time he saw Abtahi alive, a man whose only crime was that he wanted to go to America and had actually scored a tourist visa.

As they were leaving, Abtahi tried to say something to Ghasem, but the MOIS men slapped him into silence and pushed him out the door.

Ghasem looked at his watch. They had been there an hour.

Jihad Day was precisely one week away. Seven days. On that morning the missiles would rise from their launchers and Israel would cease to exist. Israel or America would probably retaliate with nuclear weapons. Ghasem could envision Mahmoud Ahmadinejad demanding that the Muslims of the world unite against the Great Satan to avenge the martyrs of Tehran, may they rest in peace.

Ghasem locked up his apartment—he paused at the door for a last look at the stuff strewn everywhere—and went downstairs. His car was where he had left it.

He drove to the ministry and went in. The guards didn't ask to see his pass; he merely walked by them.

The light was on in the minister's office. He saw his uncle on his prayer rug, bent over. His uncle didn't seem to notice that he was in the room.

Minister of Defense Habib Sultani was doing a lot of praying these days. As he had all his adult life, he started by reciting passages from the Koran, which didn't take much thought. He merely put his mind in neutral and the words flowed out.

Tonight, though, the words slowed to a trickle and finally stopped as images formed in his mind of missiles roaring into space and flying a huge parabola, finally turning slowly to fall straight down toward the earth, like a spear hurled at the earth's heart. Then the missile became a fireball that grew and grew until it consumed everything. Everything . . . cities, people, buildings, the sky, the earth . . .

Afterward . . . there was nothing. It was as if the world and humans had never been.

In his mind's eye were only images. Horrible images.

When he could stand the images no longer, Habib Sultani opened his eyes and levered himself to a sitting position on his prayer rug.

He was drained, yet the images in his mind refused to fade.

"Are you all right, Uncle?"

The voice was Ghasem's.

Sultani looked around slowly. His familiar world appeared intact, undamaged.

He reached for a table and touched it. Its solidity reassured him.

Ghasem was standing there with a worried look on his face.

"Yes," Sultani said, slightly surprised by the sound of his own voice. It seemed to be coming from a great distance away.

When he was a young boy, Habib had loved birds, had tried to imagine what it would be like if he could fly with the birds. He could feel himself flying along now, looking down, the birds accompanying him, looking down at the buildings and people, who were staring up at him and pointing, as the missiles fell toward them.

"Uncle, what is the combination to your safe?" Ghasem again.

He heard the words and understood them, but he was still aloft, still flying along as the missiles fell, missiles with warheads that he had helped create. He could turn his head and look up and see them coming down, closer and closer and closer . . .

"Uncle, you must concentrate," he heard Ghasem saying. "You must tell me the combination to your safe. I need to know that combination so that I can open it."

By great force of will Habib Sultani formed the words for the first number and uttered them aloud. Then he saw the missiles falling again.

"Now the second number," Ghasem said.

The second number . . . oh, what was it? Something with a three . . . oh yes, thirty-two. He made his lips move, forced the words out.

"And the third number?" Ghasem said softly. He was right there, near him, even though he was suspended in midair, but his words were coming from so far away. Soon Ghasem would be dead, and his cousin Davar, and Khurram and the daughters of Israr Murad, dead, as if they had never been, because he, Habib Sultani, had created the missiles and warheads to murder everyone on earth.

Now he felt a hand on his arm. And another on his back. Ghasem again, whispering about a third number. Even though he was far away, Habib heard the whisper, heard the urgency, the pleading, the desire to know.

"Fifty-six," he said, forcing his lips to form the words and his diaphragm to push air out around them.

"Thank you, Uncle."

Ghasem Murad left his uncle sitting on his prayer rug and turned to the safe. He spun the dial and carefully stopped it on the first number. Back the other way . . .

When he had put in the third number and turned the dial back until it stopped, the heavy latch lever clicked. He seized it and applied steady pressure. He felt the locks move. Then he pulled on the door of the safe. It opened.

Working quickly, he began hunting through the contents of the safe. He found a file labeled JIHAD MISSILES. Opened it. The third document in the file was a list of twelve locations defined by latitude and longitude, numbers a GPS guidance system understood. The list was headed TARGETS FOR JIHAD MISSILES. Someone had written in pencil the names of the cities or military bases that the coordinates defined. Two of them were Tel Aviv. One was Tehran, and the rest were American military bases in Iraq, Qatar and Kuwait.

Staring at it, Ghasem realized he was holding a copy of an original document. The names of the cities appeared to be in his uncle Habib's handwriting. He scrutinized the paper. Yes. It was a copy, with no number; apparently someone ran a classified document through the copy machine and handed out copies, probably to people who were not cleared to see the original.

Perhaps that someone had given a sheet to Habib Sultani. The Minister of defense might wish to know where the missiles were going to go, but arguably, he didn't need to know.

Ghasem was stunned by what he saw. He expected Israel or America to retaliate against Tehran with a nuclear weapon if Ahmadinejad destroyed Israel and these American bases, but no. Ahmadinejad was going to launch a missile at the city. Ahmadinejad was going to destroy Tehran and blame it on the Jews.

One of the warheads would detonate over the city. Two hundred kilotons of nuclear energy would form a fireball above the city hotter than the sun, a fireball that would expand until it almost touched the ground. The thermal pulse would cremate the people under it, set mud and wood, brick and concrete and steel afire, and the concussion would push over everything as it rushed away. Then, as the fireball rose and cooled, air would rush back into the vacuum in a tidal wave that would destroy any buildings or bridges or other structures still standing and carry thousands of tons of combustibles into the center of the fire, which would rage uncontrolled, destroying everything that would burn, even dirt.

Ghasem Murad hunted through the file. *Where are these damned missiles? Where will they be launched from? And when?*

He found no piece of paper to answer those questions. None. Not a scrap.

Ghasem glanced back at his uncle, who was still seated on his prayer rug, staring fixedly at nothing.

It beggared belief that the minister of defense would not know where twelve missiles armed with nuclear warheads were stored. Or where they would be launched from, which was the other side of the same coin, since all the missiles were on transporters and hidden in hardened tunnels carved from solid rock.

The information had to be here, in this safe. Ghasem carefully folded the target list with the cities' names in pencil and placed it in his pocket. He replaced the JIHAD MISSILE file in the safe and checked the name of every other file.

When he couldn't find a file that looked hopeful, he began randomly flipping through the folders, looking for . . . anything.

Damn!

If Sultani didn't have the information, then the minister of weapons of mass destruction might. Hosseini-Tash. That fool.

After Ghasem replaced all the files in the safe, he used muscle to swing the heavy door back into the closed position. He turned the great latch lever, then spun the dial until the safe locked again.

If Habib Sultani were to be sent to a sanitarium, Ghasem's access to the building would be terminated. He needed to get the information Tommy Carmellini wanted, or get Carmellini in here to crack a safe, before that happened.

Ghasem stood staring at his uncle, who was sitting rigidly on his prayer rug, lost in his own private hell. Sultani's eyes were completely unfocused.

Ghasem pulled the door shut behind him and stood in the empty waiting area trying to think.

Ghasem knew that he didn't have any more time. Sometime later today people would discover that Habib Sultani had suffered a severe mental breakdown.

Now. He had to get Carmellini in here now to open the safe in Hosseini-Tash's office.

If you've ever contemplated how a condemned man might feel as he stands against the wall puffing his last cigarette, with the firing squad at order arms ten paces away and the officer holding the blindfold standing nearby looking at his watch, then you might have a fair idea of how I felt those days in Iran.

I woke up that morning, looked out the window at the eastern sky turning pink, wondered if I would be dead in a week or wishing I were and sat on the edge of the bed contemplating my toes.

There were ten of them. This was not due to any virtue of mine or choice that I made but was dictated by the human genome. I assumed my genes were also heavily influenced by the fact that my parents and grandparents apparently liked people with ten fingers and ten toes and chose mates accordingly. Or maybe the people they liked just came equipped that way. I made a mental note to ask Charles Darwin about that if I ran into him anytime soon.

I put on my running duds and pulled socks over those ten little masterpieces.

I put on my fanny pack, stuffed diplomatic passport, hotel room keys and car keys in there, and let myself out into the empty hallway. No one else was stirring at dawn in Tehran.

The lobby was empty. At this hour, even the MOIS man was still home in bed.

I was out on the street working up to cruise speed when a car slowed beside me. I glanced over and saw Ghasem Murad at the wheel. He jerked his head, telling me to get in.

I glanced around to see who was keeping tabs on me. I knew in my bones that someone was, and that someone would report seeing Ghasem and me together. I got into his car anyway.

He handed me a copy of the Jihad missile target list. I hadn't seen anything like that before, although Jake Grafton told me about it. Tel Aviv, Baghdad, all those American air military bases and Tehran.

Tehran!

So Jake Grafton was right. Ahmadinejad was going to murder his own people to give himself a political boost worldwide.

"Where'd you get this?" I asked Ghasem as we rolled through traffic.

"The safe of the minister of defense. It's not in the format of a classified document that must be accounted for. That blob at the bottom? Someone has blacked out the original document control number."

"Where are the missiles?"

"That information wasn't in the safe."

"Bummer, dude," I muttered. Can you imagine a government having missiles with nuke warheads ready to go, targets picked, the date set, and not telling the minister of defense where the missiles were? "I hope your uncle has his postretirement years all planned out," I added. "Looks like he's there."

"He's having a nervous breakdown."

I stared. "That's one way to spend those years, I suppose. He in the hospital?"

"In his office. I believe you Americans and British might say that he's 'flipped out.'"

I kept my mouth shut.

"You need to get into the safe in Hosseini-Tash's office right now," Ghasem continued. "This morning, while I still have access."

Ransacking a safe, sorting through hundreds of files written in a language I barely understood, looking for The One, which might or might not be there, was impractical. It would take all night, and I couldn't stay anywhere near that long. What I needed was computer hard drives . . .

"Where else can the information be?" I asked Ghasem. "Targets get picked, then someone must do a ton of math for the ballistic missiles, plan routes for the cruise missiles . . . Where do they do that?"

"The Targeting Office," he said. "It's in the basement of the senior officers' wing." He described its exact location, even drew me a map, showing me the number of doors from the end of the hallway and the Targeting Office's location in relation to the stairwell.

"What's on the door?" I asked.

He drew the inscription in Farsi.

"Have you ever been in there?" I asked.

"No. Access is very restricted."

Well, it sounded more promising than the head dog's office. Hell, Hosseini-Tash was probably just another paper pusher.

"I'll go in with you," Ghasem said.

I glanced at him to see if this was a serious offer or a social one. He looked serious as an undertaker, but through the years I had found I worked best alone. I told him that now.

He didn't say anything, merely stared at the cars in front of us. When we came to a red light, he leaned forward, put his forehead on the top of the steering wheel and closed his eyes. "The MOIS took my roommate away early this morning. Mostafa Abtahi. He said you were the one who gave him his visa. For a little while he was the happiest man in Iran. Thank you for that."

The truck behind us beeped its horn.

When Ghasem straightened up and got the car in motion, I said, "Tonight you need to be in a very public place with lots of people who know you. Now let me out at the next traffic light."

I crawled into my telephone booth at the embassy and called Jake Grafton. I told him about my conversation with Ghasem and the Jihad list he showed me. I also told him that Mostafa Abtahi, one of the guys he finagled a tourist visa for on my behalf, had been arrested by the MOIS.

"What about Qomi?" he asked.

"I put him on a plane. He should be over the Atlantic or in America."

"You can't save the world, Tommy," he remarked.

We chatted a bit about the schedule for the evening, then said our good-byes.

I sat in my little cocoon breathing deeply.

Jake Grafton hung up his satellite phone and looked across the table at Sal Molina. "Tommy is going into the Defense Ministry building tonight," he said.

"Is that wise? If he's caught . . ."

Jake Grafton reached onto the table behind him for a large-scale map of Iran. He placed it between himself and the president's aide. Using his finger, he began pointing out symbols. "Using satellite photography and single-side band radar, we have verified eighteen sites where these people have missiles. We believe there are at least twenty-five sites. There may be more. We must know which of these sites has nuclear weapons and which doesn't. Tommy is going to try to find out."

"He's going to dig through a safe for an Iranian government document which may or may not be genuine?"

"Get real, Sal. He'll be stealing computer hard drives."

"How do you know he's getting the real thing?" Molina demanded. "Maybe it's a setup. Maybe these assholes are jerking us around like Saddam did. We can't afford another Iraq, Jake—that would sink this president."

"There is no way on earth to be absolutely certain about anything," Jake Grafton shot back. "If we demand an impossible standard of proof, we will only be certain that we know nothing at all."

"You're a fucking ray of sunshine, Grafton."

The admiral smiled. "What are real friends for?"

When I left the embassy I didn't go to the hotel. I spent the next two hours ditching any tails I might have; then I stood in front of an Armenian church waiting for G. W. Hosein. He was driving a battered old pickup. He was only ten seconds late. He stopped just long enough for me to get in, then popped the clutch and had us rolling again.

"You clean?" he asked.

"I sure as hell hope so," I said. "We'll find out, won't we?"

"We will indeed," he said, and pointed to a backpack lying at my feet. I pulled it into my lap and unzipped it. It held a nice Kimber 1911 .45 caliber automatic with two magazines loaded with jacketed hollow-point bullets—man-stoppers. I checked the slide, trigger and safety, then shoved a magazine into the thing and chambered a shell. Then I lowered the hammer. A lot of people carry these things cocked and locked, but I didn't have a holster, just my pocket, and besides, cocked and locked is a tad too trendy for me.

"Tell me about this safe house you have in mind," I said.

"It's under the city," he said, "in an old metro tunnel that didn't get built."

"Really?" I said. This sounded wonderful to me. Nothing stops radiation like rock and dirt.

"The Tehran police chief got arrested a couple of years ago for frequenting a whorehouse in one of these tunnels, so that got me interested. I did some exploring." He made a gesture of modesty.

"Did you find the women?"

"No, but I found a nice hideout. You'll like it."

"The police chief?"

"He was fired and prosecuted. These people are so uptight."

The safe house was actually a modest hotel, run by a German, that catered to foreign businessmen. It was on the edge of the business district and had real guests coming and going, so G. W. and I blended right in.

The German, Helmut Kremer, was, of course, in the pay of the CIA. He was working the desk, as usual—it was a small hotel—and I introduced myself with a code name. He was in his fifties, balding, with a modest tummy, and looked tired. I wondered what in the world he was doing in Iran, and he probably wondered the same about me. Hell, I asked myself that question three times a day.

Kremer glanced around to ensure the lobby was empty, then handed me a key to a room, and G. W. and I went up the stairs to find it. It was that simple.

Maybe too simple. When we got into the room I motioned to G. W. to remain silent, and I began to inspect for bugs. It was actually a nice room, with two beds and a French door that led to a small balcony. Fortunately the sewer pipes were European-sized, so unlike many Iranian hotels, this one didn't have a basket strategically placed beside the commode to receive used toilet paper. Some people savor the adventure of a third-world vacation, but it's really an acquired taste.

I didn't have my electronic antibug kit with me, so I worked the old eyeballs. I doubted that Kremer had sold out to the other side, yet after a session with Hazra al-Rashid, he might have. So I checked. Found nothing.

"Where do we meet the others?" I asked G. W.

"They'll be in the tunnel. We go in from the basement of this place."

"Okay." I looked at my watch. Four hours until the meet.

George Washington Hosein lay down on the bed and put his pistol on his belly. "Relax, Tommy," he said. "Try to get a nap."

I was too keyed up to relax. In a few minutes I went over to the window and looked out at the Tehran that Ahmadinejad was willing to sacrifice. There were maybe twenty million people, more or less, in Tehran, and Ahmadinejad didn't give a rat's ass if they all went up in a mushroom cloud as long as he could do it to the Israelis and Americans first. Twenty million people . . . and Ghasem and Davar were two of them.

I flopped on the other bed and shut my eyes. I couldn't get Davar out of my mind. She wasn't soft and sexy with a figure that would stop traffic, and she wasn't one of those dazzling personalities that I always found so charming.

She knew what she believed in and was absolutely convinced she was right. Not that that was a unique quality, to be sure; half the young women I had ever met thought they had life figured out and didn't want to hear any facts that might complicate their world. On the other hand, Davar's courage made her unique. It is easy to be brave if the dangers are unknown; yet she knew the dangers, the evil. She had lived her life with it and saw it every day. Still, she was ready to fight, to confront it head-on. Smart, committed, tough as leather, Davar was a woman to face the storms of life with.

No wonder the guy from Oklahoma had fallen for her! If I had been him . . .

How would a guy win a heart like hers?

As if there were time and a future in which to try . . .

I felt as if I were on the bank of the River Styx, and Charon, the boatman, was poling over to ferry me across to hell. Through the fires and smoke and stench of burning flesh, I could see him . . . coming relentlessly, mercilessly on, closer and closer.

A hole in the basement wall just large enough to wriggle through formed the entrance to the underground world. As G. W. flashed a light around, then wormed his way through the hole, I said, "I feel like we're crawling into an Indiana Jones movie."

"Don't forget your bullwhip," he muttered and climbed through to the other side. I had no choice but to follow.

There was a ladder against the basement wall on the other side, so I went down it as G. W. held the flashlight. Once on solid rock, I used my light to look around. We were in a tunnel, all right, that certainly looked as if it had been carved out for a subway. It was cool down here, and I could just feel the barest hint of a breeze on my cheek.

"This way," G. W. said. He led the way, into the breeze.

We walked for at least ten minutes—I estimated we had gone perhaps a half mile—making gentle turns and climbing and descending gentle grades, when we saw a light ahead. As we got closer, I saw that it was made by a Coleman-type lantern sitting in a huge cavity cut into the wall of the tunnel. This might be a future subway station.

Three men wearing Iranian army uniforms were gathered around the lantern, and they were armed to the teeth. All wore pistols in holsters and had submachine guns dangling from straps over their shoulders. One of them was Joe Mottaki, the Mossad agent, and the other two were American covert

CIA officers, Haddad Nouri and Ahmad Qajar. Nouri had been in the country for three years and was burrowed in like a tick on a dog. He made an excellent living as a computer consultant during the day. Ahmad Qajar spent his days traveling around the country updating foreign guidebooks . . . and the CIA database on the country.

After we had shaken hands all around, we examined the pile of equipment they had laid out in the lantern light. It had come from a stash in one corner of the room, a large cavity that had been hollowed out of rotten rock with a pick. The boards that usually covered the hole lay beside it.

Qajar handed both G. W. and Nouri simple, stamped, Russian-made submachine guns with four loaded magazines taped to them and silencers on the barrels. He offered one to me, but I refused. If I needed a submachine gun, my mission was a bust and I was doomed. Just in case, Qajar handed two grenades to each of his colleagues and put two in his own pockets. Everyone got night vision goggles. I received a backpack containing C-4, fuses and primer cord.

"Gentlemen," I said, "tonight's target is the Ministry of Defense. Joe, your job is to provide me with a diversion big and bad enough that you pull the Revolutionary Guards and uniformed army people out of the hallways in the executive wing. I intend to go in through a window in that wing. G. W. and his guys will deliver me there and pick me up when I come back out."

"How much time will you need?" Joe Mottaki asked.

"Fifteen minutes, at least."

"Dream on, fool. There is no bloody way. I can try for ten, but after that you're solo."

"Ten minutes, then." What else could I say? My life's ambition was to be a live spy, not a dead burglar.

No one asked what I was after. They didn't need to know.

While we were discussing the night's festivities, I stripped to my underwear and donned black trousers and a black shirt. I was wearing boat shoes tonight, with black uppers. I strapped an army web belt around my middle, one that held two pistols in holsters. One was the Kimber 1911 auto and the other was a Ruger auto .22 with a silencer on the barrel.

All of this stuff had been parachuted into the country, including a duffle bag with a T.D. marked on it.

As I rooted through it, checking to make sure everything was there, Joe Mottaki asked, "How come they used those initials?"

"The letters stand for Tulip Delany," I told him. "She's a girl I used to date occasionally in high school."

"You're really full of it, Carmellini."

"Don't ever forget it," I told him proudly. I hoisted the bag to my shoulder, just to see if I was stout enough to handle it. For a short distance, anyway.

"Let's get the rest of this stuff stowed and get on with it," I said.

We climbed a ladder to get out of the tunnel and ended up in the basement of some kind of warehouse. G. W. led the way through the place using only a sliver of light from his flashlight. I almost tripped twice.

Behind the building in an alley was a large tracked vehicle with a humongous cannon. The engine was ticking over slowly, and I caught a whiff of diesel exhaust. A man in Iranian army fatigues carrying a submachine gun was standing by the thing smoking a cigarette.

"One of my guys," Joe Mottaki said. "We borrowed this earlier this evening. It's a one hundred and fifty-five millimeter self-propelled howitzer, a Raad-2, or Thunder-2."

"Didn't you guys use something like this in Indonesia?"

"You are remarkably well informed," Joe said slowly. "Let's hope this thing comes as a surprise to our Islamic Revolutionary Guard friends." He glanced at his watch. "You have precisely twenty minutes, Tommy, then we open fire."

I checked my watch, nodded once, then threw my stuff into the backseat of the car that G. W. was driving. I got in beside him and he fired up the tiny motor. "Hi-yo, Silver," I said.

He gunned the engine and away we went. I glanced behind us. The car with Ahmad and Haddad was following right along.

In truth, it wasn't much of a plan, but it was all we had.

"You feeling lucky tonight?" G. W. asked.

"Oh, yeah."

"Well, tell you what, Kemo Sabe. You better be damn quick with the knife and gun tonight. Don't take any chances. They waylay you in there, you're on your own. We ain't riding to the fucking rescue."

"Yeah."

"Kill anything that moves," G. W. added.

"Yeah."

"You nervous?" he asked, glancing at me.

"Yeah."

CHAPTER TWENTY-ONE

Motoring through the night streets of Tehran in an Iranian army self-propelled, tracked howitzer drew no attention from anyone, a circumstance that caused Joe Mottaki to smile grimly. The possibility that someone might steal a howitzer in order to do evil, nefarious things obviously seemed so remote as to be ludicrous to people living in a police state, which Iran certainly was. One of the reasons, doubtlessly, was the certain knowledge that anyone caught doing so would have a short, grim life expectancy as an enemy of God.

Joe Mottaki certainly didn't suffer from illusions about the Muslims, who in the Middle East often taught their children that Jews were cursed by God, who would never again be satisfied with them. What the Iranian holy warriors would do to a Mossad agent, if they caught him, was something that couldn't be printed in a family newspaper. To be sure, Joe had no intention of being caught; the pistol he carried was not for shooting nasty Iranians but himself. Or his two Mossad colleagues, if it came to that.

Tonight he directed the man at the wheel with short commands as the lightly armored vehicle rolled through the streets at 25 mph, well short of its top speed. Unfortunately, it was leaving a trail in the soft asphalt that a blind man could follow; tracks were notorious for that. So far, no one was following. That would soon change, and Joe knew it.

He had the driver stop the Raad-2 in an intersection on a low hill, over a mile from the Defense Ministry, which was just visible between the buildings. This was almost point-blank range for the artillery piece. Joe Mottaki glanced at his watch.

He growled at the gunner, who swiveled the barrel of the 155 mm howitzer and adjusted his aim with the telescopic sight.

"There's two tanks in front of the building," the gunner said. "Look like cold iron. Military sculpture, maybe."

"The crews are around, someplace," Joe Mottaki said. After thirty years of life, he was a confirmed pessimist. Which was good—as everyone in the Middle East well knew, pessimists usually lived longer. If nothing else, they got a running start. "But our target is the building," Joe told the gunner. "Tell me when you are ready."

"Ready now," the gunner said.

Mottaki checked his watch. "One minute," he said. Then he grinned again.

George Washington Hosein and I put on small radio headsets and clipped the transmitter/receivers to our belts. We tested them as we drove up to the Defense Ministry.

He let me out of his car on the empty sidewalk by the ministry. The heat of the day had dissipated some, but the sidewalk still radiated the heat. I opened the rear door of the sedan, pulled out the duffle bag and hoisted it to my shoulder. Then I walked over to the side of the building, which was also still warm. It was built in the shape of a giant U, and we were adjacent to the southern wing. The main entrance was on the crosspiece, which faced west.

Ghasem Murad had drawn me a crude map, and I had committed it to memory. Fifteen windows from the east end of this wing, he suggested, might be best. Despite congenital paranoia, which I had assiduously cultivated from puberty onward, I believed him.

I counted windows, then stepped to the proper one. The window was at least ten feet off the pavement, perhaps eleven, and the wall was poured concrete, ugly as hell and smooth, without a handhold.

I glanced at my watch. Thirty seconds.

Fortunately for me there wasn't a soul out and about except for me and my friends, all three of whom were standing near their cars holding their submachine guns, ready to kill somebody. The sight of them bucked me up a little.

I pulled the rope and grappling iron from my bag—it was right on top—and flaked it out. Tied the end of the rope to the bag.

Ten seconds. I counted them down.

At zero nothing happened. Uh-oh.

Just when I was ready to toss my trash back in the car and boogie, something big crashed into the building. Sounded like it hit the main section.

Then I heard a deep, muffled boom, a heavy weapon some distance away. I didn't know where Joe parked his howitzer, but he sure knew how to shoot it.

I twirled the grappling hook and threw it through the window over my head. It smashed the glass and went in. I tugged and it came right back out. Threw it again . . . and this time it caught on something. I steadily tightened the rope, the hook held, and I went up the rope hand over hand.

Got through the window and found myself in an empty office.

Something else crashed into the building. I could hear running feet, shouts.

I grabbed a good handful of rope and began pulling the duffle bag up.

When I had it inside, I untied the rope and dropped it. G. W. and his guys were in their cars going down the street. They would return in ten minutes, I hoped.

I lifted the bag to my shoulder, got the silenced Ruger out and pointed forward, just in case, and set out for the basement, where the Targeting Office was located.

After the gunner sent the third round toward the ministry, Joe Mottaki had the driver put the Raad-2 in motion. The crew stopped in another intersection a hundred yards along and swiveled the giant gun to point at the ministry.

"Any time you're ready," Joe told the gunner, who pulled the trigger ten seconds later. The recoil rocked the vehicle and the noise nearly deafened them, even though they were wearing intercom helmets that were supposed to muffle the blasts.

The door to the Targeting Office was locked. Only one lock—and an American one at that. I guess ol' Habib Sultani never thought anyone would be wandering around in here trying to go where he shouldn't.

Wearing my miner's headlamp, I attacked the lock with picks. About that time another howitzer shell smashed into the building and exploded, sending a tremor through the structure and causing a power failure. The corridor I was standing in became dark as a grave.

Ah yes, a dark building, a lock on a door, me standing in front of it with a torsion wrench and a pick—*this* was the story of my misspent life. I tried several picks before I found the one I thought would do it.

The seconds ticked by . . . how many, I dunno. I always think these delicate operations take longer than they do. Two more howitzer shells exploded

244 — Stephen Coonts

in the masonry above, one far away, one closer. I hoped the guardians of this fine building had evacuated and taken cover, as G. W. and Joe Mottaki and I intended. In this stubborn age it is difficult to get people to behave the way you want them to. No doubt Mahmoud Ahmadinejad, the Devil's disciple, would agree with that sentiment.

Bang—I got it. The lock turned. I tried the door. As I did, I heard the sound of running feet in the corridor. Boots slapping on concrete. I snapped off the miner's light.

The door opened when I twisted the knob. I pulled the silenced Ruger from its holster, got a good grip and opened the door. Grabbed the duffel bag, stepped in and pulled the door closed behind me and turned the knob on the lock.

Standing there in the absolute darkness listening to my heart and the feet pounding the corridor, coming closer, I confess, I was nervous. Scared, even. What a hell of a way to make a living!

The running men—I thought there were at least three—went pounding by the door without slackening their pace. When the sounds of their feet had faded, I keyed my radio and told G. W., "I'm in."

"Make it snappy," he said. "Joe's shooting into a hornet's nest."

I snapped the miner's light back on and took a look around.

I was in a large office with four desks and a large safe. Three of the desks had computers on them. The entire wall on the side away from the door was covered with a black curtain. I stepped up to it and pushed it aside, revealing a map of the Middle East.

All of Iran was there, Iraq, the Persian Gulf, Lebanon, Jordan, Israel . . . and the northern half of Arabia. There were stars all over Iran and numbers. Triangles here and there. I examined Tel Aviv. A heavy black triangle was penciled over it, with numbers beside it. The same for our airbases in Arabia and Iraq. I suspected that everything Jake Grafton wanted to know was right here on this map, and if I photographed it and beat feet, we would have Ahmadinejad's Jihad plans. But I couldn't be sure. I wanted the info from the computers, too.

Those computers—planning flight paths for nine hundred conventional cruise and ballistic missiles, and for a dozen nuclear-armed ones, from known locations to precise targets, without interfering with each other in flight or when the warheads detonated, was not a task for the ignorant or careless. It would take a lot of calculating by someone who knew his stuff. Ghasem Murad had told me about the head targeting guru, a mathematics PhD from one of the local universities, and assured me he was competent and capable. Again, I believed Ghasem.

I checked my watch. I'd been in the building for four minutes.

I turned to the safe. First I turned the dial gently in the hope that whoever had closed it last had failed to lock it. Well, they hadn't. Working as quickly as I could, I got out a small computer and several rods, which I clamped to the door of the safe. Put six electronic sensors around the combination lock, then hooked them to the computer. Finally, I clamped a small electric motor with a set of jaws protruding from it to the rods over the combination dial and tightened the jaws over the dial. The last lead went to a twelve-volt battery, the heaviest thing in the duffle bag.

This gizmo could open most of these older safes, given enough time, which was in short supply tonight. An electrical current induced into the door created a measurable magnetic field. The rotation of the tumblers inside the lock caused fluctuations in the field, fluctuations that the computer measured and displayed on the screen. Finally, the computer measured the amount of electrical current necessary to turn the dial of the lock, an exquisitely sensitive measurement. Using both these factors, the computer could determine the combination to the safe and open it. I manually zeroed the dial and started the computer program.

I didn't have time to watch it work. These other computers might have information we could use. I pulled a battery-driven saw from the duffle bag and attacked them, cutting them open and removing the hard drives, which I placed in my backpack. I had all three hard drives in about two minutes.

I checked on the computer opening the safe. It had one number already.

Satisfied that the magic was initiated, I went back to the wall map and snapped off a dozen pictures with my Cyber-shot. Time was marching right along, and I heard a few more howitzer shells smash home.

I hoped those shells were beating hell out of the top of this building. Mottaki had assured me they would.

I went back to the safe. Second number was up. The dial was slowly turning . . .

"Lots of military milling around the front of the building," G. W. told me. "It's just a matter of time before they come down the street where you went in."

I clicked my mike twice in reply.

I opened the duffle bag, which contained twenty pounds of C-4 explosive, fused, with a detonator attached. I cranked the detonator around to ten minutes and flipped up the guard on the on-off switch. Turned the switch to ON. The red light illuminated.

I had just stuffed the duffle bag under the big boss's desk and stowed my camera in my backpack when I heard noises in the hallway. The footsteps stopped at the door, and someone rattled the knob.

Muffled voices. There were at least two of them, maybe more.

I hunkered down behind a desk and pulled the Ruger from its holster. Turned off the miner's light and stowed it, then put on the night vision goggles. The world turned green.

"They are firing up the tanks," the gunner told Joe Mottaki.

"Smack 'em," was the immediate answer.

Mottaki was in his third position, still on the ridge looking down another long avenue at the Defense Ministry, which was now on fire. The howitzer shells had done their work. Glancing through the IR scope, Mottaki could see the heat from the fire as white light. He was studying it when he saw the first tank, coming toward them up the boulevard.

The self-propelled howitzer was covered with very light steel, just enough to stop rifle bullets and shrapnel. A tank shell would go through it like a bullet through paper. Not having armor plate on the vehicle made Joe Mottaki feel naked. On the other hand, the howitzer was an artillery piece, and the shells in the vehicle were general purpose. In theory, they should penetrate a tank's armor. If the gunner could hit it.

He could. The gun bellowed, the tracked vehicle rocked from the recoil, and the tank on the boulevard, almost a mile away and head on, coming straight for the howitzer, disappeared in a tremendous flash.

When the IR scope cleared and Joe could see, the tank was not moving. The gun barrel was pointed down and to the left.

"Where's the other one?" he asked the gunner.

"Dunno."

Joe looked at his watch. Eight minutes had passed since the first shot. Carmellini wanted ten.

"Put another one in the ministry. Shoot at something intact."

"Roger that. By the way, we only have seven more rounds."

"Counting the one in the breech?"

"Yes."

The gunner bent to his weapon as Joe Mottaki wondered about the second tank. Where could it be? He used the IR scope to scan the avenues he could see . . . and found them empty.

The footsteps receded. The tiny whine of the electric motor on the safe door had stopped.

I checked. The combination was there. I took the apparatus off the safe door, took a deep breath and tried the handle. It gave. I pulled the door open.

Oh yes! There was a laptop in there. I grabbed it, pulled out stacks of paper and threw them around. If there was another computer in there, I didn't want to overlook it. No, there was only the one. I added it to the backpack, pulled the straps around my shoulders, went to the door to the office, put my ear against it. Silence.

There was no way around it—I had to go through that door. Since the office lacked windows, that door was the only exit.

"*Hurry up, Tommy!*" That was G. W.

I pulled the goggles back on, looked through the door to see if I could make out figures in infrared. The hall appeared empty.

With the Ruger in my hand, my thumb on the safety and the backpack on my back, I twisted the doorknob slowly and pulled the door open.

Nothing happened.

I looked across the corridor at the blank wall, then eased my head out so I could see down to the left. Pulled the door completely open and looked right. The hallway appeared empty. Of course, the darkness was Stygian, but the goggles allowed me to see in IR. What I saw was a corridor empty of humans.

No more impacts from howitzer shells, so the big building was relatively silent. I hoped and prayed all the people had bailed.

The staircase I had descended was two doors down on the other side of the hallway. I took a deep breath and came slowly out of the Targeting Office, pulled the door shut behind me and walked along the corridor toward the stairs. I paused there, looked up the stairs . . . empty. Empty all the way to the landing. There I would have to turn 180 degrees and climb another flight to the ground floor, where I had come in.

Perhaps I should go back, put the C-4 against the outside wall. It would blow a hole I could pop through to the sidewalk. Where I might be gunned down by someone at one of the building's windows.

When that C-4 went off, I decided, I wanted to be as far from this building as possible and running for the toolies. And it would go off very soon. The clock on the detonator was ticking away. Just when it was going to blow, I didn't know. I certainly couldn't read my watch with these goggles, and I wasn't going to take them off. Of one thing I was sure—time was running madly on.

I started up the stairs. Got to the landing, stood and listened . . . and heard nothing. So I went around the corner—and found myself staring at the business end of an AK-47 held by a soldier sitting on the stairs.

He wasn't wearing night vision goggles, but he had that weapon pointed right at my belly button and he was staring straight at me. He said something in Persian that I didn't catch.

I froze. For about half a second I thought about shooting him, but the thought didn't get far. The Ruger fell from my grasp and made a metallic clank as it hit the steps.

A flashlight illuminated me. The holder of the light was at the top of the stairs. That much, at least, I could see in the goggles.

The sitting soldier turned on a flashlight, studied me for a moment, then rose and picked up the Ruger and helped himself to the Kimber 1911, which he pulled from the holster on the left side of my web belt.

The man at the top of the stairs said something loudly, then came down, carefully keeping his light pointed right in my face.

One of them pulled out handcuffs while the other stood on the second step up, about five feet in front of me, with his submachine gun leveled on my belly button. He gestured with the barrel for me to raise my hands higher.

I wondered if they were told to bring me in alive regardless, or to shoot me dead if I resisted.

The other came down the stairs and approached from my right. He released his weapon, which hung on a strap slung over his neck and shoulder, and reached for my right wrist. Snapped one of the cuffs over it, then reached for my left.

I drove my left hand under his chin as hard as I could, with the fingers curled back halfway. Drove my knuckles into his Adam's apple with all the force I could generate, which was quite a bit since I had enough adrenaline in my blood to run an Olympic athlete for a month, and I managed to turn a little, getting my weight into the blow. I tried to drive my fist right through his neck, intentionally not trying to stop the punch. I heard his Adam's apple snap, crushed, as he fell away from me.

"Tommy?" I heard G. W.'s voice in my ear; then I lost the headset.

I didn't let my guy fall. I had him with my right hand now and pushed him with all my strength toward his pal, who had tried to back away and tripped and was now sitting on a stair. He triggered a burst right into the guy's back.

I followed the handcuff man right onto the gunman, who went over backward even as he tried to get out of the way.

I was on him like a cat, pushing the gun barrel aside and smashing him with my right fist. The first blow shattered his nose, sending blood flying everywhere. I hit him again and again as fast as I could. The third punch snapped his neck. I felt it go and released the body.

I got up breathing hard. This whole encounter had taken no more than fifteen seconds. As I groped for my pistols, which were on the floor, another shell exploded in the building and the windows rattled.

A police car pulled up fifty yards from the Raad-2, and the man at the wheel jumped out. He had an AK-47 in his hands and ripped off a burst. The bullets pinging against the armor alerted Joe Mottaki to the cop's presence.

He had the gunner spin the howitzer barrel and depress it. With his eye on the telescopic sight, the gunner soon lined up the police car. He triggered the gun . . . and the shell went through the car without detonating. Didn't matter. The impact literally exploded the car, sending pieces flying in all directions. The shell smashed into a building a hundred yards down the street and blew out half of a wall. There was so much dust and smoke that it obscured the truckload of masonry falling into the street.

The cop with the AK was hit by some of the pieces of the car and thrown for twenty feet. He didn't rise from the pavement.

Mottaki had the gunner send one more shell into the Ministry of Defense, then turned away from the ministry and headed for the top of the low hill they were shooting from.

The third floor of the building to his left exploded, showering the street with brick and dust.

That tank! Or another one.

Mottaki looked around wildly, saw one two blocks ahead, sitting in a side street. "Gunner!"

"I've got him."

As the words left the gunner's mouth he pulled the trigger, and the howitzer's recoil rocked the vehicle again.

Amazingly, the gunner missed. The shell might have glanced off the turret armor, but in any event it exploded in the building beyond the tank, pulverized it and made the brick, mortar and wood rain down. In seconds the tank was nearly buried and all that could be seen was the tip of the long gun barrel.

"Shoot him again," Mottaki shouted. "You missed the first time."

The tank was rocking back and forth, the visible gun barrel vibrating from the efforts of the tank crew to drive it out of the pile of rubble, which was still growing.

The barrel got longer . . . then the front of the tank appeared, and the barrel began to swing toward them.

"Let's get with it," Joe Mottaki growled.

The words were no more than out of his mouth when the howitzer vomited out another round, rocking the vehicle as the muzzle blast broke windows up and down the street, those that were still intact.

The tank was hidden in a fireball that grew and grew.

"Driver, any old time."

The vehicle jerked into motion. In seconds it was clanking right along, working up to its top speed of over forty miles per hour.

The driver turned a corner and aimed the vehicle down a narrow street lined with parked cars on both sides, heading away from the ministry. The howl of the diesel engine in the tracked vehicle filled the urban canyon with thunder as curious people leaned out their windows to see what was happening. Two police cars rounded the corner ahead and slammed to a stop, blocking the street.

Revving the motor to the redline, the driver drove right through the police cars, smashing them out of the way as the Iranian cops ran for cover.

With my backpack in one hand and the Ruger in the other, I ran for the office with the open window, and my rope. I wanted out. Unfortunately, that was about the time I realized that the Targeting Office, with twenty pounds of virulent C-4 about to explode, was only a couple of doors down, on the floor immediately underneath the room where I had entered. Can I do it to myself, or what?

I threw open the door and charged in, right into an ambush. Five people launched themselves at me. I got off one shot before they piled me, rifle butts swinging. I went out under the onslaught.

The building was visibly on fire, with heavy smoke rolling out, when G. W. Hosein rolled into the street beside the Defense Ministry and coasted to a stop directly beside the broken window where Tommy Carmellini had made his entry. Haddad Nouri was at the wheel of the car behind him, with Ahmad Qajar riding shotgun.

Ahead of Hosein, on the cross street in front of the main entrance, he could see fire trucks rolling in and police cars with sirens moaning and lights flashing.

"Tommy?" he called on the radio. He received no answer.

When I came to—I don't know how long I was out; probably no more than a few seconds—the room was lit with flashlight beams darting about. One was on my face. Someone had ripped off the night vision goggles, I guess, because they were gone.

I tried to move, but there was a man sitting on each arm and leg.

"Well, well, well, Mr. Carmellini," I heard a woman's voice say, filling the heavy silence, which reeked of gunpowder. "We have you at last. Oh, I am going to enjoy getting to know you, Mr. American Spy. I am going to enjoy watching you die."

Shit! It was that bitch Hazra al-Rashid.

She started to say something else, but didn't get it out, because the C-4 in the Targeting Office went off with a mighty crash and the wall blew in, filling the air with dirt and dust and the stink of explosives. I felt the floor sag, and thought we were going to the basement, but we didn't. The guards lost their flashlights, dropped and probably broken—I don't know—and the solids in the air glowed from what little light there was coming through the window.

People went tumbling, some on top of me. I fought with all my strength to get loose. I felt bodies moving, and then I was on my knees, then onto my feet, although I was having a hell of a time breathing with all the crap in the air.

Someone aimed a rifle butt at me, and I took it on the shoulder.

I heard Hazra shouting in Farsi and realized she was telling her men not to kill me. I launched myself at her. Or what I thought was her—I couldn't see much, let me tell you. I smashed my head into her face, felt her going down with me on top. I got my right hand up and was strangling her when three or four of them jerked me off her.

They swarmed me. There were just too many of them. They cuffed my hands behind my back and finally yanked me to my feet. Someone shined a flashlight right in my face.

"Oh, yes," I heard Hazra whisper, forcing the words out. "I'm going to enjoy killing you."

G. W. Hosein was looking at his watch when the C-4 in the Targeting Office exploded. Glass blew out of windows in the floor above, and smoke and plaster dust were ejected, as if from mini-volcanoes. Carmellini had been in the building for fifteen minutes.

He glanced at the broken windows and the crap spewing out of them, just in time to see someone stick a rifle barrel out.

Bullets thudded into the sedan, and the windows shattered as G. W. popped the clutch and jabbed the accelerator to the floor.

The guy in the passenger seat of the second sedan hosed off a poorly aimed burst at the window as G. W. threw the car into a U-turn and accelerated away in the other direction. The second sedan was right behind him.

G. W. kept the pedal to the metal as he shot along the nighttime streets of Tehran with the wind rushing in through the shattered windshield. The sedan with his two colleagues followed faithfully a hundred feet behind. G. W. knew precisely where he was going; he and Joe Mottaki had a rendezvous.

Police cars were converging on the area. G. W. saw one racing in from a side street with siren blaring and slowed to let it cross the intersection ahead of him. It went through from left to right and kept going. The traffic light changed, and G. W. ran it anyway.

At the top of the boulevard he saw a tank and two police cars. As he approached, the tank blew up. Pieces showered the street. A big piece of the turret flew lazily through the air in his direction—and G. W. Hosein swerved just in time as it crashed into the street and shattered into three pieces.

He glanced in the mirror. The other car made it by, too.

Ahead were the police cars, both out of action. Iranian police were bailing from the car as he raced up and threaded his way through the wreckage. Behind him, several of the police decided to shoot at Nouri and Qajar, who leaned out the windows and hosed them with several bursts from a submachine gun.

Then both cars were through and running as fast as their drivers could make them go.

When they topped a gentle rise, they saw the howitzer trundling along. Then it turned left, onto a smaller street.

G. W. swung the car into a high-speed turn onto a parallel street. Nouri stayed with him.

Suddenly a police car roared up alongside Nouri and Qajar. Qajar aimed his submachine gun at the front tires and squeezed off a burst. The driver fought the wheel, then crashed into a parked car.

At the next big boulevard G. W. swung right and found himself right behind the Raad-2 howitzer. One of the crewmen was standing up, manning a tripod-mounted machine gun.

They didn't have far to go. The streets were narrow and lined with parked vehicles. The sidewalks were also narrow, with buildings towering three or four stories over them.

The howitzer slowed and turned into an alley. G. W. and Nouri pulled in right behind it. All the men bailed out.

In front of the howitzer were two old SUVs, a Land Rover and a Chevrolet. Joe Mottaki jumped behind the wheel of the Land Rover, which was in front, and G. W. got in beside him. Ahmad Qajar got in the rear seat; the other men got into the Chevrolet. In seconds they were out of the alley on the other end and driving at normal speeds through the streets.

"They got Carmellini, I think," G. W. said.

Joe Mottaki muttered an expletive as Qajar handed G. W. the rucksack containing the satellite phone.

"They'll get the location of the safe house from him," Joe said, "and he'll tell them about us."

"Not for a while," G. W. said. He had the satellite phone out of the bag and was getting it set up. "Carmellini is tough. But eventually . . ."

"Find an open area and stop," G. W. directed. "I've got to report in."

CHAPTER TWENTY-TWO

Helplessness and frustration swept over me as they dragged me from the partially collapsed room into the corridor, which wasn't in good shape either. That C-4 had really done a job.

Using just flashlights since the power was off, we walked the length of the corridor, into an area where I smelled smoke, then saw it in the flashlight beams. Apparently Joe Mottaki's howitzer shells had done some serious damage. Actually, the main wing of the building, which was on fire, had been pretty much pulverized by the big explosive shells, but I didn't know that then.

They led me across some fire hoses—those guys were still flaking them out, and they had no water in them—and down some stairs, then stuffed me into a van. I didn't see Hazra.

Four men got in the back of the van with me. They had clubs, and every now and then as the van went through the streets one of them would give me a love pat with his to ensure I behaved myself.

As if resisting would do any good. The cuffs were tight, there were four of them, and they were not happy. They gabbled back and forth in Farsi, and I got some of it. I had killed one of them in the room with my pistol while we struggled, and there were two dead men on the stairs. Three dead. They were looking forward to watching Hazra cut me to shreds while I screamed.

That ride was the low point of my life. If I were a betting man, I wouldn't have wagered a used condom on my chances of living another twenty-four hours.

Twenty minutes later the van stopped and they made me get out. I was going willingly, since there was no use resisting. They poked me with their sticks and whacked me some anyway.

We ended up in an ill-lit, wide corridor. We walked and walked, went down some stairs, walked some more.

My nose was full of dirt, so I couldn't smell anything. Which was perhaps a blessing. I had been in third-world prisons before, and they stink to high heaven of human excrement, vomit and fear.

We went through some doors and entered a well-lit area that looked somewhat like a hospital emergency room, with gurneys and medical instruments. Then I saw the bloodstains, on the floor, the gurneys, everywhere. Here was where they slowly and painfully eased people out of this life into the next.

I was shoved into a large room with six gurneys. In my quick glance around, I saw that a corridor led away, and I glimpsed a cell. Two of the gurneys were occupied. I looked to see how bad these people had been treated.

Oh, my God! A woman lay naked, strapped to one gurney, and Ghasem lay naked on the other. They had been cutting on his legs and privates, and he had done some serious bleeding.

The woman saw me and shrieked, "No, no, no."

Mother of God! It was *Davar*!

They must have known I was waiting for someone to remove the handcuffs so I could kill a couple of them with my bare hands, because they didn't do it. I felt a needle go into my arm. Then the darkness came.

When I awoke I heard Hazra al-Rasid's voice and tried to turn my head. I couldn't. Some kind soul had placed a leather strap across my forehead, welding me to the gurney. My arms and legs were strapped down, too. I flexed them . . . and found that I was well and truly trapped.

I could hear Hazra—I assumed it was her, a female voice, in command and obviously enjoying herself—questioning someone, Ghasem, I think. She was questioning him in Farsi, something about a book, and his answers were shouts. No, no, no! Then he screamed, paused to inhale and screamed again at the top of his lungs.

"Hey, bitch," I roared.

Her face appeared above me.

She was naked, as least as far down as I could see.

"I hope you have had a nice nap," she said, and I felt her hand stroking my chest and penis. Apparently I wasn't wearing a stitch either. "And awakened rested and refreshed."

She smiled. "I have some questions for you, Mr. American Spy." She went away for a moment and returned with my backpack, which she placed on my stomach. From it she removed my camera. "What did you photograph, spy?" she asked in good English.

She played with the camera a moment, looked at the photos that came up on the little monitor, then put it back in the pack. She had a great figure, nice chest and breasts, wasn't carrying more than five or ten pounds extra weight.

"My, my," she said. She began pulling out stuff, looked at the computer I had stolen from the Targeting safe and the three hard drives, fingered my pick pack and opened it, then rooted some more in the bag. She pulled out the small burst transmitter and examined it. "What is this?"

I didn't say anything. I thought my goose was well and truly cooked. I figured she was going to kill me anyway, and the less I said, the sooner it would be over. To tell the truth, the idea of telling her what she wanted to know and going straight to the denouement, a bullet in the head, didn't occur to me, then. It's amazing how the human mind works, or mine anyway. Right then I was thinking about that son of a bitch Jake Grafton, who had asked me to go to Iran, and blaming myself for being so fucking stupid that I said, "Okay, yeah, being a loyal American and obedient civil servant with nothing better to do this year, sure, I'll go."

"You are just chock-full of secrets that I am sure you are *dying* to tell me," she said with a smile. I like a pun as well as the next person, but I was in no position to enjoy that one. I didn't like her smile either.

I had never been so scared in my life. I was literally trembling. Trying to get a grip, I asked, "Did anyone ever tell you that you have a nice set of tits?" I figured that any woman who likes to inflict pain while naked should enjoy a compliment like that. "I guess nice Iranian boys don't say things like that. Of course, I doubt that you're a nice girl."

She smiled again as she put the burst transmitter back in the bag. "Oh, you and I are going to have some serious fun," she said, and I almost lost control of my bladder.

She started talking about what she wanted from me—information on the CIA, our safe houses, other agents, and so on, all the while running a hand over my private parts. That was when I started doing some serious figuring. I had no doubt that she could inflict more pain than I could stand, and that I would eventually tell her everything she wanted to know . . . hell, everything I knew or could make up. This was when the idea of spilling my guts came to me.

"Maybe you and I should just sit down like adults and talk this over," I suggested.

She squeezed my balls, hard, which hurt like holy hell. "How would I know if you were telling me the truth?" she asked. "I have a great deal of experience in these matters. When the pain reaches a certain level, every-one tells the truth. When they try to lie, I adjust the pain level to refocus them."

"Better just kill me now," I gasped out.

"And spoil all my fun?" she asked. "Oh, I think not."

She gave my balls one last squeeze, which drew a grunt from me and caused every muscle in my body to contract as far as possible. She disappeared, al-though I could hear her somewhere in the room.

I was trying to get my breath when I heard a door open, then close.

"Major Larijani," she said, her voice hard as a billy club. "I gave orders that I was not to be disturbed."

Oh, great! Larijani was that ugly security asshole who worked for the MOIS.

He shot back something about Ahmadinejad, and then I heard her say, "No." She paused, then said it again, almost begging, "No, no, no," and then I heard a pop.

It wasn't very loud.

The pain from my balls was lessening, and I could breathe normally again. I tried to turn my head. Larijani's face appeared. He started working on the straps that held me down.

"Mr. Carmellini," he said. "I am going to get you loose. Then you must quickly dress and help me with Davar Ghobadi and Ghasem Murad. They are in terrible shape."

It didn't compute. What was going on?

When the strap over my forehead and the ones over my arms were loose, I sat up and looked around while he worked on my legs.

Hazra al-Rashid was lying on the floor. I couldn't see her face; just a pile of brown hide and legs and bare feet, and on the other end, a hank of hair.

"What happened?"

"I shot her," Larijani said. I caught the glimpse of a pistol butt protruding from his belt. "There was no other way to get you out of here."

He was working on the strap across my ankles and had his back to me. I reached around him and jerked the pistol free. The barrel wore a silencer. I put it against his head. He froze.

"Tell me why I shouldn't pull this trigger," I said.

"Jake Grafton asked my boss to give you some in-country help," he replied. "I'm it."

"You and who else?"

"Joe Mottaki is one."

Larijani must be Mossad. At least, he knew someone that was. It looked as if I had been handed a Get-out-of-Jail-Free card, at the last possible moment, but my faith in the good guys was at low ebb. I pointed the pistol at Hazra, who was still sprawled on the floor, and pulled the trigger.

The gun made a nice pop, and as a spent cartridge was ejected, I heard the thump of the bullet striking flesh.

Well . . .

"I'll keep your shooter for a bit, just in case," I said. "Hurry up on that strap. I want to see what that bitch did to Davar and Ghasem."

"It's bad," he muttered.

By God, it was.

Davar was covered with bruises and welts. Her pelvic area was a mass of blue and yellow and purple. They had also pounded her face, which was so swollen and discolored I hadn't recognized her when I first saw her. She was semiconscious; probably with a concussion.

She groaned as Larijani and I got her loose from the gurney.

"Why did they rape her?" I asked Larijani.

"The Koran tells them not to kill virgins," he said, "so they rape the women before they kill them."

"Makes you wonder why Muhammad ever bothered," I muttered.

With the pistol in my left hand, I picked Davar up, put her head on my shoulder and held her like a large baby while Larijani worked on Ghasem, who was bleeding freely. The knives Hazra had used on him were right there. I selected one of the larger ones while Larijani used a towel as a bandage to try to stop the bleeding.

I walked over to where Hazra lay on the floor. He had shot her high in the chest, over her right breast. I could also see a growing spot of blood on her lower torso, apparently where my bullet had prodded her. I turned her over on her back with my foot. Her eyes tracked and she wore a frightened expression, so she wasn't dead yet.

I could help with that.

I bent down, still holding Davar against me with my left arm, looked Hazra right in the eyes and said, "Tell Hitler I said hello." Then I buried the knife between her breasts, right up to the hilt.

Our clothes were lying on a bench, along with everything from our pockets. Working as fast as I could, I got clothes on Davar and skinned back into mine while Larijani worked on Ghasem. I could see from the way the towels were soaking up blood that he was in a really bad way.

Leaving Davar on the bench, lying on her side, I went over to the gurney where Ghasem was.

Larijani had three towels packed around his pelvis, and they were slowly turning red. When he moved one, I saw that Hazra had sliced away much of Ghasem's scrotum and cut so deeply into his thighs that he was bleeding from a major artery.

"I don't think we can get the bleeding stopped," Larijani said bitterly. "He's going to bleed out in a few more minutes." He exchanged one of the soaked towels for a clean one.

Ghasem's face was pale and drawn from loss of blood. Still, his eyes fluttered open. He saw me and apparently recognized me. "Save Davar," he whispered.

I nodded.

"The book . . . get it published."

"Yeah. Sure." I couldn't think of anything else to say.

His eyes focused on the pistol, which I still had in my hand. Larijani had freed both his hands, and now he lifted one, held it out. "Give me the gun," he said.

I handed it to him, butt first. Larijani backed off a couple of steps.

Ghasem Murad looked at Larijani, looked at me, then raised the pistol to his temple and pulled the trigger.

The gun fell onto the floor as the spent cartridge skittered along the stone, making a tinkling noise.

I picked up the gun and handed it to Larijani.

The backpack was on the floor by my gurney. I made sure everything was there and zipped it shut, then put it on. Then I picked up Davar. I put her over my left shoulder, too, in order to have my right hand free, and said to the major, "Let's get the fuck outta here."

Larijani screwed the silencer off the barrel of his pistol and pocketed it, and kept the pistol in his hand, pointed at me. "You in front," he said. He pulled the door shut behind us.

In the anteroom were four guards. Larijani said something to them, and I caught the phrase "doesn't want to be disturbed."

The guards were curious as hell, but they knew better than to question orders. They looked at me, at Davar, then back to Larijani and nodded. He growled something, and they stiffened to attention.

We walked out, with me leading the way, carrying Davar.

When he was satisfied we weren't being followed, Larijani said he was taking us to the safe house. He didn't have much to say after that, and I didn't either. We walked out of the building and got into his car. I put Davar on the backseat and got in beside her.

Maybe I shouldn't have given the pistol to Ghasem. I knew he was going to shoot himself, and I knew damned well we couldn't stop the bleeding. Hell, that could have been me on that gurney—and it would have been in another hour or so if Larijani hadn't come in and shot the hell bitch—and if it had been me, I'd have wanted the pistol, too.

I tried to put Ghasem out of my mind and focus on Davar. One eye was swollen completely shut. She could see a little out of the other. Her nose was broken, and she breathed through swollen lips. She was conscious enough to know what was going on.

"Hazra told me she knew everything," she said, so softly I had to put my ear near her lips to hear. "Knew who I saw, what I did . . . knew about me and you." She drew a ragged breath. "She said she was the one who serviced the drop."

My brain was frozen. I couldn't come up with words to comfort her.

After a bit she continued. "Said I thought I was committing treason, and since I wanted to, I had to suffer and die . . . Then she laughed. Said I had helped fool the Americans, the Great Satan."

"That's enough," I said. "Save your strength."

"All the time she was talking they were cutting on Ghasem and he was screaming."

After a few minutes, she added, "They came for me during the morning. When I got to the prison Ghasem was already on the gurney."

She fell silent after that, and I held her as tightly as I could.

After we got her into a bed in the tunnel under the hotel, I had a little talk with Larijani. "I must use this burst transmitter," I said.

"On the roof of the hotel. Do it now."

I couldn't get to the roof. I did find an empty room on the top floor that had a window I could open, so I used it. I sent everything I had photographed to Jake Grafton. Unfortunately, I had no way to get the data off the hard drives I had stolen. They were going to have to be flown out of Iran, then flown to the United States.

I sat there at the window looking out at the rooftops of Tehran. The buildings ran on and on, getting smaller and smaller, until they disappeared into the haze. All these people . . . and Ahmadinejad and Khamenei wanted to murder them, make them martyrs for the greater glory of Allah. I almost puked just thinking about it.

Unable to sit still, I went into the bathroom to steal some towels. There was a little mirror there; I stood transfixed, staring at the strange face I saw reflected in it. Bruised, scraped, with a goose egg on my forehead and an eyebrow cut that had leaked blood until it scabbed over, I looked like a creature from the fiery pit. Felt like it, too. Every muscle ached from the beating I had taken. I felt old and tired and defeated.

I wet the towels in the sink, then headed down the stairs to put them on Davar's face.

Joe Mottaki and G. W. Hosein and their guys were there in the tunnel when I got back. Mottaki hugged me, and G. W. shook my hand with both of his. G. W. had the satellite telephone in his hot little hands.

"We thought—" he began.

I waved it away. "Have you talked to Jake Grafton?"

"Yes. He is sending a helicopter to pick up your hard drives."

"One? Call him back. Tell him we're hot to trot. Send three or four choppers to extract us all. We want out of this damned hole."

CHAPTER TWENTY-THREE

I should be dead, you know, like Ghasem," I said to Larijani. "If you hadn't showed up in the nick, I would be."

Larijani didn't say anything to that. His face showed no emotion.

We were sitting on folding chairs in the underground safe house. Davar was stretched out on a cot twenty feet away. Sheer exhaustion, plus physical and emotional trauma, had finally claimed her.

"How long have you been in country?" I asked Larijani, who sat there with his hands on his thighs, apparently thinking of nothing at all.

He had to tot up the time before he answered. "Ten years and seven months, this time," he said finally. "I grew up here, left when I was twenty. Fought with the Israelis. They wanted me to come back, so I did."

"How did you work your way into the inner circle?"

His eyes shifted to mine. "Take a guess," he said.

"Well, you pulled my chestnuts out of the fire. Saved my life, and I thank you for it. Saved Davar's, too. Hell, I know that Ghasem was also glad to see you."

"I blew my cover. Blew ten and a half years of sheer bloody hell. Are you worth it?"

I blinked.

"I don't think that twit over there was worth it," he continued slowly, his voice low and hard. "She wasn't worth a day of it, I can tell you that. You—I am still trying to decide how many days of that ten and a half years you are worth."

I couldn't think of an answer to that, so I didn't try. Just sat there looking at him. He was an ugly son of a bitch, no two ways about it.

He opened his hands and stared at them. "I had to be the competent, ruthless spy-catcher. That's what the Iranians wanted and needed to protect their nuclear program. My bosses in Israel wanted a man inside who could protect the agency's inside technical boffins, the men who were telling them precisely what Iran was doing and how they were doing it. So I found spies for the MOIS and al-Rashid, framed innocent people and delivered them up as human sacrifices."

His eyes swiveled again to mine. "I murdered them, as surely as if I had pulled the trigger. Delivered them up for torture and agonizing deaths to enhance my reputation, so that I would be trusted. *Innocent men!* You see that, don't you?"

"What was the alternative?" I asked.

"Toward the end every one of them admitted whatever al-Rashid was accusing them of, just to end it." He thought about that for a bit, then added, as if he couldn't believe it were true, "And the bloody bitch believed them."

His eyes left mine. After a moment he reached into a pocket and extracted a pack of foul little cigars. He pulled one out, then remembered me and offered me the pack. I refused.

"It's a filthy fucking world," he muttered.

When Larijani had his cigar going, he sat silently, savoring the smoke. His face was a mask that he had learned to live behind. I suspected that behind that mask he was weighing the sins of the world, and his own, on a scale with an exquisitely delicate balance.

Sometime later G. W. Hosein came in. He sat down beside me and whispered, "I talked to Grafton. He wants us to put the hard drives on the helicopter, and Davar, if you can get her to go. But he wants us to stay. He's going to need us on Jihad day, he said."

Disappointment washed over me like a wave. I tried to keep control of my face, but it was difficult.

"That Grafton . . ." G. W. said.

I promised myself that if I lived long enough to see Grafton again, I was going to strangle him.

When Jake Grafton got home from Langley, he found Callie in the living room with two colleagues from Georgetown University. She introduced her husband to them. One, a woman named Anna Wolfe, taught Arabic. The other professor, Peligro Sanchez, was a theological historian.

"Peligro?" Jake asked. "Doesn't that mean danger?"

Professor Sanchez smiled. "I was in the service for a while and could never shake the nickname."

"Oh," the admiral said.

"I was in explosive ordnance disposal."

The admiral's smile widened to a grin.

"Professor Wolfe has read Dr. Murad's manuscript," Callie said when they were all seated. "She translated twenty or so pages, and Professor Sanchez has read them." She offered the pages to Jake, who took them and scanned the first page, then put it back on the pile.

"This manuscript," Sanchez began, carefully weighing his words. "This manuscript is easily the most original work on man's relationship with God and the cosmos since Martin Luther wrote his theses."

Jake Grafton glanced at Callie, who nodded her concurrence.

"The book is divided into twelve chapters," Professor Wolfe said, "which expound upon and explain things like man's relationship with God, man's relationship with nature and his fellow man, and so on. The twenty pages are excerpts from four chapters and are, I think, extraordinary. Amazingly, the whole book is of this intellectual and literary quality. This book *must* be published."

"What can you tell us about Israr Murad?" Sanchez asked Jake.

"He was a professor of comparative religion at a university in Iran."

"Was?"

"He died under interrogation."

Callie broke the silence that followed that remark. "Professor Wolfe would like to translate the whole work. Professor Sanchez wants to write a foreword. A former student of mine works for a literary agency in New York. Tomorrow morning I am taking the train to New York, and she and I will have lunch together. I hope that when she reads those pages, she'll take Professor Murad's book as a personal project and try to find a publisher."

Her husband merely nodded.

"If I may ask, Admiral," Professor Sanchez said, "how did you get possession of the manuscript?"

The admiral glanced at Sanchez, who got a good look at those cold gray eyes. "Legally," Grafton said flatly.

"Uh-huh," said Peligro Sanchez, who decided he had no more questions.

Jake saw the look on his wife's face. His expression softened and he added, "A member of Murad's family asked a friend of mine to send it to me."

The thought occurred to Peligro Sanchez that he was tiptoeing into a minefield. "I see," he said.

"I am sure the literary agent will require permission from the heirs to represent them," Callie said to Jake.

"I'll work that problem," Jake told her, his face warming up as he met her gaze. "Have you asked these folks if they want a drink? I could use a beer."

Peligro Sanchez decided a beer would be perfect, and both the ladies agreed they could drink a glass of white wine. Soon they were sipping their drinks and discussing the work of Israr Murad.

When the academics departed, Jake poured himself a glass of whiskey and sat down to read the twenty pages translated by Anna Wolfe.

In the light of the early morning, before the heat became stifling, Mahmoud Ahmadinejad and his aides stood in front of the still-smoking ruins of the main section of the Ministry of Defense as an IRGC colonel explained what had happened. While the howitzer was shelling the building, an American spy was at work in the Targeting Office in the west wing. He had been caught, of course, and was now being interrogated.

With the stench of the smoke in his nostrils, Ahmadinejad walked a few steps from his aides and stood looking. The Targeting Office. Well, the spy was captured, so the Americans knew nothing of what he found. Hazra al-Rashid had him and would squeeze everything he knew from him before he died—she could be relied upon to do that.

The effrontery of these infidels—to destroy the ministry!

He turned and looked up the boulevard at the low hill where the colonel said the howitzer had fired from. Almost a kilometer and a half away!

Across the street the police had a line set up to restrain the curious. Ahmadinejad looked at the crowd filling the sidewalk in both directions. Easily several thousand people were over there, looking at him and the ruined hulk of a building behind him.

He motioned to an aide. "A news release, I think," he said. The aide removed a notebook and pencil from his pockets. "The savage effrontery of the infidels is here on display for the citizens of Iran, and the devout sons of Islam everywhere, to see and contemplate. This building was destroyed by agents of Zionism and the Great Satan." He knew nothing about the participation of Mossad agents but decided to blame the Israelis anyway. A dearth of facts never slowed down a good politician.

"The strength and depravity of our enemies makes our cause glorious," he continued, "worthy of our best efforts. The glory of the martyrs will shine like a sun in Paradise." There was more, a lot more, because Mahmoud Ahmadinejad really thought like this, and because he knew the newspapers, controlled by the state, would print every word. Perhaps he could stiffen the spines of those whose faith was less than his.

He was finished with his peroration when another aide, still holding a cell phone, came to him and said, "Al-Rashid took the spies to Evin Prison. She is there now, interrogating them, but she left strict orders she was not to be disturbed or interrupted."

Ahmadinejad knew Hazra al-Rashid's proclivities and methods, so he wasn't surprised. He did, however, decide to go to Evin Prison to see these spies in person and find out what she had learned. Perhaps he could even offer a helpful hint or two to his interrogation expert. After all, he had some experience, and he, too, enjoyed the process.

So it was that he found himself in Ward 209 of Evin Prison, yet the door to the interrogation room and cells was firmly closed. Not wishing to embarrass Hazra, who he knew often liked to work naked, he used the closed circuit telephone to call in. When no one answered, Ahmadinejad looked from face to face. "Has anyone been in there since the spies were taken in?"

"Major Larijani went in," the senior guard told him. "He came out with the big American, who was carrying the woman over one shoulder. He told us not to interrupt al-Rashid."

These fools! What was Larijani doing in there? Taking the big American out?

"Open the door," Ahmadinejad ordered.

So that was how Mahmoud Ahmadinejad became the person who discovered the naked corpse of Hazra al-Rashid, with the hilt of a knife protruding from between her breasts.

He also discovered the corpse of Ghasem Murad. A glance at the young man on the gurney told him the story. Someone, either Murad or Larijani, had given him a merciful coup de grace. It certainly couldn't have been Hazra, who would never have lifted a finger to ease a victim's pain.

Mahmoud Ahmadinejad stood silently looking at Hazra, with the brown eyes open and frozen.

Oh, too bad, too bad. His life would not be the same without her. She understood the role of pain in human life. Still, they would meet again in Paradise, wreathed in glory, with the blood of infidels on their hands, and walk hand in hand to meet the Prophet.

Larijani! Traitor or spy?

As he walked out, Ahmadinejad gave the orders for a manhunt. *Find Larijani and that American spy, Carmellini. Bring them here, alive, and then call me.*

When Davar regained consciousness, I made her drink some water; then I sat on her cot and held her hand. Some of the swelling in her face had gone down, but now the bruises were turning various colors, with yellow and purple joining the black and blue.

She listened to my recount of our rescue without a word. That Larijani was a Mossad agent didn't rate a comment. Still, when I ran down, she whispered through swollen lips, "Is Ghasem dead?"

"Yes."

"I had to listen as she butchered him. I didn't think there were people like that on this planet."

Apparently she had been unconscious when Ghasem shot himself, and I didn't want to tell her how he died, so I changed the subject. "Who beat you up?"

"The guards who raped me. I didn't resist, gave them no pleasure, and that infuriated them."

I merely sat there holding her hand. After a while she asked, still whispering, "Where are we?"

"In a tunnel under the city."

She didn't say anything to that.

"We need to get you to a doctor," I said. "There is a helicopter coming this afternoon. It will take you out of Iran, take you to a doctor."

"Why a doctor?"

"You've had a concussion, and you were bleeding some. I don't know if it's stopped. A doctor might want to look you over and give you some antibiotics."

"To save me? For what?"

"To prevent you from getting a raging infection."

"I'm not going to die from this," she said fiercely. "Persian women have been raped since the dawn of time. Greeks, Arabs, Mongols, the men all did it . . . a lot. We're tough, we can take it."

"I see," I said. I didn't tell her that while she was unconscious Larijani and I had injected her with a massive dose of antibiotics. I wondered if that dose was enough. I also didn't tell her that if an artery let go in her brain, she was going to die immediately or be crippled for life.

"When I'm well," she said, "if those guards are still alive, I'm going to hunt them down like the animals they are and kill them."

"Everyone should have a reason to get out of bed in the morning," I agreed.

"I'm going to look them square in the face and ensure they know who I am. Then I am going to kill them."

"Right on."

"Don't be condescending, American spy." She pulled her hand from mine.

"I'm sorry," I said.

Somehow that conversation had gotten away from me. I was going to tell her she would get well and someday this experience would be only an ugly memory, but even I didn't believe that crock of Pelosi, and I certainly didn't have the guts to say it aloud.

Maybe she was right. She *should* get a gun, find the bastards and drill them right between the eyes. After shooting off their dicks, of course, and watching them scream for a while.

The more I thought about it, the more I liked the idea. Maybe if I was still alive a week from now, after Ahmadinejad's Jihad Day, I'd help her do it. A man also needs a reason to get out of bed in the morning.

I pulled another cot alongside hers and put my backpack on it to use as a pillow. There was a blanket on the cot. I kicked off my shoes and lay down. I reached out and touched Davar's hand.

"No," she whispered, so softly I almost missed it. "Sleep beside me."

So I moved over to her cot. There was just enough room if I lay on my side with her head on my arm. I managed to get the blanket over both of us, and then I surrendered to exhaustion.

Amazingly, I slept without dreams.

Sal Molina found Jake Grafton in a conference room in the Pentagon standing in front of a huge map of Iran. He was examining locations on the map and referring to a list he held in his hand as two senior NCOs plotted locations and drew lines.

When he saw Molina, Grafton motioned to him and showed him the sheet of paper in his hand. "Here are the locations for the nuclear armed missiles. The lines show their route of flight to their targets."

After looking at the list, Molina handed it back and asked, "How reliable is this information?"

"Tommy Carmellini got it out of the Iranian Defense Ministry Targeting Office. He was caught and would have been tortured to death, but he was saved by an Israeli agent. He sent us this a few hours ago."

"Do you believe this is genuine?"

Grafton paused and stared at the map. "Probably."

"The Iranian Defense Ministry was attacked by someone with a cannon about twelve hours ago. The Iranian government is outraged. They are making big threats. Is this list what it was all about?"

Grafton turned to the presidential aide and looked him in the eyes. "Tommy needed a diversion."

"Do they know we have this list?"

Jake Grafton led the way to two chairs in the back of the room. "Probably. Tommy was caught before he could get out of the building, and he left a bomb in the Targeting Office, so they know he was in there. They know he escaped from custody."

"So if they know we have it . . . ?"

"They have two choices," Jake Grafton said. "They can move the missiles or reprogram them to new targets. Or try to do both. We have satellites and drones overhead and AWACS planes in the Gulf and over Iraq, so if they try to shuffle missiles around we'll know it. As for changing targets, they've already picked the best dozen they could find." He made a gesture of dismissal. "I don't think it matters whether they believe we have this list or not."

Sal Molina had known Grafton for years; he well knew that Grafton looked at problems from a different perspective than most of the military brass and all of the politicians, which was why he was so valuable. He could solve problems that appeared to be hopeless tangles, and had done so repeatedly for years. The rub was that his solutions were often tough medicine to swallow.

"What matters is what they do or don't do to protect these launch sites," Grafton said, glancing at Molina to see if the lawyer was with him. "They don't know if we really have this list, or if we do, whether we think it's genuine. If they rush troops out to these twelve sites, that will tend to confirm that these are indeed nuclear weapons launch sites."

"They could scatter troops all over," Molina suggested.

"Indeed, and that would tend to confirm that launch is imminent."

"So what are they doing now?"

"Nothing. So far. That could change any minute."

Sal Molina rubbed his face, then put his palms flat on his thighs. "Okay. What is your plan?"

"We can't take out these sites before they roll out the missiles. The president wants us to react to Iranian aggression, not to be preemptive."

Molina nodded, once.

"The problem is they have nine hundred missiles. *Nine hundred!* Some of them are going to be launched—that is inevitable. Our job is to minimize the damage from conventional warheads and try to prevent the launching of nuclear missiles or shoot them down."

"Okay," Molina said slowly.

"So here is how we're going to do it." Jake Grafton led Molina back to the map and launched into an explanation.

If I had been arranging a helicopter rendezvous with clandestine agents in Iran, I would have picked the most godforsaken place I could find, as far from the Iranian military and any civilians as possible, and I would have done it in the dead of night. I even suggested two such locations that I picked from a map when I talked via satellite phone to Jake Grafton.

"This afternoon at three twenty-five your time in a park," he said, and named it.

"I don't want to rain on your parade, but I am the number one most wanted man in Iran. They are looking for me all over."

"One suspects," he said.

"How about a vacation? Maybe I just jump on the chopper and head for France. I know a woman there, and—"

"I have a job for you," he said. "Here in a few days Ahmadinejad and his buddies are going into that executive bunker. Once they are in, I want you to ensure they don't come out."

"Sounds like a job for the air force."

"Oh, they'll do a permanent job. You and our people there must keep them inside until the concrete sets."

Oh boy.

"What do you think you'll need to do the job?" he asked.

"A tank."

"You'll have to get that locally."

"And a couple of satchel charges and a couple of submachine guns and ammo."

"Okay," he said. "I can do that."

So at the appointed time G. W. Hosein and I sat in a car on the edge of the park waiting for the chopper. We were both togged out as Iranian army colonels, complete with sidearms and fake beards.

As we waited, we watched Revolutionary Guards wearing slovenly uniforms and carrying AK-47s stroll along, eyeing everyone.

"They're looking for us," G. W. said as he watched four of them standing on a corner a hundred feet away.

I merely grunted. I was keeping an eye on them, too.

I looked at my watch. "Fifteen minutes," I said.

As I watched, the knot of four accosted a group of four women wearing those long coverings and scarves. The boys wanted to talk and strut. They couldn't have been much over twenty years of age, with scraggly little beards and pimples. For all I knew, they were four future ayatollahs.

The women looked properly respectful.

Between us and the IRGC boys, a sidewalk vendor was selling food to the local civilians, who were out with their children. All in all, it looked like another day in Tehran to me.

As we watched, a truckload of IRGC soldiers went past us.

"Let's go," I said and hoisted the backpack from its position between my feet.

The IRGC boys ignored us as we walked into the park. G. W. took a beacon from his pocket, triggered it, then put it back.

We walked toward a tree on the edge of a large grassy area and stopped beside it. We had been there about three minutes, watching the kids play, when I heard the chopper. After another minute I saw it, a Russian-built Hind with Iranian army markings. The Hind was the easiest helo in the world to recognize because it had two counterrotating rotor disks mounted on the same mast. It went right over our heads, then swung out in a wide turn. It circled the area as it bled off speed, then came slowly down toward the open area, its nose into the breeze. Kids and parents scattered to get out of the way.

When the machine landed, I walked briskly over. The only man in the chopper was the pilot, who was wearing an Iranian uniform.

"Carmellini?" he asked loudly, over the roar of the engine, which was still turning at 100 percent. This guy wasn't taking any chances; all he had to do to take off was lift the collective.

"Yeah," I said, and checked to see that the rotor wash hadn't loosened my beard.

"I was told there might be a passenger."

"She decided to stay."

I tossed the backpack on the floor beside him as I looked around for IRCG soldiers. Two knots of them were watching, their AKs cradled in their arms.

"Those duffel bags in back are for you," he shouted, pointing.

I reached for the nearest one, which weighed about thirty pounds, I guessed. When I had them both on the ground, I said loudly, "Have a nice flight."

Hoisting my bags, I walked out from under the rotors back toward G. W., who was still under the tree. The rotor wash increased in intensity and played with my clothing. I felt a corner of my beard coming loose.

In seconds the chopper was off and climbing.

As I walked up, G. W. said, "Let's get the fuck outta here."

"Amen to that."

Ignoring the gawking IRGC soldiers, we walked back to the parked car, got in and drove away.

I'll admit, you gotta have a lot of balls to order a stunt like that. That Jake Grafton . . .

In the Hind, U.S. Army Warrant Officer John Pepper skimmed the rooftops of Tehran. He brought the chopper around to a northwest heading and checked the portable GPS that he had mounted on top of the glareshield. His route from Iraq to the clandestine refueling depot inside Iran, and from there to Tehran, had been carefully chosen by the intelligence officers to avoid known military bases and antiaircraft missile sites. Mostly, Pepper had flown up and down canyons at low altitude, popped over ridges and skimmed across fields and forests with his skids almost in the trees. He was going to fly the reciprocal of that course to get out of Iran.

As he flew over the city, his helicopter was of course being swept by search radars. He glanced at the ALQ-199 display: this box had also been stuck on top of the panel. The box revealed every radar sweep, yet the green light stayed illuminated. The green light, according to the major who had briefed Pepper, meant the gadget was working and the Iranians couldn't see him.

Still, sitting alone in a Russian-made Iraqi chopper skimming across Tehran, John Pepper fought back the urge to look over his shoulder for Iranian fighters. He also fought back a powerful urge to pee.

Oh, baby! Who knew, when he was a jug-headed kid and volunteered for army flight training, that this adventure was in his future?

John Pepper glanced down at the backpack on the floor and wondered what it contained. Something important, no doubt, something they would never tell him about.

He automatically ran his eyes over the gauges one more time, checked that he was indeed on course, then set the autopilot and removed a pack of cigarettes from the sleeve pocket of his flight suit and lit one as the rooftops of Tehran sped by beneath his machine.

CHAPTER TWENTY-FOUR

Mahmoud Ahmadinejad knew the magnitude of the risks he was taking. He intended to wipe Israel and the largest American bases in the Middle East off the globe, send everyone in them to Paradise or hell, as Allah chose. And he was willing to obliterate Tehran, kill or maim the twenty million people in it, and blame the atrocity on the Americans. When the dust settled, he, the new Mahdi, would lead the Muslims of the earth in a holy war against the infidels. This would be the final war, the war between good and evil that would decide the fate of the human species and the planet.

"But we will have no more nuclear weapons," Ayatollah Khamenei said. "What if the Americans massively retaliate, destroy *all* our cities and holy places? What if Iran ceases to exist, becomes only a memory?"

"All the believers will be in Paradise."

"They are all going there anyway, without a nuclear war," the ayatollah pointed out with impeccable logic. "What if there is no Iran to lead the believers of the earth in this holy war?"

"I believe Allah wishes for us to struggle until the end. The words he spoke to Muhammad that he wrote into the holy Koran leave no other interpretation."

Khamenei didn't want to debate theology. In truth, he and his fellow mullahs lived a comfortable life in Iran, paid for with petrodollars, and he doubted that his friends wanted to trade their comfort for the glories of martyrdom. To be sure, Ahmadinejad wouldn't say it quite that way, but he was steering the ship of state in that direction, and want it or not, martyrdom was visible just ahead.

Not that Khamenei had any intention of sitting in his office in the capitol waiting for a nuclear warhead to explode over his head. He and his key religious and political allies would all be in the executive bunker with Ahmadinejad and the senior officers of the armed forces.

As he thought about it, he opened a drawer in his desk, took out the list of people who would be in the bunker and scrutinized it. Almost four hundred names were on it; most, admittedly, were the wives and children of the religious, military and political elite.

His eye stopped at the name of General Habib Sultani, minister of defense. The general had suffered a nervous breakdown and was in a private sanitarium. It would be impossible to put him in the bunker, a man already unhinged. No, the merciful thing was to let the gods of war end Sultani's life quickly, and Allah would usher him into Paradise.

Khamenei's eyes continued down the list, considering each name, weighing what they could bring to the monumental task before them.

The fate of Habib Sultani's family didn't get an iota of thought from the great man. He didn't waste an erg on the twenty millions of people who were to be sacrificed in Tehran; he gave not a thought to the people in Palestine, Jordan, Lebanon and Syria who would die if the missiles aimed at Israel missed a little bit, nor did he spend a second or two contemplating the fate of the people in Iraq, Kuwait and Qatar who would be cremated alive by missiles aimed at the military bases there. Like tyrants throughout history, Ali Khamenei rarely, if ever, thought about anyone but himself.

Khamenei put the list back in the drawer and closed it. Ahmadinejad was on the other side of the desk, seemingly lost in his own thoughts.

The ayatollah had approved the tens of billions of dollars that had been spent on the nuclear program, not because he contemplated using nuclear weapons on anyone but because possession of such weapons would cause Iran's prestige to soar, raising the nation from the status of a rich third-world oil producer to first rank among the world's nations. Today he reminded himself of the sniveling, cowardly responses of the major powers to Iran's nuclear program. Once Iran had nuclear warheads on its missiles, it would be the major Islamic nuclear power—and the undisputed leader of the Islamic world.

Unfortunately, Khamenei thought, Ahmadinejad wants to trade diplomatic and moral leadership for a military quest, which might or might not turn out as he hoped. He glanced at Ahmadinejad now, and saw a dangerous fanatic.

Khamenei realized that he had five days until Jihad Day, and of course he could postpone the launches at any time, or stop them altogether, right up until the rocket motors ignited. *If* the armed forces would obey him. If they refused, Ahmadinejad would have won, would have reduced him to a figurehead without power, like the Japanese emperor or the queen of England.

Of course, if Ahmadinejad was dead, the armed forces would have no choice. They would have to obey him. And he could lead the Islamic world into a new, brighter future.

In the silence of Khamenei's office, Ahmadinejad was also doing some serious thinking. His strong right arm, Hazra al-Rashid, was dead, and the American spy, Carmellini, and the traitor, Larijani, were at large somewhere in the city. They had undoubtedly learned the truth about Jihad Day, and one had to assume they had communicated it to Israel and America.

Still, what could the Zionists and the Great Satan do at this stage of the game? If they could even find the backbone or political will to resist the inevitable.

No, those agents of the devil were not his most virulent threat. The most dangerous threat he faced was the ayatollah, sitting there like one of Muhammad's sons, certain that his was the proper vision for Iran's future. Khamenei knew the words of the Prophet, certainly, and yet he still hesitated to take up the bloody flag of martyrdom and go forth as a soldier of Allah.

However, Mahmoud Ahmadinejad thought, not for the first time, what if the Zionists were to strike the Supreme Leader down before Jihad Day? The act would infuriate Muslims worldwide, would prepare them for the great holy war to come.

Suddenly certain, Ahmadinejad knew that was the way the future should be written. He had had dedicated holy warriors willing to do the job ready for months. All he needed to do was issue the order. The time, he decided, had come.

When I called Jake Grafton that evening, he asked me to get Davar and call him back. As usual, I was in the attic of the hotel. I closed up the phone, repacked it and took it with me, just in case. The hotel was empty of guests, and the staff had been given several days off with pay, so the hallways were empty. In the basement I moved the stuff that hid the hole, wriggled through, then pulled the stuff back into place and descended the ladder to the tunnel.

Davar was awake and alert. She was sitting up on her cot. Her swollen face showed every color of the rainbow. Still, she tried to smile when she saw me. Then she arranged a scarf over her face so that only her eyes were visible.

I reached with both hands and gently removed the scarf. "I know you look a mess," I said, "but I want to see your face, just the same. The time for hiding behind scarves is almost over."

"Oh, Tommy," she murmured.

We chatted for a bit about this and that, carefully avoiding mentioning our recent adventure, or Ghasem.

Finally I said, "My boss wants to talk to you on the satellite phone. Now, if possible. We'll have to climb clear up to the attic of the hotel that sits above this tunnel. Are you up for that?"

"Do you mean, can I do it?"

"Yes."

She used both hands to lever herself erect. I could tell she was one sore female. Still, she didn't complain. I stood beside her and kissed her as gently as I could. She wrapped her arms around me and stood like that for a long moment.

Then she said, "Let's go." She reached behind her for the scarf, and this time I helped arrange it. If she ran into any IRGC guys, we didn't want them to see her face.

I got Joe Mottaki to run interference. Twenty minutes later Davar and I were back in the attic, and Joe was on the floor below, ensuring we were not interrupted. Davar sat on the only chair and caught her breath as I set up the satellite phone, checked the encryption device and made the call.

I could only hear her side of the conversation, which consisted mostly of yeses and noes. After a while, she handed me the phone. Grafton's voice sounded in my ear, distorted as usual by the encryption gear.

"I want you and G. W. to do a scouting expedition, then lay low until Jihad Day."

"Yes, sir."

He briefed me on what he wanted me to do. I merely sat and listened. When Jake Grafton is giving you a mission, he covers everything you need to know and most of the foreseeable contingencies. I had no questions. My face must have turned pale, however, because I felt Davar take my hand and give it a gentle squeeze. I looked down at her. Through the gap in the scarf, I saw tears leaking from her eyes.

After I severed the connection and was packing up the phone, I asked her, "Do you know any of those folks who will be in the executive bunker?"

She nodded yes. "Girls I went to school with," she whispered. "Some of them are friends."

I took a deep breath. "If the Iranian missile forces manage to launch that missile aimed at Tehran, everyone in this city not in that bunker will be dead, cremated alive or killed by heat or radiation or fire, or crushed under the rubble. Including you and me. All *twenty million* of us. Once that thing is in the air, we are all dead."

"Yes," she whispered, so softly I almost missed it, and lowered her head. She looked so forlorn. She wasn't telling me all of it—I could see that. "Who else will be in that bunker?" I demanded.

"My father and brother."

I stared.

She raised her head. "My brother, Khurram, is a follower, one of the herd who follows the fundamentalists because they prey on the weak. They make him feel big." She shook her head, then continued. "My father believes in money. He built that bunker—that obscenity—because they paid him. I asked him once what they were going to use it for, and he looked at me as if I had lost my mind. 'In the event of an attack,' he said, 'the leaders must be saved.' 'And who else?' I asked. 'If Iran is attacked, who else will be saved?'

"He merely looked at me and said, 'Don't worry. We will be in the bunker.'

"That was his answer. *We* would be in the bunker."

I went to the window and stood looking out. The part of the city I could see looked surreal, a mixture of old and new, atrocious architecture and stunning old buildings. I could hear the traffic, a living presence, and feel the people. The day was hot, and the heat made everything shimmer. The horrible pollution, which limited visibility to about three miles, smelled familiar, comfortable.

In a week I would probably be dead. Jake Grafton hadn't minced words or tried to dress it up. As he spoke I remembered how that Hind helo had looked that afternoon, choppering off for Iraq. I wished to Christ Davar and I had been on it.

Staring at the doomed city, I realized that the best I could hope for was getting vaporized in the initial fireball.

Would I go to heaven? After all I had done? Or would I get to shake hands with the devil in hell?

Is there a heaven, or only blackness?

I turned and glanced at Davar, who was still sitting with her head lowered, lost in her own thoughts.

Maybe there was something I should say to her, but for the life of me I couldn't think of anything.

When the Israeli ambassador called on the president, Sal Molina came to the conference room across the hall from the Oval Office and motioned to Jake Grafton, who was staring at a wall-sized chart that had been made from the photos Tommy Carmellini sent from Tehran with the burst transmitter. Other charts lay upon the table, along with sheets of paper setting forth the orders of battle.

The ambassador was speaking when Jake and Sal lowered themselves onto a couch at the side of the room.

"My government has decided on a first strike. Two missiles with nuclear warheads, each with two hundred kilotons of explosive power, are to be fired at Israel. If even one of them explodes over Israel, the population will be murdered where they stand. Israel will cease to exist. Quite simply, the risk is too great. We must act before the Iranians can fire those missiles."

The president was standing in front of his desk, facing the ambassador, with his feet spread slightly and his hands in his pockets. His head was down, as if a great weight were pressing on him. "No," he said.

"No?" The ambassador's voice rose. "No? You stand here in Washington, half the world away from those madmen, and you tell us *no?*"

The president's head came up. "Israel's survival depends on more than surviving a nuclear blast. If you make a first strike on Iran with your limited assets, you will use nuclear weapons."

The ambassador stiffened. "The military has not—"

"I know, I know," the president interrupted. "Your government hasn't shared a strike plan with you. But I am telling you, without transports and commandos on the ground and enough planes, the only possible way Israel can neutralize those missiles before they are pulled into the open for launch is to use nukes on the tunnel entrances."

The ambassador took the blow in silence. The president continued relentlessly, "If you do that, the Islamic world will never forgive you; Europe will never forgive you; and, truthfully, most Americans will never forgive you. Israel will have ignited World War III—*which is precisely what Ahmadinejad hopes to accomplish*—and no power on earth could save it from the holocaust that will follow."

The ambassador looked around for a chair. He sank into the nearest one.

After a moment the ambassador said slowly, "I merely deliver the message from my government. I do not make the decisions."

"I understand."

"The weight of responsibility is not on my head."

The president waited until the ambassador was looking up at his face. "*I am responsible*," he said. "The weight of responsibility is upon *me*."

The president turned back to his desk, his hands still in his pockets. Finally he parked a cheek on the polished mahogany. "When I ran for president, I never thought I would have to make decisions like this." He rubbed his chin with his right hand, then wiped his forehead with it and dried it on his trousers.

"Be that as it may," the president added, "*I know I am right*. You know it, too."

The ambassador nodded.

"An airburst over Tel Aviv *or Iran* will doom Israel," the president continued remorselessly. "That choice is simply between a quick death or a slow one."

"Show us an alternative."

The president glanced at Jake Grafton. "Let's go to the conference room. You can brief us."

Jake Grafton rose from the couch and led the way.

An hour later, after the ambassador had left, the president stood looking at the charts. "I pray to God, and Allah, that your plan will work," he said to Grafton, who merely nodded.

"Come on, Sal," the president said, looking at Molina. "Let's go next door and call the Israeli prime minister. Now I have to sell him." He and his aide walked out of the room, leaving Jake Grafton alone with the charts and maps.

After a while, the admiral packed up all the charts and maps, locked them in his briefcase, chained the briefcase to his wrist and went home.

Grafton was home alone that evening—his wife was at a faculty function at the university—sitting in his den sipping whiskey, when the telephone rang. He picked it up.

"Grafton."

"Jake, this is Sal. The Israelis agreed to hold off."

"Uh-huh."

"They said that if one nuke goes off over Israel, they'll massively retaliate. There won't be two bricks left stuck together anywhere in Iran."

Grafton shot back, "Of course the president told them that we would have airplanes over the country and boots on the ground."

"He did," Molina replied.

"Yeah," said Jake Grafton, then slowly lowered the telephone onto its cradle.

That night G. W. Hosein and Joe Mottaki stole some army vehicles. They didn't tell me where they got them or who they had to kill, and I didn't ask.

The following morning Davar, G. W. and I set forth in an SUV painted army colors. We wore uniforms, even Davar, who had a heavy beard glued to her swollen face. At least the swelling was going down. Still, she looked as if she had been in a car wreck and smashed her face on the dashboard.

Joe Mottaki followed us in an army truck. His men, Haddad Nouri and Ahmad Qajar, rode in the back with AK-47s in their arms. They had a machine gun on the floor of the bed, near their feet, that they had liberated somewhere.

After a half hour of inching through traffic and avoiding roadblocks, we found ourselves in an area of finger ridges that came down from the mountains to the north. The Parliament building and other large government buildings were about half a mile to the south.

"The executive bunker is under that ridge," Davar said, pointing.

"The main entrance," she continued, "is under that prayer ground there." She pointed again. "The Mosalla Prayer Grounds. It's like a park, except one goes there to pray. The entrance to the bunker is in the basement of that small mosque. There is a tunnel that the people walk through to get to an elevator shaft. The head of the shaft is under twenty-five feet of reinforced concrete. Then they covered the concrete with ten feet of dirt."

I looked at the buildings, trying to visualize the underground complex. "The main tunnel—it slopes down to the elevator room?"

"Yes," Davar said. "It is precisely seventy-two meters long and ends at the top of the shaft. There are two elevators to take people up and down. Winding around the shaft is a staircase, in case the elevators cannot be used. The elevators take the people down seventy meters, then there is another room. Bombproof doors divide the room in two. Once through the doors, one finds another elevator shaft, and stairs, descending to the ground floor of the bunker. The floor of the bunker is a hundred and forty meters below the top of the elevator shaft." She pointed. "Most of it lies there, under that ridge to our left. Between the top of the bunker and the surface is over three hundred meters of solid rock."

"Okay," I said.

"There are three air shafts, which will be sealed off when the bunker is occupied. The air in the bunker is recycled through scrubbers, and oxygen is added as necessary. It is submarine equipment we purchased from the Russians."

"How long can four hundred people live down there?" G. W. asked.

"There is food, water and air for six months. A shaft drilled down from the floor of the bunker holds human waste and garbage. It is three hundred meters deep."

"How big is this bunker?" G. W. wanted to know. "How much floor space?"

"Almost two acres. It is cut up into living units, which are separated by fireproof doors. Each living unit has its own fire detection and suppression system. My father was worried that a fire in the bunker might kill everyone, so he designed the units and fire suppression systems. Each is self-contained."

"Electrical power?"

"It is provided by diesel generators, which suck air down four shafts that are not sealed. The air is sucked down and passed through a complex filtration system to scrub out the dust and dirt, then sent to the generators and finally exhausted back to the surface. Even if the intake air is contaminated with radiation, the diesels should still run as long as they have fuel available. A tank in the bunker area contains enough for six months' judicious use."

"Communications?"

"Wires in a pipe laid in a buried trench. Of course, the trench is only ten feet deep, and it only runs to the nearest boulevard. Then the wires are on poles and go to the local telephone exchange."

"Doesn't sound as if they thought that out very carefully," G. W. said.

Davar shrugged. "The blueprints called for a pipe buried fifty feet underground, running to a military switchboard in a bunker under the Alborz Mountains, but that installation was never funded or built. Consequently an airburst over Tehran would wipe out the radio stations and landlines, and the bunker would be isolated anyway."

"Have the bunker's self-contained survival systems been tested?" I asked.

"My father has spent the last six months supervising the tests and repairing discrepancies," Davar said. "He was satisfied."

"Is there only one way in or out?"

"There is another way," she said, "on the other side of the ridge. The heavy equipment and material needed to excavate the cavern for the bunker came in from a ramp dug on the other side, and the dirt had been removed that way. At the same time, the river below the ramp was straightened and widened, a construction job that provided cover for the bunker construction. When the bunker was complete, the ramp to the bunker was filled with reinforced concrete. A walkway, or ramp, runs through the concrete from the bunker to the riverbank. It is sealed with three bombproof doors, one just inside the entrance, one midway along it and one just outside the bunker. The walkway is almost a kilometer long."

"Is your family going into the bunker?" G. W. asked.

"Yes," she said simply, without inflection.

G. W. lit a cigarette with shaking hands. He sucked on it, then flipped ash out the open window, as Davar continued to describe her father's creation. The ceiling of the bunker had been reinforced with lag bolts and massive steel beams.

"The elevator shaft lies fifty-two meters directly northwest of the center of that wall of the mosque," she continued and pointed again. "It's right under that parking lot."

G. W. flipped his cigarette out the window and glanced at me. After our eyes met, he grabbed the steering wheel and put the truck in motion.

"I want to see the secondary entrance," I said.

We had to drive a couple of miles through streets that led across the main ridge on top of the bunker, then cross a bridge over the river to get to the best vantage point.

With the truck stopped, I looked the entrance over with a set of binoculars. It was recessed under a rock shelf, set in the middle of what looked like a large highway tunnel filled with concrete. In fact, that was precisely what it was. I could see the roadway along the river where the big trucks had come and gone. The road had been bulldozed and the ground contoured, yet I could see where it had been.

"How long is the secondary tunnel?" I asked Davar.

"Over a kilometer. There are cutouts and bombproof doors at three places in the tunnel to ensure that a blast at the door doesn't reach the bunker."

I raised the binoculars and studied the ground above the entrance, which sloped away toward the crest of the ridge at perhaps a twenty-degree angle. The only place I could see that would allow a person to see both entrances was directly atop the brush-covered ridge, right over the center of the bunker. I wondered if that spot was too close to ground zero.

Well, sure as hell, I would soon find out.

As I was looking through the binoculars, G. W. asked Davar, "Who designed this bunker complex?"

"My father." I sat frozen, staring through the binoculars, trying to control my face.

When I lowered the binoculars G. W. was looking at me with a bemused expression on his face. Apparently the irony of old man Ghobadi designing and building his own tomb had gotten to him, too.

As head of state, the Supreme Leader Ayatollah Ali Khamenei was not involved with the day-to-day political affairs of the legislature. His public appearances were mostly ceremonial and, since he was also guardian of the state religion, often religious. His visits to mosques were shown on television. However, he was the leader of the Party of God, the ruling political party; the IRGC and its intelligence arms answered directly to him; he was the commander-in-chief of the military; he controlled billions of petrodollars off budget; and Ahmadinejad's government ruled at his pleasure. In short, he and Ahmadinejad were the two most important men in Iran and, some said, the entire Islamic world.

Today, outside the mosque, a television crew waited to film Khamenei as he exited the building. The cameraman began recording when a member of Khamenei's security team gave him a Hi sign from the doorway, indicating the Supreme Leader had finished his prayers and was making his way toward the door.

He got Khamenei centered in the viewfinder, with people right and left, as the Supreme Leader walked slowly toward the camera, looking right and left, nodding to acknowledge the cheers of the crowd. There were always cheers. This was, perhaps, because Khamenei's crowds usually consisted of handpicked members of the nonuniformed paramilitary force, the Basij, busloads of whom were ferried around to appear on camera at the proper moment.

The cameraman was taking it all in as the camera automatically focused on the central figure. So he saw the hand and pistol come out of the crowd, and he saw Khamenei recoil from the punch of the first bullet.

He heard muffled shots and saw that there were at least three men shooting into Khamenei, who went down under the fusillade. Still, the guns continued to fire at the figure sprawled on the steps.

Then the shooting stopped. The cameraman could see the crowd milling—he actually lost sight of Khamenei lying on the pavement—and hear the animal sounds from hundreds of human throats.

Then, almost as if by a miracle, a lane cleared and he glimpsed a dozen men stabbing one to death. He tried to keep the scene centered, but the jostling was too much. In seconds the crowd knocked him down.

Mahmoud Ahmadinejad was in conference with his generals, trying to decide upon the hour of the launch. He thought perhaps a night launch would be best, but his generals were trying to talk him out of it.

"Americans fight best at night," one said. "Every soldier wears night vision goggles, the pilots of their airplanes and helicopters wear them, they have infrared sights . . . If they should for any reason come over Iran to oppose us, we will give a better account of ourselves during the day."

"The night doesn't hide us from them," the general in charge of antiaircraft defense said. "It merely hides them from us."

Ahmadinejad frowned. He had bet everything that he could pull off a massive first strike on Iran's enemies without the Americans getting wind of it. Literally, *everything*! Yet his generals assumed that such a deception was unlikely. Worse, they assumed that even though Iran knew how the Americans' latest ECM magic worked and were prepared to defeat it should the Americans attack, they needed even more of an edge. The moral ascendancy of the infidels over his generals infuriated him. He opened his mouth to blast them, then thought better of it.

"There is a storm moving into the deserts of central Iran," one general said. "Winds will exceed fifty miles per hour in places, gusts much higher, with a lot of dirt in the air. We hope it will dissipate by midnight Sunday, but it might not."

Iran was full of foreign spies, and Hazra al-Rashid was dead, Ahmadinejad mused. Only Allah knew what the Americans believed now. Or if they would find the courage to fight Allah's warriors. It certainly wouldn't hurt to give his generals the advantage they sought.

"We will launch on Monday, two hours before dawn," Ahmadinejad said. "If the enemy chooses to counterattack, they must do so during the day."

The generals nodded their heads. This compromise seemed wise. A chart was consulted to determine the moment of sunrise. Dawn, they decided, could be defined as thirty minutes prior to sunrise. The first wave of missiles would lift off two and a half hours prior to official sunrise.

"Perhaps there will still be enough dirt in the air to hide the launches from the American satellites," one general said.

Ahmadinejad looked Hosseini-Tash squarely in the eyes. "The missiles will be ready? The nuclear warheads installed?"

"Yes, Your Excellency."

"I want you to personally inspect each nuclear warhead after it is installed."

Hosseini-Tash swallowed hard and nodded.

Only Hosseini-Tash knew the targets of the missiles, Ahmadinejad believed. His skin was pasty, yet covered with a thin layer of perspiration. Ahmadinejad could smell him. None of the others seemed overly concerned.

As the meeting was breaking up, Ahmadinejad asked for Hosseini-Tash to wait a moment. When the others were out of earshot he looked the general in the eyes and said, "I want you and your family in the bunker. Promise me. We will need you for the war to follow."

"Thank you, Your Excellency. I promise."

"Very good."

Hosseini-Tash was walking out when a breathless aide came running in. "Your Excellency, Mr. President. Zionists have murdered the Supreme Leader. Three of them shot him down as he was coming out of a mosque an hour ago. The crowd killed the assassins on the spot."

Ahmadinejad feigned surprise. "May peace be with him," he muttered.

"A television camera was there and filmed most of it. With your permission, we wish to air the scene."

"How do we know the assassins were Zionists?"

"Witnesses have come forward and swore they were Israeli agents."

Ahmadinejad paused for a moment, as if to collect his thoughts, then said, "Of course, air the footage. Tell the world what the Zionists have done, and pledge revenge."

"Yes, Excellency," the aide said and hurried away.

When he was alone, Mahmoud Ahmadinejad smiled. Of course he had betrayed the killers, who had been told they would be allowed to escape, but they were worth infinitely more as dead Zionist assassins than as live, loyal MOIS thugs.

They were just three more unwilling martyrs for the glorious cause.

On the other side of the world, Jake Grafton heard about Khamenei's assassination before he arrived for work in the morning. The director, William Wilkins, called him with the news.

"Well, that move was on the board," Grafton said. "We wondered if and when Ahmadinejad would make it."

"He's doing a rant on CNN right now," Wilkins said. "Iranian television was kind enough to provide them with a high-quality digital feed. The Iranians also passed along footage of Khamenei being murdered."

"A story is a story, I suppose," Grafton said. "But cooperation like that—isn't that nice?"

"I thought so, too," Wilkins said and hung up his phone.

Jake Grafton went back to perusing the weather forecasts for the Middle East.

CHAPTER TWENTY-FIVE

Tension was ratcheting tighter at the Pentagon. Ships were at sea, airplanes were fueled and armed, Special Forces teams were ready and sleeping near their transports. Parachutes were packed, guns loaded and missiles ready.

"Everyone knows their job and precisely how to do it," Jake Grafton told the U.S. Central Command commander, a U.S. Army four-star. Jake had planned the operation; the CENTCOM commander had the job of executing it. He and his key staff members had flown in from Kuwait to Washington for this briefing. Sitting in the back of the room was the president's man, Sal Molina.

The four-star, General Martin H. Lincoln, stared at the chart of sites, targets and predicted flight paths. The Americans had done their own simulations and compared them with the information from the computer drives Carmellini had stolen, which had arrived in Washington the previous evening. The job had only been completed an hour ago. "Ahmadinejad is bugfuck insane," Lincoln said.

"Most religious fanatics are," Grafton remarked from his place at the podium.

"So there are only eight sites that will launch nuclear missiles?"

"Yes, sir. The flight paths of the nukes are depicted on the chart in red. We are going to try to track any missiles from those sites, using satellite assets and AWACS. Theoretically, it should be possible to identify fast movers against ground return, yet the terrain is so mountainous . . ." He left the phrase hanging.

"I don't see any antiship missiles targeted for our task forces."

"We don't know what, if anything, they plan to do with their antiship missiles. They bought some from the Russians, but their plans—that is one of the unknowns."

"Has Admiral Bryant received the information you do have, and been briefed on the unknowns?"

"Yes, sir."

"When is Ahmadinejad going to launch these missiles?" the general asked, gesturing at the charts.

"We're not sure, sir," Grafton replied. "Our listening posts around the world are monitoring Iranian army and IRGC tactical transmissions and trying to keep tabs on taxi and police calls inside Tehran. AWACS planes are watching vehicle movement to and from the launch sites and keeping tabs on Iranian air activity. We have a geosynchronous satellite overhead, and drones up twenty-four hours a day watching the launch sites in infrared and regular light. There is a big cold front moving through Iran this weekend, and the forecasters say it will kick up lots of wind and dust. Indications are the front will dissipate by Sunday night, but who knows?

"Our best guess is that the Iranians will launch after the storm dies, late Sunday night or Monday morning. We'll know more as the clock ticks down. The leadership locking themselves in the bunker will be the tipoff that the attack is imminent."

General Lincoln's eyes swept across the map once again and stopped moving when they got to Tehran. "Tell me about the bunker."

"One of our agents was there today, twelve hours ago, and there was a lot of activity around the entrance. Supplies were being delivered in trucks."

"Preparations at our bases in the Middle East?" Lincoln asked crisply.

It took Jake Grafton fifteen minutes to answer this question. To minimize loss of life at these bases, should any Iranian missiles get through the cordon of fighter planes and antimissile defense systems that had been deployed, an exercise was set to occur on Sunday night. All personnel would be required to don antiradiation suits or take shelter in designated areas. Food and water was to be available in the shelters, along with medical supplies. In other words, the bases were going to be in the middle of a full-blown nuclear, biological and chemical exercise when the Iranian missiles arrived, if they did. To prevent word from leaking back to the Iranians, the exercise was highly classified, and early in the weekend the bases would be sealed.

An hour later, all the questions answered, the CENTCOM staff filed out of the room. A limo was waiting to take General Lincoln to the White House; then they were all getting on a plane to Kuwait. The multimedia tech gurus who had generated and displayed the charts and computer presentations followed the brass out, leaving Jake Grafton alone with Sal Molina.

Grafton walked up the aisle and sat down in the last row, with an empty seat between himself and Molina.

"We don't even know if this fandango is really going to happen," Molina groused.

Grafton didn't bother to reply. Molina knew as much as he did about the agency's sources and what they had said.

Molina adjusted his butt in his seat. "The president is thinking about making a secret trip to Tel Aviv."

"Going to sit on ground zero with the Israelis?"

"He's thinking about it. The National Security Council is throwing a duck-fit."

"Umm," said Grafton.

"Someone suggested we send the vice president instead."

"I see."

"He refused to go."

Grafton put his feet up on the back of the seat in front of him. "Most of this angst wouldn't be necessary if we hit the launch sites the instant they rolled out the first launchers."

"We've been through all that. The United States cannot strike the first blow. It's a political impossibility. Neither can Israel."

"That may be political reality. Now let me state the military reality. We cannot launch a Tomahawk or cross the Iranian border until the first missile is in the air. Due to the distances involved, they will get at least an hour or two to launch missiles without opposition, and we must then try to shoot them down."

Grafton stared into the president's aide's eyes. "If just one nuke gets through and obliterates Baghdad or Doha or Kuwait City or Tel Aviv, not to mention Tehran, this administration is toast. Hundreds of thousands of people will be dead, maybe millions. Maybe tens of millions. The president will be impeached, if he doesn't resign. You understand that?"

"I do," Sal Molina said smoothly.

Grafton wriggled his feet. After a bit he said, "And I thought the era of gunslinging gamblers was over."

"There's a few left around," Molina replied carelessly. "Like you."

Grafton snorted. "I'm no gambler. I learned long ago that the guy who takes the first aimed shot usually wins. I can get that happy truth embroidered on a pillow if you'd like to refer to it from time to time."

Molina ignored that comment. "Tell me something that I don't know," he said, "something that will make me feel better."

"The Nationals are at home tonight and tomorrow. Go home, fix yourself a tall, frosty stiff one, and after you've polished it off, take your wife to a baseball game."

Molina said a cuss word, got up and left. Grafton sat in the briefing room by himself. In his mind's eye he could see the deserts and the cities, the towering cloud formations over the mountains, people strapping themselves into cockpits, donning parachutes and climbing aboard transports . . .

Soon, he thought. *It will happen soon . . . then all of us will live with the aftermath.*

On Friday night during the wee hours I crawled out on the ridge above the executive bunker, found myself a handy shrub and got under it. The ground was still hot from the day's heat, and thunderstorms were around. I could see flashes in the darkness, way off on the horizon.

I settled in and used my binoculars to see what I could see.

Since we were in the Abbas Abad suburb of Tehran, there was just enough light for binoculars instead of night vision goggles, which was good, because I wanted the magnification. After quickly checking the ridge to ensure that I was indeed alone, I glassed the Mosalla Prayer Grounds and the small mosque that disguised the main entrance, examined two trucks in the parking lot being unloaded by soldiers working in slow motion . . . examined everything within my range of vision.

Then I shifted my gaze to the other side of the ridge. Even in the middle of the hot summer, the riverbed was carrying water down from the mountains.

Finally satisfied that I was alone and no one was looking for intruders, I got out the laser designator and put it on my shoulder. Turned on the batteries and fired it up. The optical sight was a nice piece of gear, with infrared and low-light capabilities for night work.

Finally I put it down and sat staring at the scene. The air force, Grafton told me, was going to drop eight bunker-busters, each of which weighed about forty-seven hundred pounds. The bomb casings, I knew, were made from worn-out eight-inch howitzer barrels, which were extraordinarily hard steel. Then the cavity was packed full of tritonal, a mixture of TNT and aluminum powder. The aluminum alloy, if you will, caused the pressure peak to occur more quickly, and go higher, than pure TNT. In effect, the weapon was an explosive spear, accelerated to terminal velocity by gravity. Nearly two and a half tons of steel and explosive would dive deep into the earth before the bomb exploded. I wondered if they would penetrate five feet of dirt and twenty-five feet of reinforced concrete.

Apparently the air force was taking no chances. Four would hit the main elevator shaft, four the secondary exit on the back side of the ridge. Then I was supposed to check the results. The parking lot that the elevator shaft lay under would be reduced to rubble by the first bomb. So would the old ramp area that housed the secondary entrance/exit. Although I wouldn't be able to see what had happened under the earth, Grafton wanted me to determine if the bunker-busters had landed more or less in the right place.

If they hadn't, no doubt the air force would be back to do it again.

Before I moved, I took a last look around. Another truck carrying soldiers, perhaps a dozen, pulled into the parking lot. The soldiers slowly exited the truck, stretched then scratched, then were herded into line for a muster by their NCO.

I crawled back to where G. W. was waiting.

When I got in the car and we were moving, I asked if he had seen the soldiers.

"Yep," he replied. "I have a sneaking suspicion they are going to patrol the area around that bunker until the bigwigs are safely tucked in."

"I can't imagine why," I told him and scratched my chin.

"Because someone told them to, I imagine."

"Grafton said the Iranian army and IRGC are to be pulled out of the city on Sunday night. Ahmadinejad is saving them for the war to come."

"They won't all leave," said the optimist in residence. "You can bet on that."

"First bomb hits, they'll be looking for holes," I mused. "Our job is to make sure Ahmadinejad doesn't have second thoughts and come rabbiting out of the bunker before the bombs land." I jerked a thumb toward the laser designator. "Grafton sent me that. There will be an armed drone overhead with Hellfire missiles. I can designate their targets."

We discussed it and decided that with so many unknowns, we were going to have to play it by ear. "Be helpful," I suggested, "if Joe Mottaki could score a tank for us when we see them going in."

"Tommy, we only have eight guys. And how will we know when the bombs will arrive?"

"They'll give me fifteen minutes' warning over a handheld radio. There were actually two of them in those duffle bags—I'll give you one, just in case."

G. W. thought about it for a moment, then said, "Has it occurred to you that if one of those things misses, it might land on you?"

"Or you," I told him. "Man, you gotta have some faith in the geeks. High tech is gonna save us, power us into a cleaner, greener world."

On Friday morning in Washington, when Jake Grafton arrived at his office in Langley, his assistant, Robin, told him to call the director.

Wilkins didn't waste words. "NSA has been listening to messages. The Iranian military is going to war alert on Sunday night. Fighter and gunboat sorties have been ordered for Monday morning at dawn."

"Has CENTCOM been notified?"

"Of course. Just thought you would like to know."

"Now that the plan has gone operational, there's nothing for me to do here but twiddle my thumbs," Grafton said. "I was thinking about going to Tehran."

"Hell no," Wilkins said and hung up on Jake.

"Via Baghdad," Grafton said into his dead instrument. "Then to As Sulaymaniyah, and by helicopter from there to Tehran." He put the telephone back into its cradle and glanced at his watch. "If I get a hustle on, I might make it by Monday morning."

He called Sal Molina at the White House. "Where did the president decide to spend Sunday night?"

"Baghdad," Molina told him. "He also decided the veep is going to Tel Aviv."

"Can I get a ride on *Air Force One*?"

"Don't see why not. Be at Andrews in three hours."

"You going, too?"

"Hell, no. I'm going to be in my office watching the war on CNN."

Jake then called Callie on her cell phone. "Hey, beloved wife. I have to go to the Middle East for a few days."

"Oh," she said. "Are you going home to pack?"

"No. I'll take my warbag along." He routinely kept a packed suitcase at the office for emergencies such as these. "The underwear is clean, and I have some toothpaste left in there."

Callie was silent for a moment, then she said, "This isn't a routine trip, is it?"

"No," Jake admitted.

"I want you to come back to me."

"God bless you, Callie. I love you."

"I love you, too. Don't forget that."

He said good-bye, cradled the phone and shouted for Robin.

By Sunday afternoon, the tunnel where we were hiding felt like a jail. It was cool enough, as the megalopolis and its inhabitants baked in the summer heat, but oppressive. It felt as if we were in a stone prison, cut off from mankind and the outside world. No sun, wind or rain, no birds or grass, just stone.

I thought about the Iranians' executive bunker, which would soon contain four hundred people, more or less, thought about it for ten or fifteen seconds, then went on to something else.

Larijani was a silent, forbidding man. Still, regardless of what happened in the next few days, the years of playing a role were over for him.

"When you get home, what is next for you?" I asked.

He looked at me deadpan, the ugly asshole I had seen from time to time during my stay in Iran, then he smiled. His face was transformed. "I don't know," he said. He shrugged. "Having to save you was a godsend. The mission is finished."

"Someday you can buy me a drink."

"Someday I will," he said and smiled again.

Davar's bruises were fading, and her face was returning to normal. She still had a big yellow place on her jaw, and her left eye was puffy, but in a few more days, the swelling and color would be gone.

"When this is over," I said, "you can get on a chopper going to Iraq, and from there, airplanes fly all over the world. I promise, I can get you a temporary travel permit that will take you to America. By God, Jake Grafton owes me."

We were sitting on her cot, which had blankets hanging from ropes around it to give her some privacy. She reached for my hand, held it in both of hers while she examined it.

"Do you have a wife?" she asked.

"No."

"Why are you here, Tommy Carmellini, on the far side of the earth, risking your life?"

I looked her square in both those big brown eyes. "Damned if I know," I said. "A character defect is the most likely explanation."

She was silent for a bit, then changed the subject. "After Jihad Day, what will happen in Iran?"

"I don't know." I pulled my hand loose from hers. "Let's hope there are some Iranians left to have a future. What it will be will be up to them."

"It will be as Allah wills it."

I was in no mood to discuss religion, which was the horse the Iranians had ridden into the middle of this mess, but I couldn't resist saying, "Perhaps. On the other hand, maybe the future will belong to those humans who fight like hell to make it happen."

That Sunday evening, I went up on top of the old German's hotel and took my last look at pre-Jihad Tehran. The evening was bloodred, which seemed appropriate, because the air was full of dirt. The wind was singing around the eaves of the building, and visibility was limited. Apparently a lot of dirt had been kicked high into the atmosphere by a windstorm in central Iran. I wondered how all that airborne dirt would affect laser designators.

I hoped Tehran would look more or less like this tomorrow evening, but that wasn't up to me. Although I didn't say it to Davar, I seriously doubted if Allah gave a good goddamn. I couldn't imagine why He, or She, should.

All over Tehran this evening, the Iranian political and religious elite were packing for the midnight ride to the bunker. No doubt they were looking at their homes, their keepsakes and knickknacks, at their neighbors' homes and the children playing in the streets . . .

It's amazing how life works, when you think about it. Somewhere babies were being conceived, babies were being born, young people were marrying, people were dying of disease, old age, murder, accident, the whole gamut . . . and somewhere people were strolling through parks, looking in shop windows, eating and laughing and loving and living. All of it went on all the time. Somewhere.

I wished I were in that somewhere where the sun was shining, couples were holding hands and birds were singing.

When the sun was gone and the black night was illuminated only by some city lights and a thunderstorm tossing lightning on the mountains to the north, I went back down to the tunnel and inventoried the stuff in the duffle bags Grafton had sent to me, checked everything. Finally I lay down on my cot and tried to grab twenty winks. Unless I got killed early, it was going to be a long night.

At 11:00 P.M., G. W. Hosein shook me awake. I had managed to doze off just a few minutes prior. "They're going into the bunker," he whispered, hoping not to awaken Davar, who was asleep inside her curtains ten feet away. "Ahmad has been keeping an eye on them. Limos arriving carrying whole families, it looks like."

I rolled out and got dressed.

I was about ready to go when Davar came out of the curtains wearing trousers, a shirt and boots.

"You're not going anywhere," I said.

"This is my country," she shot back and set off along the tunnel to where G. W. and the others were making coffee and heating MREs.

I followed her—and thought, *What the heck. Who am I to tell her how to run her life? Maybe she'll run into a couple of prison guards she recognizes.*

Joe Mottaki was there with his two guys, decked out as Iranian soldiers, complete with AKs and sidearms. With their beards, they looked as Iranian as Ahmadinejad. I scratched my own stubble, four days' growth, as I surveyed them. Joe was drinking coffee and looking sour.

"You going to try for a tank?" I asked.

"Yeah."

"We only need it in case things go bad. All we have to do is lay low until the bunker bombers do their thing."

Mottaki gave me a look I couldn't classify.

"Are you thinking about those people in the bunker?" I asked.

His lips curled into a sneer. "You ass! I've got a wife and kid in Israel, cousins, my parents, uncles and aunts, none of whom ever lifted a finger against Iran. All they want is to be left in peace. I'm thinking about *them*! These raghead jihad bastards would kill them all if they could and dance on their graves." He leaned into my face and hissed, "I don't give a bloody fuck about the people in that hole."

Using binoculars, G. W., Davar, Larijani and I watched from beside a cluster of abandoned apartments as limo after limo arrived carrying whole families, who lugged suitcases and boxes and bundles into the mosque at the prayer grounds. Then the limos drove away. Some people arrived in their own cars, which they parked willy-nilly in the lot next door, after they had off-loaded their stuff. Kids wandered around; a few young mothers were carrying babies.

"I count two dozen soldiers down there," G. W. said. "One big truck, which probably hauled them in."

"See any armor anywhere?" I asked as I scanned the area.

"Nope."

I wondered how the locals would feel if they knew their fearless leaders were taking cover. I glanced over at Davar, who was leaning against a wall to steady herself as she peered at the mosque with binoculars. Although no one had told her in so many words, I think she knew why G. W. and I were so interested in that bunker. I got out my satellite telephone and spent five minutes setting it up. Then I called the folks at Central Command and gave them the word. The guy I talked to merely grunted. No doubt he was getting information from a variety of different sources.

I broke the connection and sat watching the people arriving. Periodically I scanned the area behind us and to both sides for troops.

Behind me Larijani sat examining his feet and hands. He seemed totally uninterested in the proceedings around the bunker. He certainly had a load to carry for the rest of his life.

I tried not to think about the children I could see going into the bunker. If I were an Israeli like Mottaki, perhaps I would feel as he did. But I wasn't.

The truth is we were all guilty, all of us: Ahmadinejad, the mullahs, Larijani, Grafton . . . me . . . and Joe Mottaki.

I lowered the binoculars and glanced at Davar, who was sitting beside the wall watching me with those deep, dark eyes, her binoculars on her lap.

Once again the ready room of VFA-196 aboard USS *United States* was packed, with an officer in every seat. At the podium, Commander Burgholzer surveyed his charges and summed up the information discussed during the previous two hours.

"Folks, I'm going to give it to you straight. We are going to have a war. With luck, it will be short, although it won't be sweet. You know everything I know; you've read the Op Plan; you've got all the information you need to fly your missions. I want you people to be careful out there. Be safe, be professionals, and make sure you know what you're shooting at. Any questions?"

One pilot spoke up. "Skipper, what's going to happen if we put a 'winder into a nuke?"

The Fly scratched his head. "Either it'll go down and you'll fly on, or your next breath will be at the Pearly Gates."

Nobody even smiled.

"If you get there before the rest of us, tell St. Peter we'll all be along sooner or later and put a keg on ice." He paused, then added, "Well, most of us will get there. I don't know about the XO . . . or O'Hare . . ."

This time he got a chuckle from his pilots.

Since no one knew Mahmoud Ahmadinejad's timetable, the carrier was going to a five-minute alert at midnight. "When we know more, we'll tell you more," the wing intelligence officer told them in the televised, big-picture brief that had been piped to every ready room.

Four of the Savage Horde's F/A-18 Hornets were loaded with missiles on the flight deck. The lucky four alert pilots donned their flight gear, arranged their kneeboard cards with frequencies and notes and trooped to the escalator for the ride up to the flight deck. Once there, they checked in with flight-deck control on the location of their aircraft, verified the predicted catapult weight and, using red lights, strolled out onto the crowded deck to look for their steeds. Pilots of another squadron were also manning four F/A-18s, and crews were manning two EA-6Bs, two KS-3 tankers, and an E-2 Hawkeye.

After careful preflights of the aircraft and weapons, the Hornet pilots manned up. The plane captains helped them strap in. Electrical power was applied to the plane and, the pilots fired off the computers and began typing in waypoints and checkpoints. They didn't, however, start engines. Once the engines were started, fuel was being consumed, fuel they would need to reach their assigned patrol areas or engage enemy fighters. Ready to launch on five minutes' notice, they would wait until the admiral gave the order before bringing their aircraft to life.

The E-2 Hawkeye, with its giant radar housing riding above the center of the wing, did start engines. Chicago O'Hare was in a Hornet cockpit, playing with her computer and generally killing time, when she felt the ship begin a turn into the wind. The yellow-shirted taxi directors worked the E-2 to Catapult Three on the waist. Chicago watched as the catapult crew readied the cat, put the plane on it, and sent it off into the night. The Hawkeye would carry its radar into the lower stratosphere, there to watch thousands of miles of sea, and Iran. The information it gathered would be data-linked to the ship to keep the decision-makers there informed, and if necessary data-linked to airborne Hornets. The buzzword was network-centric warfare; and it worked.

After the Hawkeye was launched, the ship came back to its original course, which was to the northwest.

The captain of *United States* and her sister carrier, USS *Columbia*, which was steaming ten miles northward with her escorts, had been told to place their ships as close to the mouth of the Gulf of Hormuz as possible while still maintaining the sea room they needed to come into the wind for launches and recoveries. Every sea mile closer to the mouth of the Gulf was a mile the airplanes didn't have to fly. Yet every mile close to the Iranian coast decreased the task force's reaction time to antiship missiles, if the Iranians launched any.

Admiral Bryant and the captains had conferred. The admiral weighed the imponderables against the requirements of the mission and decided where he wanted the ships. As with every military decision, he and the people he was responsible for would have to live with the outcome, whatever it was.

Chicago sat in her cockpit looking at the other planes on the deck, the sailors, the night sky, savoring the gentle rise and fall of the ship as it rode the back of the sea and the smell of the night wind, rich with salt. She also thought she could detect a hint of the land on the wind, but perhaps it was only her imagination.

Air Force One was somewhere over the North Atlantic when an aide woke Jake Grafton, who was napping in a seat near the rear of the cabin. The president wanted to see him.

Jake found the president in a thoughtful mood. He wanted to talk, and did so. Jake sat and listened as the president discussed the political forces that had molded modern Iran. Merely thinking aloud, he ruminated on Mir-Hossein Mousavi, the Iranian presidential candidate who apparently won the last presidential election and had been under loose house arrest ever since.

Jake sat silently listening. The president obviously realized the personal risk he was taking by going to Baghdad, and Jake admired him for it. Yet the president didn't mention it. Nor did he mention the danger Grafton would face in Iran.

"Mousavi is the future of Iran," the president remarked at one point, glancing at Grafton, "if he lives to see it."

Jake nodded his agreement.

Finally, after nearly an hour, when the president had run dry on Iran, he changed the subject. "I personally owe you a debt of thanks, Admiral, for your efforts, regardless of how all this turns out. Wisdom is hard to find these days. I wanted to thank you to your face."

Embarrassed, Jake Grafton merely nodded.

"Let's both try to get some sleep," the president said. "I suspect we're going to need it."

After *Air Force One* landed in Baghdad and the president had departed with the military brass that had been hastily summoned to meet him, Jake Grafton slipped away. Soon Grafton was in a helicopter on his way to As Sulaymaniyah, on the northeast border of Iraq.

At As Sulaymaniyah, the chopper circled the field, then landed beside a dilapidated hangar sheltered by trees on the side of the field away from the main parking ramp. Grafton got out with his warbag, and the helo departed.

He pounded on the personnel door, which was opened by a man in a rumpled army flight suit and dirty white socks, holding a 1911 automatic in his hand.

"John Pepper?"

"Yeah."

"Jake Grafton. I want to go to Tehran."

Pepper snapped on a light and looked Grafton over. The admiral was wearing jeans, a short-sleeve shirt, tennis shoes and no hat.

"Admiral Jake Grafton?"

"Yep. That's me." Jake passed Pepper his CIA ID card. Pepper scanned it, passed it back and tucked the pistol in its holster at his waist as he stiffened to attention.

"Relax, relax," Grafton said. "I'm a civilian." He held out his hand for a shake.

When they had shaken hands, Pepper led the way toward the only desk in the room. He had been sacked out on a couch that had seen better days. "I got a message today from Washington," he said. "Seems the director of the CIA wants to personally talk to you, if you show up. The message was classified, so I sent it back to the command post for safekeeping."

"I'll call him when I can," Grafton said. "In the meantime, how about a ride to Tehran in your Hind?"

"Terrible night for flying a chopper—lots of wind—and Tehran is a damn long way. Have to refuel at a clandestine fuel depot on the Khar River. Dangerous as hell to use it."

"Right."

"I hear they are about to have a war over there," Pepper added cautiously, and glanced at his watch.

"Bad news travels fast," Jake Grafton said and threw his bag on the couch. "If they're gonna have a war, be a shame to miss it. So, when can we go and how long will it take to get there?"

CHAPTER TWENTY-SIX

U.S. Army Staff Sergeant Jack Colby and his three Special Forces colleagues were sitting in a hide two miles from the entrance to Tunnel Hotel, one of the twenty-five Iranian missile launch sites identified by the Americans. Just now Colby was examining the troops around the tunnel area with an infrared telescope mounted on a tripod. He and his three colleagues had parachuted in two nights ago and worked all night on their hide, which was under a cliff and concealed in front by brush. They were ninety miles and a chain of mountains from the Iraq border.

The soldiers used the satellite network to talk hourly with the CENTCOM controller for Special Forces on the ground in Iran. The controller relayed the message from headquarters, which was that the general and staff believed that tonight was the night, but Jack Colby was already convinced.

Yesterday, during the daylight hours, three army patrols had searched the area with the aid of dogs, no doubt looking for any Special Forces team that might be in the area.

Fortunately the chemicals the team sprinkled around the hide masked their scent from the dogs. Two searchers had actually stood ten feet from the entrance to the hide and pissed on the rocks, but the American team remained undetected.

One team, at another tunnel, had been flushed yesterday and got into a shooting scrape. A helicopter had plucked them out after they had run for twelve miles and twice ambushed their pursuers. This news Colby learned from the CENTCOM controller.

Colby turned the telescope over to one of his mates while he crawled outside for a look around. The wind had definitely eased up, but the air still contained a lot of dust, which made the image in the telescope fuzzy and indistinct.

Maybe the Iranians will postpone their launch, Colby thought. *Man, why can't we have a war in a nice place, with good weather?*

When he crawled back into the hide, the man at the binoculars said, "Better take a look, Jack. They're rolling out a missile."

Colby glued his eye to the telescope. Adjusted the focus knob a tad . . . and there it was, big as life: a truck pulling a trailer with a big missile on it. As Colby watched, the truck crept perhaps a hundred yards away from the tunnel entrance and turned ninety degrees, so that the tip of the missile faced southeast and the exhaust was directed well away from the entrance. When the truck came to a halt, half a dozen men who had been following along on foot began lowering mechanical feet on the sides of the bed, to stabilize it.

While this was going on, another truck pulling a missile crept from the tunnel.

It quickly became apparent that only two missiles were going to be launched. "How many missiles do you think are in that tunnel?" one of the soldiers asked Colby.

"I don't know. Pick a number."

"Well, at two at a time, these guys are going to be at it a while."

"Call CENTCOM," Colby said. "The bastards are really going to do it."

At the CENTCOM Operations Center in Kuwait, General Martin Lincoln was monitoring reports from his Special Forces teams in Iran and from air force units operating MQ-1 Predator and MQ-9 Reaper drones over Iran. These unmanned aircraft carried sophisticated sensors, including high-tech video and infrared cameras, the data from which was data-linked via satellite back to the control sites, which saw the data in real time. He was also getting data-linked information from AWACS aircraft aloft over Iraq, the Persian Gulf and the Gulf of Oman, and summaries of satellite surveillance, although that data was sometimes hours old.

Unfortunately, the storm in central Iran had played havoc with the drones. The wind had kept all of the ScanEagles, the smallest, unarmed drones, on the ground. Only now were the Predators and Reapers airborne and getting back into position. Still, airborne dirt would degrade their capabilities. General Lincoln also suspected that, at dawn, with clearing weather, the Iranian air force would launch fighters to hunt for and shoot down the larger drones. Ground control interception (GCI) frequencies were being monitored, so he would know if and when the fighters launched.

Finally, he was keeping track of four flights of four F-15E Strike Eagles that had just launched from Balad. These planes were carrying GPS and laser-guided bombs, and they were going to attack northern Iranian missile sites. Their tactical electronic warfare system had been expanded to include the ALQ-199 black boxes, the mystery boxes that Jake Grafton hoped would fool the Iranian antiaircraft missile systems. The men in the planes would soon find out how successful Grafton's deception operation had been, although they knew nothing about it. General Lincoln, however, did know, and he had his fingers crossed.

Inevitably, the Iranians would get some nukes in the air, and then Lincoln's forces had to intercept them. The cruise missiles armed with conventional explosives were essentially decoys, since they weren't very accurate, didn't pack much of a punch and couldn't do strategically significant damage even if they hit the military bases where they were aimed. Their purpose, as Grafton had pointed out, was to overload the American defensive system and mask the nukes. The key to a successful defense was to get ordnance on those missile sites as soon as possible after Iran had fired the first shot—and, if possible, to prevent the Iranians from launching a second wave.

Just now Lincoln sat wondering how many nukes would be in the first wave. All of them? One or two? Another unknown in the equation . . .

Now, as Lincoln received reports from Special Forces teams on the ground and the drone control room in Iraq that missiles were being rolled out and positioned for firing, he used the encrypted voice link to the National Command Center to call the president.

"They are rolling them out," General Lincoln said. "I expect first launch within minutes."

The activity at the entrance to the executive bunker in Tehran was frantic. Cars continued to arrive in front of the mosque in the Mosalla Prayer Grounds and disgorge their passengers, who each grabbed a suitcase or bag or child and rushed off toward the entrance, where a knot of soldiers apparently consulted a list and waved them through.

"Looks like folks fighting for lifeboats on the *Titanic*," G. W. said.

I looked at my watch. It was pushing two thirty in the morning. Dawn would come about five, and the sun a short time later. I wondered when the bunker was going to be locked down.

"Do you know anything about the executive survival plan?" I asked Davar, who was glued to a set of binoculars. Probably watching for her father and brother, Khurram, to arrive, I figured, although I didn't ask.

"No," she said curtly.

"Like how many kids are going in there?" I instantly regretted that remark, but once it was out there was nothing I could do about it.

"I don't know." Her voice was flat, unemotional, which irritated me a little, which, I suppose, is why I changed my mind.

"Seen your father?"

She didn't take her eyes from the binoculars. "Some people arrived. He might have been one of them. I could not be sure."

"Khurram?"

"No."

At about three in the morning a motorcade arrived at the entrance to the executive bunker. Four limos, with police escorts with flashing lights. The distance was too great and the light too dim for me to identify him, but I thought this had to be President Mahmoud Ahmadinejad, with family and kids and favored household staff, those the great one chose to save from the nuclear furnace.

With the staff pushing their stuff on a cart behind them, it took about four minutes for the honchos to get into the mosque. Then the police cars led the limos away.

I got on the sat phone again, gave CENTCOM the word. When I hung up, the army troops were driving away in their trucks. Precisely two soldiers were left standing around in front of the prayer factory, presumably to tell late arrivals, if there were any, that the gate to the bunker had been closed and locked.

"Let the party begin," I said to G. W., very softly, so Davar couldn't hear.

Joe Mottaki went about getting the tank the same way he had acquired the self-propelled howitzer. He and his men drove to the army base and waited for a tank to come out. Since the army was leaving Tehran for a rendezvous in the desert, he didn't have to wait long.

A column of old Russian-made T-54s soon came out of the gate and took the road to the south. Mottaki had driven captured T-54s in Israel and knew every lever and bolt.

He waited a few minutes, then told the man at the wheel to drive along the column. When Joe thought he'd found a tank that was the last in a group, the driver slowed to match the tank's speed. Mottaki, leaning out the passenger window, shouted to the tank commander, who was standing in the turret hatch, to pull out of the column and stop. Since Mottaki was wearing an Iranian army captain's uniform, the commander spoke into his mouthpiece, telling the driver to do so.

Mottaki climbed from the truck and strode behind the stationary tank. He went up over the right tread fender and walked along it until he was adjacent to the turret, on the side away from the passing column. Since the tank's diesel engine was idling loudly, he leaned toward the commander to be heard. As he did, the tank commander pried one earpiece away from his head to hear what Mottaki had to say.

The Mossad agent grabbed the man's shirt as he drew his pistol. In one fluid motion he jammed the gun into the man's chest, against his heart, and pulled the trigger. Scrambling onto the turret, he shoved the body down into the tank, then leaned in and shot two of the crewmen as fast as he could pull the trigger. He went into the tank feet first; the driver turned and shouted something. As the man tried to get his pistol out, Mottaki shot him twice.

With the driver's foot off the brake, the tank lurched forward.

Joe Mottaki jerked the dying driver from his seat and sat down. He let the tank continue forward, then fed it some fuel with the accelerator. The truck was already ahead of him.

Looking through the driver's slit, he followed the truck when it turned from the highway and went up a side street. There he and his men passed the bodies up through the turret hatch, put them in the bed of the truck, climbed back into the tank and headed for the Mosalla Prayer Grounds.

When Mahmoud Ahmadinejad stepped out of the elevator at the bunker level, armed soldiers escorted him to his suite. His military aide was already there, taking telephone reports from the various commands around the country and updating a status board. American planes were aloft over Iraq and the Persian Gulf, as usual. Well, perhaps a few more than usual, but all in all, tonight looked fairly typical. Within minutes, Hosseini-Tash and the other military commanders entered, picked up telephones and spoke to their commands. Everything, they agreed, was ready. Nothing remained to be done except for the president to give the Execute order.

Satisfied, Ahmadinejad went next door to see the small knot of mullahs who made up the brain trust of the Party of God, the fundamentalist Islamic political movement that had ruled Iran since the fall of the shah, over thirty years ago.

"All is in readiness," Ahmadinejad said. "We are ready to take the final glorious step to national martyrdom, to launch our jihad against Zionism and the Great Satan, and, incidentally, get revenge for the murder of the Supreme Leader, Ayatollah Khamenei, may he rest in peace."

The senior mullah led them in a short prayer; then the president went back to the command center to order the doors of the bunker sealed and give the Execute order. He also ordered Iranian national television to broadcast a prerecorded message in which he called for the Muslims of the world to join the Iranian faithful in jihad.

It was a sublime moment, the zenith of his life. A thousand years from now, when all the people of the earth prayed to Allah, they would remember his name and call him holy.

Staff Sergeant Jack Colby was on the satellite telephone talking to CENTCOM when the solid-fuel booster of the first cruise missile lit with a roar and the missile shot forward off its launcher into the air, its rocket booster spewing fire. A minute later, the second missile followed the first.

When both launchers were empty and the noise of the last missile had faded from the night sky, men ran from the tunnel and jumped into the trucks, which they drove for a quarter mile, then parked. Through his infrared telescope, Jack Colby watched another truck pulling a missile on its launcher ease its way out of the tunnel.

Five large surface combatants of the U.S. Navy, which were cruising slowly in line astern formation five miles off the harbor entrances of Kuwait, turned to an easterly heading and began working up to ten knots. The squadron consisted of two guided missile cruisers and three Arleigh Burke–class destroyers. The crews had been at general quarters—battle stations—for over an hour.

Within four minutes of the launch of the Iranian cruise missiles from Tunnel Hotel—and six other Iranian missile sites—the first of a hundred Tomahawk cruise missiles leaped from their launchers. The ships were firing at a careful, deliberate rate, so it would take almost ten minutes to get the entire hundred in the air.

The fiery booster plumes ripped the night apart. People on shore and aboard oil tankers and service vessels watched in silent awe and amazement as the missiles vomited forth like fireworks into the dark heavens. Finally, after all the missiles were airborne, the moan of receding turbojet engines echoed across the area. After a long moment that sound also faded and the night sea was again silent.

In the Gulf of Oman, surface combatants were also launching Tomahawks against the missile sites on Iran's southern coast. Twenty missiles rippled off the ships, hurled aloft by their solid-fuel boosters; then the cruise missiles' turbojet engines took over and they flew away, guided by their internal computers.

The yellow-shirted taxi director used illuminated wands to taxi Chicago O'Hare onto USS *United States'* Number Three Catapult. She ran through the familiar checks and, on the director's signal, shoved the throttles forward to the stops. The engines spooled up with a howl. She cycled her controls, then glanced at the launching officer, who was signaling burner. She moved the throttles sideways and forward, igniting the afterburners.

One more sweep of the engines' temperatures and pressures; then she put her head back into the headrest and used her left thumb to snap on the Hornet's exterior lights.

One potato, two . . . and the catapult fired. The G pressed her straight aft as the plane roared forward, accelerating violently. Two heartbeats later her wheels ran off the deck into the night air and she was flying, the stick alive in her hand. *Establish climb attitude, check instruments, gear up . . .*

Soon the four Savage Horde Hornets were spread out in a loose night formation, every plane with its exterior lights on, heading for Oman, then into the Persian Gulf. Ten miles astern, four more Hornets from VFA-196's sister squadron were following along. All eight planes carried a max load of AIM-9X Sidewinders.

Like all the pilots, Chicago was extremely busy changing radio channels, keeping track of the navigation problem and making sure her computer was receiving data-link updates from the E-2 Hawkeye, the eye in the sky.

Sure enough, within ten minutes or so, the first blips of airborne cruise missiles, heading from Iran to Qatar, appeared on the tactical screen.

Gonna be an interesting night, Chicago thought.

David Quereau was the pilot of one of the F-22 Raptors aloft over Iraq. He had been in the air for four hours, had refueled twice and was damn tired of flying circles in the sky on autopilot waiting for something—anything—to happen. Obviously, whatever it was hadn't happened on his watch, and probably wouldn't, which is about the way things go for a junior captain in the U.S. Air Force.

Good stuff always happens to the majors and colonels, which is why they get the medals and walk around like their balls weigh ten pounds each. On the other hand, as all the world knows, captains don't have any balls, or if they do, they must keep that fact carefully hidden in the new American air force . . . and good stuff never happens for them. Just bad. Like a tour in Iraq, for God's sake!

Last week, just another week in the life, and wham, bam, thank you ma'am, you guys are ferrying a dozen F-22s across the pond to Iraq. *You* get to go, Quereau, because you're junior. A little time in Iraq will look good on your record.

What a ball-buster that was, twelve hours at a stretch in the cockpit, arrive yesterday, and now, sitting here droning circles in the sky. Big whoop.

The truth was, using the F-22 Raptor to support troops in Iraq and Afghanistan was like using a Stradivarius as a doorbell chime. The plane was the über-fighter, the absolute best dogfighting airplane ever constructed, capable of supersonic cruise in basic engine, without afterburner, with vectored thrust that made it the most maneuverable airplane that had ever left the ground, able to make a sustained 5-G turn at sixty thousand feet, for Christ's sake, higher than most fighters can even fly. Yet it was also an electronic marvel that could detect enemy airplanes at extraordinary distances while remaining stealthy, receive data-links from other fighters and share its information with them and, finally, shoot down enemy airplanes with its missiles at distances of up to one hundred miles. After the pilot ran out of missiles, it even had a gun. It was a bomber, too, capable of dropping GPS-guided bombs from forty to fifty thousand feet with pickle-barrel accuracy.

No bombs aboard tonight, though. Quereau was carrying six AIM-120D AMRAAMs (advanced medium-range antiaircraft missiles) internally. As usual, his 20 mm Vulcan cannon in the right wing root was fully loaded, 480 rounds, enough for five seconds of squirting.

A turkey shoot, his section leader said. Tonight they were going to a turkey shoot.

Well, so far, no turkeys. Only one very sore butt.

Then, without a word on the radio, the section leader straightened out and added power for the climb. The wait was over. These two Raptors were going to Tehran.

The second missile the ground crews at Tunnel Hotel pulled from the tunnel for their second salvo was different from the others. It was larger, and the only fins were in the back. "That's one of those Ghadars," Colby told his mates. "It's an ICBM."

"Could be the nuke. They told us these clowns might launch one out of this tunnel."

Colby watched through the telescope as the launching crew slowly raised it into an erect position on its launcher. There it stood, pointing skyward like the finger of God, about two miles away.

Colby made his decision and announced it. "Gimme that fifty. I'm gonna take a poke at it. You guys get ready to boogie. Bill, tell CENTCOM."

"Just a thought," said Bill nervously, clearing his throat. "Say you actually get a bullet in it—it might go Hiroshima on us. Thought about that?"

Staff Sergeant Jack Colby thought about that now. About instant self-cremation. He glanced at the three faces of his mates. "You never thought you were going to live forever, did ya?"

They stared at him for a second, then swung into action. One of them passed Colby the .50 caliber sniper's rifle they had brought along. Fortunately it had the starlight scope on it, so he should be able to see the missile through it.

As Bill talked to CENTCOM, Colby got the bipod positioned and found a solid rest, then aimed the rifle. Yes! He could see the missile—still a country mile away, but if he aimed at the top of it, the big half-inch slug should strike somewhere down on the missile body. Might even have enough energy left to penetrate the skin of the thing. On the other hand, the slug might just bounce off. If it did penetrate the skin, it wasn't going to cause the missile to detonate right there in front of his eyes. Of course not! Wouldn't do the missile any good, though. If only he could dope the wind . . .

Well, Colby's best guess was that the wind was out of the southeast, maybe ten knots gusting to fifteen or sixteen occasionally.

He shoved a shell into the rifle, closed the bolt and snuggled in behind the butt. "Here goes nothing," he muttered and began taking up slack in the trigger.

The recoil and report came as a surprise. Yeah. He looked through the scope to see if he could spot the bullet striking. Might make a little spark. Nope.

One of the guys, Buddy, was looking through the telescope. "Guys around the missile are looking around. You woke them up."

Colby worked the bolt and inserted another round.

After the fifth shot, Buddy said, "I don't know if you're hitting that garbage can, but you got the ground crew all worked up. They're running for cover."

Colby stopped shooting. "Maybe they won't launch it," he suggested.

"Maybe they'll come looking for us," was the reply.

"Or maybe they won't," Colby mused. The men who had been tending the missiles had vanished into the tunnel, and they had not come out again. Just a few shots from the sniper rifle scattered them like quail. Why? *Perhaps*, he thought, *they expect the Americans to counterattack against this site, and they don't want to die.*

Behind him Bill said, "What I want to know is where the hell are our guys?"

G. W. Hosein took a truck with him when he went looking for the place where the bunker's communications cables came out of the ground. He saw no army in the streets, no police, no paramilitary militia. However, he did see vehicles piled with baggage and people, careening dangerously, presumably heading out of town. Only a few now, but G. W. suspected the exodus would soon become a flood.

One wonders precisely how many people were awake to personally watch or listen to Ahmadinejad's exhortation on television and radio, but no doubt those who heard it spread the word. After twenty years of listening to the regime's nuclear power arguments, the urban population well knew what its fate would be if Iran traded nuclear warheads with its enemies. The rumor that the political and religious elites had taken cover in the bunker would galvanize them into action. Those who could were leaving.

G. W. rolled right up to the com junction. It was housed in a little hut with padlocks and warning labels. While his men stood guard with AK-47s at the ready, G. W. used a set of bolt cutters on the padlocks. He shined a flashlight on the works. The cables came out of a pipe and were spliced into junctions of some kind. He wasn't an electrician, and it all looked like spaghetti to him.

"Oh well," he said to no one in particular and pulled the pin on an e-grenade. He set it like an egg on top of one of the junction boxes, closed the door and climbed back in the truck.

"Around the block, boys, and make it snappy."

The e-grenade was actually a small bomb. When it detonated, it would convert the chemical energy of the explosion into one large spike of electro-magnetic energy, which would glom onto any wires it found and race along them, destroying any electronic circuits it came across that were not properly protected. Circuits such as truck electrical systems, two-way radios, satellite radios . . . and, down in the bunker, computers, television cameras and so on.

The minor explosion of the e-grenade also knocked out some of the nearby streetlights. "Back to the box," G. W. told Ahmad, who was at the wheel. This time when he went into the small building, G. W. armed and left a satchel charge of C-4 lying against the pipe that contained the wires, right where it came out of the ground.

Hosein and his men were two blocks away when the satchel charge exploded.

"There are ninety-two cruise missiles in the air, General," a colonel told General Lincoln, who was trying to make sense of the presentation on the large map that covered the wall in front of him. Symbols showed the missiles' locations . . . as of a few minutes ago. Their tracks were depicted, where they had come from and a computer prediction of where they were heading. Yet the chart of nuclear missile tracks was still blank.

"Where are the nukes?" Lincoln asked.

"We don't believe they've launched yet, sir. The AWACS is trying to sort them out."

"People, all these conventional missiles are just decoys. They want us to tie ourselves in knots chasing them, and then they will slip the nuke missiles through. I don't want our interceptors to go Winchester shooting down conventional missiles when we may have a nuke in the air we will need them on." Winchester was a code word that meant the plane was out of ammunition.

"The Strike Eagles are en route to their targets, sir. One plane had to abort for mechanical problems."

Lincoln took a deep breath. *And the president hoped there would only be a few missiles!* "Where," Lincoln asked, "are our drones?"

"We are getting those locations plotted as fast as we can, sir."

He could see the locations of our cruise missiles. The AWACS and satellite sensors, plus information from the E-2 over the Persian Gulf, were posted as arrows heading toward the Iranian missile sites. Because he was a religious man, Lincoln decided the best thing he could do just now was to say a little prayer, and he did so.

He was just getting to the "Amen" when someone said loudly, "The Iranian interceptors are launching, sir."

Staff Sergeant Jack Colby was looking through the telescope when he saw a streak come out of the sky and explode against the ballistic missile launcher. It was a small explosion. *Hellfire*, he thought. "There's a Reaper or Predator drone up there," he told his mates. "Just hit that big missile with a Hellfire."

The drones were armed with AGM-114P Hellfire II laser-guided missiles. Designed for helicopters, the Hellfire had been adapted to the drones. The small Predator carried two of them, and the much larger Reaper carried six or eight, he wasn't sure. Although Hellfire only carried a twenty-pound explosive warhead, it could certainly take out a cruise or ballistic missile sitting on its launcher—and apparently just had.

Colby was grinning when the second Hellfire smacked the cruise missile and apparently ignited its liquid fuel. The fireball was quite spectacular.

The Green Berets were congratulating each other when they heard the subtle sound of a jet engine. The sound silenced them.

They heard it, then they didn't, then they did, a swelling sound, louder and louder. Four pairs of eyes were glued to the entrance of Tunnel Hotel and the wreckage of the two missile launchers in front of it when the first Tomahawk dove into the launching area and its five-hundred-pound warhead exploded.

"I think the Iranians are done for the evening," Colby said gleefully. "Let's grab our shit and get the fuck outta here."

He and his men had covered two hundred yards of the rough, arid terrain when the second, third and fourth Tomahawks targeted for Tunnel Hotel exploded on the launch area in front of it. Five minutes later, they heard a dull thud. The small satchel charge around which they had piled the gear they didn't want to carry had detonated.

The Tomahawks launched from the waters off Kuwait and the Gulf of Oman had struck the launch sites closest to the Persian Gulf first. As the missiles hit their targets, surveillance sensors captured the flashes and reported it to CENTCOM. The plotters decorated the map with little stars.

Unfortunately, Tomahawks cruised at about five hundred knots, so the northern sites all the way to Mahabad were going to take some time to reach. "How much time?" Lincoln asked his staff.

"Another hour and a few minutes to the last one, Tunnel Yankee."

Lincoln grabbed his command phone and was soon talking to the drone control squadron in Iraq.

"Lots of turbulence and a head wind, sir, but we are starting to get Hellfires on target."

"Tunnel Yankee, and those south of it. How soon?"

"Fifteen or twenty minutes, sir."

"Keep me advised," Lincoln said and rang off.

"The B-2s are airborne out of Balad, sir. ETA for Tehran is an hour from now."

"Very well," the general said and glanced at his watch. Dawn was still an hour away. "Tunnel Hotel had a ballistic missile targeted for Tehran. What's its status?"

"Special Forces team on the ground said it was destroyed on the launcher by a Hellfire. Then four Tomahawks pulverized the area. The Iranians are in the tunnel and not coming out. The team leader is withdrawing. Reaper remains over the site."

"November and Yankee?" Those sites had ballistic missiles targeted at Israel.

"They are launching cruise missiles, sir. Two from each site every fifteen minutes."

"What's the ETA for the Strike Eagles?"

"They should hit those targets within thirty minutes, sir."

"Keep me advised." Lincoln reached in his pocket for his roll of Rolaids as he stared at the nuclear missile chart. The Iranians still hadn't launched any, and F-22s in Iraq and F/A-18 Hornets were expending missiles knocking down the conventional weapons. He told the staff to order a flight of F-22s to break off and return to base to refuel and rearm, then return to their stations.

"Joe's here with a tank," Larijani said. "On the ridge."

I looked with naked eyes and saw nothing out there in the darkness. Using the infrared scope, I saw the tank creeping along the ridge, right on top of the bunker. It turned until its nose was pointed more or less at the entrance to the prayer grounds, then stopped amid the scrub. I could just make out its exhaust plume from the idling engine.

If we needed serious firepower, we had it.

"We have company." G. W.'s voice sounded in my ear. We were wearing headsets with small radios clipped to our belts. G. W., Joe Mottaki and their men were stationed as perimeter guards. "Looks like young men in a technical," he continued. A technical was a pickup truck mounting a machine gun. They were the rides of choice for young Islamic studs in the Middle East. "Basij, most likely," he added.

"You know what to do," I replied.

Indeed he did. He would do nothing if the technical went on by. If it stopped, he would take out the vehicle and kill the men, and he would do it quickly.

I looked behind me. I could see the vehicle cruising slowly along the boulevard, the three or four guys in the back looking every which way. It was at least a hundred yards from where Davar and I sat with our backs against a tree, watching the mosque in the prayer grounds. I didn't think there was a chance in the world that the people in the bunker would leave now; if they did, they were going to spoil the morning's entertainment. I kinda suspected a few of them might be rethinking their presence there. Even so, I doubted that Ahmadinejad would let them leave, and he was the guy making the decisions.

"They're stopping by the remains of that com shack."

Terrific!

"Couple of them are out looking it over, what's left of it . . . Uh-oh. They're having an argument, pointing at the bunker. Looks like someone is advocating a look-around."

I bent down and checked the safety on my AK, made sure the magazine was seated firmly. Davar watched me. She wasn't wearing a headset, so I told her about the technical and nodded in that direction. She hunkered down behind the tree.

"They're all out of the vehicle. Spreading out. Going to make a sweep toward the mosque, looks like. We'll take 'em out when they are between us and you, Tommy. Keep your head down."

I motioned to Davar with my hand—down—and stretched out with the AK pointed in their direction. Then I looked at her. Couldn't see her features in the darkness, but I wondered what she was thinking. I pulled out my pistol and nudged her arm with it. Her head turned, then she reached for it.

I saw flashlights coming . . . six flashlights, flickering randomly about as their holders searched the area and checked the footing . . .

They were about twenty-five yards in from the boulevard amid the scattered trees when the guys let 'em have it. A roar of AK fire, strobing muzzle flashes, and the flashlights fell to the ground. Some of them went out. Two people were screaming.

The F-15E Strike Eagles were as complex an airborne weapons system as the United States possessed. Designed to give the pilot and a weapons system operator—WSO, or wizzo—multiple options in the complex, harrowing environment of ground attack, in any weather, day or night, while providing for its own electronic and fighter defense, the planes' state-of-the art computers and avionics demanded a lot from its crewmen. As usual, the Strike Eagles that flew tonight against Iran's nuclear missile launch sites contained some highly experienced crews, some with the green just worn off and some new people just rotated in from the states.

First Lieutenant JoAnne Rodgers was the WSO in one of them. Two months into her first tour in Iraq, she was being bounced around by turbulence in a night black as a whale's tummy while voices on the radio overloaded the frequency. It seemed everyone on the freq had something vital to say to somebody—and what it became was merely distracting noise. To make matters worse, some of her gear wasn't working. The INS velocities were too large or small, and that affected the computer's calculations of the aircraft's present position and the proper direction to the target, Tunnel November. In addition, the radar's primary mode wasn't working properly and she was forced to use it in a degraded mode. And, although she didn't know it, her ALQ-199 wasn't working at all, although it had passed its built-in tests on the ground and the little green light glowed comfortingly.

"This techno-magic is taking a shit," JoAnne told her pilot on the ICS. Ladylike language was not one of her virtues.

"We can cancel or do the mission," the pilot, Major Dick Hauer, growled. "Make up your mind."

Rodgers didn't reply. As she would put it, she was up to her ass in alligators, severely overloaded, and she had downed a system the day before yesterday. She didn't need a reputation as a candy-ass who would only fly on VFR days with a perfect system.

Hauer didn't appreciate her problems since he was nursing one of his own as he flew the aircraft, monitored the electronic warfare panel and tried to make sense of the radio chatter. Fighter attack was the toughest mission in the air force, where only the best were good enough, and to do it right you needed lots of testosterone, plus a quart. Here he was flying with a woman who didn't have any. She was foul-mouthed, butt ugly, twenty pounds too heavy, obviously smarter than he was and yellow; in toto, the perfect person to push every one of his manly buttons. To be sure, words to this effect had never passed his lips and never would, not in today's air force. A few cracks like that could kill a career.

At precisely the planned time, he lowered the aircraft's nose and began a descent to attack altitude. He made sure the infrared sensors were working and put a ground avoidance display on one of his screens—and saw nothing. Dirt in the air degraded the infrared. Well, he would get a reading in just a moment, when he got a little lower.

That thought had no more than passed through his head when he realized he wasn't seeing the target symbol on his nav screen. "You know where in hell we are?" he growled at Rodgers as the plane did the turbulence bump-and-grind.

"No," she said. "I told you the velocities were running and the radar is in backup mode. I'm looking for something I can identify to get a position update."

Automatically Hauer's eyes flicked to the altimeter. The plane was descending through ten thousand feet—and there were peaks in this mountain range that reached well above eleven. Just then he saw a shape materializing on the infrared. Something damn solid. A mountain! Dead ahead. He pulled the stick back and jammed the throttles forward, and the F-15 pointed its nose at the sky.

JoAnne Rodgers jerked off her oxygen mask and vomited into her lap.

Three nuclear-armed cruise missiles were in the air, according to the AWACS people. They had launched from the predicted sites and were flying the predicted flight paths to three nuclear targets: Mosul and Al Asad in Iraq, and Al Jaber in Kuwait. As General Martin Lincoln listened to the AWACS controller direct F-22s onto these specific missiles, he wondered if there were any other nukes that had been misclassified. Or the intelligence wasn't perfect. Or . . .

To be sure, Tomahawks were crash-diving Iranian missile sites, drones were beginning to pour in Hellfires, and Iranian missile launches had slowed to a trickle.

THE DISCIPLE — 317

Only 142 cruise missiles were airborne. *Only*. He scanned the projected flight paths on the laptop computer on the desk in front of him.

Well, one or more missiles, regardless of warhead, were on the way to every Iranian target, except Tel Aviv. The F-22s were banging away, but missiles were getting through. Two cruise missiles with conventional warheads had already exploded on Tallil Air Force Base, one on Baghdad and two on Balad. Some might have missed the military bases and crashed in the desert or a city or town—no one knew for sure. So far, damage was minimal.

Being only human, Lincoln found his eyes drawn to the symbol of the cruise missile with the Jihad warhead flying toward Kuwait. It was only a hundred miles out, mere minutes away.

One of the colonels leaned down to whisper, "Sir, one of the plotters has asked if you plan to have the staff go to the bombproof."

Lincoln looked at the colonel in disbelief. "The bombproof won't withstand a nuke hit. *You know that*. Now tell these people that I'll court-martial any son of a bitch who leaves this room."

When General Lincoln looked again at the inbound missile, he saw that the AWACS was reporting it destroyed.

Captain Quereau sighed nervously. His Raptor was cruising along at Mach 1.6 without use of the afterburners—super-cruising, the public affairs people called it. He couldn't decide if this airborne CAP, or combat air patrol, over northern Iran was a good deal or not. The other F-22s were shooting down missiles by the handful, and he wouldn't even get to squeeze off an AMRAAM.

The short end of the stick again, he thought, just as he realized his leader, out to his right, was pulling back his power as briefed, slowing to max conserve to save fuel.

After five minutes of that his data-link began spewing targets. The AWACS controller's artificially calm voice sounded in his ears. "You have bogeys out of the Tehran area headed west. They're low."

That was followed by the section leader's truly calm voice. The man must be on drugs! "Q-man, do you have them?"

Quereau tried to make his voice matter-of-fact. "Affirm. F-14s, apparently."

"They're yours."

"Breaking off."

Quereau lowered his nose and turned to point his plane a little ahead of the bogeys, which were still at 150 miles distance. He was coming in from their right forward quarter, closing rapidly as his speed increased through Mach 1. His electronic warfare suite had analyzed the radiation from the bogeys and classified them as F-14s, then displayed that fact on one of his screens. He recalled that during the days of the shah, Iran had purchased several dozen of the swing-wing fighters from the United States. The Iranians had kept a few flying for the thirty years since the revolution by cannibalizing parts from those too worn out to repair.

Quereau locked up both targets in sequence and shallowed his dive. Checked the electronic countermeasures. His plane was being painted by search radars—had been for the last twenty minutes—but it was doubtful the Iranian on the ground saw the stealthy fighter. Certainly the F-14s, with forty-year-old radars, did not. He reminded himself to make no violent maneuvers that would present his planform to any of the probing radars.

He armed two missiles and waited. Coming down through thirty-five thousand, descending gently, speed Mach 1.2, the range counting down . . .

At one hundred miles, David Quereau squeezed the first one off manually. He felt the weapons bay doors slam open and closed as the missile was ejected from the bay; then it ignited and shot forward. The target progression was automatic. He squeezed the trigger again. The doors opened and closed again, and the second missile followed the first. They looked like stars in the blackness, fading as they pulled away.

Quereau shallowed his dive—and stared at the symbols on his screen. Since he and the F-14s were on closing flight paths, the distance between the planes was decreasing quickly, and the missiles were leaping the gap at Mach 2.9. The missile symbols quickly merged with their targets.

In a few more seconds the bogey symbols vanished.

Death in twenty-first-century air combat sure isn't glamorous, he thought as he began a slow turn to the heading that would take him to Tehran.

At least, he reflected, *it's quick*.

Chicago O'Hare was flying an airplane several technical generations behind the F-22, and she had short-range heat-seeking Sidewinders on her rails. Still, the largest challenge she faced was closing the five-hundred-knot missile in front of her and locking it up. In the darkness over the night sea, she would never see the cruise missile, of course; this interception was being conducted based on the symbology on her HUD, or heads-up display—symbols created and driven by her computer, which was fed data-link info from the E-2 and AWACS and raw data from the radar in the nose of her plane.

The Iranian missile was flying at five thousand feet above the sea, headed for Qatar. She was only dimly aware of that—it was an Iranian missile, according to the E-2, and that was enough.

The distinctive Sidewinder rattle sounded in her ears, and she squeezed the trigger on the stick. The missile shot forward off the rail in a gout of fire. *Now, to see if it tracks.* Sidewinders were very reliable, approaching a 90 percent effective rate, but that meant one in ten would go stupid or fail to explode. If the first missile didn't bring down the target, she would fire a second. *Unless the cruise missile has a nuclear warhead that detonates*, she thought. *If it does, then I'll just be dead.*

Through the HUD, she saw a flash, which blossomed as fuel spewing from the ruptured tank caught fire. The missile began descending toward the water.

Chicago didn't watch. With the radio chatter of other pilots talking and the Hawkeye calling out targets for them as background noise, she turned left to intercept another missile. This would be a ninety-degree left-to-right shot, which was fully within the AIM-9X's capabilities. With vectored thrust nozzles, the missile could almost fly a square corner. She got the lock, squeezed the trigger and watched the exhaust of the missile as it flew a high-speed curve to intercept. Another flash, then nothing.

She checked her radar scope as she turned left again to pass well behind the enemy missile, and saw that it was disintegrating into a cloud of small targets.

The radio chatter continued on. She paid only enough attention to catch her call sign, War Ace 307, if and when.

Ten minutes later she picked up another cruise missile coming at her head-on. The Sidewinder might be able to hack the angle, but why waste one? She turned right into a four-G pull and let the cruise missile pass her. When she rolled out pointing toward it, it was tracking at a thirty-degree angle to her left, an angle that was increasing. The Sidewinder went after it like a starving wolf.

What am I going to do when I run out of Sidewinders?

Captain Fereydoon Abassi of the Iranian navy stood on the pass overlooking the Gulf of Oman and listened. He could hear jet engines, not too far above. "American," he said, then swore.

He was here to launch five antiship missiles, which the Iranians had purchased from Russia. SS-NX-26 Yakhonts, the finest antiship missiles in the world. The Russians had, of course, loudly advertised that fact, and even though they were Russians, infidels and users of alcohol to excess, Abassi believed them, because he had seen a demonstration of the Yakhont with his own eyes.

Even listening to the American planes overhead, looking for him, he felt privileged. The admiral had personally chosen him to deliver this mighty blow to the American navy. This was, he well knew, the zenith of his career. No honor he would ever receive in this life or the next could compare with the pride he felt at this moment.

There were, he knew, two American aircraft carriers in the Gulf of Oman. With a little luck, he would hit them both and do massive damage. With just a smidgen more luck, he might even sink one, which would be a feat that would be remembered for many generations. However it worked out, the American navy would be taught a bloody lesson, one that would humble its pride, one it would never forget. He mouthed a prayer to Allah that He might make it so.

The missiles were fire-and-forget; they carried their own radar, the latest Russian design, and they were extraordinarily fast, between Mach 2.0 and 2.5. They also flew low, jinking flight paths to their targets, so they would be extremely difficult to knock down with defensive weapons. In short, the Yakhont antiship missile was the U.S. Navy's worst nightmare.

Although they were capable of carrying a one-hundred-kiloton warhead, the Supreme Leader had refused to release one or two for these missiles, so tonight they carried conventional 750-pound warheads, which could still punch deep into an unarmored ship and do massive, perhaps fatal, damage.

All Fereydoon Abassi had to do was ensure the American carriers were within range and launch the missiles properly.

He went from launcher to launcher, checking everything. The semitrailer launchers were stabilized with hydraulic feet; the missiles themselves were housed inside closed-end containers, which had been properly elevated; a course was set into their computers. The diesel engines in the launchers were running, providing electrical power.

He looked at his watch. It would soon be dawn, and he and his men must be off this ridge by then—and the missiles must be in the air.

He sent his launcher crews marching away north, down the road out of the pass. Then he walked a hundred feet south, past the launchers, along the road to the mobile radar van. One man, the operator, was manning it. The diesel engine was snoring nicely; the lights on the panel were on.

"Are you ready?" he asked the sailor, who stood at attention.

"Yes, Captain."

"Let us proceed. A very short look. I want the distance and azimuths to the two carriers, and the instant I get it, I will tell you to cease radiating. You must stop radiating immediately, shut down the diesel engine and run after the others."

"We will abandon the equipment?"

"If the Americans do not destroy it, it will still be here tomorrow."

"Yes, sir."

Abassi straightened his uniform as the operator threw switches. Over the man's shoulder Abassi could see the scope, which glowed. Even as he watched, blips appeared.

"Over a dozen ships," the operator said, staring at the scope as he manually moved the azimuth cursor.

"The largest ones," Abassi said, "in the center of the formations." The Americans were so predictable.

"Range ninety kilometers, bearing one-seven-two degrees"—the operator turned the knob—"and range ninety-five kilometers, one-six-five degrees."

"Cease radiating. Shut down the engine and run."

The operator quickly did as directed. The diesel abruptly died, leaving only the faint sound of the diesel engines in the launchers.

In an EA-6B Prowler, the radiation from the Russian-built mobile radar was detected and recognized for what it was. These radars, the U.S. Navy intelligence officers believed, were often used by the Iranians to aim cruise or antiship missiles.

The EA-6B operator informed the E-2 Hawkeye circling over *United States* and her sister ship, USS *Columbia*, even as he flipped a switch to jam the radar. However, the few seconds it took for the jammer to go to that frequency proved to be too much. The Iranian radar had ceased radiating.

In the flag combat control spaces aboard *United States*, Admiral Stan Bryant gave the order. "Possible missiles inbound. Code red. Notify all ships."

The warning would merely sharpen the troops already at battle stations. Bryant had ordered battle stations, and the closure of all watertight doors, throughout the task force prior to the first launch earlier this morning. Buttoned up tightly, all internal air circulation in the ships was now secured. In the red-lit passageways the damage control parties stared at the bulkheads and each other.

Captain Abassi walked quickly—he refused to run—toward the first launcher, which still had its prime mover attached. The lid for the control panel was already open. He checked the switches and settings one more time, then manually tuned the azimuth control to one-seven-two and range control to ninety kilometers. Satisfied, he raised the covers of the two fire buttons and simultaneously pushed them both. Then he jumped into the cab of the fireproof prime mover, pulled the door closed and jammed his fingers into his ears.

Ten seconds later the missile's solid-fuel booster engine ignited in a stupendous roar and a blast of white-hot flame that illuminated the area as the missile shot forward off the launcher. It raced away toward the dark ocean, accelerating quickly so that the liquid-fueled ramjet engine could ignite when the booster burned out. It rapidly became a receding star.

Abassi fought the temptation to watch it and climbed out of the cab. He ran to the next launcher and repeated the process. One-seven-two degrees, ninety kilometers. Pushed the buttons and climbed back into the cab. This missile followed the first.

On the third, fourth and fifth missiles, he dialed in one-six-five degrees, ninety-five kilometers. In less than three minutes, they had followed the others on their way to glory.

Fereydoon Abassi jumped from the cab of the last prime mover and raced off down the road after his men, as fast as his feet would carry him.

"Missile launch!" The sensor operators in the EA-6B were the first to detect the distinctive radiation from the radar in the nose of the Yakhont missile. "Missile in the air."

A moment later, an F/A-18 Hornet pilot flying above the coast of Iran, invisible to antiaircraft radar thanks to its ALQ-199, spotted the brilliant plume of a Yakhont coming off the launcher and shouted to the E-2 controller, "Missile in the air. Headed south. We are attacking the launch site."

He jerked his plane around, stuffed the nose down and pushed the throttle forward. His wingman, well out to his left, followed him down. As he descended and flipped switches on the stick with his thumb to select the proper ordnance, he saw the last of the Iranian ship-killers lift off and go streaking southeast. He already had the MASTER ARM switch on and the crosshairs of his bombsight pointed at more or less that spot, so now he sweetened his aim and designated that spot as the target.

Within seconds his computer began giving him steering to his release point. His eyes flicked to the panel. He was going to salvo all his ordnance, six five-hundred-pound cluster bombs, two at a time, at minimum intervals. The clamshell housing on the bombs would open well above the ground and scatter a cloud of bomblets, each of which would detonate and spray shrapnel when it hit something solid.

Heart pounding, he concentrated on following the computer's steering commands. Passing four hundred knots, six thousand feet, the computer released the bombs with a short series of trip-hammer thuds.

He pulled up and left, out to sea, to clear the area for his wingman while he watched the ground. He saw multiple flashes as the bomblets scattered over the empty launch vehicles and mobile radar van. There were no explosions on the ground since all the missiles were in the air.

Running down the road, Captain Abassi heard the swelling noise of jet engines at full throttle, and the whip-cracks of the cluster-bomb containers opening. The noise of the jet peaked when the bomblets went off, so he didn't hear them. He did hear the second plane roll in, and he heard the containers open. This jet had dropped a little long—and several of the bomblets hit the hard road around him and exploded with white flashes. Shrapnel cut into his legs and body, scything him down.

He was lying in the road, bleeding and laughing, when the sound of the jet engines finally faded. He had done it!

Yessss! *For the glory of Allah, and Iran!*

CHAPTER TWENTY-SEVEN

Dick Hauer and JoAnne Rodgers were still flailing around in the darkness over western Iran in their F-15E, trying to find their target, Tunnel November, even though they were twelve minutes past their target time. Rodgers refused to give up, and Hauer wasn't about to abort the mission unless his WSO suggested it first.

Both of them were startled when a missile plume came up out of the darkness several miles off to their right. Their first reaction was that the Iranians had launched a surface-to-air missile at them, but they quickly realized that wasn't the case. The exhaust plume illuminated the thick air with a dull glow as the ballistic missile rose on its pillar of fire, going straight up, accelerating.

"They just fired that thing from our goddamn target," Dick Hauer said heatedly over the ICS. "Our fucking target is right down there, right where they launched that thing!"

His positive statement did little to help Rodgers. The INS was worthless, the radar was only usable in an area search mode, and even with the position inputs she was getting via data-link from AWACS, she couldn't get the system to update her current position. She was doing everything right, she thought, but tonight, in the darkness and turbulence, flying with Mr. Major Asshole, the system had taken a shit.

"Turn toward that spot," she told her pilot, who dumped the right wing and pulled, which caused the radar picture to go blank for a second or two as the gimbel limits were exceeded. As he was turning, another ballistic missile came up out of the gloom, following the first into the heavens.

"I'm going to fly over those shitheads and dump the load, armed," Hauer said. As good as his word, within twenty seconds, all his bombs were on their way.

Even as the bombs were falling, he keyed the radio and reported the two ballistic missile launches to the AWACS, who already knew about them from sensor data and had yet to give him the word.

Cussing silently to himself, Hauer turned the Strike Eagle westward. "Think you can find our goddamn base?" he asked his WSO, who didn't reply.

Behind him in the darkness the bombs exploded on a hillside about a mile from Tunnel November, injuring no one, hurting nothing.

The F-15 was fifteen miles away heading west when the first of the Tomahawks fired at November exploded right in front of the tunnel, killing the launch crew and destroying the empty missile launchers. Within three minutes, three more Tomahawks arrived to flail the area with blast and shrapnel.

Approaching the Iranian border, the MISSILE LAUNCH light began flashing on the instrument panel in front of Hauer, and an audible warning assaulted their eardrums. According to the threat indicator, the missile was coming from the left. Hauer jammed the left wing down and turned hard toward it as he manually pumped off chaff, just in case the automatic system was malfunctioning.

In the soupy darkness, the missile's exhaust plume was starkly visible as it rose toward them.

"What the fuck happened to the ALQ-199?" Hauer demanded of Rodgers, who didn't have time to answer before the missile hit.

Neither crew member managed to eject from the out-of-control, flaming plane as it plummeted from the sky.

The Iranians had scored their first kill of the night.

Aboard *United States*, the incoming Yakhont missiles were not picked up by the carrier's surface search radar. Nor did *Columbia* see the three aimed at her.

One of the Super Aegis cruisers four miles north of *United States*, USS *Hue City*, picked up the incoming missiles on its radar, and the tactical action officer rippled off a salvo of four SM-2 missiles, hoping they would connect with something. But the Yakhonts were too low and traveling too fast—over fourteen hundred knots—and all but one of the Standard missiles failed to find its target. That Standard struck its Yakhont a glancing blow and failed to explode; still, the forces of impact were so great both missiles disintegrated.

USS *Hue City* failed to get a firing solution on any of the three incoming Yakhonts. They were too low and too fast, and their flight path was too erratic.

Aboard *United States*, Admiral Bryant watched the computer symbols that depicted the incoming ship-killers with a growing sense of horror. He knew these symbols were merely computer estimates of the Yakhonts' position because none of the radar systems airborne or shipboard had managed to get a sustained lock. The computer derived a theoretical position, course, speed and time to impact based on very fragmentary data.

Twelve seconds, eleven . . . the missiles were traveling at 2,341 feet per second, moving a statute mile in a little over two seconds. Bryant fumbled for the microphone on the wall and pushed the button for the ship's loudspeaker system. "Incoming missiles," he roared, "forward, aft, amidships! Brace for shock."

He felt the two port-side Phalanx Gatling guns open fire. Those 20 mm weapons were directed by their own radar and internal computer, which aimed and fired them automatically whenever the system detected an incoming target. Each gun vomited out three thousand depleted uranium bullets a minute, a river of heavy metal. They made the deck vibrate at a high frequency, so inside the ship they were felt rather than heard. Bryant's heart threatened to leap from his chest. Maybe, just maybe . . .

Then a missile hit. In the flag spaces, Bryant felt a dull thud. The Yakhont arrived at an eighty-degree angle from the bow and hit *United States* fifty feet above the waterline, below the flight deck, almost exactly amidships. It punched through the steel side of the ship and buried itself deep in the aluminum bulkheads under the flight deck, almost reaching the Number Two Elevator, before it detonated. The explosion blew a hole in the flight deck and blasted a cavern in the offices, bunkrooms and passageways. It also blew a hole in the ceiling of the hangar deck. The blast wrecked two planes on the flight deck, blowing one thirty feet into another plane and collapsing its gear, and smashed three on the hangar deck. And it ignited a thousand square feet of aluminum within the ship. Bodies and body parts were quickly consumed by the flames.

Columbia's Phalanxes knocked down one of the incoming missiles. The first one to hit crossed above the flight deck too fast for a human eye to follow and smashed into the island superstructure, doing catastrophic damage and killing over fifty men outright. The other went through the opening for Number Four elevator, crossed the hangar deck and blew a hole in the starboard side of the ship. The explosions of both warheads started fierce fires.

Columbia's bridge was shattered; half the men there were dead or disabled, and the helmsman lost control of the rudders. The massive carrier began a gentle turn to port. She did a complete 180-degree turn, almost colliding with a destroyer, before Damage Control Central managed to get the helm shifted and regain control of the rudders from the after steering room. Fortunately, aboard both ships, the propulsion systems were still intact and functioning flawlessly. The nuclear reactors, also sited below the waterlines, were also undamaged.

Like the well-trained professionals they were, the crews of the giant ships responded immediately to the disasters. On the flight decks, men began moving aircraft forward to escape the fires while other men flaked out fire hoses. Flames, poisonous fumes and severe battle damage to all systems near the blast sites wreaked havoc with ships crammed with explosive ordnance and jet fuel. The battles to save the carriers would last almost twelve hours before the fires were brought under control.

Chicago O'Hare had fired her last Sidewinder and had declared to her flight leader, who was at least forty miles away, that she was Winchester and Bingo fuel. She had to head back to her tanker rendezvous now or she was going to be swimming home. Fortunately the sky seemed empty of cruise missiles. She stuck her hand up under her oxygen mask and wiped the perspiration from her face. Then she wiped her eyes and eyebrows. Her flight suit and underwear were soaked with sweat.

Holy mother!

The E-2 controller came up on the radio. "Ninety-nine Battlestar aircraft, ninety-nine Battlestar aircraft, divert to Qatar." Ninety-nine was the jargon for all, and Battlestar was the call sign of *United States*.

O'Hare laid her plane into a lazy turn in the general direction of Qatar and worked on her nav computer while she climbed. Oh, joy, Al Udeid Air Base at Doha was only 110 nautical miles away. She had plenty of fuel for that little jaunt. She looked up the frequency for Al Udeid Approach on her Bingo cards and dialed it into the ready position on her radio.

She wondered how many cruise missiles she and her fellow Hornet pilots had failed to intercept. Well, in life there is always an accounting. She hadn't seen a nuclear explosion light up the night to the south, so if any got through, they had conventional warheads.

Her next thought was more practical. Were there any more missiles crossing the Gulf?

Just to be on the safe side, Chicago ran her radar scope out to max range and began a slow 360-degree turn.

She was pointed toward Iran when she saw them, two blips heading south. Low. Making about five hundred knots.

She didn't even pause to think about her fuel; she advanced the throttles, lowered the nose and turned to intercept. Using her thumb on the stick, she selected GUN.

Dear God, don't let these two be nukes.

Now the Hawkeye controller called these targets out to her. "Tally," she replied.

O'Hare came in on the nearest one in a classic high-side bounce. She wanted to get behind it, so she could see the glow of its exhaust pipe. Without that she would have to fire on radar, would probably use more ammo, and she needed to stretch her supply to ensure she got them both.

As she approached, she realized she could see the missile through the HUD, cruising at about three thousand feet, a dark little cigar shape against a darker ocean. The sky was just light enough. It was a while before dawn, but with the sliver of moon in the east and the brightening sky, she could see it.

She didn't bother to slacken her speed—just closed, put the gunsight pipper on it, waited until the last possible moment, then waited another second and squeezed off a tiny burst. As she went over the missile she saw it begin to tumble. Must have hit the autopilot.

The next enemy missile was already well ahead and above her at five thousand, so she had to use the afterburner to catch it.

As she closed she was aware of the fuel pouring into her exhausts to give her extra power. Well, she had a little extra; she could make Qatar.

Somehow she missed with her first burst. *Fired too soon,* she thought and kept closing. This time she waited until she was way too close before she pulled the trigger. The missile exploded, and she yanked on the stick to go through the top of the fireball. Whump, and she was through.

Checked the engine instruments and came out of burner. Everything seemed okay. She pulled the nose into a max range climb and told the Hawkeye dude she had splashed these two.

"War Ace Three Oh Seven, roger that." His voice sounded tight. "We think we have a nuke headed toward Al Udeid. We want you to go to max conserve and intercept it."

Uh-oh. The LOW FUEL light was already illuminated.

"How far out is it?" she asked.

"It's still over land, and we don't yet have it on the display. Wait."

She had only a few minutes to stooge around if she planned on bringing back the navy's jet. She told the controller that and got no answer. She throttled back anyway and turned slowly right, inscribing a circle in the sky.

A minute passed, then another.

"Hey, man, War Ace Three Oh Seven. I am about outta gas. Don't you have anybody else?"

"War Ace, the tactical commander requests that *you* intercept."

As she honked the plane around, she said, "I go in the drink, buddy, and you're going to be buying me beer until you retire."

So she flew northward, away from Qatar, at max conserve. After a couple of minutes, she decided to just wait until the nuke came to her. She pushed the stick over, and the autopilot held it there. She began circling again. *At least after I drop it*, she thought, *I won't have so far to swim.*

"War Ace Three Oh Seven, Black Eagle. Bogey will be along in ten minutes if you hold your position."

It was only then that she realized most of the other planes she had launched with were no longer on the frequency. The silence was broken only occasionally by pilots telling Black Eagle that they were switching to Al Udeid Approach.

Each of the minutes seemed to take an hour to pass. Desperately thirsty, Chicago took a baby bottle full of water, now warm, from her survival vest and chugged it. When it was all gone, she recapped the bottle and replaced it in the vest.

The fuel gauge told the story. She wasn't going to make dry land. No way, José!

Chicago wondered how many cannon shells remained. Not many, that's for sure. Maybe one good squirt. She was going to have to be right behind this guy, sticking her nose up his tailpipe, when she pulled the trigger. Every shell had to count.

What if it goes nuclear when I shoot it?

Well, she would be dead before she realized the warhead had detonated, even if she gunned it from half a mile away. She took a ragged breath and exhaled explosively. Took off her oxygen mask and swabbed her face, then replaced it.

What if a bullet punctures the warhead and it squirts out a cloud of radioactive plutonium, and I fly through it?

Hell, it won't explode. I won't get slimed. The missile will go into the water, and a few minutes later, so will I. I'm probably going to drown.

"War Ace Three Oh Seven, Black Eagle. Say your fuel state."

She told him.

In a few seconds the controller said, "Qatar is launching a rescue chopper your way. After engagement, look for him and try to rendezvous."

She didn't know whether to laugh or cry. "Roger," she managed.

General Martin Lincoln called the president. As he was waiting for the call to go through, someone turned on the television mounted high in the corner of the Ops Room. Lincoln caught the picture out of the corner of his eye. The face he saw was the president's, talking to an interviewer! Christ, he was on CNN. He watched, mesmerized, with the phone against his ear. CNN was broadcasting from Baghdad! The president was in Baghdad!

Now someone off-camera spoke to the president, and he took off his mike. The camera followed him as he walked to a table to the camera's left and picked up a telephone. The president's voice sounded in Lincoln's ear. "Yes, General."

"Mr. President," the general began. "The Iranians launched two ICBMs, which probably have nuclear warheads. They are apparently on their way to Israel. We're tracking them."

"All right," was the president's response. Looking at his back on television, Lincoln could see that he had taken the punch well. His posture didn't change. The man had ice water in his veins.

"Another nuke is on its way to Qatar aboard a cruise missile. We've shot three down. Those six seem to be all they launched. About a hundred and seventy cruise missiles total. We think we have taken out all the launch sites. There haven't been any more launches in the last five minutes. Our two carriers in the Gulf of Oman have been hit by conventional antiship missiles—they are fighting fires."

The president didn't ask a single question. "Thank you, General," he said, and the connection broke.

Lincoln slowly replaced the telephone on its cradle as he watched the president walk back to his stool beside the interviewer and someone pin his mike back on.

Unable to look away, Lincoln listened as the president talked about the future of Iraq and Iran. These countries had to join the international community, he said, and build their nations as members of the world family. They owed that to all their citizens.

Another general was mesmerized by the CNN broadcast and the sight of the president of the United States talking to a CNN reporter in Baghdad as a handful of cruise missiles assaulted the town. As General Aqazadeh, the Iranian chief of staff, watched from the Ops Room of the Defense Ministry, a room untouched by the recent assault by Zionist terrorists with a howitzer, an aide told him that two of the six missiles that had reached Baghdad had been shot down by American forces, one had hit a runway at Baghdad International, and the other three had crashed into the city's suburbs.

An ineffectual assault, Aqazadeh thought dejectedly. *And now the American president is in Baghdad, making political hay of the Iranians' best efforts.*

He turned from the television and studied the reports. Apparently all twenty-five of the missile sites had been the targets of U.S. Navy Tomahawk cruise missiles. While many cruise missiles and a few Ghadar ICBMs remained in the tunnels, the crews refused to push them out onto the launch areas for launching, according to those people who had reported. Some of the missile sites could not be raised on landline or by radio. Whether the communications had been destroyed or the crews had panicked and refused to answer HQ's calls, Aqazadeh didn't know. *Not that it mattered*, he thought. *Regardless, the result was the same.*

Nor could he contact the president in the executive bunker. His staff had tried repeatedly. That was certainly odd. The president and other national leaders had taken shelter in the bunker in case the Americans retaliated after a nuclear burst. They hadn't yet done it, even though at least two Ghadars with nuclear warheads were in the air heading toward Israel. Aqazadeh didn't know that one of his own nukes was targeted on Tehran; Ahmadinejad hadn't shared that tidbit with him.

Aqazadeh realized that Iran had probably lost the shooting war and was in danger of losing the political war, even if the Jihad missiles obliterated Israel. *The president should know of this,* he thought, *so that he can make a statement to counter American propaganda efforts.* He decided to personally go to the bunker and appeal to the president to come out and lead his nation.

The blip blossomed on Chicago O'Hare's radar scope. Hell, it was still almost a hundred miles away, over the Gulf, and would pass ten miles to her left. She glanced at her fuel gauge. Five hundred pounds remaining. There was water in her immediate future.

She turned west on a course to intercept, resisted the temptation to advance the throttle now. She would have to wait until the very last moment to increase her speed to match the missile's.

"Black Eagle, War Ace Three Oh Seven has the target and is intercepting. Hope you have that chopper on the way."

"It's airborne and crossing the coast."

"Roger that."

She checked her switches, then eyed the radar as the target marched down the scope, coming closer. She had to accelerate and turn before she got to the missile so she wouldn't end up in a tail-chase. Not enough fuel for that happy crap.

Finally she advanced the throttle. Her speed began to build. O'Hare timed her turn well and ended up closing from the missile's port side. Looking for the missile through the HUD and not seeing it, she realized she had made a mistake. Couldn't find it against its background. She was almost on top of the thing. She popped her speed brakes and pulled up in a yo-yo, then lowered her nose and checked her radar as she dropped into trail behind it. *There*, at a half mile.

Closing deliberately from astern, Chicago crept up until she saw the exhaust glow and centered that in the gunsight. Her breath was coming in quick gasps, as if she were running. This was *it*!

She checked the range. Less than a hundred yards. Pulled the trigger. Felt the cannon vibrating . . . and the missile's engine glow disappeared. She kept the trigger down, but the cannon stopped abruptly. Out of ammo.

She yanked hard on the stick to avoid a collision. Found herself going almost forty degrees nose up. Stuffed the nose and turned so that she could again acquire it on the scope. Halfway through the turn she saw a little plume of fire, then a splash.

Amen.

When she was again heading to Qatar and climbing, she called the E-2. "Splash one nuke. Give me a heading to intercept the chopper."

"One-seven-five. It's twenty-five miles from you."

"Have a nice life," she said.

She sat staring at her fuel gauge, which read zero. *Maybe the gauge is wrong. Maybe there is more juice in there than you think.* Even she didn't believe that. She pushed the button on the IFF to squawk 7700, Mayday.

The altimeter read six thousand feet. She was still doing five hundred knots. She pulled the throttle back to max conserve, and the airspeed bled off.

Oddly, her next thought was about the skipper, Fly Burgholzer. *He is going to be so pissed.*

Then her right engine died. She had arrived at the end of her rope.

"War Ace Three Oh Seven is flaming out. Ejecting." Even as she said it the left engine died and the cockpit went dark and silent.

Sitting in that black coffin that the cockpit had become as the plane decelerated, O'Hare took a deep breath and pulled the ejection handle over her head. She yanked the face curtain all the way down and the seat smacked her in the ass and whoom! she was out and tumbling through the black night sky.

The opening of her chute almost split her pelvis.

She fumbled with her oxygen mask bayonet fittings, got it off, then threw it away as she drifted down toward the black ocean. She could see the surface now. The first traces of dawn were arriving. *Just another navy day*, she thought as the water rushed up toward her boots.

Betsy "Chicago" O'Hare was sitting in the little one-man raft that had been in her seatpan waving a flare when the chopper found her.

My handheld radio squawked to life. "Tommy Carmellini?" a tinny voice asked.

"Yes. This is Carmellini."

"We're fifteen minutes from drop."

I looked at my watch, which I could see quite plainly in the early dawn. "Got it," I said. "Make some bull's-eyes."

"Oh, we will, we will. You can bet on it."

That was the problem. I was betting on it. Betting my ass and the ass of everyone here with me. I didn't tell him that, though.

"Thanks," I said.

He didn't reply.

As I put the radio back in my pocket, I looked around. Joe Mottaki and his tank were sitting on the ridge to the left, on top of the bunker. G. W. was behind us, across the access road, nearer the gate to the prayer grounds. Larijani, Davar and I were still at the base of the trees, where we could see the boulevard behind us. Haddad Nouri and Ahmad Qajar had a machine gun set up on our right. They had gone back to the boulevard, then crawled forward until they found a slight depression where an old tree had been. They set up the gun there, about a hundred yards from the entrance to the mosque, where the two Iranian soldiers stood a sloppy guard. One was sitting in the dirt, his weapon across his knees; the other was smoking at the corner of the building. Obviously, there were no officers or NCOs about to check on them.

Behind us, civilian traffic packed the boulevard, all of it going one way—out of town. The military was already gone, and the civilians were doing their best to get gone, too.

"Gonna be over soon," I whispered to Davar and Larijani, neither of whom replied.

The kids in that bunker were still on my mind. I lowered my forehead onto the cold steel of the rifle receiver and tried to think of something else. Like going home. I didn't give a damn what Grafton wanted; first chance I got, I was going home.

Deep in the bunker, Mahmoud Ahmadinejad was a worried man.

After the computers, telephones, televisions and camera equipment for television broadcasts went dead, instantly, all at the same instant, he had sat in his command room in silence, watching the three technicians attempt to figure out what was wrong and restore communications. After about ten minutes, one had brought a computer that he had taken apart over to him. "Excellency, we have no electrical power on the circuits, and the computers have been destroyed." He pointed to the circuit board, which was black in places. "The whole thing is burned up from a voltage overload."

Ahmadinejad walked out, went to his private office. That was several hours ago.

He had waited there for the jolt of the nuclear burst over Tehran, which hadn't happened. Waited and waited and waited.

Now he wondered who had severed the communications line with the bunker. Zionists? Or his political enemies? The possibility that his political enemies had staged a coup after he went into the bunker could not be overlooked or discounted. The entire leadership of the Party of God was in the bunker, all the prominent clerics and leading citizens.

His enemies couldn't get into the bunker, of course; all the bombproof doors were sealed from this side. What if they were up there now, patiently waiting for him to emerge . . . to assassinate him? Of course, if they decided not to wait, they could call him on the telephone beside the entrance door in the basement of the mosque. Thus far, no one had called.

So he sat by himself in his office, very much alone, waiting for the airburst that would flatten Tehran, wondering if the Jihad missiles had destroyed their targets and pondering the venality of his enemies, of whom he had many.

The B-2s were already over Tehran, thirty thousand feet up, making practice runs on their targets. Painted repeatedly by search radars that never locked on them, the stealth bombers cruised back and forth undetected in the sky as it lightened to the east. The pilot of the lead bomber was certain that the Iranians didn't even know they were there.

Since the mission resembled a training exercise, they did a complete practice run and a simulated drop, then circled back to do it again for real.

The bomber was on autopilot, which was slaved to the computer, which the copilot was monitoring. The pilot didn't have to do anything except turn on the MASTER ARMAMENT switch at the proper moment and be ready to take over if the autopilot refused to obey the computer.

This is like flying the simulator, the pilot thought, *without all the failures the sim operator likes to create.*

The two ICBMs launched at Israel had reached apogee and were now hurling downward toward their target. Steaming slowly toward the Israeli coast, just offshore of Tel Aviv, USS *Guilford Courthouse* was at battle stations, and had been for hours. She picked up the two small missiles on her radar while they were still almost five hundred miles away. This technical feat was only possible because the missiles were so high above the earth.

The tactical action officer, a commander, was in charge of the ship's weapons systems. He telephoned the bridge. "Two targets inbound, sir. One behind the other."

"You are cleared to engage according to plan, Commander," the captain told his TAO.

The ship was equipped with six SM-3 antisatellite missiles. Using one, a Super Aegis cruiser had successfully destroyed a failed satellite in orbit 110 miles above the earth. Hitting a target that high traveling at eighteen thousand miles an hour was a stupendous technical feat, one that many scientists and physicists said couldn't be done. Yet it had been done, just a few years before.

Still, the commander was nervous. Theoretically, the incoming ICBMs should be within the SM-3's capabilities. Yet the angle wasn't ideal. In fact, head-on was the worst possible angle of approach to the target; the slightest angular error in the missile's radar and computer would result in a miss. Consequently, he and the captain had decided to shoot three Standard-3 missiles at each incoming ICBM, all they had. If they missed, the accompanying cruiser, USS *Stone's River*, would launch her SM-2 missiles at them.

General Lincoln said the Iranians had only launched two ICBMs, but certainty in war isn't possible. Besides, they could launch another in a few hours. Or two or three. Yet rather than wait for the blow that might not fall, the TAO and captain had decided a few minutes ago to give these first two their knockout punch. And pray.

The clock hands in Combat swept mercilessly on as the ICBMs raced downhill toward their target. Actually, the lead one was slightly off course. It appeared to be headed for Gaza. The angle differential might actually help, the commander thought as he watched the blips that were the missiles race toward the center of his presentation, which was this ship.

When the ICBMs were two hundred miles away, the SM-3s came out of their vertical launchers riding a plume of fire. Their exhaust blasts shook the ship. Away they blazed into the lingering night, until they became stars racing away into the brightening eastern sky. One by one they departed, six of them, and when they were gone the sea was dark and silent again.

A Flash message was immediately sent to General Lincoln. "SM-3s launched."

The ship was in shallow water, actually too close to the coast for comfort, but the captain dared not turn her. The best radar reception was in the forward quadrant. He ordered the ship slowed to two knots and heard the bells as the engine room responded. Ten knots would be better—the ship more stable—but it wasn't possible.

The captain wondered if he should tell the crew to prepare for a nuclear blast. He reached for the 1-MC mike, then changed his mind. No.

He was sitting there, staring at the lights of Tel Aviv on the horizon, when the squawk box came to life. "TAO, sir. First missile missed."

The captain didn't acknowledge.

When the squawk box spluttered again, he jumped. "TAO, sir. Direct hit on the first enemy missile."

Automatically his eyes rose and probed the darkness to the east. The sky was cloudless; he saw all those stars . . . but no explosion. Too far away.

He waited, feeling every thud of his heart. Scratched his forehead, wondered if there was something he should have done but failed to do.

"Captain, TAO. Fourth missile, a direct hit."

As relief washed over the captain, he said to the OOD, "Right full rudder. Five knots through the turn. Steady on course two-seven-zero and work up to twenty knots. I want to get away from this coast."

"Aye aye, sir."

As the giant warship slowly heeled into the turn, he picked up the 1-MC microphone and spoke to the entire ship's crew. "This is the captain speaking. We have just destroyed two ICBMs targeted at Israel. Well done, shipmates."

He hung the mike in its bracket. For some reason he felt a vibration. And heard a noise. What was *that*? Several seconds passed before he realized that every man and woman on the ship was stomping their feet and cheering, even the bridge crew.

The captain put one hand over his forehead and wiped his eyes.

Five minutes later he was down in Combat looking at a map. The locations of the two missile kills were plotted on it. Both were destroyed over Jordan. He wondered whether the warheads had broken up in the air or when they hit the ground. Either way, radioactivity was going to be released.

The captain sent a Flash message to Washington with the coordinates of the kills.

David Quereau was at fifty thousand feet, flying at just above Mach 1, in a slow turn, letting his radar sweep the sky over and around Tehran. He shouldn't be this slow—he well knew that in combat speed is life—but the silent sky had seduced him into this gas-saving measure.

The stealth B-2s at thirty thousand feet were giving him their position by encrypted data-link, so they were on his tactical screen, as was his lead, who was at thirty-five thousand feet over the city, providing close top cover. He watched the bombers in trail make their turns and begin their bomb runs.

He was thinking about death, about the two pilots and two back-seaters he had shot down earlier in the evening, just a few minutes ago. He wondered if any of the four men had gotten out of their planes. Since he was a young cynic, he thought probably not. AMRAAM warheads do horrible things to fighter planes.

He had killed them. Oh, they would have killed him if given the chance, but the aircraft designers and technical wizards in the States had given him a superior airplane, so he lived and the other fellows died for their country. Just like that.

Now he had to live with it.

Quereau was thinking about that, about living after killing, when his peripheral vision picked up something on his left. Something moving . . . He looked. A fighter, coming in on a bounce! Now a missile streaked from under a wing.

He slammed the left wing down and lit the burners at the same time. He manually triggered his chaff dispenser, which included flares to attract heat-seekers, which is probably what this guy launched.

He watched the missile as he turned a five-G corner. The incoming heat-seeker went behind the F-22, perhaps decoyed by a flare, perhaps because it couldn't hack the turn.

He kept the turn in. The other fighter was creeping forward on the canopy, so he was out-turning him. He could see vapor trails off the other fighter's wingtips.

He was canopy to canopy with the other fellow now, who was about a mile away. He was looking at its planform. MiG-29.

The F-22's vectored thrust made this a lopsided contest. As maneuverable as the MiG was, the F-22 was even more so. The MiG was in his forward quadrant now. He was winning, getting behind the guy.

It would have to be a gunshot. He had only AMRAAMs aboard, and the MiG was too close for them to arm. Yet his thumb didn't move to the gun button on the stick.

Turning, turning, the MiG pilot knew he was dead if he tried to dive away. The G was bleeding off the MiG's airspeed, so the F-22 appeared to be closing. Quereau pulled the throttles back out of maximum burner, so he wouldn't overshoot, kept the G on.

He also stole glances at his threat indicator and tactical screen. If this guy had a wingman, Quereau couldn't afford to play. Apparently he didn't. Or if he did, Quereau hadn't seen him yet.

Now the MiG pilot reversed his turn, half a roll, and jammed the stick forward, going into serious negative G, the classic escape maneuver. He had waited too long—Quereau was directly behind him and followed his every move.

Normally, in fighters of roughly equal performance, the lead fighter could escape with this gambit. But the fighters weren't equal. The F-22's superior roll rate and responsiveness more than made up for the lag due to the pilot's reaction time.

Quereau couldn't believe this encounter was happening. The F-22 was an artifact left over from the Cold War, or so the politicians said. And every living expert had solemnly pronounced the dogfight dead as dollar gas, yet here he was in one.

The MiG pulled positive and negative G, turned and rolled and climbed and did a Split-S. Quereau stuck to him like glue, even closing on him a little; less than fifty yards separated them now.

This guy doesn't have a wingman. He's out here solo looking for a fight. The realization hit like a hammer. Even if there were another Iranian fighter up here stooging around, the guy would never get a weapons solution on a target maneuvering this wildly or risk a missile shot with his victim this close to an Iranian fighter.

Quereau grinned under his oxygen mask. The ride was vicious, but the experience was sublime.

"Uh-oh! We got company," G. W. said on the tactical net.

I looked behind us. Dawn was here, and I could see fairly well. Two vehicles were coming down the access road toward the mosque. The lead vehicle looked like a limo. For sure, it was a long, low car. Behind it was an army truck with an open bed. I could see helmets in the bed. Troops.

"Can the door to the upper elevator chamber be opened from the outside?" I asked Davar, who was hunched down beside me.

"No," she said, "but there is a telephone by the door, a direct line to the bunker command center. They can talk to the people inside, and they can take the elevator up and open the door."

I thought about that as the vehicles drove toward the mosque. What if the B-2s didn't drop their bombs, or the bombs missed the elevator shaft? What if Ahmadinejad came out?

One thing I knew for certain—Jake Grafton didn't want that to happen, and he had told me to prevent it.

I glanced at the infrared designator lying in the grass beside me. A Hellfire or two on the mosque would lock Ahmadinejad in, but there wasn't time.

"Haddad," I said on my tactical radio, "we gotta take these people down."

The vehicles stopped in front of the mosque. As the rear passenger door closest to the mosque opened and someone got out, troops came pouring out of the truck and raced away in all directions to set up a perimeter.

Nouri and Qajar opened up with the machine gun, cutting them down. Still, some of the troops escaped the kill zone. At least four of them ran into the mosque behind the limo passenger. Our guys concentrated on taking down the exposed troopers.

I keyed the tac net radio again. "Joe, take out the vehicles. Don't let them escape."

"Okay," he said.

The limo blew up, literally disintegrated right before my eyes, with pieces going everywhere. Then the booming report of the 100 mm tank gun reached me.

The truck driver wasn't waiting to see what happened next. He popped the clutch and floored the accelerator. He managed to get the truck turned and pointed toward the access road before the second shell from the tank blew the cab clear off the truck. The carcass rolled forward for about fifty feet, then came to rest with the fuel tank ablaze. Smoke boiled up.

"Get those soldiers," I roared into the mike and grabbed the satchel charge.

"No," Davar screamed and grabbed my arm. "No. Don't go down there. Wait for the bombers!"

"They might miss," I told her, shrugging out of her grasp. I put my hand on Larijani's shoulder. "Give me cover."

Then I started running, bobbing and weaving, trying to keep low, carrying that satchel charge in my left hand. My AK was on a strap over my shoulder, flopping around. I had the pistol grip and trigger with my right, and the strap was so loose I might even be able to shoot the thing one-handed.

I lengthened my stride and ran like the wind toward the mosque. Bullets snapped in the air around me. The machine gun was vomiting bursts, I could hear several AKs going . . . I was going to get it any second.

For some reason I didn't care. I had reached the combat plateau and no longer gave a damn.

I quit jinking and just flat-out sprinted. I went through the door with the AK going. One soldier was inside, maybe one of the guys who had sat outside the door for hours. He was just a mite too slow, and I gave him a burst right in the chest.

I slammed my back against the wall and waited for my eyes to adjust. The entrance to the bunker was in the basement, Davar had said—but where were the stairs down?

I heard running feet and turned just in time to see Larijani come flying through the door. He landed on his face. I rolled him over and saw he had been hit twice.

"You don't run fast enough," I said.

In the basement of the mosque, General Aqazadeh grabbed the telephone on the wall adjacent to the entrance to the bunker, which was sealed with a steel bombproof door. "The president," he shouted at the man who answered. "This is General Aqazadeh."

In two seconds Mahmoud Ahmadinejad came on the line.

Against the background noise of machine-gun bursts and random bursts from AK-47s, the general tried to tell the president how the war was going. "We couldn't communicate with you," he said, "and thought you might not be aware of events. The Americans have attacked all the sites. The American president is in Baghdad, on television, making political propaganda of our efforts. We have two missiles on the way to Israel. You must come out of the bunker and talk to believers worldwide."

"What is that noise I hear?"

"A firefight," Aqazadeh replied. "Commandos have surrounded the bunker. I have a radio in my automobile. You must summon troops back to the city to kill them." Aqazadeh didn't realize that his limousine had been destroyed.

Of course that is what he would say, Ahmadinejad reflected. *The military is staging a coup, and the loyal troops are being attacked by the traitorous ones. Aqazadeh is part of the plot to kill me. If we open the bunker door, we will be murdered by these traitors to Allah.*

"You are Zionist swine," the president of Iran told his general. "If you are alive after the war, we will execute you as the traitor you are."

Then Ahmadinejad hung up the telephone.

"Bombs away."

The words sounded in Quereau's earphones. In front of him the MiG was flying straight and level—and slowing rapidly. *This jock's a real sport! He's going to see if he can fly slower than I can.*

Quereau grinned inside his oxygen mask, retarded his throttles and deployed his speed brakes. He let his fighter creep up onto the MiG's right wing, where he could look over into the cockpit.

"Number Two, bombs away. And we're RTB." Return to base.

"Roger." That was Quereau's lead. "Outlaw Two, you copy?"

"Roger that," Quereau responded. "I'll watch the back door and be along shortly."

The MiG-29 and F-22 were in close formation now, each pilot looking at the other, the throttles at idle. The guy who flies the slowest in this kind of game gets a free guns shot when his opponent moves into the lead. Quereau knew that, and knew that with his vectored thrust and a partial flap deployment, his fighter could fly level at a sixty-degree angle of attack. He doubted the MiG-29 could match it.

Gonna find out, by golly!

I left Larijani and went around the corner. Found the stairs down. Some-body fired a shot up the stairs, which spanged into the wall beside me.

I didn't know what those guys were doing down there, didn't know how much time we had before the bunker-busters landed, and I couldn't afford the time to study my watch.

I pulled the igniter on the satchel charge and tossed it down the stairs. Then I ran around the wall back toward the entrance. I was pulling Larijani over against the wall when the floor turned to jelly, sweeping me off my feet. The trip-hammer concussions of the four five-thousand-pounders jackham-mering their way into the earth demolished the mosque; the walls came apart and the ceiling fell in.

Davar was lying down, shooting at an Iranian near the mosque, when the bombs hit. The bombs were falling too fast to register on her retinas, and she never saw them.

As the first shock wave punched her, she scrunched her eyes shut and grabbed the shaking earth with both hands. The four bombs took about two seconds to detonate, from first to last, four vicious impacts that set the earth shaking. Davar held on tightly to the earth as dirt and rock rained around her. The small rocks hitting her were painful, and she knew that if a big one hit her she would be instantly dead, yet she couldn't move. Only when the earth stopped moving and things stopped falling did she slowly, carefully, open her eyes and raise her head.

Although she didn't know it, the entire first elevator shaft down to the in-termediate chamber, and that chamber, had been destroyed and filled with rock. The lower elevators had been torn from their mountings by the vibrat-ing earth and had fallen to the bottom of the partially collapsed shaft. It would take months with heavy excavation equipment to dig down to the bun-ker entrance.

Davar stood and wiped the dirt from her face.

She walked down the slope toward the smoking crater in the parking lot. The hole was almost a hundred feet in diameter, and it was surrounded by a debris field of loose dirt and stone that had been ejected from the hole. In places, the debris was over two feet thick.

She was almost to the edge of where the asphalt had been when she came across the first body. It was a dead Iranian soldier. Trickles of blood had come out his ears. He was lying on his side, half buried, staring life-lessly.

She walked on, past bodies that had been machine-gunned and bodies that had been crushed by falling stones and were now almost buried. She tried to see into the gigantic hole. The bottom of the crater was still smoking, giving off fumes and atomized dirt. She could see nothing.

She walked on across the debris field toward the pile of rubble that had been the mosque. Saw a head sticking out of the rubble. Carmellini, lying motionless.

"No," she screamed and attacked the rubble with her bare hands. She threw rocks, pieces of masonry, dug through piles of plaster, trying to free him. "No," she said, "no, no, no."

Tommy stirred, looked into her face. Tears were streaking the dirt.

She saw his lips move. She couldn't hear him. The concussions had tempo-rarily deafened her. She bent down, kissed him, worked on getting the dirt out of his hair.

G. W. Hosein roared up in a technical. He leaped out and helped her pull Carmellini from the crumbled bricks and mortar.

"Larijani's in there," Carmellini whispered. "Get him out."

Haddad Nouri and Ahmad Qajar were also there now. A stone had bro-ken Qajar's right arm, which he held with his left. G. W. told him to sit in the pickup's passenger seat. Together, the other three burrowed into the rubble with their bare hands while Tommy crawled out.

Subtly adjusting his throttles and trying not to move the stick, David Que-reau kept his F-22 in formation on the MiG's right wing. Both planes flew with their noses pointed up at steep angles, riding their exhaust gases like rockets, teetering on the edge of stalls.

Yet the MiG pilot was not decelerating anymore. The pilot must have sensed that he was as slow as he could go, and the loss of another knot or two would result in a departure from controlled flight. He was at the far left edge of the performance envelope.

On the other hand, the American pilot had a few more he could scrub off, if he wished. If he did, he would fall behind the MiG and could eventually put a cannon burst into the Iranian, when he finally began to accelerate again.

The MiG pilot looked over at Quereau, who of course was looking at him as he flew formation. Quereau saluted with his throttle hand, then pointed east, repeatedly, jabbing his finger. Then he waved good-bye.

He saw the MiG pilot acknowledge the salute and gesturing. The MiG-29 accelerated smartly, and the nose dropped so altitude could be quickly converted to airspeed. Flaps coming up, both men stayed in formation a moment as their speed increased and wings and controls bit solidly into the air.

Then, with a little wave, the Iranian lowered his left wing to turn east and dropped his nose even more. He raced away in a descending left turn.

Quereau watched the MiG until it was lost in the vastness of the sky; then he turned a complete circle as he checked his radar picture and threat indicators. He saw the B-2s' symbols and the lead F-22. With a grin he lowered his nose to help him accelerate and headed west.

He savored the past few minutes. Whatever else it is, squirting missiles is not dogfighting. The thought occurred to him that he might have been in the very last dogfight in the history of the world.

He and that Iranian pilot were the only guys who knew about it.

Cool.

Every muscle I had screamed in protest. I sat up, found that nothing was broken and slowly worked my way erect. The others were tearing bare-handed at the rubble. I joined them. We dug until we found a trouser leg, then dug more frantically until we finally uncovered Larijani's head. He was dead, with dirt in his eyes and mouth. I kinda figured that the bullets killed him, but maybe it was the collapse of the building.

I straightened up as I looked at him. Another unnecessary death. I felt tired and sore. I turned and walked slowly, painfully, over to the technical. I felt like I was a hundred years old.

In a moment Davar joined me. She was trying to wipe the tears and dirt from her face. "Why did he follow me?" I asked her.

"He didn't want to live anymore," she said. "Couldn't you see that?"

We left him there and piled into the technical. I didn't even look into the massive hole, which was still giving off visible smoke with an acrid odor. G. W. got behind the wheel and fed gas.

He didn't waste any time getting us going. Nobody wanted to be here when the Iranian army eventually showed up to see what happened.

I leaned forward and shouted, "Give us a look at the secondary tunnel on the other side of the ridge."

A helicopter went right over us as we roared up the access road toward the boulevard, a Hind. It circled the crater, then landed beside it. A figure stepped out and walked over to the edge.

Grafton!

I reached though the gap where the rear window in the pickup used to be and grabbed G. W.'s shoulder.

"Go back. Go back," I shouted. "It's Jake Grafton!"

G. W. slammed on the brakes, made the turn and roared back.

Grafton watched us come. He must have recognized us, because he waved at the Hind pilot, who lifted his machine off and flew away. Grafton threw his duffle bag into the back of the technical and climbed in. G. W. peeled out.

Grafton grinned at me, grabbed my hand and said, "Jesus, you look bad, Tommy."

I lay down in the bed of the pickup and tried to sleep. Amazingly, I dropped right off. It had been a long night.

General Martin Lincoln called the president to report that all the Iranian missiles had been shot down and all the launch sites seemed to be out of business. "We have drones over the sites monitoring them, and the people inside the tunnels have been dribbling away. Most of the tunnels seem to be abandoned, and both entrances to the executive bunker in Tehran have been sealed."

"So it's over," the president said, his voice pregnant with relief.

"The shooting, anyway," Lincoln admitted. "The Israeli missiles were destroyed over Jordan, so there may be a serious fallout problem there."

"Bomb the Iranian reactors," the president told him.

"Radioactivity will be released. The environmentalists will howl."

"That's unavoidable, but we're not doing this again. Bomb the reactors."

"Yes, sir," said General Lincoln. After he hung up, he gave the appropriate orders.

CHAPTER TWENTY-EIGHT

Jake Grafton had an agenda, which should have been no surprise to me, but to tell you the truth, I hadn't been thinking much beyond the vaporization of Tehran or sealing the executive bunker. Call me shallow.

When I awoke from my nap in the back of that old pickup, I saw Grafton in the passenger seat talking to Davar, who sat between him and the driver, G. W. Hosein. Haddad Nouri was standing tall behind the machine gun, and Ahmad Qajar was sitting in the bed of the truck, cradling his broken arm. Haddad passed me a canteen; I guzzled some water. Actually drained most of it.

Finally I took a look around. Not a soldier did I see on the streets, nor were there very many people or vehicles.

"The empty city," Ahmad said, grinning.

Hosein took us to the embassy annex. He, Ahmad and Haddad got out. "You stay here," Grafton said to Ahmad. "They'll set your arm, and you can stay until we arrange for transportation to get you home."

Grafton shook hands with the three of them, then climbed behind the wheel. We finally came to a driveway that went into what appeared to be an old estate. The building was a huge, ramshackle place, with bricks and ivy and lots of windows. The truck pulled up right in front; Jake Grafton got out, then helped Davar out. She was almost as much of a mess as I was, filthy from head to toe.

Jake Grafton paused and grabbed my hand. He looked me in the eyes, grinned and said, "Thanks, Tommy."

Then he released my hand and took Davar's elbow. They went in, and I trailed along. About a hundred things bubbled up that I wanted to ask Grafton, but I sensed that now wasn't the time. He did murmur to me that this place was a mental institution.

They conferred with the man on the desk, who led them away. I located a men's room and tried to wash some of the dirt off.

When I came out, the lobby, if that's what it was, was empty. I found a chair and sat in it.

About a half hour later Grafton and Davar came back with a medium-sized fellow wearing a bedsheet. He seemed somewhat dazed. Grafton introduced me. He was General Habib Sultani. "General Sultani has been a patient here," Grafton said, "and he wants to see the bunker."

We piled into the truck. Grafton got behind the wheel, and Sultani sat in the passenger seat. Davar sat between them to act as translator.

Away we went. I was feeling better by this time. My head was clearer, and every muscle I had hurt like hell, but I was alive and I felt pretty good about it.

Grafton drove us along the ridge where Joe had parked the tank, then downslope toward the bunker's back entrance. We found the holes where the bunker busters went into the ground, two hundred yards upslope from the entrance, twenty feet apart. They were in the center of a gentle depression. The earth had subsided, filling the tunnel below, sealing it.

We went back to the Mosalla Prayer Grounds. Several dozen young adults in civilian clothes, men and women, were staring into the hole. Grafton parked as near to the remains of the collapsed mosque as he could get and led Sultani and Davar across the loose earth and rock to the edge. I trailed along. The four of us stood on the berm of earth that marked the rim and looked in. The crater wasn't very deep; the bottom was full of packed dirt and rock, yet fumes were still wafting up. Maybe the bombs had ruptured the ceiling of hell.

"Iran has a choice," Grafton told Sultani, through Davar, as the other spectators looked at us curiously. "You can dig Ahmadinejad and his political and religious allies out of there, if they are still alive, and he will use his thugs to retake control of the country, make some more bombs and rant on about 'Death to America'; or you can see that he stays in that hole and let the politicians who remain aboveground rechart the nation's course."

I looked around, in all directions. There wasn't a single soldier in sight. The other kibitzers were whispering among themselves as they surveyed the scene. Maybe they sensed that something terrible had happened here. Or something hopeful, depending on your point of view.

"It *is* possible to be a Muslim nation," Grafton continued, "tolerate dissent, argue about the political choices the nation faces, and sell oil to the world and use the proceeds to build a new Iran. Instead of spending money on nuclear reactors and weapons and a comfortable life for the mullahs, build schools, roads, sewers, factories and hospitals, loan money to entrepreneurs who will build companies to manufacture goods for domestic use and export, build a brighter future for every Iranian. The choice, quite simply, is up to you."

I didn't know where Sultani had been emotionally these last few months or weeks, but as Grafton talked I could see him mulling the possibilities.

"Regardless of our personal wishes," Grafton continued, almost talking to himself, "it isn't possible to withdraw from the world. Nor is it possible to remake the world into what we want it to be; that's a fool's errand. We must accept the world as it is and live within it as best we can, as our conscience dictates."

Sultani said little and promised nothing. He kicked a rock or two into the hole, watched the fumes leak out, and finally asked to be taken to the Ministry of Defense.

We dropped him off in front. The central wing of the building was half demolished, but he didn't even look at that. He got out, glanced at Davar and said something to her, then turned and walked into the building without a backward glance. Only one soldier was stationed at the door, and to his credit, he stiffened to attention and did a Present Arms as the minister, still wrapped in a bedsheet, passed him and went inside.

Then Grafton drove away. Davar was in the front with him. I sat in the bed immediately behind the cab, which had no rear window, and listened to Grafton. Mainly he wanted to know which politicians in the political opposition he should talk to. Davar was full of names, and Mir-Hossein Mousavi led the list.

Finally he turned and spoke to me. "Tommy, I am going to drop you and Davar off at her house. She needs to clean up, change clothes and so on. I will pick you up in about two hours."

"That might be a real bad scene for Davar," I said.

She glanced at me with those big brown eyes.

"I will be all right, Tommy," she said.

There wasn't a car in the driveway. No staff. The house was apparently empty. Davar lowered her head and walked inside, with me right behind her. Grafton fed gas and drove away. Fortunately the front door was unlocked, so I didn't have to crawl though a window to unlock it.

She walked into the house and took the stairs for her room. I knew where it was, but I had never entered this way.

I trailed along, just in case.

Four flights of stairs later, she opened the door to her room under the eaves. The place was trashed, with every book, sheet of paper and scrap of clothing lying in the middle of the floor.

A lean young man in his twenties, with a short beard, was prying boards off the back of the bookcase with a crowbar. He looked startled to see us.

"I thought you were in the bunker," she said.

"I'm looking for a book."

"A book? Which one?"

"The blasphemous manuscript that Grandfather wrote. I know you and Ghasem had it. The Basij didn't find it in his apartment, so it must be in this house. Where did you hide it?" He took a step toward her with the crowbar in hand.

"You were the one who betrayed Grandfather to the MOIS," she said evenly.

He paused, and I could see by the look on his face that she had said the truth.

She turned and grabbed the butt of the pistol in the holster on my belt. She was trying to get it out when I stopped her.

"Who is this guy?" I asked with my hands on top of hers.

"Khurram," she hissed. "My brother."

"Who are *you*?" he roared at me. "Who are you to come to my house with my sister and enter her bedroom?"

"It isn't here," Davar told him. "Ghasem and I sent the book to America to be published."

That rocked him. He looked from her to me, back to her.

"You slut! Whore!" His voice rose to a shout. "Grandfather was possessed by the devil. He insulted the Prophet, insulted everyone who believes with blasphemy, heresy, apostasy." He took another step toward her and raised the crowbar threateningly.

"Whoa," I said. "Why don't you let Allah worry about all that? You've got a full plate right here. And lay off your sister."

He turned toward me. "Who *are* you?"

Truthfully, I had had enough. It was time to send Khurram on his way.

"I'm an American spy," I told him evenly. "I work for the CIA."

He swung the crowbar at me as if it were a cutlass. It whacked the ceiling but kept coming at my head. I caught it and pulled him in, then used my right elbow on his chin. He went down amid the trash, out cold. I laid down the crowbar and hoisted him over my shoulder.

"You bathe and get dressed," I said to Davar. "Pack some clothes. I'll get rid of this."

I took him down the stairs, all the way to the ground level. Carried him out onto the lawn and tossed him down.

The sun was well up, a nice breeze was delaying the summer heat, and a thunderstorm was building to the north, over the mountains.

I squatted in the shade and waited for Khurram to awaken. Got out my pistol, unloaded it, checked it for dirt, worked the action and blew through the barrel, then reinserted the magazine and chambered a round.

Finally Khurram stirred. He sat up and shook his head and rubbed his eyes and his chin. Then he saw me.

I pointed the pistol at him. "If I kill you," I said conversationally, "who do you think will care?"

He tried to get up. Got tangled in his feet and sat down hard. Then he tried again and succeeded. He stood swaying, looking at me and the pistol.

"You won't be anything but dead," I said.

He massaged his jaw, which didn't appear to be broken.

"Leave, and don't come back. Go. If you return here, I will kill you."

He walked out of the yard onto the street. "Hazra al-Rashid will take care of you," he shouted and shuffled off in a trot.

I watched him until I lost sight, reholstered the pistol and went back inside.

Davar packed a suitcase. She and I were sitting on the front steps when Jake Grafton rolled up. G. W. Hosein was standing at the machine gun, and Hadad was sitting in back, cradling an AK-47.

There was more traffic on the streets. Some of the families that had evacuated last night were trickling back; it looked as if they hadn't even unpacked their vehicles. Rolling along a boulevard, Grafton said, "I talked to the chargé at the American Interests Section. She had some names she thought Davar should talk to. We are going to drop you there, Tommy, and the chargé will arrange for you to get on the next Air France flight out. I think you said something about Paris."

"Yeah," I said, so overwhelmed with relief that I couldn't control my face. "Yeah. I'm ready to go."

So that is what they did. On the sidewalk in front of the Swiss embassy annex, I handed my pistol belt to Jake Grafton, shook his hand again and had a brief moment with Davar.

"You are staying?"

"For a while. Admiral Grafton wants me to introduce him to people I know."

"You deserve better than this, Davar."

She passed a hand across her face.

"Remember that guy in Oklahoma, who wanted to spend his life with you."

"I haven't forgotten," she whispered and kissed me on the cheek.

I eventually wound up at the airport, waited twelve long hours, and that night found myself in a window seat heading to Istanbul, then Paris.

I called a woman I knew, Marisa, and she came to the airport to get me.

After I had been in France for three days, I finally picked up a newspaper, which was full of the goings-on in Iran. The Parliament met and elected Mousavi as interim president. He had the full backing of the minister of defense, Habib Sultani, who was using the army to disarm and disband the MOIS and the Basij. The first act of Parliament was to renounce the nuclear weapons program and invite international inspectors to Iran.

Jordan and Iraq had nuclear contamination problems. Most of the plutonium from the destroyed warheads had landed in uninhabited desert, but the areas were sizable. Several nations had agreed to participate in the decontamination efforts.

All that was very far away from summer in France, with lunches in the garden and mornings and evenings in bed with a beautiful woman whom I adored. Perhaps even loved. If there is a heaven, and if I ever get there, I hope it will be like that ten days I spent in Paris.

In odd moments I thought about leaving the agency, moving on to the next chapter in my life, but no matter how hard I tried, I couldn't imagine what it would be. So I stopped thinking about it and let my time with Marisa just happen.

When I finally got back to the States, my apartment was so empty I almost cried. Then the telephone rang.

"Tommy, this is Jake Grafton. I heard you were coming home."

That Grafton—he knew everything.

"Come over to our place tonight for dinner," he said. "Callie and I want to see you."

So I did. Imagine my surprise when I walked in and there was Davar, wearing a chic dress, makeup and a smile. She held out her hand and let me hug her, but she didn't kiss me. She had come to the States three days ago with Jake Grafton and had been staying at the Graftons' and shopping.

At dinner we talked about her grandfather's book, which a publisher in New York had agreed to publish, and what she should do with the royalties. Davar wanted to use them to fund an orphanage in Iran, but Jake Grafton counseled against it. The book would be very controversial in the Muslim world, he thought, and the orphanage might become a lightning rod for protests. Perhaps, he suggested, the royalties might be donated to an international agency that specialized in the adoption of orphans. Davar agreed.

The conversation turned to her plans. She was going to Oklahoma tomorrow, she said. She had talked to her guy, Jim, and he was waiting. He wanted her to meet his parents.

"Just that?" I asked, watching her facial expression.

"He wants to marry me," she admitted with a smile.

I sat there watching the life in her face, the anticipation of the future, and I realized my Iranian adventure was over. Life was marching on.

The next morning I went down to the newspaper vending boxes in front of my apartment building and bought a newspaper to read with my coffee. I was stretched out on the couch, drinking java and perusing the Metro pages, when I found an interesting news item.

Yesterday, according to the *Washington Post*, a professor at Georgetown University named Aurang Azari had been stabbed to death in a university building by a woman wearing an ankle-length coat and a scarf that concealed most of her face. The coat, scarf and knife had been found later stuffed in a sidewalk trash can a block from the university. Azari was well known for publicizing inside information about the Iranian nuclear program. The police were investigating.

"Good-bye, Davar," I whispered.

On the afternoon that General Syafi'i Darma retired in Jakarta, the officers under his command threw a party for him. It was a very pleasant
affair. He had been in the military for thirty-five years, been promoted to in-
creasingly responsible commands, distinguished himself by uncovering and
foiling an assassination attempt on a foreign head of state and, although his
officers weren't aware of it, piled up a rather nice fortune in bribes and gifts.

Darma was looking forward to his new life, one without responsibilities,
with horses and beautiful women to play with and admire.

He left the party in his armored limo with his son at the wheel. The son
drove out of the capital headed for the general's estate in the country. The
road was familiar, a two-lane that was being upgraded to a four-lane, partly
in response to the general's persistent lobbying of the government.

They came to the construction area and slowed down. They crept along
for a bit, past the construction equipment on the new grade to their left, until
the limo was forced to stop by queued-up traffic. A dump truck of some
kind eased up behind them.

They sat there a moment, the son laughing at his father's jokes, enjoying
the moment, completely at ease. Then, without warning, the vehicle ahead
backed into the limo, struck it hard. At almost the same instant, the truck
behind them smashed into the limo's trunk.

As the occupants of the limo recovered from the surprise crashes, they
saw that the drivers of the trucks had climbed from behind the wheel and
taken station near their vehicles. Each of them held a submachine gun and
faced the limo.

"Oh, my God," the general shouted. "Call the police," he yelled to his son. "Use the radio. Get someone here *now*!"

His son fumbled with the radio, which had been off, grabbed the mike and held it in his hand while he pushed buttons.

General Darma stared at the gunman beside the left side of the truck ahead. He was merely standing there, holding that submachine gun. Perhaps he didn't know this vehicle was armored. Then again, maybe he did—he had made no attempt to shoot the windows out.

Darma glanced behind. The other driver was behind the limo on the right side. Any attempt to exit the vehicle on that side would also lead to a shoot-out, and probably be fatal.

As his son shouted into the radio microphone he held in his hands, something coming from the left attracted Darma's attention. He looked. It was a giant bulldozer, one that had been on the grade of the new lanes. The blade was raised, and it was coming straight for the limo.

It wasn't going to stop. It came steadily on. Now he could hear the roar of the diesel engine, hear the treads clanking.

There was just sufficient room, Hyman Fineberg decided, between the two trucks that had pinned the limo, so he drove the bulldozer, a giant Caterpillar, right up onto the limo. He could feel the car being crushed under the dozer's weight.

The gunmen climbed back into their vehicles and moved them away from the trapped limousine. Fineberg pivoted the Cat ninety degrees on its right tread, screwing the limo right into the earth, then moved the dozer forward until it was back on the ground.

Now he glanced over his shoulder. The tires of the car had blown out, and the vehicle sat on its frame in the road. The roof was crushed; most of the glass was missing.

"A job worth doing . . ." Hyman Fineberg muttered to himself and ran the dozer back up over the car. It was getting flatter, no question.

Still, Fineberg wasn't satisfied. He used the blade of the dozer to flip the car's carcass upside-down. Then he ran the dozer over it again. And again.

When he finally shut the dozer down and climbed down from the operator's seat, the limo was only about fifteen inches thick in the engine compartment. The rest of the vehicle was less than a foot thick.

Hyman Fineberg looked the wreck over, then climbed into a dump truck beside the driver and rode away.

ACKNOWLEDGEMENTS

This book is a thriller, not a travel guide. Still, to get the flavor of fundamentalist Iran, the author did extensive reading. Three books proved most helpful: *A Concise History of Iran,* by Saeed Shirazi; *Know Thine Enemy*, by Edward Shirley; and *The Iran Threat*, by Alireza Jafarzadeh. A heartfelt thank you to these authors.

RADM Stanley W. Bryant, USN (Ret), read and gave helpful comments upon the action scenes in this book. As usual, the author's wife, Deborah Coonts, offered cogent advice on the plot and characters. A special tip of the flight helmet to Stan and Deb.

Finally, the author would like to publicly thank his editor at St. Martin's Press, Charles Spicer, whose enthusiasm for adventure fiction and patience are unsurpassed. Thanks, Charlie.